SAM CRESCENT

EVERNIGHT PUBLISHING ®

www.evernightpublishing.com

SAM CRESCENT

Sam Crescent

Copyright © 2017

Chapter One

"Come on, Hope. I need you," Dwayne Carson said.

Staring into her locker, Hope Miller wondered if there was any way that she could get out of helping the most popular guy in school. If it wasn't for her college applications, she'd have told him no, but tutoring always looked good. Tucking some hair behind her ear, she took a breath and finally turned toward him.

"What do you need?" she asked.

Even though he'd bullied her when they were younger, and they never, ever moved in the same crowds, she couldn't bring herself to be a bitch. Rubbing at her temple, she waited for him to answer.

"Math, English, and also history. I really, really need to get these right, as otherwise my ass is on the line."

She rolled her eyes but didn't argue.

"Fine, fine. I've got to work at seven, but I can

help you for a couple of hours after school." She closed her locker.

"Great. You're okay to come by my place, right?"

She paused, not really liking the whole idea of being around his place. She'd heard a lot of rumors about the Carsons. Most of them she'd put down to being bullshit. She didn't like gossip, especially as a lot of it had been about her in recent months. All she wanted to do was keep her head down, use whatever of her trust fund she was allowed to, go to college, and put all of her family's mess behind her.

Living with her aunt wasn't what she wanted to do for the rest of her life. She knew Aunt Tay only put up with her because of the small amount of money she got paid to look after her. Her mother had known something bad was going to happen, so she'd put all of her money in a trust for Hope.

"Can't we go to the library or something?"

"I won't bite, Miller. Believe me. I won't get anything done if I go there. You may as well cave. You know you want to. You'll get to see my pad; it's totally the shit."

"Great," she said, trying to find the excitement but failing. "Call me excited."

He chuckled. "You're a star. See you after school."

She watched him walk away, rolling her eyes as some of the girls nearly fainted as he winked at them. High school boys didn't appeal to her. They were ... disgusting.

Grabbing her bag from out of her locker, she made her way to calculus and put the whole Carson drama out of her mind.

All she wanted to do was focus on her work, getting the best grades that she could so that she didn't have to stick around town anymore. She was done being "that girl." The one that people pointed at and whispered about the crazy daddy who'd killed her mom, and also tried to kill her.

Yep, that was her secret. Her father had developed a drug addiction which made him completely paranoid, crazy, and insane. He'd believed his wife was having an affair, and that Hope wasn't even his daughter.

He'd kept them chained up in the basement for two weeks. That's how long it had taken for people to be alerted that something was amiss. During that time, she'd watched her father shoot her mother before he shot Hope in the stomach, and then he'd put a bullet in his brain. She'd screamed, begging for help.

Rubbing at her temple, she tried to focus on her teacher as the memory danced across her vision. She was considered a bit of a freak because she'd not broken down. The fear, the memory of it, she was able to put it in a little box and seal it away.

Her aunt sometimes stared at her like she was weird. Not the best feeling in the world, but not a lot Hope could do about that. She could sit and cry about it, or get on with her life, and her mother had told her what she needed to do while they'd been chained together. Even when death was certain, her mother had done everything she could to take care of her.

Moving from calculus to PE, Hope drifted from one class to the other, ignoring some whispers and stares. At least they weren't talking about her dad. Nope, these whispers were because of Dwayne, the hot guy who'd been caught talking to her.

She wished they'd grow up.

Hope didn't bother to get changed out of her shorts and large shirt. Leaving the campus grounds, she found Dwayne sitting on the hood of his car, chatting with some of his friends. Squaring her shoulders, she made her way toward him, folding her arms as she did.

"Babe, it's about time."

"I'm not your babe. Do you want the classes?" she asked.

"Sure." He opened her door, and she thanked him for it, climbing inside. Pushing some of her hair out of the way, she leaned back in the leather seat and admired the comfort of the vehicle. It had to be expensive, but Dwayne belonged to a wealthy family, so she didn't expect anything less.

Tapping her fingers on her knees, she watched the scenery passing her by, wondering how tutoring him would be.

"I'm really grateful you're doing this for me. I saw your name on the tutor list thingy, and I figured you're my best bet. I know you tutored Frank last year, and he said you're all about the focus and not about the bullshit."

"Don't you have your grades in the bag or something?" she asked.

"My uncle demands that I earn every single grade. He doesn't want me flunking out of school or getting someone else to write my essays. Believe me, I'd do it, but my uncle knows this shit, and I got to impress him if I want to join the family business."

She shrugged. "It's fine. Do you have your grade sheets so I can take a look?" she asked.

He reached behind him, pulling out a list. "The classes I'm flunking, I got them to point out what I needed to work on."

She opened it up, shocked the teachers would do that. Whenever she tutored before the teachers always told her the kids knew where they were going wrong or fucking up.

Scanning through the list of places that were his weaknesses, she knew where to get started. The easiest subject would be history, but seeing as he was also failing math, she figured it would be best to start at his weakest point and work up to his strongest.

Twenty minutes later they arrived at one of the largest houses she'd ever seen, especially when it came to security. Four men stood at the main gate, each wearing pristine suits without a mark on them. She was very aware of her surroundings, so she felt out of place. Her mother had a small fortune but nothing like this, and by the time Hope finished college, she wouldn't have anything left. Her mother wanted her to be something, and she was determined to grant her wishes.

Dwayne climbed out, and she hated the way her stomach rolled. This was not a place for her. She wasn't rich or important.

"Come on," Dwayne said, leading the way into the house. She followed behind him, feeling like everyone was staring at her, knowing she wasn't meant to be here. This wasn't where she belonged.

Pushing those thoughts aside, she hiked her bag higher on her shoulder, releasing a breath as he made his way inside the house, which was far more beautiful on the inside than out. She spotted several men standing in various places, but Dwayne walked past them as if they were ghosts, completely invisible.

"I think here would be a good place to start," he said, opening a large door, which led into a large library. She saw a couple of desks and computers set up.

Placing her very scruffy bag onto the table top, she tried to be careful not to leave a single mark. She missed the library in town where names were carved into the desks along with lewd comments.

As she took a seat, Dwayne dropped into another

and pulled out his book. She hadn't expected him to take this so seriously, and yet here he was, grabbing books, leaning forward, and waiting.

"I wasn't joking around or anything. I need to pass high school."

She smiled. "Why now? If you don't mind me asking."

"I don't. I never took shit seriously, and let's just say that someone I know made me very aware of the fact people don't follow a fuck-up. They don't like someone who can't lead for shit. So I'm getting my head down and trying to make up for lost time."

Nodding, she pulled out his book, finding where he was going wrong, and flipped to it. "Could you work out this algebra equation for me, please?"

He already had some paper in front of him, and she waited for him to complete it. Once he was done, she glanced over it, and saw the problem. For the next half an hour, she got him to complete the first equation, but he still didn't seem to understand how it worked, and as she was about to go through the second one, his cell phone started to ring.

Each time she tried to show him, it would ring … and ring … and ring.

"Why don't you pick it up?" she asked.

"It's fine. Really. I want to learn."

"Yeah, but it could be important, and it's starting to drive me crazy."

He grabbed his cell phone, turning it over. She didn't see the name of the person flash across the screen, and he was gone, telling her he'd be back in a minute.

Standing up, she stretched out her tight muscles, raising her hands above her head, and walking toward one of the large walls.

Books were … heaven. No matter how many she

read, she always found comfort in their scent, and how they were able to transport her away from her reality. The moment she entered a book, she wasn't Hope, the daughter of a murderer. No, she wasn't anyone.

"Who are you?"

She spun around, pressing a hand to her chest when she caught sight of a much older man. He had short, black hair with grey tips at each temple. He was tall, taller than Dwayne.

Her mouth went dry, and she looked past him toward the door. Dwayne wasn't anywhere in sight.

"Dwayne brought me here?"

"You're not Dwayne's type."

She frowned, shaking her head at the same time. "I'm not Dwayne's girlfriend." She tucked her hair behind her ear. "I'm here to tutor him."

Who was this man?

****

Beast Carson didn't like having strangers in his house. In fact, he was really fucking pissed that not one of his men told him Dwayne had a girl over, but also that she'd been left alone in his fucking library.

He was … angry.

Clenching his hands into fists, which she couldn't see as he had them in his pockets, he stared at her.

This woman … girl was not his nephew's type. First, she was on the chubby side. She had a lot of curves, and even in the large-ass shirts there was no way she could hide that body. With her tits pressing against the front of her shirt and her hip cocked to the side with her hand on it, she was all woman in the right places. Again, his nephew didn't appreciate curves, nor the luscious brown hair falling in waves down her body. It was long, and Beast liked long hair. Something to wrap around his hand as he took control.

What he found even more interesting was the look in her eyes. There was pain there, and something else. Something he couldn't quite put his finger on, which he didn't like. At thirty-seven years old, no one had been able to hide from him. He discovered their secrets within seconds. It's what he'd been doing for a long time, but when everyone turned to him as their leader, he didn't have much of a choice. His father had once been the head of the family. They weren't related to the mafia, but they had their own set of illegal dealings. Chaos and shit rolled through his life like it was natural. He made the decisions. In his world, he was the judge, jury, and executioner, which raised the question—why was she here?

"You're here to tutor?"

She nodded, moving toward the desk and pointing it out.

"You're not here to screw my nephew?"

"Ew, no. He came to me to help him. I'm just trying to help." She shook her head folding her arms around her body as if she was protecting herself. He didn't know what she was trying to protect herself from, but he didn't like it.

"I see you're grossing out my tutor. Hope, I'd like you to meet my uncle, Beast."

"Your name is Beast?" she asked.

"Let's just say my mother thought it would be a joke to my father." He shook her hand, feeling the strength within her grip. There was something alluring about her.

"It's nice to meet you," she said.

"Likewise. I appreciate my nephew taking an interest in his education."

"I'll help where I can."

He held her hand a little longer than was

appropriate, but she didn't show any nerves at the action, which he found alarming. Anyone else would have been worried. Glancing at Dwayne, with one look he let the kid know that he was going to want a word with him. No one came to the house. It was his rule.

Moving toward the back of the library, he glanced back over to see Hope lower herself into her chair and watched for a few seconds as she tutored his nephew. Dwayne's father was six feet under, and had been for over ten years. Beast had gotten custody, dealing with the boy's father the only way he dealt with traitors, killing them.

It hadn't cost him anything to put a bullet in the bastard that was beating his blood. Dwayne had sported black eyes, fractured ribs, and other pains. For that, Beast had made sure his brother was made an example of. Anyone who threatened or hurt what belonged to him, what he considered his, he'd kill. Simple as that.

Dwayne was his nephew. Beast had gotten attached to the kid years ago, and he wouldn't have anything happen to him.

She didn't flirt with Dwayne. Instead she kept a distance and simply tutored him. *Hope.* He'd never heard his nephew talk about her.

Leaving them alone, he made his way into his office to deal with the legal side of his businesses.

His father was long since dead, but all of the businesses fell to Beast, and he'd spent all of his life learning everything.

He had to have strong sons, and Beast being the oldest of three, he'd had to learn the ropes. Rafe, Dwayne's father, was dead, which left him and Caleb. His youngest brother entered the office and took a seat.

"Since when do you have guests around?" asked Caleb.

"I don't have guests. He has a tutor. You've seen them?"

"Yep. Do you know who she is?"

"Haven't got a clue."

"She looks older than high school age."

The warning was clear. It wouldn't be the first time a cop has tried to pose as something to get into his home, and he wasn't going to allow it, not today or any other day. He'd find out everything he needed.

"I take it you'll deal with it, and with Dwayne, if she turns out to be a cop."

"I don't think she's a cop."

"Can you be sure?"

He just knew she wasn't a cop.

"Are you here to question me or to conduct business?"

Caleb threw the keys down on the desk from one of their brothels. "I had to get rid of Howie. He was abusing the women. I won't have that."

Picking up the keys, Beast turned them over in his hands. The brothels were one part of the business his father owned that he really wished he could get rid of. He didn't like it.

They brought in a shit ton of cash, but he didn't like making his money from women who lay on their backs, spreading their legs.

"This is your problem. You deal with it. I don't want to hear about it again until you've found a suitable replacement."

Caleb left, and Beast got to work. He'd returned from one of his warehouses where his men had found a rat trying to escape the city. No one ratted on a Carson and got away with it. No one.

Time passed, and as it grew dark, he turned the lamp on over his desk, working through his files, making phone calls, and doing everything he needed to do.

"She's gone," Dwayne said. "I took her to where she works."

He stared up at his nephew, leaning back in his chair. He nodded at Dwayne to put the light on.

"Before you start freaking out and doing that shouting thing you like to do, I'd like to say she's not a cop, or anything dodgy, okay? She's just a girl at high school."

Beast locked his fingers together, staring at him.

"I know you weren't around last year, but did you hear the story of the guy who killed his wife and shot his daughter?"

Beast was more than aware of it. He'd been the one to supply the lunatic with a gun. Information he kept to himself.

"I'm aware of it."

"She's the daughter that got shot."

"Excuse me?" He didn't like that. He'd made sure his men covered all traces of where the gun was purchased. Mr. Miller hadn't had a license, but he'd had the money to pay for what he could provide.

"She wasn't in school for a month. For two weeks her dad kept her locked up with her mother in the basement. The story is everywhere. He'd gotten paranoid or something, and had decided to take it out on mother and daughter. He killed her mother and shot her. That's the story around high school anyway. People are a little freaked out by her though."

"Why?"

"Because she still attends school. She's still a star pupil. She tutors, works at the local diner, and is normal. After shit like that wouldn't you go a bit crazy?"

When he'd first got Dwayne back, the little fucker had been a nightmare to deal with. It hadn't taken long for Beast to put him straight. Threats, regardless of if they were idle or not, worked.

"That will be all."

"I need her to tutor me. If you want, we can use the main library in town."

"That's fine. You can be here. Where does she live?"

"What?"

"Her parents are both dead. After he killed his wife and shot his daughter, he shot himself in the head. Who does she live with?"

"I think her aunt or something."

He watched Dwayne go. The moment he was gone, Beast picked up his cell phone, dialing a number. "I want every single little detail you can find on Hope Miller, extending it to her parents as well. Everything."

Chapter Two

Listening to her book, Hope glanced around to make sure no one was around to hear her moan. It had been a week since she'd begun to tutor Dwayne, and she had a horrible feeling in the pit of her stomach, but she put that down to walking from the diner in the dark. She probably shouldn't be listening to her current romance book, but she didn't have much time to read the "drivel," as her aunt called it.

Romance was her weakness. She put it down to two weeks of being chained up thinking she was going to die a virgin and not experience love. She still believed she was going to die a virgin.

No guys had ever asked her out, but that was okay. She could live with that. So long as she had her books, at least she could pretend, for however long it took her to listen to one story, to believe she was the heroine in the book. The one that got the guy, even if he was an ass, and she loved it when they groveled in books.

She wouldn't take anyone back who treated her like shit, but that didn't matter much.

When a black car pulled up alongside her and a door opened, she let out a gasp, pulling her earbuds from her ears.

She recognized Beast straightaway. He stared at her a few minutes.

"You know it's not safe for a woman to walk the streets alone," he said.

Glancing up and down the street, she frowned. Yeah, she got that it wasn't all that safe, but no one was around. "It's fine." She clicked her story off, hoping he didn't hear anything that was being said. It had gotten to the really sexy part, which she hated to admit she loved. She was a sucker for a sex scene. Romance was great, but the books that had the fire, the dirty sex, she loved them.

She was a freak, just like her peers called her. "Is everything okay?" she asked.

"Do you even consider the possibility of being attacked?"

Again, she looked down the street and shook her head. "I don't really think it could happen." She held her arms open, showing her very manly attire. "I don't think attackers would be bothered by what I'm wearing."

"Are you being stupid on purpose?" he asked.

"That's the first time anyone's ever called me stupid." She reached into her pocket and pulled out a can of mace. "I hear this is effective, and once I spray this, I'm quite heavy. I intend to slam my foot down, and then run." She shrugged. "I figured that's all I need."

"I don't like your lack of respect for your own personal safety."

"Who's going to attack me?" she asked.

He stepped toward her, and she couldn't help but take a step away. He was so tall, and he seemed to completely take over everything he touched. His presence made her heart pound as she hit a wall. When did that appear?

"You see, when it comes to men there are some that don't care if a woman says no. They will take what they want, regardless of what you want." One of his hands pressed against the wall, and the other touched her neck. The tips of his fingers stroked over her pulse as his thumb pushed her chin up so she had nowhere else to look or to go. She held herself completely still, staring into his dangerous blue eyes.

In that moment, she knew the rumors she'd heard about the Carsons had to be true. There was something deadly in his gaze, the way he commanded attention, and she had no choice but to listen, to stare back and wait for him to decide what he wanted to do with her.

"You see how easy it is for me to take what I want. I could fuck you right now against this wall, press a hand against your mouth to stop you from screaming." He placed a hand against her mouth, and she was confused.

She didn't feel afraid of him. Now she really believed herself to be a freak.

"Or, I could choke you, taking what I want, and killing you in the process." His fingers wrapped around her throat, but didn't tighten or squeeze. The touch felt more possessive than dangerous.

You're a freak. This man is dangerous, and you're just standing there, staring.

Freak.

"You need to take more care of yourself." He stepped away, and she hated that she missed his heat, his warmth. It was the first time she'd been close to someone, and she'd enjoyed it, even if it was one of the single strangest experiences in her life. "Get in." He moved toward his car door, holding it open and waiting.

"I can walk. Honestly. I don't live too far from here."

She wanted to get in the car, and that scared her. This man was different. She didn't like the feelings he inspired inside her, and the sooner she got herself back under control, the happier she would be.

"Get in the car, Hope. That's not a request."

A thrill ran down her spine at how he'd remembered her name. He didn't strike her as the kind that would remember trivial matters like a name.

Seeing no reason to argue, she slid into the back seat of the car. He had another driver, and heat flooded her cheeks at what he'd seen.

Beast climbed into the back seat beside her, and the car seemed too small to her. She didn't say anything though, staying on her side as she looked out of the window, but then glancing over at him, she saw he stared at her.

She forced a smile to her lips, wondering what he thought as he looked at her.

"You've not been around the house this week," he said. "Why?"

"Erm, I've been tutoring him at school on breaks and after it."

"Next week, and every week after that, I want an update. Every Monday, Wednesday, and Friday. It will piss him off that I have control, but again, I don't care so long as I know he's doing what is right."

"You care about him?" she asked.

"Of course I care about him. He's my nephew."

She smiled. "I can work with that. He's not too bad. His cell phone is always buzzing though."

"I'll deal with his cell phone."

She liked that he cared, and she missed it. Having someone to care about her. Seeing they were close to her home, she let the driver know, and he pulled up at the smallest house on the end of the street. It wasn't great. The front lawn was overgrown, and the windows were dirty on the outside. Her aunt didn't care for presentation.

"This is where you live?"

"This is home."

It was a far cry from the home she was used to. Her mother had cleaned every single day, and believed the key to a happy life was a good home.

"Thank you for the ride, Mr. Carson," she said.

"It's Beast. You can call me Beast."

She smiled at him, and climbed out, making her way toward the house.

Opening the door, she glanced back, seeing Beast stare at her. She liked his gaze a little too much. Closing the door, she turned around, and saw her aunt stood there.

"Are you behaving like a whore now?" Aunt Tay asked.

"No. It's just a friend. He didn't like me walking home."

"Back in my day any woman could walk home and not need a lift. You know I don't want that kind of behavior in my house. It's the reason your father had issues with your mother. She didn't know when to keep her legs shut."

"Don't," Hope said. "Don't talk about my mother like that. You're more than happy to take the money she had to take care of me, so don't you dare speak about her like that. Your brother, my father, was the sick one. He couldn't keep his cravings at bay." She glared at her aunt, once again thankful that in those final hours, her mother made her aware of the stipulations of the trust fund, and the allowance that would be granted in the event of her and her father's death.

If Aunt Tay so much as laid a finger on her, everything would be gone. The money she loved so much, and Hope could leave. Part of her wanted Tay to hit her, so then she wouldn't feel obliged to stick around. This was what her mother wanted, and she'd do whatever it took to make her wishes come true.

****

The day was bright, and from his office, Beast stared out into the garden, watching as Dwayne and Hope were lying out on the grass. It was too hot for them to be inside, cooped up in the library. He watched as Hope tucked some hair behind her ear, and he was curious about her.

The report he had told him she didn't even go to a counselor after the event. For two weeks, she'd listened to her father's rants, watching as he beat her mother before turning onto her. There hadn't been any indications of a sexual assault, and no rape kit had been required either.

Her father simply lost it.

She laughed at something Dwayne said, and it completely lit up her entire face.

Beast had gotten every single detail on her aunt as well.

Once again, he watched as Dwayne grabbed his cell phone, leaving Hope alone. For several seconds, he watched as she pulled out her own books, and started to work on her stuff. She nibbled her lip, and he saw the focus in her gaze. Leaving his office, he stopped by the kitchen on his way outside, grabbing a soda for Hope.

As he made his way toward her, she still hadn't looked up, and only when he stood over her, casting her in shadow did she finally glance up.

"Beast," she said, smiling.

"I figured you could use a drink." He handed the soda down to her.

"Thank you." She opened the can and took a sip.

"Where's the student?"

"I think the student has a girlfriend who doesn't like him being tutored by me. She's probably worried my weirdness will rub off on him, and she's going to have a weirdo for a boyfriend."

He sat down on the grass and stared at her. "What makes you weird?"

"The fact I still go to school. That I don't do drugs or get high. I work." She nibbled her lip.

"I know your history, Hope."

"Everyone seems to know about it, and of course

because they know, they think they're an expert in how a person deals with it."

"And you hate it?"

She paused, licking her lips. "I hate that they think they know what's right."

"You have to admit it's strange. Your father kept you locked up, chained to a wall, and you're sitting here, drinking soda, looking like everything is normal."

She averted her eyes, but he saw the tears in her gaze. She started to speak but stopped as her throat sounded full. He watched as she gained composure. "My mom, she didn't want me to think about what happened. She told me that I would get out, and when I did, I wasn't to make mistakes. I wasn't to let it beat me. She wanted me to make her proud." Her eyes watered again, and she quickly dropped her head.

He couldn't resist reaching out, tucking some hair behind her ear. She didn't pull away from his touch, and she glanced over at him.

The yearning in her gaze was clear.

Beast wondered how many people had taken the time to touch, to take care of her. The information on her aunt wasn't exactly flattering. He didn't for a second imagine life was easy for Hope.

"You're not alone," he said. "There are always people who can help."

She laughed. "I know. What happened to me wasn't as bad as what some people go through. It wasn't the best, but … it could have been a lot worse." She gritted her teeth. He saw the telltale sign of her jaw clenching.

"You can talk to me," he said, offering his support even before he knew why he was doing it. He didn't owe this woman—girl, he had to remember that— he didn't owe her anything.

"I really don't need to talk about it, but thank you. I really appreciate it." She tucked some hair behind her ear.

"I'm so sorry about that," Dwayne said.

"I'd like you to tell your girlfriend you'll deal with her when you're not studying, as otherwise I'll take your phone."

"Beast," Dwayne said.

"No, your education comes first. Miss Miller could be anywhere else in the world. She doesn't need to be helping your lazy ass. Give her the respect she's due."

He got up and walked away, not glancing back.

Heading to his office, he grabbed his jacket, looking outside once more to see them both studying. His nephew looked pissed off, but he didn't care.

Leaving his office, he stopped at the doorway, seeing Levi standing there. "Make sure Hope Miller gets home safely. I don't want to see a bulletin about her being lost or dead."

"Yes, sir."

Beast climbed behind the wheel of his car, taking off into the city.

The few occasions he'd spoken to Hope, he'd found himself drawn to her. The darkness in her gaze, the need, no one else saw it, but he did. Hope Miller craved attention. Her family was dead, and that left her alone. Not for the first time, he wondered how long she'd been wanting attention, touch.

She wasn't acting out for it, nor was she showing any outward signs of needing it, but he saw it.

The way she leaned against him, begging for his touch with her gaze. At the same time, she pulled away, not wanting what he could give.

She was pushing and pulling with equal measure.
Eighteen years old.

She's a high school student.

She's already had something fucked-up go on in her life.

Even as he tried to list every single reason that he had to stay away, he was once again drawn to her gaze. She wasn't afraid of him. He also believed she didn't have a clue of what he was capable of. What he could do.

He wasn't a good man.

He hurt people.

Anyone who betrayed him found themselves a gruesome death.

Beast had never taken shit from anyone.

"The key, son, is fear. Make everyone afraid of you, and it will keep them in line. Anyone tries to take that power away from you, show the world why they should fear you."

He'd watched his father torture men and women, anyone who thought they could have a life without him.

Each lesson had created the person he was today. His own mother had told his father she'd named her son aptly, because that was exactly what he was going to turn into, a beast.

Parking up outside of Sarah's apartment block, he made his way inside, nodding at the man on the main desk. It wasn't the first time he'd been here, and he knew it wasn't going to be his last either.

Sarah was a first-class slut. She took anyone's money, and so long as they paid her high fee, she'd make every single man's dream come true.

He's seen her in action. Fucking an entire line of fifteen men and loving every second of it.

As he knocked on her door, she opened it with a smile on her lips.

"Hey, Beast," she said.

He shook his head, opening the door the rest of

the way. She loved it when he took charge. Closing the door behind him, he wrapped his fingers around her neck, pushing her against the wall.

"You don't say my name. You don't say fucking anything. I don't even want you to look at me right now."

She instantly closed her eyes. Her nipples were rock-hard points, begging for his attention, her body already on display with the sheer dress she wore. She loved the attention and the shock value she gave. He'd watched her walk down a street, seeing men and women turn to look at her.

Tearing the dress from her body, he cupped one of her breasts. They were a little small for him, but for now they would do.

Moving her from the wall, he pushed her down so that her ass was pointed up. He didn't want to stare at her. Grabbing a condom from his pocket, he tore into the wrapper, rolling it down his cock. Once he was protected, he didn't touch her nasty pussy. He never did. Sarah was just a tool to be used, and if he didn't fucking need her right now, he wouldn't be here.

Slamming his dick deep inside her, he closed his eyes, not liking the other face he saw. He was royally fucked.

Chapter Three

Chewing her gum, Hope picked up the three jars of salt, making her way out to the main diner to place them on her table. It was late, after eleven, and she still needed to finish writing two assignments before Monday.

The biggest problem she had was that weekends were always so busy at the diner, but the extra money came in handy. She worked so that her trust fund went further. If she didn't withdraw too much, she'd be able to pay for college and leave debt-free, with a good job. That was her plan, and she intended to stick with it.

Coming to a stop, she saw Beast Carson with a couple of men huddled around a table. They looked so out of place in a diner like this. Their suits gave away their wealth. Each one had to cost more than she earned in a year. Not only that, one suit alone would probably fund her entire college tuition for a year.

"I'm not serving them. I don't want to register on Carson's radar," Chloe, a single mother said, coming toward her. "I've got kids to protect."

Before Hope could comprehend what was happening she was shoved toward the table. Taking out her notebook, she stared at the table of men, who fell silent the moment she approached. When she was around Beast he never made her feel uneasy, but right now she wasn't exactly getting any of the good vibes. Her stomach was somersaulting, and she felt afraid.

"Is there anything I can get you?" she asked.

"There's not enough menus. Bring us some."

"A coffee for each of us to start, Hope," Beast said.

There he went, his voice calming her. She gave a quick nod, leaving them alone. Entering the kitchen, she began to make two pots of fresh coffee.

Chloe came up to her. "Do you know him?"

"I tutor his nephew in school." She waited for them to fill, and turned to give Chloe her undivided attention. "What's the big deal?"

"The big deal? You know who Carson is, right? You know what he does?"

"I've heard the rumors."

"If I was you, I'd get a new tutor for his nephew. Nothing good comes from sticking around a Carson. They're bad news."

Hope watched as Chloe walked away, and she bit her lip, hating that sick feeling beginning to start in her stomach.

Once the coffee was filled, she grabbed a handful of menus and went to serve them. Once again, the table went quiet, and she hated how nervous that made her. Silence meant what they were talking about was top secret.

Or dangerous.

She finished serving them coffee and left them alone, going to deal with other customers. The diner had pretty much emptied out the moment Beast Carson entered.

The rest of the shift went by without much incident. The men ate. Her boss looked shit scared, and she had to serve them since no one else would.

Not bothering to change out of her uniform, she pulled out a jacket and headed outside, stopping when she caught sight of Beast, alone. He leaned against his car, and he was smoking a cigarette.

"I didn't know you smoked."

"I rarely do anymore. It just seems like the night for a smoke." He offered it to her, and she shook her head.

"I don't smoke."

"You don't party."

She stared at him. Dwayne had invited her to his party, something about a pool house, and it being a rare occurrence for him to allow people to his place. She'd declined, as it wasn't really her scene.

"I'm going to keep my brain cells active while I can. Last I heard I kind of need them to get out of town."

Folding her arms beneath her breasts, she stared at him. At the table surrounded by men, she'd been afraid of him. Now, she wasn't. She felt drawn to him.

"Why aren't you at the party?" she asked.

"Kids don't appeal to me."

If words could hurt, that sure did, and she didn't know why. "I better get going."

She made to turn away, but he spoke, stopping her.

"Why do you want to get out of town?" he asked.

Glancing over her shoulder, she saw he'd turned to look at her. "Didn't you get the memo? I'm a freak."

"I know about your past, Hope. You just don't strike me as the kind of woman that runs."

She took a deep breath. "There's nothing here for me, Mr. Carson. No one at school or at home. I've got … nothing. I'm just waiting to graduate high school, get the hell out of town, and away from the memories. The whispers."

"The whispers?"

"People know what happened, and even though I can pretend for a time that it doesn't bother me, I get tired of it. My dad killed my mom, and I'm what's left." She held her arms out. "Not a lot really going for me here."

He moved toward her, staring into her eyes. "You're eighteen."

"I know."

"I have to keep remembering that."

She tilted her head to the side, watching him. He didn't look away from her. The warmth seemed to radiate off him, and if she could, all it would take was putting her hand against his chest.

He's older.

Much older.

She didn't care.

There was something about Beast Carson that had her thinking about him at really inappropriate times. One of those being when she was standing in the shower, water dripping down her body, and she imagined him there with her, holding her, touching her.

She took a deep breath, knowing she had to get out of there. None of the guys at school had ever made her feel this way. Beast looked at her as if he really saw her.

He's an uncle.

Still, as she tried to think of all the reasons she should probably be grossed out, nothing came to mind. He was older, but again, she didn't care.

She didn't want to think about what his words meant. "Dwayne is doing really well with his studies. I think a few more lessons and he'll have cracked algebra. Yay!" She did a little fist pump, and saw his lips quirk a little as if he was suppressing a smile. "You can smile. It's good. Your nephew is doing great."

"That's good to know. Why don't you make new memories?"

She paused, hoping he'd forgotten about their little conversation. "Memories are hard to make. I miss my mom."

"Find someone to make new memories with."

She chuckled. "You make it sound so easy. Like it's not difficult to find someone to share your life with."

"Everyone has a price."

"I'm not going to force someone to share memories with me." A gust of wind rushed over her, pushing her hair onto her face. She went to move it out of the way. Beast's touch stopped her. He pushed her hair off her face, and she couldn't move, not that she wanted to. Staring up into his eyes, she was struck once again.

She loved that shade of blue more than anything in the world.

You've got a crush.

Yeah, just to add to another of her freakish tendencies, she had a crush on a guy's uncle.

"Why are you walking home?" he asked, holding her hair to her face.

His touch felt so good, his hands warm against her skin.

Licking her lips once again, which she couldn't seem to stop doing, she shrugged. "I, erm, I always walk home."

"I've told you before these streets are dangerous."

"It's late, Beast. I've got to be getting home."

His jaw twitched. Was she pissing him off? She didn't mean to. Was he worried about her? He'd be the first guy who worried about her in a long time.

"You're not walking home. Come on."

He released her hair, and she missed his touch, wanting him to hold her again, or at least touch her.

Get a grip, Hope. Nothing is happening here.

It's all in your pathetic imagination.

He opened the door, and she climbed inside.

Beast leaned in, securing her seatbelt in place and pulling back. "You need to start learning to take care of yourself."

He was so close, his breath fanning across her face.

Sitting back, she closed her eyes, waiting for him to get in the car. She had to get a grip. This wasn't good for her at all.

Opening her eyes, she stared out as he climbed in.

"You know, everyone is afraid of you," she said.

He started the car, and she chanced a look at him, seeing the smile on his face. "Fear can be a great motivator."

"It can also cause a lot of people a lot of pain."

"I'm not here to hold anyone's hand," he said.

"Are the rumors true about you?" she asked.

"Don't ask questions you don't want the answers to."

Did she want to know the truth? Was she ready to go down that road?

No, she didn't want to know. For once she wanted her little bubble to remain intact, and that was exactly how she was going to leave it.

****

Beast should have left. He shouldn't have gone to see her, or stayed behind to wait, knowing she didn't have a ride.

With Dwayne having his little pool party, the house was off-limits, every single door and window locked. Beast didn't mind his nephew using the pool house, but he wouldn't allow any little shits into his home. They weren't invited.

Out of the corner of his eye, he saw Hope twisting her fingers together, and he wondered what she was thinking about. He liked the way she looked at him. The haunted look in her eyes, the way she held herself, in her mind and body she was a lot older than her eighteen years.

"Have you ever been back to your old house?" he asked.

She tensed up. She shoved her hands between her thighs, pressing them together. He turned on the heat, not wanting her to be cold.

"No, I've not. My stuff was packed and the house sold. I don't know what happened to it. My aunt took care of that."

"She doesn't take care of you though, does she?" he asked.

"It's not her job to take care of me. I'm old enough to take care of myself."

"You're not used to it though, are you? Being alone. I heard your aunt is from your dad's side?"

"She's my dad's sister."

He wondered how that went.

"We ... tolerate each other."

He pulled up outside of her aunt's house, and he saw the lack of desire to go inside. She didn't want to go home. He watched her, waiting.

"You hate her?"

"She hates my mom. Says that everything that happened is her fault. She wasn't there." Hope snorted. "I don't even know why I'm telling you this. I don't want to talk about it."

"Sometimes strangers are the best people to tell our secrets. It's why some go to confession."

"I have no intention of telling my fears or my memories to a priest. Aunt Tay ... hates me because I remind her of my mom. I was there, and no matter how often she tries to blame everything else, it was her brother who pulled the trigger."

He noticed she placed her hand on her stomach. "You were shot as well."

She nodded. "Yeah, I was bleeding out. I think the doctor said I died on the table for a few seconds. I don't remember anything."

Beast gripped the steering wheel tighter, not liking the thought of a world without her in it.

"Everything happens for a reason, right?" she asked. Her gaze moving from the house to land on him. "Why do you think I had to lose my parents? Why did he kill her?"

"You hate him?"

"He killed my mom. Took away the one person in the world I could talk to. I didn't have to put on a happy face. I miss her more than anything." She wiped away the tears, and laughed. "I'm sorry. You've got more important things than talking to me."

"Would you move out if you could?" he asked, stopping her from leaving as she reached for the door handle.

"What do you mean?"

"If you had somewhere to go that meant you didn't have to go home to that."

She stared at the house, and he saw how tempting his offer was.

Plans began to draw up in his mind. "I'd move out in a second. I really would. I ... I've thought about it. I've got a trust fund, but the more of that I save, it means I can go to college. I don't want to spend too much. It won't be much longer, you know. Just a few more months." She smiled at him. "Thank you for the ride."

He waited for her to leave.

She gave him a little wave, which he returned before he headed back toward his home. Cars were parked in his driveway, which only served to piss him off.

Yes, parties for teenagers bored him. Climbing out of his car, he made his way inside, and found Caleb standing at his office window, staring out toward the garden.

"I think we should get Dwayne tested for some kind of STD, or even STI. I've seen those skanks he's got on his lap making out with three other boys."

Moving toward the window, Beast watched his nephew. Dwayne was living the life a high-schooler should be living. He was getting laid, flunking his classes, but also making up for lost time.

He'd seen the transformation in just the few weeks that Hope had been tutoring him. She was good at what she did. Patient, talented, and … beautiful.

She saw herself as a freak, but he saw her as beautiful.

She's eighteen.

That was his only problem. At thirty-seven years old, he was too old for her. Nearly twenty years her senior.

Yet, he couldn't seem to stop thinking about her. Even when he was away from her, he thought about her. Tonight, he'd gone to the diner because he knew she'd be there. He also knew she'd walk the streets alone because she didn't have a car, and he fucking hated that. She shouldn't be walking alone, not now, not ever.

The streets were dangerous. She had absolutely no care at all for her own safety.

"There's something I want to do," he said.

"Are you telling me to ask for my advice, or because you just want me to hear it out?"

"I want to bring Hope Miller here to live while she finishes out her high school days."

"Is this because of the gun?"

"This is because she doesn't deserve to live with a first-class bitch." He turned to look at Caleb. "You can make that happen?"

"I'll call our lawyer tomorrow. I'm sure he'll draw the papers up."

"When she goes to the diner to work, I want you to keep an eye on her."

"Why?"

"I'm going to see her aunt. I think she and I have a lot to discuss."

He watched as Dwayne picked up both girls and threw them into the pool. Turning his back on the party, Beast went back toward his desk, wondering what it was about her that wouldn't let fucking go.

****

Armed with the necessary papers, Beast parked his car outside of Tay Miller's house. She'd never been married, and was known for being the sister of a murderer. She also had a reputation for being a bit of a slut.

"Do you want me to go in for you, boss?" Donny asked.

"No. Stay here."

Climbing out of the car, he saw most of the houses in the neighborhood needed some kind of care. Buttoning up his jacket, he made his way toward the house, lifting his hand to knock.

"I'm coming. I'm fucking coming." Tay opened the door. Curlers were in her hair, and the scent of cigarettes hung heavy in the air.

The moment she caught sight of him, she paled. He liked that.

Fear.

He could do whatever he wanted. People were so easily controlled by fear, by the unknown, and he loved to do that.

As he stepped over the threshold, she backed away, and he pulled the papers out of his pocket.

"I've done nothing," she said. "I don't have anything to do with your type."

He held out the pen for her to take. "Read it."

She took the pen and glanced down. She started reading through the emancipation order he'd drawn up. "What has Hope done? We had an agreement!"

"You should have been grateful that you had another person to share your life with. Your brother took away a great deal inside her. Made her have to deal with what a small town does to an outsider. You're a despicable human being. Sign her over, and you get this." He held up some rolled-up notes, seeing the greed in her eyes.

Hope wasn't thriving here. She deserved better, and he was going to make sure she got it. "Where's her room?"

"First bedroom down the hall."

He went to the room, seeing that she didn't have that much in the way of possessions. Picking up the picture frame beside her bed, he saw her mother. The only person who really mattered to Hope. The one person he couldn't bring back.

After packing up her stuff, he made his way downstairs and checked over the signed paperwork. Seeing that it had Tay's signature, he handed her over the cash. She took it greedily, and he smiled. Heading toward the house, he heard her shout.

"You bastard." Spinning around, he shot her with a glare. "You ... it's one-dollar bills."

"I know. Next time maybe your greed won't get in the way." He'd put a large bill around one dollars to make it look like they were all the same.

Chapter Four

Hope once again stepped out into the cool night. The weather at the moment was all over the place. One moment it was boiling hot, the next so cold a jacket wouldn't do to protect her.

When she spotted Beast leaning against his car once again, she stopped. Should she go to him? He confused her, his presence making her nervous as she wanted things she never wanted from a man before, from anyone. Just by being near him, she felt the changes inside her, the craving, burning need, like fire building.

"Hey," she said, not moving closer.

"I've got a present for you."

"Oh," she said, finally stepping closer. It was rude not to, right?

She held onto her bag tightly, not wanting to let it go.

He pulled out some papers from his pocket and handed them to her. He stood beneath a streetlight, so as she took them, she was able to read.

"Emancipation orders." She shook her head, flicking to the back. "No, no, I don't want this. I told you the money I have is for college. I can't afford to live on my own." Didn't he know that she'd looked into everything these orders could mean? She'd done multiple calculations, seeing if there was any way she could be free of the woman who liked to spit up the past. Every single cent would be gone within a couple of years, and she'd have to turn to scholarships. She didn't want that. Her plan kept her focused. She knew what she wanted, and this right now, wasn't it. "She signed." Tears filled her eyes, but they were happy. "Why? I don't want this. I told you I didn't want this."

He took hold of her arms, but she was so

distracted that any pleasure she'd have gotten from his touch rolled off her. She didn't want his touch in that moment.

"You're safe, Hope. She'd given you your freedom, but I've got a room for you at my place."

This made her pause. "What?"

"I didn't want to have to deal with a screaming aunt telling the world I stole her niece."

She doubted Aunt Tay would ever do that.

"This way, she's given you your freedom, not that you really need it. At eighteen, you can do whatever the hell you want, but I just wanted to have that piece of paper just in case. You're going to live at my house. I pay for food, utilities, and I own my property. I deal with all the finance. You can still continue to work here if you wish, but I'll have a driver escort you to and from. No questions asked."

"Why?" she asked. "Why are you being so nice to me?"

"I've got a feeling that not many people have been all that nice to you, Hope."

She didn't get it. This man owed her nothing. There was nothing she could ever give him to repay him, and yet here he stood, holding a chance for her future to be a whole lot better than it had been.

Staring at him, she knew in her heart she fell a little bit in love with him right then. Everyone was afraid of him, but he'd only ever showed her kindness, and she didn't care what other people said. All she worried about was how he made her feel. She refused to care about anything else, especially right now.

"Thank you. Erm, I better go and get my stuff."

"I've already got it." He opened the car door. "If you climb inside, I'll go and show you where you're going to sleep."

She climbed into the car and held still as he secured her seat belt. There was something sexy about the way he took charge, plugging her seat belt in.

Let's face it. You've got a crush so damn big on him that rivals any kind of movie star crush.

He sat behind the wheel, and she watched as he pulled out of the parking lot, heading in the opposite direction of her old home, and instead, toward her new one.

I can totally handle this.

Out of the corner of her eye, she kept watching him, not wanting to miss a moment. Biting her lip, she couldn't help but smile. Everything felt so charged, so different. She took a deep breath and wondered what her mother would think of Beast Carson.

It didn't matter really. She felt amazing when she was around him.

"I'd like to keep my job if that's okay."

"I said it was. I'll arrange for a driver to get you there and back safely. I don't want you walking the streets."

"Because it's dangerous?"

"You don't know when the bogeyman may come out and scare you."

She chuckled. "I've not heard 'the bogeyman' in so long."

"Did your parents ever tell you about it to make you go to sleep?" he asked.

"Nah. I was a very good kid. I always did as I was told. The only time I heard about the bogeyman was at Halloween, and my mom did it to be scary. I used to love Halloween. She'd get us both dressed up, and we'd go out trick-or-treating. I loved it."

"What happened?"

"I got older, and all the magic with an addict dad

just went out of the window. It was easier to stay in. We'd watch a few horror movies, and leave it at that."

He pulled into the open gates. "I've never celebrated Halloween. Dressing up felt pointless. There's no reason to be scared of those things that go bump in the night when you're one of them."

"I'm not even going to think about that right now," she said.

He parked the car, and she was pleased she didn't have to ask him anything more. Holding her bag tightly to her, she stared up at the house and followed Beast. He placed a hand at her back and began to move her into the house.

Guards stood at the door, and he nodded at them. It was only then she heard another car entering the grounds.

"I always have men following me," he said as she'd stopped to look behind her.

Beast didn't linger, and they were making their way up the long staircase. In fact, he moved toward the end of the hallway where she saw a second staircase.

"Dwayne's room is down there. I'll be having a word with him tomorrow. He won't bother you. I'm going to get him to take you to school though."

"I don't mind walking."

"And I don't mind getting people to drive you to where you need to be."

He stopped at the far room, and she stared at the door he stood at.

"This is my room?"

"Yes."

She reached past him, gripping the door handle and twisting it. The door opened, and Beast flicked on the lights.

The room was huge. It easily had to be the size of

an apartment. The bed was one of the largest she'd ever seen.

Beast moved past her. "En-suite bathroom so you'll have your privacy. A walk-in closet, and over here is a storage area."

She saw her clothes had already been hung up, and the few possessions she had were stored in the closet. The picture that she'd kept by the side of her bed was already there, waiting for her.

"Thank you," she said, feeling incredibly touched.

"I hope you find some happiness in your stay here, Hope." Next, he pulled out a cell phone from his pocket. "This is now yours. I've already placed numbers in it—mine, Dwayne's, and several of my men. You call them at any time, and they will come for you."

She nodded, and smiled. "Thank you."

"If there's anything you need. Don't hesitate to ask."

He moved away, and she watched him leave.

"Wait, where do you sleep?" she asked.

"At the end of the hall. I'm a light sleeper, so I'll know if Dwayne tries to sneak up here." He winked at her, and she got a little thrill knowing she shared an entire floor with Beast.

"Thank you, for everything."

He nodded, closing the door as he left. Sitting on the edge of the bed, she didn't care about the time. Not right now. She was … in shock.

Her aunt was finally in the past, and she didn't have to hear the crap coming from her mouth. Staring down at her cell phone, she flicked her thumb across the screen and scrolled through contacts. She smiled as she saw a contact for the local Chinese place.

She had to keep herself in check. There's no way

she could let her crush shine through. No way.

****

Beast stared at the security screen in the library. Dwayne was taking a test, which Hope had been helping him with seconds before. She now stood at one of the bookshelves, staring at the array of titles he had on them.

Today she wore a pair of shorts that fell to her knees, and a crop top. They were having hot weather once again. It had been a couple of days since he picked her up. She'd already gotten used to the routine, and Dwayne didn't mind having her around. The two rarely spoke to one another unless she was tutoring. Neither of them moved in the same high school circles.

Dwayne had told him Hope was a loner, and a lot of people considered her a weirdo. Beast didn't think she was a weirdo. More misunderstood than weird.

"Have you told her your part?" Caleb asked.

"No, and I'm not going to." He didn't look away from the screen. She'd climbed up to the second floor of books, the ones that were far more intimate.

He watched as she pulled a book from the top shelf. Now this one interested him as she opened up the book. The camera angle was just right to see the page she'd flicked to. Dwayne had gotten him that book three Christmases ago. It was a book on sexual positions, with rather detailed pictures. In response, he'd gotten Dwayne a checkup at the hospital, and a supply of condoms. He didn't give a shit if people didn't agree with his parenting methods. It worked for him and Dwayne.

Hope's cheeks were on fire, but she didn't close the book as if she was too shocked to see what was there. Her hand landed on the book, and he watched as she slowly traced her fingers across the picture. She turned the page over, and once again, she was met by a rather explicit display of sex.

What was she thinking?

He wished he was there right now. He'd ask her everything he could think of to know and understand about her.

"You're a little … obsessed by this girl."

"She's not a girl. She's a woman," he said, not really paying attention to Caleb.

The way she looked at him, it was like a fucking drug, and he was growing more addicted with every single passing day.

She was of legal age.

Not once had Hope made him think of a child or a teenager. She was all woman. Her body was made for sex, and seeing as she was flicking to the next page, he knew her mind was as well.

He watched as she closed the book and looked down. Dwayne held a piece of paper up, and she nodded.

She placed the book back, but held the spine a little longer. She didn't want to leave it alone.

Finally, Beast stood watching her for another few minutes as she marked Dwayne's test, and he had no choice but to pull himself away. He couldn't keep staring at her, watching her, even though deep down he knew that was all he wanted to do.

"We've got to head out to the warehouse," Caleb said. "Business needs to be taken care of."

Leaving the house, Beast didn't need to give the order for his men to take care of Dwayne and Hope. He'd given them that update days ago.

Climbing into the back of the car, he pulled out his cell phone, checking through the texts before giving Caleb his undivided attention.

"What do we know?" Beast asked.

"Frank has been spending some time with the local cops."

Gritting his teeth, Beast nodded. Frank was one of the guys who helped with the lending side of the business. He knew a great deal, but what Frank also had was a problem with gambling.

Just in Beast's casinos he owned nearly a million bucks, and that was just for the past few months.

If Frank thought for a second he was going to get away with trying to rat to the cops, he was in for a shock, not that it should be all that much of a shock, not really.

"I've already paid William off. Gave him ten grand," Caleb said.

William was their informant within the police force, who helped to turn a blind eye to certain activities. He'd been working for the Carsons for a long time now, and they'd helped get him a nice big retirement settlement, just like he deserved for helping friends.

"What's the deal with Hope Miller?" Caleb asked.

"Just helping a girl out."

"You and I both know that's not true."

"We're the ones that gave her father the gun."

"So? We've given plenty of crooks guns. They've killed a lot of people with them as well. What is it about this girl?"

He glanced over at his brother and didn't say a word. Caleb held his hands up.

"Look, I've never seen you look at a woman the way you look at her, and I say 'woman' and not 'high school girl' because I know you. I've seen her. She's older than her years. I also know you've used Sarah a lot more in the past few days since you've met Hope. She gets to you, doesn't she?"

Beast wasn't about to tell his baby brother exactly how an eighteen-year-old girl had him feeling. Just watching her look through that sex book had given him a fucking hard-on that took all of his self-control not to do anything about, which pissed him off.

When he looked into Hope's eyes, he saw her yearning for a man, especially the way she looked at that fucking book. She'd been staring at it as if she wished *she* was the woman getting a nice, big, fat cock.

"She's nice," Caleb said. "I've seen her, and she's not like your usual women. She's innocent."

"How about you stop thinking about the woman living in our house and start focusing more on your work?" He didn't want to hear any more bullshit about her innocence. Even though it wasn't bullshit, he was very much aware of how naïve she was to her current situation.

She now lived in a house full of monsters with the only exception being Dwayne, but his time would come as he grew older. His own father had already destroyed what little innocence he had by the time he was fifteen.

Maybe he should be running Dwayne, but he couldn't do it.

His nephew wouldn't know the kind of life he lived growing up, and he'd taken him away from a life of violence, so he didn't have to.

Time would come for his training. Until then, Beast, Caleb, and his men were capable of running the family business.

Pulling up outside of the warehouse, Beast climbed out, buttoning his jacket and pushing Hope and Dwayne to the back of his mind. He didn't need to be thinking about the innocence in his life right now.

Stepping into the warehouse, he saw his men holding back as Frank stayed tied to a chair. This wasn't new for Beast. Everyone who tried to rat on him ended up on this chair.

"Mr. Carson, I swear I don't know anything. My wife!"

"Your wife is in the hospital with her jaw wired shut, Frank." He grabbed a chair, spun it around, and straddled it. "Here's the thing, she got there long before we got you, so I have to wonder if she was the one warning you about crossing me."

He glanced down at the man's knuckles, which were tied to the arms of the chair. The telltale signs of a fight were evident there with the split skin.

"You beat your wife, Frank?"

He'd met Delia a few times. A beautiful woman, a little ... slow at times, but he imagined that was down to one too many punches in the head.

His own mother had gotten slow over the years, and then of course when body parts weren't given the right amount of care, it made walking difficult. He'd been sitting at the table while his father mocked his mother's inability to walk. He wouldn't even let her have crutches to help, and he'd seen the tears.

Of course, his father had beaten her one time too many, and when Beast came home and saw the bloody mess on the carpet, he'd decided to give his father a taste of his own medicine.

He'd not stopped, and spent an entire week humiliating his father, making him go through the agony he'd put his mother through before he finally got bored and simply killed him.

His mother got a beautiful resting place, which he maintained every single Sunday. His father got cremated and his ashes pissed on in the back garden. As far as Beast was concerned, it was justified.

Reaching out to the weapons on display, he picked up a steel hammer and tested the weight of it in his hands.

"Please, Beast, I swear. I didn't—"

"What did your wife say?" Beast asked. "You see, I've got a real problem with men who beat their wives, especially when those wives are only trying to help their men. Women do that, Frank. There are a rare few out there that are only there to help you. To guide you, to warm your bed, and give you children."

He brought the hammer down with force, shattering Frank's hand.

"And those women don't deserve to get hit."

Chapter Five

Making her way downstairs, Hope hummed to herself, happy for the first time since her father took everything away from her. Entering the dining room table, she stopped when she saw Dwayne, Caleb, and Beast all sitting there.

"I'm so sorry. I didn't realize I was late." She quickly glanced at her wrist to see she was right on time.

"I'm hungry," Beast said.

"Please take a seat."

Caleb sat opposite Beast at one end of the table. With Dwayne on one side, she went to the only place that was set, taking a seat.

It had been a long time since she'd shared a dinner with anyone. Her mother always made sure there was a meal on the table, and it brought a smile to her face thinking about it.

"You've got a math test next week. How are your scores?" Beast asked, looking directly at Dwayne.

"If I remember everything that Hope's taught me, I should ace it."

She smiled. "Don't stress out, and look out for those trick questions. The ones that make you think well, duh that's right, but when you look at it again, you just know it's something else." She frowned. "I've just made that sound way more complicated."

"It's fine. I'll probably fail," Dwayne said. "Useless tutor."

He was smiling as he said it.

"Hey, that's not fair. You know I've got one of the highest successes as a tutor."

"Yeah, we'll see, hot-shot."

She giggled. The food came out, and out of the corner of her eye, she noticed Beast staring at her. She liked that, having his gaze on her, which of course made her think of that damn book. Why would he have that kind of book anyway?

"Did you have a good day?" she asked, finally chancing a glance over to him.

"It was a good day. I think I finally taught someone the error of his ways."

She heard Caleb snort, and she glanced down the table to see him trying to contain his laughter. Dwayne, of course, chewed his food and stared at his uncle. Something was going on here, and she didn't think for a second she'd like whatever kind of secrets they were hiding.

For the rest of the dinner, she stayed silent, not wanting to ask questions. The rumors about the Carson family kept ringing around her head. He had so much security, and every time she walked into a room, conversation between the men always seemed to stop.

After dinner, she made her way to her room, taking a quick shower and changing into pajamas. Sitting on her bed, she stared at her books but couldn't find the energy to study, even though that was all she did.

She was curious about that damn book.

Climbing off the bed, she made her way down the flights of stairs and entered the library. She flicked the switch for the second floor of lights and climbed the stairs, finding the book once again.

She stared at the spine and gritted her teeth.

It's just a book about positions and sex. You've learned all about this in sex ed.

Still, she reached out, taking hold of the book and turning it over. Opening the page, she stared down at the man holding onto his cock. It wasn't a real-life drawing either, but a sketch.

"You really like that book."

She gasped, spinning around, and came face to face with Beast.

He was still in his suit.

"You scared me."

"Were you worried about being caught in the library with a dirty book?" He took a step closer, and the response with her body was instant. Her tits became sensitive, and her pussy grew wet.

She was a virgin, but that didn't for a second mean she didn't know what was going on with her body.

Beast was a very attractive man, and she was attracted to him, no doubt about it. Her little crush wasn't so little, not right now.

They were alone, in his library, and she held a book that suddenly felt like fire within her grasp.

"I…"

"It's okay to be curious. What do you like?" he asked.

She stared down at the book, and he moved her so that her back was to him. She wasn't able to see his face, which unnerved her a little.

"You like seeing a man take his cock into his hand."

"It's a beautiful drawing," she said.

"This is more than a drawing, Hope. It's a temptation. Don't you see that?" He reached out as she held both hardback covers, and he turned the page. It was hard for her to not gasp. That same cock was seen running through the lips of a woman's pussy. "Our bodies are made for fucking. These are just pages, giving a glimpse of the real thing."

She closed the book up, not even wanting to deal with that temptation, and slid it back into its spot. Her emotions were all over the place because all she could think about was a cock sliding inside a woman's pussy as perfectly as that book did in that space.

When she turned around again, Beast was close. He placed one hand on the books beside her head along with the other one, staring down at her, trapping her against his hard body and the books. She didn't mind at all.

In fact, there was nowhere else she'd rather be.

"You're a curious little thing."

"What more is there to be?" she asked, tilting her head back, staring at him. She couldn't look away, nor did she want to. With how close he was, she wondered if he was going to kiss her. His body was so close to hers, and she didn't want him to back away. She craved his touch.

They were the only two people in the world as far as she was concerned. Anything could happen.

Her gaze went to his lips, and she bit her own. What would it feel like to have his mouth on hers, to take what he wanted without any thought from her?

No one had ever kissed her before, and she'd never wanted anyone's kiss. Slowly, she placed her hands on his chest.

He was rock-solid, and she'd seen the gym that he kept near the pool house at the bottom of the garden. She had yet to see him work out in it, but that didn't matter.

"You're playing with fire, Hope."

"I don't care." She didn't have the first clue what she was doing, only that she couldn't stop herself as she stepped close, bringing her body to his, finally feeling him against her.

One of his hands fisted inside her hair, tugging on the length, making her gasp as he pulled her head back. She didn't look away, nor was she afraid. Something told her that Beast couldn't hurt her.

His other hand still rested on the bookcases behind her. The angle that he held her meant her body was in full contact with him, and she felt the hard ridge of his cock pressing against her stomach.

"You have no idea what you're doing."

"Then teach me, Beast. Teach me what I'm doing."

Slowly, she drew one hand down, cupping his cock. This was the most blatant she'd ever been in her life. She didn't have a clue what to do, but it was like she was running on instinct, and that alone charged her actions, making it hard for her to think past anything else.

She gasped as his lips crashed against hers, pressing her against the bookcase, making her moan and ache all over just with the power of his kiss. Wrapping her arms around him, she never wanted to let him go, and refused to give him up. His cock pressed urgently against her pussy, and she cried out, needing everything he could give her, and more. There wasn't a second that went by that she didn't want more.

There was no fear, just need.

Her pussy was on fire, her nipples rock hard, begging for his touch, and for more.

Beast shoved her against the bookcases, taking both of her hands and holding them above her head, keeping her trapped as he kissed her.

His tongue trailed across her lips, and she closed her eyes. When she opened her lips, he plunged inside, and she tasted the coffee on his breath.

"You taste so fucking good. I bet every single part of you tastes like perfection."

One of his hands let go of her wrist, and a finger trailed down her arm, across her breasts, toward her pussy.

"You want me to teach you?" he asked.

"Yes." She didn't have a clue what was happening right now, but she didn't want it to stop.

"Friday night, come to my room. Dwayne's away for the weekend. We'll have the whole house to ourselves, and cancel your shift at the diner. You'll belong to me."

Before she could ask any questions, he was gone.

****

The rest of the week went by without any event whatsoever. Beast often contemplated what the fuck he was doing. He watched Hope from afar, seeing the way she turned toward him. Her curious eyes always drove him crazy, wanting to know more. What was she thinking half the time that she stared at him? He honestly didn't know. There were times he caught her in the library staring at that same book, which gripped her attention. Each time, it made his damn cock thick imagining her spread on his bed, begging for his cock.

"You know, she's a strange one," Dwayne said, shoving a few of his bags in the car. Caleb was taking him out camping for the weekend, which was more than fine with Beast. "No one understands her."

Out of the two of them, Caleb liked to get back to nature. It seemed to balance him between the monster he became to the outside world.

"No man is ever supposed to understand a woman, Dwayne. That's the point of them being different."

Dwayne laughed. "Yeah, but she's more than that, and it scares a lot of people at school." He shrugged. "You sure you don't want to take her with us?"

Beast glanced back at the house and saw she was standing in the library. When she caught them both looking, she held her hand up, giving them a wave.

"I'm sure."

Keeping control of his patience, he waited for Dwayne and Caleb to both be gone before he headed back into the house.

There was no soldier in sight, as he'd asked them to keep a perimeter outside. He didn't want any interruptions this evening.

She stood at the top of the open staircase, and he caught sight of the ankle-length skirt she wore. She also had on a shirt. Even as she covered every inch of skin, he knew the curves of her body, how big her tits were as they strained against the buttons holding them together.

The skirt dipped in at her waist, highlighting her hips and thighs.

It wouldn't be long before he had them wrapped around him.

Neither of them spoke as he grabbed hold of the banister and began to make his way toward her. With each step he took, he imagined her backing out, telling him she'd changed her mind.

She didn't say a word even as he climbed the last step, closing that distance between them. He'd not spoken to her since their conversation in the library, nor had he shared a meal with her. In fact, he'd purposely left her alone to see how she could handle what was going on between them, and if she'd back out.

Taking her hand, without a word he made his way back to where their rooms were. Once outside his door, he pressed her against it, cupping her cheek, running his thumb across her lip.

"I've not brought a woman here before," he said, finally breaking through the silence. "I never bring women here."

She nodded.

"Do you want to come into my room?" he asked.

"Before you answer that I want to warn you. I don't always play nice. I'm not a nice person, Hope. Don't think this is more than sex. It's not."

"I'm not asking for anything else, Beast. I'm not wearing my heart on my sleeve. I'm not sticking around, remember? This isn't going to change that."

"Good girl." He opened the door. Reaching in, he flicked the light on and closed it behind him.

His room was basic. The layout was the exact same as hers, only his bed was a little larger and more rounded as he liked plenty of space when he slept. His sheets were black silk, and the walls pure white.

He didn't need anything more than a bed and doors which opened, leading onto a veranda where he could overlook the garden.

She spun in a circle, taking in everything.

Finally, her gaze returned to him. Removing his jacket, he placed it on one of the chairs he had in his room.

"Strip."

"You're not big on romance."

"I'm not going to have you believing shit that doesn't exist."

"You don't think romance exists?"

"I know it doesn't."

"Then you've not been around the right people. You love Dwayne."

He stared at her. "I never said I love him."

"But you take care of him. You always make sure he's okay."

"That's not love. It's obligation."

She smiled. "Okay." He was sure that wasn't really okay. Her gaze remained on him as she began to open the buttons of her shirt. "Are you trying to scare me off?"

"No." He wasn't. Tugging his own shirt off, he advanced toward her, halting her progress, realizing that he wanted to be the one to take her clothes off.

He took charge, opening the buttons of her shirt and moving the fabric down her arms. The simple white bra lace against her skin reminded him that she was new to all of this, that she could believe in hearts, flowers, and all the crap the rest of the world wanted to believe.

"I'm not running," she said.

"That's your mistake, but now I'm not going to let you go." Cupping her face, he slammed his lips down on hers, tasting her once again. She touched his hips, and he pulled her against him, needing her close.

The bra covering her tits was an obstruction he didn't want. With a single snap of the strap, he had it undone, and her tits fell free. Cupping the mounds, he relished her cries, wanting them to never stop.

Kissing down her neck, he held her still, watching as her head tilted back just a little, her mouth opening slightly on a gasp as her eyes closed.

Running his thumb across her lips, he slipped it inside her mouth and moaned as she sucked him.

He shouldn't be here, not with her, but no matter what he said, he couldn't bring himself to pull away.

Staring at her virgin tits, he flicked the tip of a large red nipple. Sucking her into his mouth, he heard her gasp and rushed moan. Smiling against her skin, he used his teeth, and she cried out his name.

The sound of his name from her lips brought a rush straight to his cock.

Sliding his tongue between the valley of her tits, he took her other breast, giving it the same attention as he'd given the first one.

His dick pressed against the front of his pants, begging to be released. He was so fucking aroused. All he wanted was to put her down on the bed, spread her thighs, and fuck her hard. He didn't do that.

Taking his time, he released her face and touched the button holding her skirt in place. In quick movements, her skirt was on the floor, and she stood in a pair of plain white panties. So virginal, so out of place in his room, and yet so tempting that he couldn't look away.

She was perfection, and she fired his blood.

Stepping back, he kicked off his shoes, removing his pants, being careful not to hurt his swelling dick.

The boxer briefs remained on, and he stepped up toward her once again. She was panting, and he noticed that she tried to cover herself.

"Don't ever hide your body from me," he said.

"I'm not perfect."

"I don't give a fuck what you think."

"I'm fat."

He couldn't help what he did next. Pushing her down on the bed so that her ass was up in the air, he slapped each juicy cheek, watching as her skin blushed beneath his touch. It was so fucking addictive he did it again for good measure.

Beast moved right behind her so that his cock pressed against her ass cheeks, their underwear keeping them both safe from each other for the time being. He didn't want to rush in taking her virginity.

Leaning over her, he took hold of her hands, pressing them down on the bed so that she was trapped underneath him. She squirmed, and he loved feeling her wriggle.

"Don't ever call yourself fat in my company. I have no problem spanking that hot ass."

"I'm not perfect. I have wiggly bits."

He chuckled, rubbing his shaft against her flesh. "Does this feel like I give a shit about wiggly bits, baby?

I don't. You ever call yourself shit again, and I swear there will be consequences."

Chapter Six

Hope stayed still as Beast continued to pin her down on the bed. She loved his spanks, the words of warning that rolled off his tongue, commanding her to do as she was told. Her weight had been an issue with so many people, and yet he'd been so pissed off that she'd been nervous around him. She liked that. She liked his attention, and the way he seemed to know exactly what she was feeling.

"I like your curves, baby. Your weight means that you won't break in my arms."

Even his threats aroused her.

I'm crazy.

She didn't care.

From the moment he'd begun his journey walking up those steps, her body had been on fire, and she didn't want to put it out, not now, not ever.

Slowly, he pulled away from her, and she missed his touch, not that she had to wait long for him to take her once again.

He flipped her over, and she stared up at him. Her breasts were naked, and the only piece of material protecting her was that of her panties between her thighs.

His fingers landed on her hip, and he stroked across her stomach. The tips of his fingers slid beneath the waistband of her panties, making her ache for more of his touch.

"These are pretty, but I really prefer you without them." He snapped them off her. The sheer force of his strength surprised her as he took charge, getting rid of the fabric as he tossed it onto the floor. "Now that is so much better, and so very pretty." His fingers stroked across the fine hairs of her pussy. "I'm a man that likes to know he's fucking a woman, so don't go waxing or doing any of that porn star shit that women seem to think men like. Some men may like it, not me."

"O-kay."

He smiled. "Do I make you nervous?"

"I think you make everyone nervous."

"I do. It's nice to know you're finally paying attention."

"I think you do it for fun though. You like to make people afraid of you."

"Fear keeps a lot of people in check. Fear of the unknown, and what crazy shit people can do."

"I'm not afraid of you."

"Then you're crazy, because you should be." He sank down to the floor, and she watched as he spread her thighs open. "Look at this very wet pussy. You've been thinking some wicked thoughts. I hope they're all about me. I don't like sharing."

There wasn't anyone else she could want. He opened the lips of her pussy, and she went to her elbows so that she could see him clearer.

"No man has tasted this?" he asked.

She shook her head.

Hope cried out as his tongue latched onto her clit, sucking it inside. The pleasure was instant, and she collapsed onto the bed, staring up at the ceiling as he took her pussy. He slid his tongue over and across, sucking and licking.

He touched over her entrance but didn't penetrate, gliding up to take her clit into his mouth, sucking it in deep again.

"You're so wet. So desperate." His hands moved to her hips, holding her down as he continued the pleasure of her pussy. She didn't know what to do, and there was no way for her to fight the feelings he inspired. His touch took it to a whole new level, and she knew without a doubt that she was about to come. It wasn't slow either. One second his touch felt so good, the next almost unbearable as her orgasm rushed over her body.

She screamed his name, and he teased her clit.

There was no way she could take much more, and it wasn't long before she begged him to stop.

He finally relented, releasing her clit and landing a kiss to her hip.

"Was that your first orgasm?" he asked.

She nodded.

"You've never tried to touch yourself?"

"I've touched myself. I've just never … completed."

"Thank you." He pressed another kiss to her hip.

When he stood up, she couldn't just lie there waiting, so she moved up his bed, sitting against the pillows and watching as he went to a stereo. Soft, melodious music filled the air.

She liked the classical music most of all. It helped to relax her.

Beast wasn't done though. He removed his boxer briefs, and she caught her first real sight of a man, and boy, was he a man.

His cock was long and hard.

He was big though, not that she'd seen anyone to compare him to, but he looked … painful. Like he wouldn't fit inside her, or if he tried it was going to hurt.

Remember sex ed. No one's too big.

Just uncomfortable.

He wrapped his fingers around the length, but he didn't dive on the bed and take her hand. She watched, unable to form any kind of words as he pulled a condom out of his bedside drawer.

"Are you on the pill?"

She shook her head.

"I'm clean, but I don't want to risk pregnancy." She watched as he tore into the condom and began to lower it over his shaft.

When his knees hit the bed, she tensed up. She couldn't help it.

"Do you want me to stop?"

She shook her head. "No, I don't." She lay down on the bed. "I want this."

He lay out beside her, his hand resting on her stomach, and once again she was confused. He didn't do love or romance, and yet his very actions said the complete opposite.

If he didn't believe in romance, wouldn't he just fuck her and get it over with?

She didn't know enough to judge, only what she imagined, and that wasn't a whole lot. This was confusing to her.

"Talk to me."

"Do you make all the women talk to you?"

"Only the ones I like hearing the voices of," he said.

She didn't like that but didn't say a thing. The thought of him with anyone else filled her with jealousy, and she hated that, hated that anyone could have that kind of control of her, and she wasn't even with him yet.

"There's been no other woman in this bed, and I don't like hearing other women talk."

"I'm not so different," she said.

"You're wrong."

She turned toward him. "What?"

"You're my first and only virgin, Hope. I told you, I'm not a good man. You shouldn't be here because I like to keep what's mine, and I don't like to play either." The hand on her stomach trailed up, and he cupped her tit. "I'm a selfish fucker."

"I don't know what to say."

"Then don't say anything, and just know that if another man or boy thinks they can take you, they're going to have to go through me."

That sent a thrill down her spine. She liked his possessive words. Never in all of her life had she ever been wanted, and even though she was eighteen she wanted to be worth something.

Cupping his cheek, she pulled him down, kissing him back.

She was more than ready to have him.

He moved over her, and she spread her thighs for him. Even though she was petrified, she didn't want to stop.

Hope wanted him to be her first, and in the back of her mind she knew she wanted him to be her last as well, but for now, she'd settle on just being her first. He was going to ruin her for every single man, but that was okay. She had no intention of being with anyone else.

Beast broke from the kiss first, and he pulled away just a little. She watched as he grabbed his cock, running the tip down between her slit, bumping her clit before he moved down. She gasped as he didn't wait. He didn't take his time.

Slamming his cock in deep, he tore through the wall of her virginity, taking her hard. The pain was instant, and he caught her hands, pinning them to the bed, keeping her underneath him, and she felt her eyes fill with tears. She always knew there would be pain, but never did she think it would be so … strong.

It was just a thin piece of skin, a hymen. She'd read it could be removed with simple horse riding, and yet here she was, ruining her first moment.

"Shh, I've got you," he said, kissing her neck, sucking on the pulse.

Slowly, as the pain began to lessen, she could think about other things. The way he held her down, the weight of him over her. She loved the feel of his body inside her.

His kisses went from her pulse to her tits, sucking on each bud before coming back to take her lips.

Each of his kisses awakened the fire in her veins. He began to pull out of her pussy, only to thrust back inside. This time, there was no pain.

She cried out in pleasure and need as he began to rock within her.

"Fuck, baby, you feel so fucking good."

His thrusts started out slow, and built until he slammed every inch of his cock inside her, and she loved it, not wanting it to end as he brought her to a second orgasm.

This time, Beast joined her, filling the condom he wore.

****

The first time wasn't perfect, but then it was never perfect for anyone. Beast continued to hold her down on the bed, and stared into her eyes as she slowly opened them. He smiled right back at her.

"You're beautiful," he said.

He meant it as well. Beast couldn't recall ever seeing a more beautiful woman than he did right now.

"Next time will be better."

"There's going to be a next time?"

"You're going to try to convince me that you're happy with just one time." He'd hated causing her pain. In fact, it had left a bitter taste in his mouth to see the tears falling down the sides of her face, and he'd wanted to fucking kill something. Instead, he'd waited, hoping that the pain would lessen like he'd read it would.

Yeah, he was so fucking gone he'd even done

research on fucking a virgin. It was … pitiful.

He was used to women who knew how to take a cock, who relished being used and fucked.

Hope wasn't like those women.

She was a virgin.

Beautiful inside and out.

Even after everything she'd been through.

"I'd like there to be a next time."

He pulled out of her, and saw the flash of pain cross her face. *No more times tonight.* "Stay there."

Entering his bathroom, he filled the bath, adding some soothing salts and lighting some scented candles. Whatever fancy shit that helped women when they were in pain. He entered the room, and moved back toward the bed, seeing Hope trying to remove the blanket. "I thought I told you to stay put."

She moved quickly, and he saw she was hiding something. Stepping up close to her, he glanced over her shoulder, and caught sight of what she was trying to hide.

There on his pristine white sheet that lay beneath the black silk sheets was the sign of her virginity. He'd already seen the blood on the condom, which he'd thrown into the trash.

"Erm, I need to clean these sheets. I'm so sorry."

Cupping her face, he kissed her lips and smiled down at her. "You've got nothing to be sorry about."

He … liked it.

Beast had always known he was a freaky fucker, and this confirmed it. The sight of her virgin blood on his bed filled him with so much fucking pleasure. Not just that, he was consumed by need to keep her that way. To keep her for his cock only.

You don't do love.

You don't do romance.

You don't do virgins.

That had all changed. He didn't even want to think about her teenage status, even though she was eighteen.

He didn't like young women.

There was something about Hope though. She wasn't like anyone else, and damn it, he wanted to take care of her.

He didn't want her to go without.

When he picked her up in his arms, she wrapped her legs around him. "I've got to clean it up."

"You've got to rest in the bath, and I'll take care of that. You don't have to worry about a thing."

He lowered her into the bath. Tilting her head back, he took her lips once again, unable to deny himself the pleasure of her kiss. "I will deal with the sheets."

"It's gross."

"No, it confirms you're mine." He kissed her once again. "I'll be back. Do not leave this bathroom."

Entering his bedroom, he removed the sheet and stared at the stain on the sheet.

A virgin.

His virgin.

His woman.

No matter what he thought, he felt this consuming need to keep her.

Even as she wanted to leave town, he wanted her to stay.

There's ways of keeping her.

He knew there were a lot of ways to keep her. The first one was fear, which he didn't want. The last thing he wanted was for her to be afraid of him. He loved it when she smiled at him, talked with him.

The moment fear entered any situation, something as easy as talking became a challenge.

She'd already had so much fear in her life, and

had seen darkness. He wasn't going to bring that to her again. The other way was pregnancy. He didn't like that one either, even though that would be the most effective.

Pushing those thoughts to the back of his mind, he threw the sheet into the laundry basket and changed the bed before entering the bathroom. She was lying back when he entered. She sat up as she saw him, her cheeks flaming red.

He didn't wait for an invitation. Sliding in the bath behind her, he wrapped his arms around her waist, tugging her back so that she was lying against him. "You have nothing to be embarrassed about when you're with me." He kissed her shoulder. "I don't want you to keep anything from me."

"I guess I'm confused right now."

"Why?"

"I don't know what this is. Doesn't protocol say that I've got to go to my own room now, and never look at you again?"

He burst out laughing. "Protocol? For what?"

"I don't know. One-night stands? I don't know what this is."

Resting his hand on her stomach, he kissed the side of her head. "I thought you wanted to be taught. All those delightful little positions you've caught sight of in that very dirty book."

She relaxed against him.

"This can be anything you want it to be, Hope. It doesn't have to be something quick and over in an instant. This can be a lot more, and you don't have to put a label on it. I know I'm not."

"I don't want it to be over." She looked up at him. "I'm … I won't be clingy or anything. I still have school, and in a couple of weeks I'm going to be looking at colleges. I don't want to leave it to the last minute."

He didn't like the thought of her leaving, but there wasn't much he could do about it, at least not yet. "I can help you with college applications."

"You can?"

"Yes."

"I don't want Dwayne to know," she said, biting her lip. "I'm not embarrassed, but we don't really get along, and I don't know what he'd say at school, and it's already weird—"

"Even if he was to find out, I'd make sure that he didn't say anything. No one is ever going to make you feel anything you don't want, Hope."

She giggled. "Does your power run to the entire school?"

"No, but I've got Dwayne. Just say the words, and you can be the most popular girl in school by the end of Monday."

Hope shook her head. "I've never wanted to be popular. It looks way too exhausting. I like being left alone. I don't make friends easily. I always had my mom."

Guilt washed over him.

Her mother had been taken away, and she'd been trying to survive on her own.

Gritting his teeth, he reached for the sponge and began to wash her body.

"I'm sorry, I don't mean to go a bit dark on you."

"You've not gone dark." He cupped her face, stroking her cheek. "I don't want you to keep anything from me. I want to know every single secret."

"What's the point of there being secrets if I tell you?"

"A lot of secrets are meant to be shared." He ran his thumb across her bottom lip.

"I can try," she said. "Will you share secrets with

me?"

"I don't like broccoli. I've never liked it. I think it's the food of the devil."

She burst out laughing, and he smiled. It was the truth. He never told anyone, and he always left it when it was on his plate. He hated the stuff.

"That's not a big secret."

"No, but it's something no one else knows."

She bit her lip and stared at him. "I wish someone had killed my dad," she confessed. "I get so angry that he was able to take the only person I've ever loved away from me. He wasn't always around, and he was always such a boring person. Miserable, and he'd take the light out of Mom's eyes."

"It's okay to want something like that."

"Is it though? He killed my mom, and I wish more than anything that he'd put the gun to his head before he came home." He saw her grit her teeth.

"Your father was a coward, Hope. Don't let him bring you down." He kissed the top of her head. He'd do everything he could to protect her.

Chapter Seven

"Look what I got," Dwayne said.

Hope pulled her bag out of the locker and turned toward him. He held a piece of paper up. "Is that your math test?"

"Yes, and I got a B. Look at that. I totally nailed it."

She smiled. "Congratulations. See, I knew you'd nail it." She clapped her hands for him, and laughed as he took a bow.

"I think we should celebrate."

"Okay, how?"

"Party."

Shaking her head, she finished grabbing her stuff from out of her locker. "Not happening. I don't do parties."

"You know that's weird, right? Besides, it'll be a party at our place."

She wrinkled her nose. "Will your uncle really go for that?"

"I'll ask him tonight. Besides, he's heading out this weekend, so we'll have the entire place to ourselves, and he doesn't need to know."

The thought of keeping something from Beast didn't sit well with her. The weekend they'd just shared meant something to her. She didn't know if Beast felt the same way, but she couldn't bring herself to lie to him.

"Come on, Hope. I've had parties without him knowing before. Don't tell him, please."

"I don't feel comfortable with all of this. He's done so much for me."

Dwayne rolled his eyes. "Come on, Hope. Live a little. It's not going to be long before you're old, covered in wrinkles, and wishing you had something to do with this party."

She burst out laughing, shaking her head. "You've got to ask him first. I'm not going to be part of making him mad."

"Whatever." Dwayne winked at her and told her he'd see her later.

Releasing a breath, she got through the rest of her day without any other sign of Dwayne, which she was pleased about.

By the time school ended, she saw Caleb waiting to take her home. Dwayne was nowhere in sight.

"Are you here to take me home?" she asked, stepping up to him.

"Yes. Beast is on business right now, and he'll be home when he's ready."

He opened the door for her, and she didn't argue even though it was in the back of the car.

Putting on the seatbelt, she noticed a couple of people paid a little more attention. The car was a nice one, and probably of a popular make. She didn't know. She'd never been one for cars.

After her parents died, she'd actually worked out the expense on running a car, and that had been put in the "never" pile.

"Beast wanted me to tell you that he hoped you had a good day."

She smiled. "Thank you."

"Did you?"

"Yeah, it was okay." She nibbled her lip.

"Do you know what you're doing with my brother?" Caleb asked, drawing her attention back to him.

"Excuse me?"

"Don't pretend that I don't know you and my brother are a thing. You're a lot younger than the women he usually screws, but I guess he has a thing for innocence and that kind of thing."

Her cheeks heated. "I don't really feel comfortable."

"Look, you're one in a long line of women he's screwed. Graduate from high school, get the fuck out, and go to college. That's my advice. Don't have feelings that you're going to get married, have lots of babies, and all that shit. Women don't deserve to be part of this life, at least not women like you."

He pulled up inside the main gates.

"I'm not being a bastard on purpose here. I think you're a great person, and that for me is the problem. Great people in this life have a tendency to find themselves dead."

She swallowed past the lump in her throat. "I … the rumors?"

"They're true. Beast is probably going to be pissed I told you, but we're not good men, Hope. There's no hope of ever finding anything good inside us so don't try. Find what you love, and then stay the hell away from us otherwise you'll be joining both of your parents at the cemetery."

Hope didn't linger. She climbed out of the car and made her way toward her room. Closing the door behind her, she leaned against it with her heart pounding. That was Beast's brother, and he was warning her about it, and she couldn't think, not right now.

Closing her eyes, she saw the smile on his lips that weekend as she made him laugh. She couldn't recall seeing him smile all that much.

Yes, she was playing with fire. Their age difference alone confirmed that, but she liked him. She'd been attracted to him from the very beginning. Even now, after Caleb's warning, she still wanted him, and that wasn't ever going to change.

Stepping away from the door, she dropped her bag, heading straight to the bathroom. Removing her clothes, she climbed beneath the warm spray, thankful as it seemed to wash away all of her worries.

Whatever was going on between her and Beast, it wouldn't last.

In time, she wanted romance and love. She didn't just want sex. Right now, she could handle his rules without too much worry. Placing her hand on the tile, she recalled the feel of his hands on her body, touching her, stroking between her thighs, building a fire that only he could put out.

The water began to turn cold, and she quickly pulled out of her haze and changed into a set of pajamas. It was early, but she didn't want to leave her room. There was comfort there and no confusion.

She was tired of being confused.

Pulling out her books, she spread them open, and for the next three hours she just sat on her bed, studying.

When she needed to clear her head, she stepped out onto the veranda that looked out over the garden.

She heard moaning, and saw Dwayne with one of the girls from school below her in the garden. Quickly stepping back into her room, she shuddered. She wasn't interested in seeing other people have sex.

Going back to her studies she didn't stare at the time until she saw that it was nearly nine, and her stomach started to growl.

Getting up from bed, she made her way downstairs and went to the kitchen. She paused when she caught sight of Beast, shirtless, rummaging through the kitchen. Staring at his back, she saw several silvery scars that looked like they came from whips.

"Who did that?" she asked.

"My dad. It was all part of his punishment, and how to keep a brat in line. I don't think it mattered if you were a good or bad kid, it's what he did." He turned toward her, holding stuff to make a sandwich. "Hungry?" he asked.

"Yes." She nodded, crossing her arms over her chest.

"Are you having second thoughts yet?"

"About?"

"Last weekend?"

She shook her head. "No. Erm, Caleb, he … said some things."

"Let me guess, he pretty much told you that my world isn't suited for women like you?" he asked.

She saw the grasp he had on the butter knife he was using. "How true are the rumors?" she asked.

He smiled, and it was then that she realized she hadn't a clue about the man he was, or who he claimed to be.

The stories were all around town. Everywhere she turned there was idle gossip, but then she compared it to the stories about what happened to her, and they were so damn wrong. Now though, she began to second-guess herself.

"Why don't you just ask me questions, and I'll tell you what you want to know, and what you're not allowed to know."

He put some ham and cheese onto a sandwich, closed it, and took a bite.

Something was happening here, and she wasn't entirely sure what it was, only that it scared her.

"Have you ever killed someone?" she asked.

"Yes."

She paused, and took a breath. "Were they innocent?"

75

"Does it matter?"

"I don't know." She took a step back, rubbing at her forehead. "I … I'm going back to my room. I can't. I'm sorry."

She didn't say anything more, and made her way to her room, a little disappointed that he didn't follow. Dwayne stood just outside of his door as she went to the next set of stairs leading her to floor.

Neither of them said a word as she began walking to her room. Everything had changed the moment she agreed to tutor him.

****

Beast was pissed. Finishing off his sandwich, he pulled out two slices of bread and began to make Hope some food. She'd not eaten, and he'd heard her stomach growling. He was pissed off, and when he was in that mood, it made him say and do things that he often regretted.

"You need to leave her alone," Caleb said.

He threw the knife he had, and it went straight past his brother's face, hitting the wall and clattering to the floor.

"You must be getting old."

"I didn't miss." He grabbed another knife and finished up her sandwich, adding slices of fruit and some cake he saw. "You're not to talk to her about shit you don't understand."

"What are you hoping to achieve with her, Beast? She's an innocent. She thought the idle talk around town was just fucking rumors."

"I don't give a fuck what anyone else says, Caleb. You're not to tell her shit, or to confuse her."

"She's eighteen."

"She's fucking mine!" He glared at his brother, and movement out of the corner of his eye drew his attention to Dwayne. "You got a problem with that?"

Dwayne held his hands up. "I don't know what is going on, and like always I'm the last one to find out."

"You're not like our father," Caleb said. "She's … weak. She didn't grow up with this, and what do you think's going to happen when she discovers the involvement you had with her parents?"

Beast stared at his brother and his nephew. "I'm not giving her up. She doesn't find out about that, and if either of you says anything, you better hope I don't feel like I need to lose a brother."

Picking up the plate of food, he made his way toward her room.

Nothing was going to make him give her up.

He didn't knock on the door; he entered and found her sitting on the bed, staring at the books in front of her.

Closing the door behind him, he watched her for several seconds. Neither of them spoke, and he liked that she didn't always feel the need to talk. He wished she would talk now, though, so he knew what was going on in her mind.

"I've killed people that needed to be taken care of."

"What about the cops?"

He shook his head. "I've got men who turn a blind eye."

She nodded. "Are you like the mafia?"

"No. I'm not."

"What is it then?"

"I'm a guy that inherited responsibilities. I have legitimate businesses, and I have some that I don't want to talk about. My father taught me everything that I know, and after he killed my mother, I took care of him."

Her mouth opened and closed.

"I'm telling you this because you've seen darkness, Hope, and you've come out of it. You've heard the rumors, and I've told you before I'm not a nice guy. I'm not the Prince Charming in this story. I never have been. I never will be. I'm the kind of guy your mother warned you about." He laughed. "I shouldn't even be here right now, and I certainly shouldn't have fucked you. I don't know what it is about you to be honest. I can't get enough of you, and even when I try to stay away, I find myself drawn back to you."

He put the plate on the dressing table and moved toward the bed. One by one, he closed her books, and she didn't fight him.

Her gaze was on his, and he saw she was taking deep breaths. Her shirt pressed against her tits, showing off her hard nipples, and his cock responded. He wanted to fill her pussy, flood her with his cum, and watch as her pussy leaked it out. There were so many dirty things he wanted to do to her, and he would.

Beast intended to make her crave him just as he did her.

He held out his hand, and without hesitation she placed her hand in his. "What I can promise you, Hope, is you'll never see this life. It'll never touch you. You're safe here, and I can guarantee that."

Putting his hands on her hips, he tugged her forward.

"Do you want me to leave? Do you want me to forget how good your pussy felt wrapped around my cock, and that you wanted me to teach you?"

"I don't want you to leave." She placed her hand on his chest, her fingers tracing over his heart. "I want you to promise me that when I graduate, you'll let me walk away."

He gritted his teeth. That was going to be next to

impossible, but he had ways and means of making what he wanted happen.

"I agree." It wasn't the first time that he'd lied, and he doubted it would be his last.

Hope called to a part of him he'd long thought dead. He wanted to be a better man for her. The women he fucked, he didn't care about, and he never had.

She was the only one that made him ache.

Teasing the edge of her shirt, he tugged it over her head and dropped it to the floor. Cupping one of her breasts, he teased the nipple, relishing her moan as he pinched the hard bud. "All I've been able to think about all day is these tits bouncing as you ride my dick. I want that. Do you want it?"

"Yes."

He took possession of her lips, pushing her back to the bed. She sat on the edge, and he stepped out of his pants, kicking off his shoes.

Gripping the waist of her bottoms, he took them off, and groaned as he saw the evidence of her arousal. She hadn't even bothered with panties, and he liked that. Skimming his hands down her thighs, he spread her open and slid a single finger inside her.

She was tight, incredibly so, and he wanted to taste her.

Going to his knees before her, he held her hips as he took her clit into his mouth. She cried out his name, and he smiled, licking and sucking at her nub, wanting her to come on his face before he got what he wanted.

Her fists at her side, he drew her first orgasm with a few strokes of his tongue. Climbing onto the bed, he guided her so that she straddled his lap. Holding his cock still, he watched as she slowly took him in deep, her cunt squeezing his dick as he went to the hilt inside her.

Returning his grip to her hips, he held her steady.

Her gaze was slightly hooded as she looked at him.

"I don't know what I'm doing," she said.

"I'll show you."

"It's not just that. I shouldn't be here with you."

He stared at her, wondering if he should be insulted by that, but saw the confusion in her gaze.

"Do you want me to let you go? I can stop, and you can live your life. I won't force you to do anything." He only wanted her if she wanted to be here. He'd been and done many things in his life, but he wasn't a rapist, nor was he an abuser.

Her hands moved to his shoulders. "I don't want you to stop. Show me what you like," she said.

Keeping hold of her hips, he showed her how to take his cock. Her hands were on his shoulders as she took over rocking her pussy on his cock. Stroking his hands over her body, he leaned back and watched as her tits bounced. He loved the way she arched up, and each time he hit that special place inside her, she seemed to purr with each stroke.

Beast saw the scar on her stomach. The single hole that had been healed, and he skimmed his fingers across the wound. They both had scars put there by others.

The only difference, hers were partly his fault as he'd supplied the gun. He'd never have hurt her, and he hadn't for a second known what that guy was going to do.

Her father had been a two-bit crook, an addict, and he'd not really cared for the reason why he wanted the gun, only that he owed more money.

Pushing those thoughts to the back of his mind, he basked in having her in his arms. His own little Hope that he never intended to give up.

Gripping her ass, he took charge, filling her

pussy, jolting her as he got deeper and deeper inside her.

Sliding his hands around to her front, he found her pussy and teased over her clit.

"You're so fucking beautiful, baby. There's nothing else I want to see than you riding my cock."

"Please, Beast."

"You want to come?"

"Yes."

Stroking her clit, he watched and felt as she came apart, giving him her second orgasm of the night.

She brought him to his first, and he flooded her cunt with his cream. Part of him hoped that she got pregnant because he finally had something that he didn't want to give up.

Chapter Eight

On the day of the secret party Beast was nowhere to be seen, but Hope had already figured he had work to do as he'd told her he wouldn't be around. Staring out of her bedroom window, she watched as Dwayne welcomed his guests. She was dressed in a pair of jeans and a shirt, but she didn't feel like joining the others.

She missed Beast.

Their time together was fleeting at most, but she relished the rare moments they shared together. He'd gone to take care of some business, and she'd spent a lot of time researching the internet on anything to do with Beast Carson. There was a great deal of information about him. He'd told her he wouldn't hide the truth, and she knew most of the rumors about them were indeed true.

He killed people.

His businesses were not always legal.

She didn't know how she felt about that.

Dwayne looked up toward her bedroom, and did that hand wave signal thing that told her to come down.

Seeing no point in staying camped out in her bedroom, she made her way toward the party, being sure to lock the door that she left through. Beast had told her that he didn't mind Dwayne having parties so long as they stayed out of the main house.

He didn't want any brat seeing something that couldn't be unseen. Again, she didn't know exactly what that meant, so she stood at the edge of the party, feeling uneasy.

Beast didn't know about this party, or at least, she didn't think he did.

"It's about time you came out and had a little fun. Have you ever been to a party before with actual human beings?" Dwayne asked, putting his arm around her shoulders.

"Did you ask your uncle about this?"

"Please, Beast won't mind. He never does. You've got to learn to live a little. Besides, we both know he's got a thing for you." He winked at her, and she just stared at him. Neither of them spoke about the fact she was screwing his uncle. Most of the time she didn't give Dwayne much of a thought unless she was tutoring him. It wasn't because she was being rude, but neither of them had anything in common. Like now, she didn't want to upset Beast. "If he's mad I'll just push you in front of him. It'll take away all of his killer instincts and I'll be safe."

She didn't like that. "Don't, Dwayne."

"Don't what? Come on, Miss Prissy. Lighten up. I know you two are screwing. I've known for some time now, and you don't think I caught you both eye-fucking each other. Just have some fun. Beast's not home, and you know what? Good. It means I get to make you have a good time." He grabbed a cup of beer, handing it to her. "Now, take a sip and loosen up. This is a party. You're safe here."

She took a sip of the beer and wrinkled her nose. It was cheap, nasty, and horrible. The music filled the air, and she took a seat beside the pool, staring at the scantily clad girls. Some of them she didn't even remember their names, but they were screaming for Dwayne to join them.

They removed their bikinis, throwing the wet fabric toward him. Within seconds his shirt was off, and he dived into the pool.

She chuckled and looked away as he began to kiss one girl, then the other, before going for the third girl.

"Leave it to Dwayne to have all the fun."

Hope turned to see one of Dwayne's friends, Micah, take a seat. "He seems to know how to throw a party."

"I've not seen you around here before."

"First party," she said, taking another sip. She missed Beast, his warmth and his passion, but she didn't say anything.

"You're the girl that has moved in here, right? The one the uncle controls."

She frowned. "No, I just live here."

"Haven't you heard what Dwayne's uncle is all about? He loves to take young women, virgins, and show them a thing or two. Rumor has it that like a real beast, he eats them up, and buries them in a secret plot he has on the land."

She stared at him and burst out laughing. "Yeah, I don't believe that for a second."

"Of course he doesn't eat them. He just kills them."

"No young girl has disappeared," she said. "It's ridiculous."

"Yeah, but what about in towns and cities, huh? They go missing all the time."

She rolled her eyes. "I've got to head back inside."

There was no way she was sitting and listening to horror stories about the man she was falling in love with.

Yeah, the deadly words that ended all magical flings. She didn't mean anything to Beast, she was aware of that.

He didn't want to keep her. They had a few moments of madness. That was all she could think of what their actual relationship was about.

Entering the main kitchen, she was about to close

the door when Micah charged inside.

"Hey, you're not allowed to be here."

"And you are?" Micah pulled the door from her grip and she glared at him, moving away and stepping around the counter, putting some distance between them. She preferred when the party was outside, so she could stay inside.

"This is my home."

"Yeah, and I've heard how you earn that. Beast is very … protective of you. I've heard Dwayne tell me all about it." Micah stood, and she didn't like the evil glint that came into his gaze. "No one's home. Beast is usually home to take care of the parties, but you and I both know this is not one of those occasions."

He advanced toward her, and she took a step back, wanting to put as much distance between the two of them as was physically possible. When he moved around the island within the kitchen, she took his spot on the opposite side.

Her heart pounded, and she knew the threat that he posed.

"You know, a lot of women are asking for it. You just got to rub them the right way to get what you want. No one will believe you. You're a no one. A freak who watched her parents get killed. Me, I'm someone important."

She just stared at him. "Leave."

"Nah, you don't get to boss me around, baby. In here, *I'm* the one that calls the shots. You should have stayed out there. I'd have picked someone else."

"You're disgusting." She wondered how many other women he'd preyed on, forced into a corner, and it scared her.

He was the secret no one spoke about, and yet she'd seen girls around high school who people whispered about.

"Beast will kill you."

"He's not even here."

She moved toward the door, and as he made a lunge for her, she ran off. She only made it to the dining room as he shoved her to the ground.

Screaming at the top of her lungs, she tried to fight him, but Micah was incredibly strong. He had both of her hands pinned above her head, and with his free one, he began to touch her up.

"I know you're not a virgin anymore. There's no way a man like Beast can leave you alone."

"Get off me." She tried to wriggle free, but his grip on her tightened.

"You know, people will never believe that a fat bitch like you could be raped by a guy like me. They'll look at you as if you're a fucking liar. It's the perfect cover. Let's face it. I'm the handsome guy. The one every girl wants. I can take what I want, and no one will say anything."

He shoved his hands down her jeans, and she screamed, thrashing beneath him.

She'd never been so terrified in her life.

All of a sudden, she saw a pair of shoes, Beast's shoes, come into view, and the weight at her back lifted. Quickly scurrying away, she caught sight of Beast holding Micah around the neck.

"So, you prey on innocent girls to get away with taking what doesn't belong to you."

He wasn't allowing Micah to talk. In fact, he was choking Micah. In that moment, she didn't care. He'd intended to hurt her, to rape her.

Beast didn't even look her way, and she wrapped her arms around herself.

"Hope, you may go to my room. I'll be up very

shortly. I'm going to take care of this piece of scum, and then deal with my nephew."

She got to her feet, and was about to pass him when Beast caught her arm, stopping her.

Slowly, she looked at him, feeling the shame wash over her.

"This is not your fault. You didn't do anything wrong. Do not let him break you."

She nodded without saying a word, and left.

****

To say Beast was pissed, put it mildly. Caleb stood beside him as he held Micah by the throat. He'd known his nephew intended to have a party, and even thought it was funny that Hope kept Dwayne's secret. What he didn't intend was for it to go on for so long. He had business within the city, a deal that he had to be part of, and so he'd been home a few minutes later, and entering his home, he'd heard what this sick little shit was going to do. What he'd already done.

Rapists, abusers of any kind, sickened him. Staring at Micah, he saw a coward, a piece of shit. Releasing him, he shoved him toward Caleb. "Keep him company, and call that little shit's father, and our guy at the police department. I want to have a little chat with him."

Leaving his home, he stepped out into the fray of the party and came to a stop. What he saw … angered him.

Kids were snorting up coke on one of his coffee tables, and he saw Dwayne fucking one girl as he licked and sucked at another.

It was time to call it off.

"Anyone who is not Dwayne fucking Carson, get the fuck off my property or I will have you all arrested, and I see a lot of evidence that your little daddies won't be able to save you from."

Within minutes they were scrambling to get away. Dwayne had stood up, and even with a hard dick, he stared at him as if he had a right to.

Beast's rage ... was not something to be trifled with right now. He was pissed. More than pissed, he was fucking ready to kill, and right now, he wanted to hurt his nephew. That little shit had brought a rapist into his home, and because Dwayne had been too busy getting his own dick wet, it had put Hope in danger.

He'd heard the terrified scream. The fear. That scream would stay with him forever. Just another to add to his list of many crimes when it came to that girl.

When they were alone together, he stared across the yard, and Dwayne didn't say a word.

"I was aware of this party ever since you began organizing it."

"Hope—"

"Hope told me nothing." He cut him off before any blaming could begin. "You're not even aware of what I just had to stop, are you?"

"What?"

"Your good 'friend' Micah, Dwayne. You know anything about him? Know of his many secrets?"

Dwayne shook his head.

"So there's never been a few tales of how he's raped girls. Taken them without their permission. You know what rape means."

"Micah doesn't have to force a girl."

Beast's hands fisted at his sides, and for the first time, he wanted to hurt his nephew. Being soft on him hadn't helped him in the least. It had made him foolish.

"I just walked in on Micah trying to rape Hope." He tilted his head to the side and let that piece of information sink in. "Believe me, Dwayne, she wasn't begging for it. She was screaming for help."

Dwayne went pale, all blood draining from his face. "Is she … is … she okay?"

"I'll deal with her, just like I deal with everything else." He glanced around the pool. The use of drugs and sex was obvious. "You know I saved you from my brother all those years ago because I found you with bruises. He wasn't doing anything differently to how we were raised. A boy that can take a few slaps can also punch, and from there, you begin to grow a monster. My brother was using our father's methods. We'd all agreed it wouldn't be the same for our children, but seeing how you abuse my trust, I know I was wrong. I'm not going to start beating you, but the playtime you had, the complete freedom to do what you want, ends tonight. This was your last party. Putting my woman at risk is the final straw. If you even think to put the blame of this on her, you'll deal with me. Do you understand?" he asked.

"Yes."

"Good." He turned on his heel, about to make his way inside.

"Is Micah still alive?"

"For now. He won't be around for much longer, but not because I put a bullet in his brain. He's going away, and last time I checked he was eighteen. Let's see how he likes being someone's bitch for a change." He was going to make sure that little shit went to prison, and got a taste of what he did to others.

When he got back inside the house, Micah was sitting in a chair with his father and a local police officer in the room.

By the time he finished explaining the situation, Micah was being led in handcuffs and a deal was struck with his father. Plain and simple. Micah's father was a businessman, and Beast knew how to make shit happen.

He wanted Micah in prison, and he did a deal with the father to make sure that happened. If it was anyone else, he'd have killed the little shit, but he didn't want Hope to feel any of that guilt.

Moving into his office, he poured two glasses of scotch, handing one to Caleb, who took it without a word. They stood in the office watching as Dwayne cleaned away the mess. It was the least he could do.

Beast had to go up to see Hope, but he couldn't see her until he had a drink. Taking another large swig, he watched his nephew.

"We could send him away until your temper is back in check."

"There's nothing wrong with my temper, brother. He needs to learn to be responsible, and having parties where he can't protect others, that's something he's going to learn." He finished off his whiskey. "I want you to start tomorrow morning, training him. We'll hone his skills, and teach him what he's missing."

He walked toward the office door. "Hope, she's different for you, isn't she?"

Glancing back toward Caleb, he stared at his younger brother, not saying anything.

"You're different around her. You've not gone to see Sarah, and I know there's no other woman in your life."

Again, he just stared at Caleb, waiting for his brother to finish what was being said.

"Do you love her?"

"My feelings for Hope are not your concern."

"They are, Beast. You and I both know they are because I'm part of this family, just like you. I know what you want, and I know what you're capable of. I'll protect her at all costs, you know that. You're my brother."

"You tried to warn her away."

"For her own good. Do you really think that anything good could come from her being with you, being here?"

He gritted his teeth. His mother had lived a life that he wouldn't allow a dog to have. No matter how hard he tried, he couldn't give Hope up. Every night that he watched her sleep he was convinced that it would be the last. Only, the morning would come, and she'd smile at him, and he'd find himself lost once more.

"I'm going to go see her."

This time he did leave, and made his way toward his room. There was no sign of her in his room or his bathroom, so he went to hers where he found her in the bath. Bubbles covered most of her body, and she looked tired. The moment he entered the room, she looked up at him.

"I wasn't asking for it. I didn't beg or anything."

"I know you didn't." He removed his clothes and joined her in the bath, pulling her into his arms. At first, she tensed up and wouldn't allow him to hold her. Beast didn't give up. He pulled her into his arms, kissing the top of her head. "You don't have to think about him anymore."

She began to cry, and her arms moved around him, holding him close. It was a good thing Micah was now in police custody, as otherwise he'd kill the little shit with his bare hands.

"How many girls do you think he's done that to? He was so confident. He knew nothing and no one was going to harm him. How? Why? He shouldn't … he can't get away with that."

"I've already got it handled. He's not going to get away with anything, baby. I promise you. I've got things in place to make sure he won't ever touch or hurt another woman again."

She nodded and clung to him.

Closing his eyes, he kissed her head. "Next time, tell me that Dwayne's going to have a party."

"I'm so sorry. He begged me not to, and this is his home."

"It's yours as well."

"I didn't think that would happen. I thought I'd be safe."

"I don't want you to be afraid inside your own home." He pushed some hair off her face and smiled down at her. "I won't let anything happen to you."

"I know you won't." She pressed her lips to his. "I trust you."

Just like that, guilt once again gripped him.

He saw the love shining in her eyes, but he didn't say anything. He just held her close.

Chapter Nine

Time passed. Days turned to weeks, and weeks turned into months, and it was Christmas before Hope knew what was happening. Her time spent with the Carsons was the happiest of her life. After the party, her friendship with Dwayne was rather … awkward. She felt guilty, and after a few weeks, Dwayne apologized to her for not being there.

She didn't say anything, just gave him a hug, and put it behind them. Beast had somehow made it so that Micah was sentenced for multiple counts of rape. A lot of girls had come forward, not just in their town, but in several others. Each of them had a story, and quite a few of them with similar claims as Hope's, where he'd told them he'd get away with it.

Just thinking about it made her sick.

"I don't do trees," Beast said, from where he was lying on the bed. He was still completely naked after his latest *lesson*. They weren't lessons, and they never had been. He didn't teach her anything, but her body certainly felt good after their time together.

She gasped, placing a hand against her chest. "How can you say such a thing?"

"I told you I don't do Christmas."

"That cannot happen." She rushed toward the bed, dropping down beside him. Even though she was naked, she felt comfortable in her own skin around Beast. Maybe that had something to do with fact he'd seen her completely naked, and had even kissed every square inch of her body. She smiled up at him, recalling how he'd trailed his tongue down her back, lifting her up so that she was on her knees as he'd stroked her pussy and ass.

"You know," he said, resting his hand on her ass. "You've been talking about Christmas a lot. Tell me why?"

"My mom always loved it." She stared down at her hands, closing her eyes as he began to stroke up her spine, then sliding his fingers down. He grazed over the cheeks of her ass. "Aunt Tay didn't celebrate it, and I guess I just wanted to have one Christmas before I went away to college. You know. It's fine though. I don't mind if you don't want to." She smiled as he tsked and slapped her ass.

"You know how to get whatever you want out of me, and you don't even try."

She giggled. "When was the last time you had a Christmas?" she asked.

He thought about it. "After Dwayne's father was born. That was the last time she put up a tree."

Hope saw the darkness swirling in his gaze, and she hated that it was there. "Talk to me."

"There's nothing to talk about, babe. My dad, he hated Christmas, but he made her do a big thing of it because he knew she loved it, but he'd spend so much time shouting at her, and tearing it down. I think he only allowed her to put it up so that he could ruin it."

She placed a hand on his chest and moved so that she straddled him. His cock already pressing against her core. "We don't have to celebrate it." She didn't like the bad memories she saw in his gaze.

He smiled. "You know if you want something you're not supposed to agree to not have it."

"I don't want you to be sad. Just as a point to mention, your dad sounds like an asshole."

"He was."

She didn't touch on the past tense. He skimmed his fingers down her body, gripping her ass and rolling her over. "I'd love to know what you've done to me."

"I have no idea what you mean."

She opened her thighs as he slid between them. His cock bumped her clit as he rubbed between the lips of her pussy.

He pulled back, holding her hips, and he stared down at where their bodies lay together. Every touch against her nub had her gasping, desperate, begging for more.

"You make me ache, baby. I want you so fucking much." He placed his cock at her entrance, and she cried out as with one hard thrust, he slammed to the hilt within her. Arching up, she felt his lips on her tits, and watched as he took one nipple into his mouth, followed by the next.

His cock pulsed inside her, and he didn't move for the longest time. "I'll never grow tired of your pussy wrapped around my cock, baby." He groaned as she tightened herself, feeling him pulse. "Damn, Hope, you want my cum, don't you?"

"Yes."

Gripping her hips, he pulled her off his cock until only the tip was inside her, and then he fucked her hard, slamming all the way within her. She cried out his name, feeling him fill every single part of her, touching places deep inside her that made her ache for more.

She was addicted to him, desperate for his cock.

Beast had a power over her, and she loved every second that he used it.

"You're all mine, baby. There's nothing I wouldn't do for you. I want you so fucking badly."

She cried out as he bit her tits, knowing he'd leave a mark.

He moved over her completely, wrapping his arms around her waist and fucking her so hard that the headboard slammed against the wall, matching their cries.

Beast brought her to orgasm first before he joined her, flooding inside her with his cum. She felt every single spurt as he filled her. He'd not worn a condom for some time, and she kept forgetting to get an appointment with the doctor. She quickly made a note of it to get it done. The last thing she wanted to do was trap him with a child he didn't want.

"What are you thinking?" he asked.

She smiled. "I can't move right now."

"Good, because I'm nowhere near done with you yet."

****

"Are you okay?" Caleb asked.

Beast glanced up at his brother, sitting back in his seat. He spent a great deal more time at home now than he ever did outside of it. Hope was the reason. Whenever she was near, he found it next to impossible to leave her. He didn't *want* to leave her.

"Why wouldn't I be?"

"Your woman is hunting for colleges, and I didn't know if the age difference bothered you?"

"Age difference?"

"She's young, Beast."

He smiled as Caleb took a seat. "The age difference? You know when I'm with her, there doesn't feel any difference at all. She's not a child, and she doesn't giggle, unless I tickle her."

Caleb burst out laughing. "You tickle your woman?"

"On occasion. I like to catch her off guard, and I'm not talking about this with you." He sat back. "Why are you asking me this?"

"Just curious. You never struck me as the kind of guy who liked them young is all."

"I don't 'like them young.'"

Hope was the first woman that had ever made him cross that line. She'd been of legal age, and he didn't doubt for a second that if she hadn't been, he'd have left her alone. He would have.

There were a lot of things he would do, but even *he* had morals and lines he wouldn't cross. Those lines his father had once told him were what made him weak.

No, his lines, his morals, were what made him strong.

"What made Hope so different for you?" Caleb asked.

"Why the sudden questions about the woman in my life?" He pressed his fingers together, watching his brother.

"You're not going to tell me anything until I tell you, are you?"

"That's the way this works."

"Fine. I may have seen or met someone. Not going to go into the details. I'm sure you're aware of everything already."

Beast smiled. He was aware his brother had met someone, and that she was indeed young. Not illegal, but still out of Caleb's comfort zone.

"Her eyes," Beast said.

"Her eyes? They're just brown."

He chuckled. "You've got to look a little deeper when you stare at a woman. Don't just see tits and ass." Beast stared past him. "I saw her ass first. She was standing at the bookcase in the library, her hands trailing across the spines of the books. That was the first time I saw her. She turned to face me, and I saw her eyes. They're deep brown, and so torn. She's seen pain and come out fighting. She's a fighter, my woman." He smiled, just thinking about it. "I know I'm the one responsible for putting that look in her eyes, but ... I couldn't look away. I was caught, enslaved by that one gaze. She left, and I found myself thinking about her."

"I know you got every single little bit of information on her."

"I watched her at the diner. She walked everywhere." He smiled, thinking about that small jacket wrapped around her.

"Dude, you sound like you're in love."

Beast stared at his brother. "It's when the little things, like age, don't matter. When you're together, and you crave her smile, or find yourself charmed by something that really annoys you in everyone else, you know that it doesn't matter."

"What does she do?" he asked.

"When she giggles ... everyone else annoys me, but with Hope, I find myself constantly making her giggle. Trying to give her a reason to hear that one blissful sound. Her giggles don't make me want to kill her. I just want to take care of her."

Silence fell between them.

"You're not going to let her go to college," Caleb said.

He didn't say a word, staring at his brother, who ran fingers through his hair.

"She's not a toy."

"I never said she was, and I don't intend to keep her on a shelf so that I can bring her out to play."

Caleb stared at him. "I thought you and I agreed that no woman would ever make us bring them part of this world. Our lives ... it's not for them."

"I run a tight ship, Caleb. It's never been safer than it is right now."

"She wants this."

Sitting forward, he glared at his brother. "From the moment she's been in my life, you've been trying to draw a wedge between us. I don't like it, and it ends now."

"I've never seen you so taken with a woman, Beast. I know you've used Sarah. You can't stand the bitch, and I get it. She's got many men rutting away in her pussy. She's never going to miss you when you're gone. Hope, she's different, and she makes *you* different. The thing is, I don't see her not wanting to leave. She's still looking for the right college. She's still wanting a future away from here. You can't keep her locked up in your little cage, no matter how much freedom you think you give her. You're heading for a fall. Be careful, brother."

Beast watched his brother get up and leave his office. Sitting back at his desk, he stared at the computer. There was a copy of the college's application form that she'd sent. There wasn't anything that Hope did that he didn't know about. He was aware she still wanted to go to college, and that she wanted out of town. He also knew that every Sunday she spent an hour tending her mother's grave while her father's went unnoticed.

Some nights she'd wake up screaming, holding her side where she'd been shot. There were a lot of secrets between them, mostly from him, but each time he intended to tell her the truth, something would happen, and he'd bide his time.

That time was running out. He didn't need his fucking younger brother to make him aware of it.

****

Staring at the window display of watches and tie pins, Hope nibbled her lip, unsure what to get Beast. She'd already picked gifts for Caleb and Dwayne, along with some of the men who'd taken her to and from school.

She didn't have to, but at Christmas it just meant

something. It was a time for giving, and she liked the thought of having gifts ready for them. Beast had caved on a tree. It wasn't a live one. He didn't want the mess, so he'd purchased a plain, fake pine one that looked great once she had it all decorated. Caleb, Dwayne, and Beast had watched her decorate it, and of course she couldn't have them staring. She'd made each of them help her, and afterward they shared a hot chocolate and a sugar cookie.

They behaved at times like they didn't know or understand Christmas, and she was determined to make it a day to remember.

Entering the shop, she found the watch that she'd been eyeing, and asked the attendant if she could have a look. It was just a nice-looking watch that reminded her so much of Beast.

She got it gift wrapped and left the shop. Passing a coffee shop, she paused as she was overcome with a wave of nausea. It took her so completely by surprise that she gripped the wall and took several deep breaths.

That very morning she'd woken up and been sick. It wasn't just that day though. No, she'd been sick for the past couple of days, and she didn't want to think what that meant.

You can't bury your head in the sand for much longer.

She'd not made it to the doctor, and they'd had a great deal of unprotected sex. Tears filled her eyes, and she forced herself to go into the pharmacy. For the longest time, she simply stood outside, staring at the shop, wondering if she could wait until after Christmas.

College was not far away, and she'd already picked where she wanted to go. Placing a hand on her stomach, she gritted her teeth and entered. Finding the pregnancy tests, she saw there were so many that she just picked the one that seemed to offer the highest accuracy.

A couple of hours later, she was back at home with the pregnancy test kit burning in her pocket. Carrying the presents she'd purchased up to her room, she made sure to lock her door before going to the bathroom.

Taking a seat on the toilet, she read through the instructions. Peeing on the stick was not something she would ever get used to, especially as her hand wouldn't stop shaking.

"Please be negative. Please be negative."

She'd put a timer on her cell phone so it would beep when she was supposed to look at it.

Her heart pounded as she allowed her thoughts to drift. A baby. Beast's baby. She had fallen in love with him—how could she not? In a weird kind of way, he was her hero. He'd taken her away from her aunt, given her a life, and a chance to finally have a future. The past few months had been a complete dream.

Going to college would cost her him.

Would he even want a baby?

He'd not once talked about a future with her.

Her alarm sounded, and picking up the stick, she saw the answer that she already knew.

She was pregnant with Beast's baby.

Staring at the stick, she placed it back down on the edge of the bathroom sink. What the hell was she to do now?

The news terrified her.

The unknown always had.

She didn't have anyone, not really.

Whatever happened, she couldn't keep it from Beast.

Chapter Ten

Washing the blood off his hands, Beast stared at his reflection. Someone who betrayed him had to pay the consequences, and the only way to stay ahead was to make sure everyone knew who they were dealing with. He wasn't a man with much patience.

He changed into a clean shirt, smoothed back his hair, and stepped out of the bathroom.

"The mess has been dealt with," Caleb said.

"Excellent." He employed cleaners of the special variety that helped to get rid of bloody mess and dead bodies. Seeing his brother wanted to say something, he paused. "What is it?"

"I got a call from Hammond."

"Yes." Hammond was the security detail he'd put on Hope. No matter where she went, someone was near her to keep her safe. He had a lot of enemies. Most of them kept their distance, but he wasn't willing to take any chances with his woman, so he made sure she was protected at all times. "Is something wrong with Hope?"

"She purchased a pregnancy test at the pharmacy."

Beast paused. "Excuse me?"

"She's back at the house. That's what I've been informed, and I figured you should know."

Pregnant.

He'd hoped she was.

He'd not worn a condom in a very long time. He loved the feel of her naked cunt wrapped around his cock, and he was selfish. He didn't want to share her with anyone.

Running fingers through his hair, he nodded at Caleb.

"Was this your plan all along?" Caleb asked.

"I think you should stay out of this."

"I've stayed by your side throughout everything, Beast. There's nothing I wouldn't do for you. I don't want to see you get hurt."

"I won't get hurt."

"This girl wants her freedom."

"You don't know what she wants, just like you don't know what that girl wants back at your house." Beast stared at his brother. He knew all about the girl that was given to Caleb as payment.

It was the same girl Caleb had been asking questions about. "You knew?"

"Of course I knew. I'm not an idiot, Caleb. I didn't get this far by having people hide shit from me. I'm aware of everything that goes down." They climbed into the car, and he told the driver to take him home.

"She's safe when she's with me."

"I have no doubt. You're many things, brother, but a rapist is not one of them," he said.

Speaking of rapists, he'd already gotten the update that Micah was being taken care of in prison. That fucker had hurt way too many girls, and Beast felt no remorse for sending him down. Some people needed to learn the fucking hard way.

Getting back home, he didn't wait around, and went straight to Hope's room. She wasn't there, and he went to the bathroom, finding the pregnancy test. Moving out of her room, he saw something in the garden, and saw Hope swimming in the pool.

It was freezing cold outside, but he paid to have the pool heated.

Holding onto the stick, he made his way outside, and he nodded at the security guard in the garden to leave. Once they were alone, he moved toward the edge of the pool. Crouching down, he held the test as she swam toward him.

Neither of them said a word, and she just looked at the stick, then at him.

She didn't come any closer, and he stared at her.

"How did you know?"

"You think I'd let you leave my house unprotected?" he asked.

"I didn't know." She stared at the stick. "Someone saw me buying the test?"

"Yes, and I found this in your bathroom."

She nodded. "I guess it makes sense you finding it. I didn't know how to tell you, and a text message didn't seem right." She frowned.

He put the test down and began to remove his clothes. The chill bit through his body, but he didn't care. Climbing into the pool was a welcome reprieve as it heated his bones. She stayed still as he advanced toward her.

Standing directly behind her, he placed a hand on her stomach. His baby, their child lay there.

His cock thickened at the thought of her being heavily pregnant with his baby. He couldn't wait to watch her grow, flourish. The mother of his child.

"We're going to get married," he said.

"No."

"You're saying no to me."

"I don't want to get married. I don't want this to change anything."

He pulled her close to him so that she felt the length of his cock pressing against her ass. "No matter how much you don't want this to change anything, it does. This changes everything, baby. Don't you get that?" He kissed her neck, sucking on the pulse beating beneath.

She gasped, melting against him.

Tell her.

He'd never told any woman how he felt, and he wasn't sure he was ready to let her have that kind of power over him.

"I love you, Hope."

She pulled away from him, spinning around to face him. "No. Don't say that. Don't say something you don't actually mean. I don't want you to say things you don't mean."

Capturing her face, he slammed his lips down on hers, silencing any protest she had. He didn't want to hear her say shit like that.

Wrapping her wet hair around his fist, he broke the kiss, and glared at her. "Do you really think that I would say shit I don't mean?"

"I—"

"I've never told another woman that I love her. I've never given another woman a fucking chance with me. I never loved anyone, don't you get that? Then you, Hope. I see your nice juicy ass, and you turn to look at me, and I'm fucking lost. I want to see your eyes on me at all times. I crave it, and no woman has ever made me make a fucking fool of myself, and yet here I stand with you. I love you, Hope. You can believe me or not, but you will never tell me what I can and cannot feel. I love you. I've loved you even before you told me about the fucking baby. I never knew how to tell you. You're eighteen. You're planning a life far away from me, and you think I want to be the lost little puppy?" Tears were in her eyes, and he hated that he'd been the one to put them there. "I'm not a good man." He stopped. For the first time he felt his own feelings breaking free, rising out of him, demanding a voice, and he couldn't stop them. "I've killed people, and not even thought about it the rest of the day. I'm not a good man, and I know you deserve a hell of a lot better than me, but I can't give you up. I can do everything else, but I can't give you up. I won't."

He pressed his face to hers. Both of them were panting, and he closed his eyes, stroking the skin at her back near her ass.

Slowly, she wrapped her arms around his neck, and her body pressed against his. The suit she wore covered up everything. "I love you, too. It scares me."

Taking the straps of her suit, he pulled them down her arms, watching as her tits sprang free.

"You're mine, Hope. You've been mine for a long fucking time, and I'm not going to let you go. Not now, not ever." He spun her around, placing her hands on the edge of the pool. The sides of the pool were high enough that he didn't have to worry about anyone seeing her.

Her body belonged to him, and he didn't want anyone to see how precious she was with her big tits, rounded stomach, and juicy thighs. Not to mention her ass. He fucking loved her ass, and how good it felt nestled against his cock.

"Now, we're going to get married, and you can still go to college, but it's going to have to be closer to home so that I can make love to you, and show you just how much I love you. I'm not going to give you up, Hope. Not now, not ever. I don't want to." He ran his hand down the front of her body, finding her pussy. Sliding a finger inside her, he discovered how wet she was.

Pulling his finger from her body, he rubbed against her clit. She gasped, and her ass rubbed against his cock.

"Do you want my dick?"

"Yes."

"Where do you want it?"

"Inside me."

With his free hand, he grabbed his cock and found her core. Thrusting deep inside her, he teased her clit at exactly the same time.

He thrust inside her, going deeper as he brought her to orgasm. Her tight cunt squeezed him as he filled her. He'd not lied to her.

Beast had fallen in love with her, and now he didn't want to be without her. Kissing her neck, he breathed her in, knowing he'd do anything to keep her safe within his world.

****

Even though Beast was determined to move fast, buying her a ring, booking the church, Hope didn't mind. Since he'd discovered she was pregnant, everything had fallen into place somehow. She'd booked a place at the local college, and she liked that she could go home, and not be in a dorm, surrounded by everyone.

She'd wanted to get out of town, but at the same time she didn't want to leave her mom, and she could go to her graveside, and tell her about the pregnancy. Her plans for Christmas were still the same, and she'd gotten all of their presents.

There were times that Beast still had to go and do his work, and she didn't question him. She couldn't.

She loved the man, not what he actually did, and everything felt … perfect.

High school had let out for the day, and she stood waiting for her ride, which was unusual. Normally someone was waiting for her.

Folding her arms across her body, she glanced down at her cell phone and began to play a game.

"So, all the rumors I'm hearing are true?"

Hope looked up to see her aunt, Tay, standing in front of her. She'd not seen her ever since Beast came and picked her up that night. Staring at the woman before her, she didn't experience any feeling of regret.

This woman had made her life miserable, and she knew her mother had hated her.

"What are you doing here?"

"Came to see what a slut my niece is."

"You can't be here."

"I mean, look at you, screwing around with a known killer. A madman. Your father would be ashamed. Ah, that's right, you don't really care about your father." Aunt Tay cackled. "That's fine. You see, dearie, that man you're sleeping with, that man you're marrying, and that has the whole town whispering behind their hands, he's the one responsible for losing your mother."

"What?" She pulled away.

There was alcohol on the woman's breath, and the stench coming from her made Hope's stomach flutter. "Your father called me after he shot your mother. I know he shot you, and he told me everything. He told me about his addiction, and that he couldn't get out. That his skin was crawling, and I asked him who had given him the gun, and he told me Beast Carson had given it to him."

Hope stared at the woman who'd meant nothing to her. Tears filled her eyes as she saw the joy in Tay's eyes. This woman got pleasure out of hurting other people.

"I suggest you step away from my woman right now, or I swear to God, I will show these kids just how accurate those fucking rumors are," Beast said, drawing both of their attention.

She turned to the man she loved more than anything. His gaze was hard, focused on Tay. "Hope, baby, get in the car."

Nodding her head, she stepped past Tay, who grabbed her arm. "Now you're having the murderer's baby."

She pushed Tay away from her, climbing into the car, ignoring what was going on. Her heart was aching, and her nerves were all over the place.

Seconds passed, and he finally climbed into the car, and she just knew it was true.

He didn't say anything, and she saw they weren't heading toward the house but in the direction of the hills out of town. She knew there were cabins that people often rented out to go hunting, not that she'd ever been interested in hunting.

"What's going on?" she asked.

"I planned to bring you here before Christmas. Work got in the way, but now I think it's best we have a private discussion with no chance of interruptions."

She didn't speak as he drove them toward one of the cabins. Tears fell down her cheeks, and she wiped them away. It hurt her to know that Tay got pleasure out of causing others pain. She'd lived with her for only a short time, but it had been enough to leave a mark.

"Stay," Beast said, climbing out of the car. She unbuckled her seatbelt, and he was there, taking hold of her hand, and leading her inside one of the luxury cabins. Snow was heavy on the ground, and it looked so romantic, so beautiful, and she felt ... numb.

"I think I'm going to be sick."

He led her toward the bathroom, and she made it just in time as she threw up everything she'd eaten, and a great deal of stuff she hadn't. Her stomach turned, but after a few minutes, and a glass of water, everything settled down.

Beast made her sit on the sofa as he collected their things. She didn't have a clue what he'd packed, but right now, she didn't want to talk about anything. Sipping her water, she watched him bring in two cases before closing and locking the door.

She sat on the chair watching as he held their things, putting them away in one of the bedrooms. Sitting there on the sofa, she felt … strange. Aunt Tay had never liked her. In fact, they'd never liked each other, even when her father had been alive. Tay was such a nasty woman, someone determined to make everyone around her as miserable as she was. She'd even heard the men say that Aunt Tay was great until she opened her mouth, and then everything got spoiled because her bitterness knew no bounds.

Staring down at her hand with her engagement ring, Hope smiled. From that very first moment she saw Beast, there'd been this fire inside her. Even before she realized it herself, she yearned for his touch, desperate for him.

Beast was now hers. She carried his child, and she had his love. They were going to get married, and she didn't for a second believe it was going to be the most perfect happily ever after, but she believed it was going to be something.

She wanted their life together. She looked forward to being with him every single moment of every single day.

He came back, and took a seat in front of her, taking her hands. She saw the guilt in his eyes, and she hated seeing it there.

"I gave him the gun."

"I don't care," she said, reaching out to touch his face.

She chuckled at the frown and cupped his face, pressing a single kiss against his lips.

"What? You looked so sad."

She shook her head. "Aunt Tay is a horrible human being. All she wants to do is make everyone around her miserable in a way to justify her own misery. I don't know. You gave my dad the gun, he paid for it whatever, and he came home, killed my mother, shot me, and killed himself. Do you see the point I'm trying to make?"

"I'm the one responsible for your mother's death."

"No. You're not." She licked her lips, wondering if she sounded crazy. "It's ... you're not the one that fired the gun, Beast. It would be like saying that someone who sold a wife her kitchen knives is the real killer of her husband. I can't think of a really good example right now, but you gave him the gun. You didn't know what he was going to do. You didn't think for a second that he was going to go home and kill his wife and try to take his kid." She smiled at him. "So you gave him a gun. Did you tell him to do what he did next?"

"No. Never."

"Then you've got nothing to feel guilty about. Guns are bought and sold all the time. I don't blame you. Do I wish you hadn't given him the gun? I can't take back what happened. But would I still have my mom? Dad was going to do all those things regardless. It could have been a knife or his hands, or anything." She took his hand and pressed it against her stomach. "This is all I know. I love you more than anything else in the world, so that I'm changing my life plan to stay with you. I'm going to get married to you, and we're going to have a beautiful baby. I don't know if it's a boy or girl, but I don't care. I only know that I love you, and I want to spend the rest of my life with you." She laughed as tears fell down her cheeks. "We'll probably get a few weird looks. You know, the age gap and all."

He pulled her close and slammed his lips against hers. "I don't give a fuck what anyone says, Hope Miller.

You are the love of my life, and I'm going to spend the rest of mine loving you, keeping you safe."

Beast picked her up in his arms and carried her through to the bedroom. "I've never belonged to any woman, Hope, but know that I am yours. Every single part of me is yours. I love you more than anything else in the world."

"Now you're really making me cry."

He lowered her to the bed and took her lips as he ran his hands over her body.

"I was just existing before I saw you in my library. Not a moment goes by that I'm not grateful you were tutoring Dwayne."

She truly believed it was the best decision she had ever made. Her love for this man knew no bounds, and it wasn't just a crush either. Her future was tied to him, and it was a life she intended to enjoy.

Epilogue

Seven months later

"You're making everyone nervous," Hope said.

Beast turned back to look at his wife. Perspiration dotted her brow, and she looked tired, way too tired for his liking. She'd been in labor now for a couple of hours, and he was about ready to lose his shit at anyone who dared comment on him being a new father.

He'd read the fucking books, and not just that, he'd also read the statistics about some women not making it through their pregnancy.

If he lost Hope ... no, he couldn't have that thought. There was no way in hell that he was going to lose the only woman he'd ever loved in this life. He would fight for her.

Finally, a doctor entered, and he tapped him on the shoulder. "A word please." They left the room, and Beast grabbed the man around the neck, slamming him against the wall. "I don't know if you're aware, but I'm Beast Carson. You're treating Hope Carson, my wife. If she dies while giving birth, I'm going to kill you, and the entire line of your family, are we clear?"

The doctor nodded. "I can see why I was assigned your wife."

Beast smiled. He'd have given the good doctor a warning in the hospital room, but he didn't want to upset his wife.

Going to the head of the bed, she gave him a glare.

"Ignore everything he says," Hope said. "He's what the nurses are calling 'new daddy.'" She smiled up at him. "Behave."

"I will as soon as I know everyone and everything is going to be fine."

She cupped his cheek, which she did every single time he was agitated. "It's going to be okay."

Her face scrunched up as a new contraction began. He held her hand as each one built until they were mere seconds apart, and the doctor announced it was time to push.

For Beast, he'd tortured, maimed, killed, but nothing could have prepared him for those moments of waiting, of being petrified that he would lose the only woman he'd ever loved in all of his life. She was younger than he was, but that didn't make his feelings for her any less. That love would last a lifetime, and as he heard the screams of his little girl being born, another love swept over him, a fatherly love.

Their little girl was placed in Hope's arms, and he felt exactly that … hope.

"Look at what we made," she said. "Our beautiful little girl."

He kissed her head.

"I must look so ugly right now," she said, laughing.

"You're the most beautiful woman in the world." Staring into her eyes as their bundle of joy wriggled, Beast knew without a doubt, he'd found his very reason for living, and he intended to hold onto the both of them for the rest of his life.

The End

HER MONSTER

Sam Crescent

Copyright © 2018

Chapter One

The sound of breaking bones didn't help Caleb Carson's need for vengeance. He stared at the man whose hand he had just shattered, and he felt nothing. This was not going how he hoped. Stepping away from the bleeding man, Caleb took the cloth from one of the men and thanked him for it.

"I gave her to you. Why are you doing this?" the man sobbed.

Caleb stared at the man who three weeks ago had given him his daughter, Faith Grey. She was eighteen years old, and quiet. She also looked at him for a long time as if he was going to hurt her. This man wanted to use his daughter to pay his debts, debts that were constantly growing as he didn't pay them off in any other way. There was no way Caleb could let Faith go, or allow this asshole loose. The only problem was now he didn't want to push Faith out onto the streets. Those were all problems he'd deal with closer to the time. He'd taken

Faith as payment to protect her. That first look at her and the fear in her eyes, and he'd not been able to say no. His instant need to take care of her had completely surprised him. He rarely cared about women, apart from the pleasure he got from them. He certainly didn't care what happened to them, but when it came to Faith, she'd broken down a wall within him that he couldn't seem to rebuild. He had to keep her safe, and that meant killing this piece of shit.

"Is it because of her scar?" the dad asked.

He turned back to the dad and glared at him. Grabbing the back of the fucker's head, he lifted it up. "What the fuck did you say?"

"The scar. I know it's ugly, but she's a good girl. A virgin girl. No one else will touch her. You can train her to be exactly what—"

Caleb plunged the knife he was holding into the man's neck. He didn't want to hear anymore coming out of his mouth. He was so fucking disgusted.

The sound of gurgling filled the room, and it didn't give him a single ounce of satisfaction. In fact, it filled him with more rage.

No one spoke, and he was pleased about that, as otherwise his need for blood would move to one of them. Twisting the blade out of the dead bastard's neck, he wiped it on the man's clothes before stepping away.

Faith belonged to him now, and there was no way he was letting her go. She'd been given to him to settle a debt, and over the past three weeks, he'd watched her, seeing the fear in her eyes every time she looked at him. He didn't like that. He didn't know what it was, but each time he looked into her pretty green eyes he wanted to protect her.

The scar ran down the right side of her face, going from her eye toward her lip. It wasn't ugly.

He'd not discovered why it was there yet, but he would.

"Clean this piece of shit up," he said, stepping out of the warehouse. The moment he was free of the building, he took a deep breath. Staring up at the beautiful clear blue sky, he smiled. He could think clearly now. He didn't know how long it would last, but until his need to kill came again, everything felt clear.

Running his fingers through his hair, he stepped toward his car and fired it up.

The moment he pulled out of the warehouse, his cell phone began to ring. His brother, Beast Carson, was calling.

"Enjoy your fun."

"What the fuck do you want?"

"I want to know if you're done killing the dad."

This was just one of the reasons why Beast was in charge. He knew what everyone was doing.

"I'm done. I want information though."

"About the girl we're not talking about."

"I want to know how Faith Grey got her scars."

"Would you like me to pay a visit, look her over?"

Caleb knew without a shadow of a doubt that Beast wouldn't hurt Faith. His brother only had eyes for one woman in his life, and even though Hope was the same age as Faith, he'd never seen his brother so smitten before.

"No. I want to know how she got it." The last thing he wanted was for Faith to be afraid of him even more. It was bad enough that she looked ready to run when he entered a room. No matter, if she was eating, reading, watching television, within a matter of seconds, she was gone.

He rubbed at his eyes.

He was a monster. There was no doubt about that, but he wouldn't hurt her. To everyone else he was the monster. Faith knew his business. She knew that he killed for a living.

Rubbing at his eyes, he pulled into the parking lot outside of his home. He lived about thirty minutes away from Beast. He could have easily lived with his brother, but he liked his privacy. Also, there were moments where he didn't want to remember what he did for a living.

They were a crime family. The Carsons had run their section of the city with an iron fist. Blood and death were what he'd known all of his life. Where other kids were learning how to grow up, he'd learned how to handle a gun, knives, and to torture the answers out of everyone.

He was good, but Beast was better.

Caleb was more than happy for his brother to take the lead. Being the head of the Carson family was not what he wanted to do. He was more than happy with taking orders.

Staring up at his home, he caught the green-eyed beauty sitting near the library window. She always sat there. Always stared out across the gardens. Not for the first time, he wondered what she was thinking about. Climbing out of his car, he pocketed his cell phone and went straight toward the kitchen, where Anne was making dinner.

She'd been part of the Carson family for decades. She knew what they did but turned the other way, cooked, and organized cleaners for them. He wouldn't have anything happen to her.

"Hello, Mr. Carson."

No matter how many times he told her to call him Caleb, she wouldn't do it. She liked to have that formality between them.

"Has our guest eaten something?"

Anne frowned. "She did. Nibbled on some toast, made her excuses, and she's been up in that library staring out at God knows what. I don't get it. She's going to start wasting away."

She'd been on the fuller side. Her clothes read a size eighteen, but in the past few weeks, he'd noticed those clothes were getting loose on her. He didn't like it.

"Make us both a sandwich," he said.

Anne didn't question him, and began doing what he asked. He waited for her to finish watching as she placed a slice of ham, cheese, and pickles on one side, spread the other with mayo, and put them on a pretty plate.

"Thanks."

He took both of their plates and headed straight toward the library on the second floor. Outside the door, he paused, wondering if she'd be able to cope with eating in the same room as him. He'd never hurt her, but that didn't mean she wasn't afraid. Caleb understood fear, and he respected it. Just because he'd never hurt her didn't for a second mean, he *couldn't*.

Opening the door, he returned her wave. She sat near the window with her knees pressed up against her chest. He felt this overwhelming need to … protect her. He didn't get it. She wasn't his responsibility, but sending her out there in the world, it didn't feel right, not to him.

"If you don't eat something soon, Anne's going to have a fit." He moved toward her, putting their plates on a nearby table and carrying a chair to sit right in front of her. "Anne's the cook."

"I know who she is," she said.

There was no attitude as she spoke. She offered him a smile. He liked the sound of her voice. It was gentle, kind, a little raspy from not being used.

Handing her a plate, he stared into her pretty green eyes. "You've got to eat."

Without question, she took the plate he offered.

Sitting in front of her, he picked up a sandwich and took a large bite. "Eat."

This time she did, and her eyes closed.

"You like pickle and mayo together?"

"Yep, love it."

This time she took a bigger bite, and he couldn't help but smile. Beast thought his sandwich combinations were disgusting. It may just be pickle and mayo, but as far as he was concerned, that equaled success.

"Can I ask you a question?" she asked.

"Sure."

"How long will I be staying here?"

He paused mid-chew. "You're not happy here?"

"It's a beautiful place, but it's not my home, and I don't really know what's going on. My dad just told me to go with you, be good, do whatever you wanted, and to stay out of your hair until you needed me."

"You won't be going back home." Caleb watched as she paled.

"Ever?"

"Ever."

"What … erm … what will I have to do?"

He saw her hand shake a little, and he didn't like it. "You're just going to have to learn the grounds a little longer. You don't have to stay trapped up here in the library. You're not a princess waiting for your prince to come."

Her cheeks heated.

"I wasn't waiting for that. I was just … I like libraries. They're usually very quiet, and no one comes in here. I can go anywhere?"

"Anywhere you like. The gardens, the pool, anywhere."

"I can't swim," she said.

"One day I'll teach you." He finished his other sandwich and watched her deep in thought. "What about school?"

"What about it?"

"Do you need me to get some books? Help you get settled in?"

"I don't go to school."

"Why not?"

"Dad pulled me out three years ago." She pointed at her scar. "We left town, and I never went back."

****

Faith knew she shouldn't be surprised that she wasn't going home. One day her father would push too hard, and he wouldn't be able to talk himself out of shit. Caleb stared at her scar. There was no disgust on his face like there had been with other people, or even her father. He hadn't been able to look at her when it happened.

Getting hit by a car had sucked, like, mega fucking sucked. What didn't help, it wasn't an accident. Nope! Her father owed a bad debt, and because he hadn't paid up, they'd struck her down. It was at that moment, getting out of the hospital, that she realized to her father she meant nothing.

He'd hated what had happened to her, but part of her had been sure it was because she was damaged goods. He'd always been on her case to lose weight, to make herself beautiful. To do things that she hated.

"And that scar?" Caleb asked.

"That was business Dad couldn't take care of."

Caleb's lips pursed. He was a handsome man. Dark, scary, but he was sexy with it. She glanced down at his hands, and his shirt sleeves were rolled up, showing off his inked arms. They were thick, muscular, and let her know without a shadow of a doubt that he could probably kill someone with his bare hands.

"Are you going to kill me?" she asked.

"No."

"Why not?"

"Because I don't kill little girls."

"I'm far from little, and I'm not a girl."

He shrugged. "You've done nothing to piss me off."

"My father has."

"Your father will be taken care of."

She frowned. "Then why take me?" She'd finished her sandwich, and he took her plate.

"Your father is a piece of shit. I'm not going to lie to you. I imagine he's in deep with a lot of people. I'm just the first guy to come calling. If he was willing to hand you over to me, what else do you think he'd be willing to do?"

She nodded. "Fair enough."

"You're not shocked by that."

"I got this because of him. Nothing that man does surprises me anymore." She wished it had. The only reason she'd remained with him after turning eighteen a few months ago was purely because she had nowhere else to go. If she had, she'd have been long gone.

Her father never scared her. His gambling habit had, and how far he'd been willing to go.

"I wouldn't be surprised if he didn't try to sell off your virginity."

She burst out laughing. "He'd have been pissed for sure on that one. You can't sell something that's not there."

Her cheeks heated when he stared at her. "You're not a virgin?"

"Did he tell you that?"

"He didn't tell me shit."

He didn't seem angry.

"I'm sorry," she said.

"You're eighteen. When did you have time to lose it?"

She smiled. "I'm sure you were younger than eighteen when you lost yours?"

"That's beside the point. There's a real difference here."

"Oh, yeah, what is it?"

"I'm a man."

"Wow, that is not sexist at all."

"It's the truth. It's different for men. We have certain urges."

She was shocked, and she couldn't help but laugh. "Yeah, well, so do women as well." Then her cheeks heated up.

"How old were you when you lost your virginity?" he asked, and she was more than pleased that he didn't want to linger on needs.

Did she have urges?

Reading romance books, at least the ones with the dirty sex that were all the rage right now, she certainly wanted to know what it was like. The men described in the books were so devoted and loyal to their women. They didn't just hump away, and leave you wanting for more.

"I was actually sixteen, and I made the decision myself."

He kept on staring at her, and it made her very uncomfortable.

"I knew Dad would one day risk doing something incredibly stupid. I don't know. I just, I wanted that to be … my choice."

Silence fell between them.

"I notice you didn't say special?"

Faith couldn't help but laugh. "It wasn't special. I promise you, it was anything but special." It had hurt, and been over way before she knew what was really happening. It had been with a guy who kept noticing her and asking her out. She'd spent a lot of time at the local library, as her father had already pulled her out of school. At first, the guy had been interested *because* of her scar, which she found weird. Then, when she realized that it was her chance to do something completely rebellious, she'd used him. She remembered it was the first time a boy had ever noticed her. The entire thing hadn't been great at all. She didn't remember much from it, not even his name. She'd just blatantly asked him if he wanted to have sex. "I was safe though. Condom, and I even made sure I went for a check-up when we moved out of town to make sure he hadn't given me anything."

"Romantic."

"It was still my choice." Her stomach gave a little turn, and she hated that she'd told him the truth like that. It was her business. Why did she have to go and tell a complete stranger about her life? It was no one else's problem, just hers. She'd hated every second of it, but she knew deep down, that she couldn't trust her father. "Look where I am now, and I bet he's not even asked after me."

"You need to forget your father, Faith. He means nothing."

She nodded. "Thank you for the sandwich."

He took the plate from her, resting it on top of his empty one. She didn't know what else to say.

"I'll be in my office if you need me."

She watched him walk away, not saying anything as he did.

Caleb Carson. She'd done an internet search on him, and some of the stuff that had come up wasn't great, not at all. Of course, most of it was rumors and hearsay, but even still, her father had never been involved in anything good. Carson had links to prostitution, gambling, illegal fighting, stuff that she didn't want to get messed up in, and yet, she had because of her father.

He had a really bad gambling habit, but he liked to drag everyone else down around him. It was his MO.

Turning back to her window, she bit her lip and waited for something to happen. Her mind was all over the place, and she really didn't know what to do or say. For most of her life she'd been on her own. Sure, her father had been there somewhere, but she couldn't rely on him to tuck her into bed at night or to read her a story.

No one had been around her for that. Nope, that had been all her. She read her own stories and tucked herself into bed, along with her bear.

She got herself to school every single day, made herself dinner, and just got through it. Now she lived in Caleb's house, and she didn't know what to do. Food was made for her, and she liked Anne, but she didn't trust any of it.

Whenever she got comfortable growing up, something would always happen to suck her down, to make her regret trusting in anything, and that was why she never did.

Wrapping her arms around herself, she watched as Caleb stood outside. He was on his cell phone.

His time in the office didn't last long.

From her vantage point, she could admire him.

Caleb was a sexy as sin kind of man. He always looked in control and confident. He was the man every woman wanted, and every mother wanted as well but told you to stay away from.

She wondered what he thought of her now, knowing she wasn't a virgin. Had he hoped for a virgin?

What would it matter anyway? He would never look at her with interest. The women that threw themselves at him were probably gorgeous model types.

She was fat and had an ugly scar down her face.

There was no way they were even in the same league, and he was older.

He glanced up at the window, and she couldn't look away from his piercing eyes. Did he always get what he wanted?

Faith couldn't handle the stare, so she looked away, biting her lip as she did.

Climbing off the window seat, she left the library, complete with the book she'd been reading, and made her way upstairs to her room. Caleb's home had a lot of stairs. Opening her bedroom door, she stared inside, once again amazed at the luxury before her. The apartments she'd lived in were nothing compared to this. In fact, this room was easily the size of two apartments.

Closing the door, she made her way to the closet and opened it up. Only a couple of pairs of jeans and shirts hung there, but she could imagine it full of clothing.

"Dream on, girl. You're not going to live the fairy tale princess dream. This is not what this is about."

In fact, she imagined once Caleb was bored, she'd be thrown out onto the street, or worse, forced to work for her keep.

Her future didn't look good at all.

Chapter Two

"I don't want you in my house," Caleb said, glaring at his nephew.

"Come on, man, please let me stay. It's gross being at home. I walked into the room, and seriously, they were fucking, and I don't need to see that shit." Dwayne snuggled down into the chair, and Caleb stared at him.

Anne had alerted him that Dwayne arrived a couple of hours ago. So far, he'd not seen Faith, and that was the way Caleb liked it.

He loved his nephew. He simply didn't trust him.

Dwayne was an impulsive, spoiled, little brat at times, and as far as Caleb was concerned, he didn't trust him, not yet.

Trust in the Carson family had to be earned, and so far, he wasn't impressed by what he saw from the youngest member.

"You're not staying here."

"Why not?"

"I work for Beast. I'm a Carson through and through. I don't have time for your bullshit parties, or thinking you can get away with shit. It's not going to happen. Not in my house."

"Come on, Uncle Caleb!"

"No. I'm not falling for that little pup lost routine. You may have Beast wrapped around your finger, but I see through your bullshit, Dwayne. I'm not interested."

This life wasn't easy.

It was fucking dangerous, and if Dwayne didn't take it seriously, then he was going to end up dead, and that wasn't something Caleb was willing to deal with. Not now, not ever. Beast wouldn't ever forgive himself if Dwayne ended up dead.

This was what made him and Beast different.

His brother had that protective feeling inside him when it came to this boy. Caleb just saw him as reckless, and in no way fit to serve them.

Dwayne sighed. "What will it take for me to become like you and Beast?"

Caleb stared at him. "Excuse me?"

"You heard me. I don't want to be the odd one out of this. I know what you guys do is the real shit, and I get it. I know it's serious, and whatnot, but I want in."

Caleb couldn't help but start to laugh, and the weird thing was, the moment he started, he couldn't fucking stop. The laughter just kept coming, bubbling up inside him, and he bent over, holding his stomach.

"I'm being serious here. Ass."

Dwayne went to walk past him. Reaching out, Caleb grabbed hold of Dwayne's neck, and pressed him up against the nearest wall.

"Being serious is realizing that walking away like that, is bullshit. Don't even think of having a temper tantrum in my house, Dwayne. I'm not interested. In fact, I'd rather shoot you and end whatever crap you're going to give us because right now, it's half-assed. All you want to do is party, fuck around, and spend the money we earn. And guess what, you have a right to that because your last name is Carson. You're not even close to being ready."

"Then how do I get ready?"

"Report to me at five o'clock, every single day. I'll see if I'm ready to take you seriously."

"In the evening?" Dwayne asked.

"No, in the fucking morning. Our days start early and end late." He released his nephew. "Get the fuck out of my house."

He watched Dwayne leave.

The young kid was throwing his arms all over the place as if he had a reason to, and Caleb found it fucking amusing.

Once there was no trace of Dwayne, he headed to the kitchen.

"Is that boy still alive?" Anne asked.

"He's alive, and gone for now. I don't want him anywhere near Faith."

Anne smiled. "I doubt that's going to be a problem. She avoids everyone who comes here, and I can't get her to do much more than mutter a few replies. I don't think she's used to talking all that much."

Caleb leaned against the wall, staring out of the window. He caught sight of Faith in the garden. She wore another overly large shirt, and a pair of jeans again. She leaned over a rose bed and inhaled the scent.

"Why doesn't she wear different clothes?" he asked.

Anne came to stand next to him, and smiled. "She can't. Those are her clothes. I thought the same thing, and then I went to check out her closet while she was waiting in the library. She doesn't have anything else, sir. Her clothes are all well-worn, and do not do her figure well at all."

"I want you to buy her clothing," Caleb said. He pulled his wallet out and handed her a credit card. "I don't want you to spare any expense."

"I certainly will. Do you want me to tell her anything?"

"Yeah, tell her to buy things she likes, and not to worry about anything else." He turned toward his cook. "Do you have her food ready?"

"I do."

He took both of their sandwiches and made his way out to the garden. Faith hummed to herself as she stroked the petal of one of the roses.

"You like them?" he asked, drawing her attention.

She nodded.

The air was cold, and he didn't like the light jacket she wore.

Putting their plates on the nearby table, he removed his jacket, and placed it over her shoulders. "I've got plenty of jackets near the door. Wear them. I don't want you getting cold."

"I don't need—"

"I'm not arguing with you over this. Pick a jacket, or don't come outside."

He left, grabbing himself another jacket and joining her at the table.

"You're very bossy."

"It's the only way to be to get things done." He sat down opposite her, and once again, they ate their sandwiches.

Caleb found it hard to look away from her. She was a bit of a mystery to him. Even in the middle of his workday, he wondered what she was doing, and if she was okay. He wasn't used to a woman getting under his skin like this, and he wasn't sure that he liked it either.

He watched as she ate her food. Every now and again her gaze would move toward the rose beds before returning back to him.

"You like roses?"

"I never really gave much thought to flowers, to be honest. They were just … there. I know it sounds weird, right? Flowers are so important to everything, and yet, I never realized how beautiful they were. Roses would have to be my favorite. They stand out. They've got thorns, so sometimes people may not want to pick them up, but if they took their time, and just held them properly, maybe they'd see how beautiful they were, too."

Caleb stared at her scar, and wondered if not only was she referring to the flowers but also her face.

"Have you been hurt a lot?" he asked.

She shook her head. "Not as much as people would think. I just … sometimes it's doing nothing that hurts the most." She shrugged. "Forget I said anything."

"Do you miss your dad?"

"Nope. That is one thing I know for a fact I do not miss." She chuckled.

"What happened to your mom?" he asked.

"You ask a lot of questions."

"I'm a curious guy."

"She died." Again, she gave him another shrug. "I don't really remember her. It was me and Dad for so long, it seems weird to even think about her at this point. I like to think she wouldn't have agreed with his choices in life."

"Your dad was selfish."

"Was?" She looked at him, tilting her head to the side as she did.

"Eat your sandwich."

She didn't need to know yet that her father was long gone, and would never be coming back.

They finished their food in silence. She wouldn't look at him, and he couldn't stop staring at her.

The scar on the side of her face didn't look ugly to him. It looked like it had hurt like a bitch, but it didn't take away from her beauty. He adored her green eyes. They held so much warmth, which to him meant a good deal.

"I wanted to talk to you about school."

"You don't have to worry about that. My father pulled me out of school a few years ago."

"Didn't you get school, you know, understand

it?"

"I got it, but I was tired of moving from place to place. Always feeling out of my depth because classes had changed. I'm not interested in that. I never knew if I was going to be in the same place for longer than a few months."

He didn't push as he already saw that she wasn't happy. Glancing down at the time, he saw he needed to be getting out.

"I'll see you tonight."

"Okay."

He grabbed their empty plates and stared down at her. "Have fun."

****

"Why do we have to go here?" Faith asked.

"You need some new clothes, and seeing as I don't trust you to come home with any of them, I guess I'm going to have to come shopping with you."

She climbed out of the car and followed Anne as they made their way into the shopping mall.

"I hate shopping."

"Which is why I'm here, and you're going to get some new clothes."

She turned toward the woman who'd ordered her out of the house, and even threatened to get one of the men to force her into the car. Anne was ... scary. She didn't see that coming. She liked the older woman, as she didn't take shit from anyone, and she also admired her for sticking around.

Anne must have seen some serious stuff working for the Carsons, but she seemed loyal to them.

"I don't have a lot of money, Anne."

"Money is not a problem." She held up a plastic credit card. "We can have a whole lot of fun without worrying about the price."

"Is that Caleb's?"

"Yes. We're here on his orders that you have some new clothes, and I'm not going to hear any bad-mouthing. Do you understand? You're eighteen, and even though you're Caleb's property now, you're going to look good."

"Property?"

"The moment your dad handed you over, you became his."

Her stomach turned. She hadn't thought of it like that, and now she was ... scared.

There was no way she was getting out of this mess. Her father was dead. She knew it. She didn't feel anything about it though. Her father had been dead to her for a long time, and there was nothing she could do to make herself care. Why should she?

All he ever cared about was finding his next gambling fix, and getting himself thousands of dollars into debt.

"How about we have some fun? I know I'm old, and you probably don't think this, but I can be a laugh." Anne held onto her arm, and smiled up at her.

Faith giggled. "Okay."

"Caleb's not going to hurt you. I hope you know that."

"I don't know what to think anymore, to be honest. I've never ... I don't know what to do."

"Learn to have a little faith, dear."

This time she did smile. "Like my name."

"I think your name is beautiful."

"Dad told me that my mom gave it to me. He didn't want her to name me that, thought it would make me too big for my boots."

"Men don't get it, sweet. They never do."

"Do you have any children?"

"Nope. I don't have any, and I never want to have any either. I'm happy taking care of my Carson boys. I've been with them for so long they feel like mine."

She laughed. "I bet you'd have made one hell of a mom. Baking cookies, and just being you."

Faith liked Anne. She felt comfortable with the other woman, more so than anyone else in her life.

"I'll never know. Now, let's get you dressed."

Before Faith could argue, or try to get out of going shopping, Anne took her from one shop to another. She'd never liked clothes shopping. There was nothing more boring than looking through piles of clothes, hoping to find something that fit. This was just another of those reasons that she never fit in.

Of course, no matter how difficult she made it for Anne, she still ended up in a changing room trying on jeans, shirts, skirts, and even dresses.

She hated it.

Some of the dresses showed off her knees. Others fit to her curves, which she didn't like. After years of wearing her father's hand-me-downs, or just buying clothes way too big for her to grow into, she wasn't used to this kind of luxury.

"You look absolutely beautiful. Now, we're going to have your hair cut."

She quickly pulled away from Anne. "No. My hair stays."

"I don't mean all the way off." Anne held up some of her hair. "Just the split ends to clean it up a bit. Don't worry about a thing, sweetheart. I'll be right there."

Faith hated being treated like a child, but seeing no point in arguing, she followed Anne toward the hairdressers, where she then sat for over an hour while a man worked. She didn't even get a woman working on her hair, which only served to piss her off.

Anne at least stayed true to her promise. She stood right there the whole time, talking, and making sure the guy did a damn good job.

By the end of the day, Faith was exhausted. She didn't want to do anything else other than collapse in her bed, far away from everyone and everything.

When she entered home though, there was no such luck as Caleb was waiting for them. Anne had asked her to dress in one of the skirts and blouses, and Faith had only agreed to one that fell below the knee. It was a blue one with flowers all over it. The white shirt went well with it, and she also wore a jacket.

"Did you have a nice day?" Caleb asked.

She looked toward Anne, who shrugged. "She hates to shop, and I don't think you should get used to it. I got as much as I could this time."

Anne left, making her way up toward Faith's bedroom.

Caleb stepped in front of her. "You don't like shopping?"

"I know. It makes me weird, right?"

His gaze traveled down her body, and she didn't like the way she responded to that look. How she *liked* it. Her nipples tightened, and she was so pleased the jacket covered her reaction so he didn't see it.

In the past few weeks, she'd noticed that she responded to him in ways she never had to any other man.

She wasn't immune to him, and she found that hard to deal with.

"You look pretty, and this really suits you."

She ran a hand down her skirt, lifting it just a little. The fabric was soft and nice. "I like it."

"But you don't like shopping."

"Nope. Anne made it fun though. She's a hard one to say no to."

"That's why I put her in charge."

"Will you be staying for dinner?" she asked, changing the subject.

"I don't know, Faith. Will you be joining me?"

She tilted her head to the side, thinking about it. "I may."

"Good, I'll stick around for dinner so long as I have you for company."

Before either of them could say anything else, his cell phone rang.

"Excuse me."

He stepped away, moving toward his office, and for a long time she just stood there, watching him.

Finally, after several minutes had passed, she shook her head and made her way upstairs where Anne was already putting away her clothes.

"I can do that."

"It's no trouble."

"I think Caleb is staying for dinner."

"Right, okay." Anne handed her a dress. "Will you be downstairs to join him?"

"Yes." Other than the few sandwiches they'd shared, this would be the first time that she had dinner with him.

She watched Anne go, and finished putting her clothes away. They were all so beautiful. She'd never had any fine things before.

Once everything was done, she sat down on the edge of her bed and simply stared into space. There was nothing else she could do.

Could she sit across from Caleb or by his side, and have dinner? It seemed almost too much for her to even consider. She didn't know why she was worried.

Pressing her thighs together, she knew why she was worried.

No one had ever gotten such a response from her. She wanted him, there was no denying that.

At eighteen years old she wasn't a fool about her needs.

Other than that one guy, she'd never had sex with anyone else, and even that one time, it had been awful. It had hurt, and it had been over within a matter of seconds.

She really didn't see the appeal with younger guys.

"You're not going to sit here thinking about Caleb, or what it means to be with him, or anything else."

Shaking her head, she finally stood up and left her bedroom. She didn't want to chicken out. The thought of having another meal by herself filled her with a loneliness she didn't want to feel.

Caleb had never hurt her, and even though he owned her, she felt safer with him than she ever had with her own father.

Making her way into the kitchen, she asked Anne how she could help. She didn't like to be useless, and sitting around waiting for something to happen was driving her insane.

She hated it.

She wasn't leaving this house alive.

Nor was she going back to her father, so she really needed to make this work, or she would end up dead.

Chapter Three

Caleb sat in the dining room, waiting for Faith to arrive. He couldn't look away from the door, and he was curious as to what she would wear. Not for the first time in the past few weeks did he wonder about her.

His thoughts when it came to this girl were starting to drive him crazy. Not only that, he'd seen Beast and Hope's relationship flourish. Faith wasn't like other women he'd met. She didn't throw herself at him, even though he'd seen the interest in her eyes.

She wasn't a virgin, but from what he'd learned from her own lips, she may as well have been. The guy didn't know what he was doing, and she'd only done it out of fear her father would make her do something later on.

Rubbing at his temple, he sat back in his chair and wondered what the fuck he was doing. He was a grown-ass man, and shouldn't be sitting with an eighteen-year-old girl at dinner. There were plenty of women out there. Women who would suck him off and not blink if he walked away without touching them.

There were women whose fathers were still alive, and hadn't been killed by his own hands.

Even as he thought all of this, there wasn't any place he'd rather be than at home with her. Then of course, Faith rounded the corner and stood in the doorway of the dining room, and there was no chance he was leaving.

The clothes Anne had bought for her fit perfectly, and now he was able to look at her without thinking of a sack of potatoes.

"Anne said you hated shopping."

"It's really not my thing." She stepped into the room, hesitant at first. He expected her to sit far away from him, but she didn't. She took the seat right next to him. "Did you have a good day?"

"Yes."

He expected more of an interrogation, but in fact, he got nothing. Anne brought their food out, and he didn't understand the smile on her lips. It was just food, and yet she looked mightily smug about something. "Enjoy your meal."

"You're not going to join us?" Faith asked.

"No. I already ate. But you two enjoy."

Caleb didn't like the look on his cook's face. Anne was up to something, and he didn't get it.

Picking up his knife and fork, he glanced over at Faith to see her doing the same. Together, they began to eat, and he didn't like the awkward silence.

"Can I ask you a question?" Faith said, speaking up first.

"Sure."

"I was wondering … if I might be able to buy some books? There are a lot of e-books out there that I'd really like to read, and well, I don't have an account or anything."

"I will get you an e-reader, and we can set you up an account then."

"Thank you."

They ate once again in silence. He couldn't take it anymore.

"Are you happy here?" he asked.

"What?"

"Would you like me to find you an apartment or something like that?"

"No. I like it here, and there's no one or anything for me to go back to. Do you want me to leave?"

"No, I don't. It was the wrong thing to say. I want you here, Faith." He reached out, touching her hand, and she stared down at it.

Just like that, he ruined dinner.

Faith excused herself, taking her plate into the kitchen and then heading outside.

"Well, what happened here?" Anne asked, coming to take the seat that Faith had been sitting in.

"I don't know what you mean."

"I know you, Caleb. Women and you have always gotten on well."

"She's eighteen."

"I've had a great many adult conversations with that woman. Eighteen or not, she knows her own mind. Sure, she's quiet a lot of the time, and it takes her a while to warm up to you, but her heart is there. She's a good woman, Caleb."

"Her father gave her to me for a debt, Anne. What do you want me to do?"

"I want you to stop feeling guilty about wanting someone younger than you. Stop trying to push her away, because Faith could be the one person to understand you. Now, go and talk to her."

"We've got nothing to talk about."

"Ugh, you men are stubborn, and it's going to drive me into an early grave."

"Early? Last I checked you were nearly sixty."

"And to a lot of people that's still young. Don't back talk me, Caleb Carson. I used to change your diapers, and your hard-ass approach is not going to work on me."

He rolled his eyes. He couldn't help it. No matter what he or Beast did, Anne had their back. Of course, she'd seen the evil within their middle brother, and would do everything she could to help him, but there really was no helping him. That's why he was dead now, and Beast was raising Dwayne, the evil brother's son.

It was one of the many reasons he didn't trust Dwayne. He didn't come from a good man, and there was nothing to suggest that he wouldn't turn out the same as his father.

"Go and talk to her."

"You know it's not going to work."

"Have you ever thought she's as lonely as you are?"

"I'm not lonely."

"Screwing whores does not make you happy or fulfilled. It gives you satisfaction for as long as that feeling lasts, which I'm guessing is not that long."

"Your mouth always surprises me."

"I had to help some Carson boys. I had to learn not to be a prude, especially when I found porn underneath your beds at such a young age. Now, be a good boy and go talk to her."

She took his plate and offered him a smile.

Anne was the closest thing he'd ever really had to a mother.

He did as she asked, and made his way outside. Once again, he found Faith at the rose bushes, her fingers brushing against the softness of the petals.

"I'm not used to having company," he said.

She offered him a smile. "I'm not either. For the most part, Dad said kids were to be seen but not heard. He didn't really like to see me all that often either."

"I killed him," he said, blurting out the words before he could even stop himself.

"I figured you had."

"A man that was willing to put his daughter in danger was not a man I wanted out on the streets for you. He could have brought a lot more complications."

She simply nodded.

"You've not got anything to say to me."

"Nope."

"I admitted to killing your father."

"He wasn't really a dad to me, Caleb. He spent most of his time elsewhere. I've been on my own for so long that I forgot what it meant to have a parent or anything like that."

"Is that why you didn't return to school?"

"Schools are full of people with parents and problems. I had a father with a reputation who was addicted to gambling. No matter where we went people seemed to know who I was related to. I simply stopped going to school to avoid the inevitable problems that would come."

"I know a woman that could help you," he said, thinking about Hope.

"What do you mean?"

"She tutors. If you'd like, I could ask her to come over here, and she can help you with your studies, bring you up to date. I'll even arrange for the high school to let you take your last exam if you don't want to go to classes."

"You'd do that for me?" she asked.

"Only if you want to. I'm not going to pressure you or anything."

"I'd love to do that."

"Okay. It may take some time. The woman I'm referring to belongs to my brother. He's a little possessive."

"I don't mind waiting. I've waited all this time, so what's a few months more?"

He smiled.

"Are you sure you don't want me to leave?" she asked.

He didn't like the little pang of guilt and regret that rushed through him. "No, I don't want you to leave.

The roses would miss you, and so would Anne."

"I do like Anne, even though she loves shopping way too much."

"She means well."

Once again, he was watching her with nothing to discuss. He didn't like this. Normally he was happy to just walk away. When it came to Faith, he liked looking at her, watching her.

She was different from the women he was around. The scar didn't detract from her beauty, and in fact, to him, it made her shine brighter than anyone else.

Faith was one of the many reasons he loved coming home.

****

The weeks went by, and one of Faith's favorite times of the day was sitting down to eat with Caleb. Of course, there were long silences, but then there would be a spark that struck a chord with each of them, and they could talk. He'd started to leave a magazine around or a newspaper, and it helped for them to find something to talk about.

She enjoyed their silences just as much as the conversations. Both were amazingly fun. He couldn't stand the silence though, and it always made her smile thinking about it.

After living in places where the walls were super thin, she appreciated peace and quiet. Not only that, being with Caleb, she felt safe, which, considering who he was supposed to be, was crazy.

He wasn't a good man, and yet he'd done nothing but show her kindness.

Before long, she'd been with him nearly four months, and one day she was sitting in the library, reading one of the many books when he brought in a beautiful woman, who couldn't have been much older than herself.

"Faith, this is Hope. She's my brother's wife."

Hope positively glowed, and when Faith looked at her, she saw that she was pregnant.

"Caleb said you needed help with studying, and I do that well."

Closing the book on her lap, Faith climbed off her seat and moved toward them. "Thank you," she said, looking at Caleb.

"Enjoy studying. I've got things to do." He left them both alone, and Hope sighed.

"Beast is always doing that. They're busy men."

"I think I make Caleb uncomfortable," Faith said.

Hope chuckled. "I find that hard to believe."

Faith shrugged. "You're a Carson?"

"Yep."

"Beast is a lot older, right?"

Hope shrugged. "I don't care. I love him, and he's amazing, and I shouldn't be babbling right about now. I need to focus on helping you study. Caleb told me that you've been out of school for a while, and to help me find where you're missing things, I've printed out a couple of tests. I can see where we need to start off."

Faith stared down at the test, and Hope placed a pencil in front of her, taking a seat. She held open a study book and started to read.

Faith saw no point in arguing as she really did want to finish high school. Being a dropout hadn't been in her plans until she got her scar. Tucking some hair behind her ear, she sat down and started to read the test.

Every now and then she found herself glancing at Hope.

She couldn't recall a time she'd seen another woman so happy, and she was married to Beast, one of the most feared men in their world.

Pushing all of those negative thoughts aside, Faith focused on the test and began to work her way through it. After answering only a few questions, she felt that rush she used to love about being in school. She loved learning new things, and she had missed it so much.

She found herself glancing over at Hope, who was working on a couple of assignments. On her finger was a wedding band, and it made Faith curious.

"Do you love your husband?" Faith asked.

Hope smiled. "It's a test. I really shouldn't be talking to you, but when it comes to Beast, I can't seem to stop myself."

"You love him?"

"More than anything in the world. I lost my mom a couple of years ago, and I was living with my aunt, and out of nowhere, Beast helped me. He had his reasons, but one thing led to another, and before I knew what was happening, I fell in love."

Faith nibbled her lip, seeing the sparkle within Hope's eyes. She was clearly happy. There wasn't a time Faith could ever recall really being truly happy like that. She'd been constantly moving, fearing the knock at the door, wondering if her dad would ever come home.

"How are things with you and Caleb?"

"I don't really know. We eat dinner together. He's always out for breakfast."

"You're not together, together?"

"Not at all. He kind of got dumped with me."

"Hmm."

Faith stared at her. "What's the hmm about?"

"Nah, just the way he approached me about tutoring you, and how he looked when he mentioned you had some gaps in high school … I thought something more was going on."

Staring at her test, Faith couldn't really see the words, and that in itself was … irritating. For a long time, she didn't give Caleb much thought, and now over the weeks, and past few months, he'd become a comfort.

"What's it like being with an older man?" The moment she asked the question, she slapped a hand over her mouth and shook her head. "Completely ignore what I just said. I don't know what the hell has come over me. I'm clearly losing it."

Hope chuckled. "Have you ever had a girlfriend to talk to?"

"Didn't stay long enough in one place to have one of those." She rolled the pencil around in her fingers and felt like an utter fool.

"It's the best feeling in the world."

Faith looked up and saw Hope's cheeks were red.

"Are you a virgin?" Hope asked.

"No."

"Oh, I was. I mean, and he was so careful and gentle, and sweet. There's … he took his time, and he made me orgasm. I'm sorry. I'm not really good at this either. I've been seen as a bit of weirdo for a long time."

"It's more than fine. I really shouldn't ask. I don't even know why I did."

"Do you have a crush on Caleb?"

Faith paused for a second thinking about him. Dinner times were her favorite out of the entire day. When she was in the garden, her heart would speed up just thinking about him. "I don't know. I don't think I've ever really had a crush on someone."

Hope laughed. "Really?"

"Again, my life hasn't always been so easy. Guys just … don't do it for me."

"How do you feel when Caleb is near?"

"My heart speeds up, and I sometimes think what

it would be like if he kissed me. Is that weird?"

"It's not weird. I think this is the first time I've ever had a girly conversation about boys," Hope said. "And I'm married, expecting our first baby."

"Congratulations."

"Thank you. Beast is very protective. He wanted me to have a bodyguard just coming here." She chuckled. "I know to some women his protective attitude is, like, serious overkill, but I love it. I love that he worries so much about me, and he doesn't want to see me hurt. I love that he holds me close at night, and when his arms are around me it feels like he never wants to let me go."

Faith saw the love shining in Hope's eyes, and she wanted that.

"I don't think Caleb would ever feel that for me."

Even as she thought it, she felt a little saddened by it.

"What about you?"

"What do you mean?" Faith asked.

"Don't you feel anything for him? Sometimes it doesn't have to be the man to start something, Faith. It could be you."

She didn't answer, and finished the test. Once that one was done, Hope gave her another, then another. For most of the day all she did was take tests.

Caleb came to the library to let them both know that Beast was here to take Hope home. Just the look on Hope's face had Faith wishing for something like that for herself. Following Hope out of the library, she watched as she ran toward a man whom she assumed was Beast.

"You ready to go?" Beast asked.

"Yep."

Hope turned toward her. "I'll go over these, grade them, and see where we can go on from there. If you want to talk about anything at all, anything, just give me a call. Caleb knows my number."

Before she could stop her, Hope had pulled her in for a hug. She saw Beast watching her, and she quickly closed her eyes.

"You better know what you're doing," Beast said.

In the next second they were both gone, and Faith stood at the door.

"My brother is very protective of his wife."

"I can see that. Hope told me he was." She held onto the pencil like a lifeline. Glancing over at Caleb, she wondered if he could have any feelings for her at all, or if he felt more obliged to help her, which made her cringe. She didn't want to be a problem that needed solving.

"How did things go with Hope?"

"They went well. She's really nice. Erm, I can't talk to her. I don't have a cell phone."

Caleb nodded and pulled a cell phone out of his pocket. "Been meaning to give you this, and this." He opened one of the drawers in the hallway that held an e-reader. "I've set you up an account. Anne has everything ready."

She stared at the device, shocked and touched.

"Thank you."

"It's no trouble at all. I want you to be happy."

Looking up at him, she thought about what Hope had said, and once again there was a stirring deep inside of her that she couldn't control. Caleb reached out, stroking her cheek. "Enjoy."

He left her alone, more confused than ever before.

Chapter Four

"This is bullshit," Dwayne said.

Caleb stared at him. He watched his young nephew bend over and take several deep breaths. It was still dark out, and of course it was cold. Caleb didn't give a fuck though. Dwayne asked for his help, and he was merely providing it.

"What do you think is bullshit?"

"This. This is not what you and Beast do. I want to know the good stuff. Not freezing my balls off just for a fucking jog," Dwayne said.

There were a million different things he'd love to be doing right now. Babysitting this pansy ass wasn't one of them.

"Go home." Caleb turned his back, ready to go home himself. He wondered if Faith was already up, or if she'd still be asleep. There were a few times he'd gone to check on her, and watched her sleeping, in a totally non-creepy kind of way.

"Caleb," Dwayne said, sounding like a whiny little girl.

The sound of his nephew's voice was really starting to grate on his last nerve. "What, Dwayne? What the fuck is your problem?"

"Is it wrong that I just want you to teach me the guns, the weapons, the business?"

Caleb rounded on him. "You can't even hack it running laps at five in the morning. You're nowhere near ready to handle the kind of shit we deal with. I doubt you ever will be. You're too much of a lazy ass."

"I can run the fucking laps."

"Then prove it," Caleb said, yelling now. They were alone in the park and had been for the past hour. "I haven't got time for you to tell me what you can do. I want to see it."

"I've been running with you for months, and you've not changed what we do."

Caleb stared at Dwayne. There had been several times over the years that he told Beast he needed to be harder with him.

He understood wanting to give the kid a childhood, but he was eighteen now. There was no way that he'd trust this little shit with his back, or the business. All it would take was someone who had a little drive to take Dwayne out, and that didn't sit well with him. He hadn't liked being born into a criminal family that owned brothels, fight clubs, drugs, and many other illegal businesses, but this was what he did. It was in his blood. Lives depended on him being tough and not taking shit from anyone.

Grabbing Dwayne around the neck, he pinned him against the nearest tree. "You may be used to getting your own way with Beast, but that's not going to cut it here. As far as I'm concerned, you're so far away from a person I need by my side, you've not got a chance of being part of this world. You can't take a simple run every single day without moaning about it. I can't have you at risk of ruining other lives. It's not just about the run. It's about being able to withstand the kind of torture that can be thrown your way, while you wait for Beast or someone else to help you out, and people want to get information out of you. So you can take the pain, the beating, a couple of stabs, hell, even a few bullet holes, waiting. You don't talk. No matter what kind of pain they deliver to you, the people you hurt, the Carson name remains strong. You don't fall against your enemies. You don't beg them to stop." He stared Dwayne up and down. "You'd crumble within the first few minutes. You don't know how to take the pain. You don't know how to keep your fucking mouth shut. You're a disgrace to the Carson name, so no, I won't have you anywhere near our line of work. The best you'd get is dishing out donuts at the mall." He released Dwayne's neck.

Without another word, he spun on his heel and left, jogging back toward his home. Beast would be pissed at him, but this was the way it had to be.

He entered the code that opened the gates to his home, being sure to lock them behind him. Nodding at his security detail, he went toward the back. Anne wasn't up yet, but he paused, catching sight of Faith as she leaned against the counter in a nightshirt. In her hands, she held the e-reader, and she looked so engrossed that for a few moments, he watched her. She'd pulled her hair back, exposing the scar for him to see.

It wasn't an ugly scar, not to him anyway. The harsh redness had long since faded, and most of the time she hid it behind her hair. To Caleb, the scar was a sign of strength. She'd been through a lot in her years, and because of that, it made her the woman she was today.

The last thing he wanted to do was scare her, so he opened the door and stepped into the kitchen.

Faith turned to him with a huge smile. "Good morning."

"Morning."

"Did you have a good jog?"

"It was ... interesting." He closed the door, relishing the warmth that wrapped around him. "What are you doing up so early?"

"I'm always up early. Anne showed me how to work the coffee pot yesterday. I was more of an instant girl, and I've seen you come and go quite early, so I figured I'd be ready with a coffee for you."

"Thank you." He watched as she poured him a cup of coffee and presented it to him.

"Anne said you liked it dark in the morning, especially after having a grueling time working out."

He took the cup from her and took a sip. "You really didn't have to do this."

"Is it bad?"

"No. It's nice." He sipped some more of the coffee so she didn't feel bad.

The smile she offered him was so damn sweet. Faith, for all of her macho attitude, was a sweet woman.

"Would you like something to eat? I make a mean French toast."

"Sure."

He sat at the counter, watching as she worked. She no longer looked skittish around him, and he liked watching her … a lot. He was as fucked-up as his brother.

Hope had really tamed something within Beast. When he stared at Faith, the only taming Caleb needed was that of his cock.

Watching her work, even looking like she'd just woken up, his cock was hard, ready for action.

There was no denying that Faith was a beautiful woman, even with her curves. She was all tits and ass, all in the right places. Sipping at his cooling coffee, he watched her ass while she stood at the stove cooking his toast.

The scent was making him hungry, but the thought of bending her over the counter and feeling her tight cunt made him even more so.

Glancing down the length of her back, he took in her fluffy white boot slippers, and even they didn't help detract from his arousal.

She finished his toast and placed it in front of him, which caused her to bend forward. The nightshirt she wore gaped at the front, giving him a good view of her tits.

Forcing a smile to his lips, he took a bite of the food, not really tasting it but feeling the need to fuck, and fuck hard.

Unable to take his gaze away from her, he waited for her to take a seat, and she did, completely oblivious to the pain he was in. He wanted to fuck her so hard.

"Is your food okay?" she asked.

"It's fine."

He hadn't taken her to belong to him as some kind of sex toy to help relieve his needs. There hadn't been another alternative, since he couldn't bring himself to leave her with a man who was willing to sell her for a debt. When it came to Faith, she made him feel so fucking much, and he didn't get it. Women were all the same, but when he was with Faith, everything felt different. Her father was going to use her in any way he saw fit, and Caleb didn't like that.

They finished their food in relative silence. There wasn't any awkwardness, or at least he tried not to show that he was in fucking pain.

The shorts he wore seemed to be getting tighter with every passing second, and it was starting to piss him off.

Once their food was finished, Faith took his plate and stood at the sink. He gulped down the final bit of his coffee and moved up behind her.

"You may not think it, but you really need to start wearing clothes downstairs." He pressed his body against her.

For a split second she tensed up as he made her aware of his rock-hard cock.

"Some men don't have as much control as me."

Before he could do anything more, he pulled away and left the room.

A cold shower was in order, and if not, he was about to have some happy time with his fist.

****

Faith stared out at the garden where Beast and Caleb were talking. There was no sign of Hope today, not that she minded. She still had a great deal of coursework to do, and that was what she was supposed to be doing right now, studying. Instead, she stood at the window, and watched Caleb. She didn't care about Beast. He seemed too … mean for her.

Caleb had that mean streak though.

No one messed with him, and she imagined he was a force to be reckoned with. Both men were.

Teasing some of her hair through her fingers, she thought about the other day at the kitchen sink when he'd pressed his body against hers.

She'd not been afraid. Far from it.

The instant hit of pleasure had taken her by surprise. Her nipples had grown hard, and her pussy so slick. She'd not wanted him to leave, and when he had, she'd mourned the loss.

What did that make her? Did it make her a whore? Wanton? What? She didn't get her feelings for Caleb.

She wasn't scared of him.

Never had been.

He'd protected her from her own father, and she even knew without a shadow of a doubt that he'd taken care of her father, killed him. Yet, she didn't care.

Over the years her father had pushed her love for him until there was nothing left. Did she love Caleb? No. The truth was, she didn't believe in love. As a child she'd once believed in fairy tales.

From what she'd witnessed firsthand, love gave men and woman an equal right to abuse each other, all in the name of love. She did a lot of people watching, and most people ignored teenage girls who were alone.

Biting her lip, she forced herself to stare down at her book.

Chemistry wasn't going through her head, nor were math equations, or the correct way to build a sentence.

Sex.

Dirty, hardcore sex rushed through her mind, and it made her once again look at Caleb. One sexual partner, one time, and she was ... needy.

Her tits ached, and pressing her thighs together did little to relieve the slow agony she felt.

"I'll be fine," she said, talking to herself.

Of course, with her need for sex, she'd started to search for something, anything that would help relieve her for just a few days, if not longer. Porn helped a little. Well, it didn't really help. It was boring, but she loved to watch the act itself. The penetration of a cock inside a pussy, and just because she was a woman didn't mean she couldn't enjoy that.

Men loved it all the time.

She still didn't understand their love of girl on girl though. She'd see that as competition, but then, she'd never been with a girl before. Not that she was attracted to girls, far from it. She could look at them and see how beautiful they were, but that didn't for a second mean she wanted anything more.

"You're really overthinking this." She closed her book and glared straight ahead of her. Thinking about sex was really starting to bug her, and not in a good way either.

Gathering her books, she made her way up to her room and placed them on the desk before sitting on the edge of the bed. There was no way she could hide up here, but right now, she didn't see any other option.

What if Caleb didn't return her feelings or her needs?

He'd given her no indication that there was even anything between them.

Finally, when she couldn't handle it anymore, she took a quick shower and changed into one of the dresses that Anne said she looked good in. She didn't think for a second that she looked good in any dresses, but she didn't want to hurt Anne's feelings. Since she'd been with Caleb, she'd grown attached to the older woman, and she loved Anne's caring nature. For so long she'd been alone, not really knowing how to be with anyone, and Anne seemed more like a mother and a parent to her than anyone else had. She didn't want to lose that.

Leaving her room, she made her way down to the kitchen, knowing the older woman would help her feel calm and more herself again.

When she got to the kitchen, however, Caleb stood at the stove stirring a pot.

Hands clenched at her sides, Faith was about to leave just as he turned and saw her. "Hey, Anne wasn't feeling very well. I think she has the flu, so we're fending for ourselves for the next couple of days."

"Does she need someone to take care of her?" Faith asked.

"Nope. Anne doesn't like anyone fussing over her. She's got a niece who takes care of her when she's like this." He covered the pot he'd been playing with and turned toward her. His shirt sleeves were rolled up, and to Faith it only seemed to enhance the thickness of his arms, and it was driving her crazy. "You weren't in the library when I came to see you."

"I decided to go to my room. Try and do some studying there." It wasn't a total lie. She'd been to her room to try to forget about her arousal. Being around Caleb didn't help.

Any other man was easy. She'd seen some of his guards, and her body was fine, even her thoughts staying calm.

With Caleb, on the other hand, she was in total meltdown, and it was driving her crazy.

"What's wrong?" He stepped closer to her, and she took a step back.

She couldn't look away from him though, and as she stared at him, she was mesmerized by how dark his eyes actually were. They were so brown and intense. He didn't stop coming toward her until her back hit the wall. Then his hands pressed either side of her head, and she found that so sexy. Trapped between his body and the wall, she didn't see a problem with that.

Tilting her head back, she waited for him to speak. Then of course she remembered that he was the one who spoke last. "I'm fine."

"You don't look fine."

"What is fine supposed to look like?"

"Why are you hiding in your room?" he asked, completely avoiding the question.

"I'm not."

He smelled so good.

The closer he was, the harder she struggled not to reach out and touch him. She wondered what he'd do if she ran her hands up his chest. He had to be as hard and muscular as he looked even beneath the crisp, white shirt.

He always wore business clothes, which to her was incredibly sexy.

The tension seemed to mount as he stared down at her.

"What are you thinking?" she asked, daring to hope it was the same as she was.

"You don't want to know."

Do it.

What have you got to lose?

He can reject you, and you just hide out for the rest of your life.

Easy peasy.

Taking that next step, she ran her hands up his chest. He tensed up just a little, but he didn't pull away. In fact, one of his hands went to her hair, fisting the length, and she released a gasp. There was a bite of pain from the tightness of his hold, but it only made her more aroused.

For several seconds neither of them moved. The only sounds she heard were those of their deep breaths, and she didn't know what to do.

Everything seemed fuzzy. Then he slammed his mouth against hers, and all came back into focus. She wrapped her arms around his neck, moaning as his tongue plundered inside her mouth. He held her head so there was no getting away.

Wrapping her arms around his neck, she refused to let go, holding him tightly as his touch consumed her more than anything.

Her pussy was on fire for his touch, or for anything.

Caleb pressed her against the kitchen wall. The hard ridge of his cock grazed her stomach, taking her breath away with its sheer size. Even confined in his pants he was a big man.

She didn't care.

She wasn't some virgin that didn't know what happened next, and she wanted this more than anything. She'd been around sex a lot in her life. Her father hadn't kept her away from some of the women he liked to pick up for the night. It had been random women who told her about her periods, what to expect when she got older, and to always make sure the boys bagged their dick up.

It had been an interesting upbringing. Some women had been cruel to her, while others had felt bad for her.

He broke the kiss, and she missed his touch. Licking her lips, she tasted him on her tongue, wanting some more. Neither of them spoke, and she was desperate for something, anything but rejection.

Of course, she should have expected it.

"That shouldn't have happened."

Chapter Five

Caleb's cock was so fucking hard right now. He didn't want to stop, and he certainly didn't think it was a fucking mistake. Far from it. He'd been trying to ignore these feelings for a long time now, but in that dress, looking so vulnerable, he wanted her more than anything.

"I'm sorry," she said.

Faith tried to leave. Caleb couldn't let her, so he grabbed her arm, pressing her up against the wall.

"What are you doing?" she asked.

He saw the tears in her eyes, and hated that he'd been the one to put them there. Did she not like that kiss?

She'd seemed to go up in his arms like fire, but what if he'd misread the signals?

"I'm sorry."

"Why?"

"I shouldn't have kissed you."

"It doesn't matter. You don't have to talk about it. You regret it—"

"I don't regret it."

"You said it was a mistake."

"You didn't enjoy it." They were going around in circles right now.

"I did."

He frowned. "What?"

"I ... I wanted the kiss, Caleb."

Okay, he wasn't expecting that. Her lips were red and slightly swollen from his kisses. Reaching out, he stroked her cheek, and she pressed her face against him. "What is happening here?"

"I don't know."

His cock was so hard right now, and he'd not had a woman in months.

Faith had been driving him crazy, but no matter

what he did, he kept trying to do the right thing when it came to her.

She licked her lips. "I wanted you to kiss me. I want you to touch me." She took his hand and placed it against her breast. "Like this."

Her tits were large and filled his hand just perfectly, making him groan. "We shouldn't be doing this."

"Why not? We can—"

He cut her off by claiming her lips once again. They were so soft beneath his.

She wrapped her arms around his neck, and as he pressed her against the wall, she melted against him. Would her pussy be wet? How tight would she be when he drove inside her, filling her to the brim? There was nothing nice or sweet about what he wanted to do to her. His nights had been filled with fantasizing about her beneath him.

He wanted that more than anything else; her beneath him, taking his cock.

Dropping one of his hands down to the skirt of her dress, he gathered it up in his fist and touched her naked flesh.

She felt so good.

He'd never been one for skinny women. He liked them to have some meat on their bones as he loved to fuck. There was nothing worse than taking a woman that would moan about how big he was or that he was hurting her.

The last thing he wanted to do was hurt Faith, but his need for her was driving him harder than ever before.

"You don't have to do this," he said, breaking from the kiss.

"I want you, Caleb. This is not about making me do anything. I want you." She gripped the back of his neck, and when he stared into her green eyes, he was completely fucking lost.

She began to undo the buttons of her shirt, and he didn't stop her. She lifted the dress up and over her head, and stood before him in lacy white lingerie. Her tits were large, she had a nice rounded stomach and hips. Her thighs were thick and juicy, and he wanted her.

Tilting her head back, he took possession of her mouth. At the same time, he ran his hand down her back, gripping her ripe ass.

He was on cloud nine, his cock so hard that it was threatening to blow at any moment.

Breaking from her lips, he trailed kisses down her neck to the tops of her breasts. She released a little whimper. Holding the straps of her bra, he slid them down her arms until her tits fell out, and they were a beautiful sight.

Her hard, red nipples poked out. Cupping her tits, he heard her gasp, and staring into her eyes, he saw she was completely into this.

"If I touch your pussy right now, will it be wet?"

"Yes."

"Show me."

"Show you?"

"Touch yourself. Show me how wet your pussy is. I want to see it."

She touched her pussy. The moment she touched her clit, he saw it as a gasp escaped her. She was so sensitive that her own touch caused her pleasure.

She held her fingers up to him, and he saw how wet she was. The scent of her was intoxicating, and he couldn't get enough. Taking her hand, he sucked on her fingers, tasting her sweetness, and he wanted more.

He'd never been one for sucking on a woman's pussy, but right then, that was all he wanted to do, have

Faith spread out on the bed so he could lick every single inch of her.

Lifting her up into his arms, he carried her away from the kitchen.

"What are you doing?"

"I'm taking you to my room."

"But…"

"No buts. I know what I want, and this first time with you, it's going to be something to remember." He didn't care if the world ended around him. The only person he focused on in that moment was Faith.

She held onto his neck as he carried her upstairs toward his bedroom. Kicking open the doors, he did the same after he entered so it closed with a bang.

Placing her on the bed, he pushed her back and grabbed her panties. He tore them from her body, his impatience finally winning the day, and he couldn't wait another second. Spreading her thighs wide, he knelt on the floor, and for a few precious moments, he looked at her pussy. So sweet. She had fine hairs covering her lips, and they were open just a little, showing off her swollen clit.

Running his fingers across her pussy, he opened her up and moaned. Her cunt was dripping, and she was so wet.

"You want me, Faith?"

"More than anything."

He'd been wanting her for a long time now, and he'd felt like a sick fuck whenever he allowed himself to think about it. She was eighteen years old, and had so much of her life ahead of her. There were so many other men she could be with, safe men. He wasn't a safe person. He killed people for a living, and he'd killed her father purely because he'd given her to him as a payment.

Yet the thought of anyone else being near her, close to her, filled Caleb with a rage that he couldn't describe. No one else would ever be able to give her the kind of the pleasure he could.

Stroking through her wet pussy lips, he teased her clit, and she gasped, arching up, her tits shaking with each indrawn breath. Finally, when he couldn't stand to *not* touch her, he spread open her lips and ran his tongue across her clit. Going back and forth across her nub, he felt her shake. The gasp that escaped her along with the sounds of pleasure drove him crazy. Releasing his belt, he began to slide open his pants, desperate to release the pressure. He was so fucking aroused. His cock was rock-hard, in so much need. He kept on licking her pussy as he wriggled out of his pants. His cock sprang forward, and he ran his hand up and down the length, pre-cum already leaking out of the tip.

With his free hand, he slid his fingers through her pussy, finding her entrance and pressing in deep. She felt so incredibly tight and hot. She was already soaking wet, and the taste of her was the best thing he could ever remember.

This woman on his bed was all his.

That was what was driving him completely crazy with need. Faith belonged to him, and he was going to treat her with so much care, and never let her go, not for a single second. He loved her being here, and feeling her responses to him only served to drive his desire for her even higher.

"Please, Caleb, I can't stand it."

"You want to come?" he asked, whispering the words against her pussy.

"Yes, please, I need it."

Thrusting two fingers inside her wet cunt, he attacked her clit, drawing her closer and closer to orgasm, feeling her ride toward it fast approaching. Her pants, her pleasure cries, all drove his arousal up. Releasing his cock, he held onto her hip, squeezing the flesh as she wriggled against his mouth.

Her pussy tightened even more, and within seconds she erupted, screaming his name as her cum flooded his fingers. He continued to suck her clit, relishing each shake and moan as it filled the air.

****

Faith had read about orgasms, and of course she'd experienced them at her own hand, but never in all of her life could she even imagine it being like that. Caleb pressed a kiss against her clit and lifted up.

Staring down at him, she saw his face covered in her cream, and she licked her own lips.

"You taste so good. I'm going to want to lick your pussy regularly."

She didn't have a problem with that, not at all. In fact, she liked the thought of him licking her pussy.

"I don't want you to stop," she said.

"You don't have to do this."

"I'm not doing this because I have to." She sat up and hesitated as she cupped his face. She didn't know why she did, only that she wasn't sure if she could touch him.

Caleb took her hands and placed them against his cheeks. "I'm yours to touch any time you want. You don't need permission."

She ran her thumbs down his face. There was a hard line of stubble that grazed her thumbs.

"Is it wrong that I want so much?" she asked.

"It's never wrong to want something." His hand stayed at her hip, and she watched him, unable to look away. "You don't have to do anything you don't want."

"But I want this, Caleb. I want you."

165

"What exactly do you want?"

"I want to … have sex. I want to fuck."

He smiled. "The stuff I know would terrify a little girl like you."

She tilted his head back, and this time, she claimed his lips. When she slid her tongue across his, he opened up, and she plunged inside, deepening the kiss. Her need for him rose with each passing second.

"Why don't you try me?" she said. "I think you'll be surprised about what I'm willing to take."

She sat on the bed, naked, completely vulnerable and open to his touch. Glancing down, she saw his pants were down to his knees. His cock was still rock-hard, the tip slick with his pre-cum.

"I'm not a little girl," she said, reaching down and taking him in her hand.

He was a lot bigger than what she thought he would be. Working her hand up and down his length, she watched as he closed his eyes.

It looked like he was in a little pain.

"Once you start this, there's no way out, Faith. You'll be my woman. No holding back. I want to know everything, and you'll be open and honest with me."

"I know you killed my father. I know you hate having me here as some kind of debt." She'd come to see that even though Caleb was a bad man, he had … standards. It seemed to contradict everything, and yet, she wouldn't change a single thing about him. She didn't care that he hurt people or even killed them in his line of work.

The world was a shitty place to be. There were men and women out there who were far more dangerous than this man in front of her.

"I'm not a good man."

"I'm not looking for a good man, Caleb. I'm not

going to judge you or ask you for anything that you're not willing to give."

"I don't do love."

This made her smile. "I don't believe in it."

She may read all about it, but that didn't mean that she was interested in it, or even for a second believed it existed. In the world she'd known, love meant nothing. Her own parents hadn't loved each other. In fact, she'd go so far as to say they despised each other, at least from what her father said. He'd often curse the woman who'd burdened him with a child.

"There won't be any other man."

Her heart sped up as it meant he was considering it. He'd just given her one of the best orgasms she'd ever experienced, and she wasn't ready to let it stop there. There was so much more she wanted.

For the longest time he stared at her, and she wondered what he was thinking.

"I'm the one in charge. You'll do as I say."

"Okay."

"I'm not a dominant man or believe in BDSM. If there's anything you don't want, say no, and I'll stop. I'm going to push you because that's what I'm like."

This made her smile. She had yet to discover any kind of secret sex dungeon, not that it would have caused her a problem. The thing about owning an e-reader, she could read whatever the hell she wanted, and there was some dark stuff around about dominants and submissives.

"Why would you ask that?"

"I see the kind of stuff you read."

This made her cheeks heat, but she couldn't contain her smile.

"You like a lot of sex," he said.

"I'm curious about it. I've had it one time, and I'd

love to do it again." Was she flirting? It felt a lot like she was flirting with him.

Everything was moving so fast right now, and her heart raced. She kept on teasing his length hoping that he'd give in.

Please, Caleb, see that I want this.

Even though she'd already experienced one orgasm, she wanted another so desperately.

He pushed her hand away and stood up. She stared up at him, waiting. He reached out, stroking her cheek. "Open your mouth."

She did as he asked, opening her lips and staring up at him.

He cupped her cheek with his thumb running across her mouth before sliding inside. "Suck it."

She did as he asked, sucking on his thumb with her gaze still on him, waiting for his next instruction.

Caleb pulled his thumb out from her mouth, and sank his fingers into her hair, fisting the length. She didn't mind the slight pain that he inflicted with his touch. Her nipples tightened.

"Get on your knees."

She sank down to the floor and stared up at him, once more waiting for his next instruction. Did he even realize that his orders were turning her on? She didn't know if she'd like being at a man's mercy, but right now, she couldn't wait for whatever he had to say. Everything felt right, and completely in focus. Did that make her a submissive or kinky?

With his other hand, he held his cock, and when he ordered her to lick the tip, she did, tasting his pre-cum.

"You've never sucked a man's dick?"

She shook her head.

"Don't use your teeth. Take me into your mouth

until I hit the back of your throat." She followed his instruction, making sure she didn't graze his dick with her teeth. She didn't want to spoil the moment.

When he hit the back of her throat, she pulled away. She bobbed on his cock, listening to his moans as she did so.

Faith loved hearing the pleasure come from him. Placing her hands on his thighs, she glanced up at him, and his gaze was focused on her. Her cheeks heated at the way he looked at her. It was like he wanted to consume her, and she was more than willing to be his.

"Do you realize how many times I've thought about you on your knees in front of me? How I've wanted you to take my cock into that pretty little mouth? Your lips were made for a cock, Faith."

She closed her eyes and moaned, the vibration of her sounds setting him off as he gripped the back of her neck and pumped into her mouth. She loved that little loss of control he showed.

"For a woman who's never sucked a cock, you're a natural. A little rough around the edges, but with practice you'll be perfect."

Pulling off his cock, she took a breath. "I'll be happy to practice on you."

He stroked her cheek, and she didn't wait. Taking him back into her mouth, she sucked him even harder, wanting him to come with just her mouth alone.

"So fucking beautiful," he said. "I'm so close. You've never had a mouthful of cum. Pull away if you don't want it, Faith."

She didn't pull away.

He hadn't when she'd been close to her release.

"Oh, fuck!" He shouted out the word, and it made her smile. In the next second his cock expanded, and she felt the first wave of his cum spill into her mouth. "Hold it, don't swallow," he said.

She didn't know how much more she could take as he filled her mouth. Finally, after a few seconds, he stopped, and pulled out of her mouth.

"Open, let me see."

Feeling incredibly aroused, she opened her mouth, and he groaned.

"Swallow it."

She did as he asked, and he stroked her cheek.

"I'm fucking doomed," he said.

"You've said a lot of fucks in the past few seconds," she said, smiling.

"You're moving into my room."

"Okay. What will Anne think?"

"I'll handle Anne. Knowing her, she thinks you'll be my salvation."

Chapter Six

"Have you caved yet?" Beast asked.

Caleb glanced over at his brother while their men brought in the traitor who had decided to not only talk to the cops, but also sell their product to their enemy.

"What the fuck are you talking about?"

"Your little teenager. I saw the way you were looking at her the few times I've seen her, or at least how you try to pretend that you can't see her."

"She's not a teenager, not like that." Caleb didn't like to think about their small age gap. He was only a couple years younger than Beast's thirty-seven years, so there wasn't as big of an age gap, but still.

Faith didn't seem to mind when he was licking her pussy. In fact, he'd still be in bed with her today if it wasn't for Beast's call alerting him to their current problem. Their informant on the police force happened to be on duty when the little fucker came in, so no crap was going to go down on that front.

It wouldn't have been a big deal, but it would have cost them a lot more money and they'd have had to bribe a lot more people.

"You really need to get over whatever issues you have," Beast said, shrugging.

"How about you stay out of my business and I'll stay out of yours."

"Ah, but you see, you didn't always stay out of my shit, now did you? If you remember, you liked to talk to my little bird." Beast raised his brow, and Caleb sighed.

"Hope is different."

"She is, which is why I won't completely mess with your life even though I really want to."

"Just leave it alone."

"We'll see. How is Dwayne getting on?" Beast asked.

Caleb had been completely surprised by Dwayne's turnaround. He hadn't expected the young man to turn up for their runs or their workout sessions, but each day at five o'clock in the morning, Dwayne was there.

"He's training really well. Surprising me with his change."

"He's not partying anymore, and there's no beer either. At first, I thought it was Hope because she can't drink anymore, not that she ever really drank. Dwayne's the one who did it, not that I've got a problem." The sound of screaming filled the air, and Beast sighed. "Why do they think they can get away with stuff like this?"

"I don't know, but it's time for us to party."

For the next two hours, between himself and Beast, they tortured the man to find out who his supplier was, who'd approached him, and where he'd been feeding their product. The moment they had everything they needed, Caleb plunged the knife into the fucker's throat, ending his life.

Grabbing his jacket from one of the men, Caleb left Beast to clean up the mess like he did every single time they did this together. He was the one who handled the final blow.

Taking a life hadn't always been so easy.

Caleb for the longest time had refused to kill anyone, but their father, and then Beast, wouldn't let him refuse. He'd seen how destructive people could be, and that no one would ever have his back other than his brother. There wasn't anyone else in the world that he'd trust with his life other than Beast.

Dwayne still had a long way to go, and Caleb

only ever trusted his guards to a point. They were paid for their loyalty, and anything bought with money he didn't trust.

He drove home, thinking about Faith and what had happened between them. He'd not fucked her yet, but he'd moved her into his bedroom as he wanted to hold her.

Anne was happy about their change in relationship. The older woman was convinced that all he needed in his life was a woman's touch. Caleb didn't know what he needed anymore.

Parking up outside of his home an hour later, he suddenly felt extremely tired.

Faith was so young, and she had her whole life ahead of her. She shouldn't be with him, or part of this life.

Entering his home, he didn't stop or linger. Instead, he went straight to his en-suite bathroom and stared at his reflection. The jacket didn't have a speck of blood on it, but the white shirt he wore beneath did.

He threw the jacket on the floor, knowing he'd have to torch it.

"I heard you come in," Faith said.

Before he could tell her to leave or close the door, she stood in the bathroom, staring at his blood-soaked shirt.

She released a little gasp. "Are you hurt?"

"No. It's not my blood."

"Oh."

He opened each button, and his gaze focused on her.

"Did the person deserve it?" she asked.

Caleb chuckled. "I don't know. Do you think traitors who sell your secrets deserve to die?"

She didn't believe in love, and he'd promised her

that he couldn't give it to her, but what if … he wanted both?

"In your world, yes."

"What?" He turned toward her, aware there was blood on his flesh that had soaked through and dried.

"You don't live with the same rules as normal people. If you're threatened, then you have to take action," she said. "This man, whoever he was, earned his death sentence. In this world and this life, your decisions have consequences. If you let this man live, then he could have killed many more. The men who work for you, people's families rarely go unscathed by the actions of selfishness."

Okay, he wasn't expecting that.

He'd anticipated her upset or her judgment.

Yet, here she stood with a shrug of her shoulders.

"I killed your father."

"You've said that already."

"You don't care?"

She shook her head. "Does that make me a bad person because I don't care? He sold me because he'd taken your money. I'm sure he'd have used me many times over if he could get out of trouble himself."

"No."

"I like being around you, Caleb. Being near you." She stepped close to him. Her hands curled around the back of his neck, gripping him. "I feel something."

"I don't do love."

This made her smile. "I know." Her gaze dropped to his lips. "I've got nowhere else to go."

"You're not going anywhere else."

He cupped her face, his thumb stroking down her face exactly where the scar was. "You became mine, remember? Right now, you're not exactly helping your cause to get away."

"I don't want to leave."

For several seconds he did nothing but stare at her. The scar seemed more pronounced now than ever before, and he didn't care. To him, Faith was beautiful with her lack of trust and love in everyone else.

He'd seen his brother fall in love. But the way Hope seemed to draw that emotion out of Beast, he didn't understand it.

Gripping the back of Faith's neck, he tilted her head and claimed her lips. She tasted like fucking heaven, and he was a man that didn't want to let her go, not for a second.

She gasped, her lips opening, and he plunged inside, tasting her. She was so fucking sweet, like a drug that only he was addicted to. Running his hand down her back, he gripped her ripe ass, holding her close.

Lifting up her shirt, he broke from the kiss and began to strip her. The clothes she wore were going to get burned as he wouldn't risk any traces on her. She didn't deserve that. Once she was completely naked, he turned on the shower and held her hand.

Helping her inside, he followed her.

Neither of them spoke.

Words were not needed right now.

Grabbing the soap, he lathered up his hands, and staring at her body, he got to work on soaping up his prize. The water from the shower landed on his back. He guarded Faith's body, starting at her chest.

For the longest time he didn't touch anywhere intimate, soaping her arms and neck, then her stomach. He couldn't wait a second longer, so he cupped her tits, holding them up and running his thumbs across each beaded nipple.

She let out a gasp, and he couldn't resist pinching the hard buds.

Her moans echoed around the bathroom, and he relished each sound. With some soap still on his hands, he lathered up the fine hairs of her pussy, and then knelt down to deal with her legs.

Once he was all done, he stepped behind her and let the water wash away his hard work, the suds slowly going away down the drain.

With his hands on her hips, and the suds gone, he kissed her neck, right over her pulse. Running his hands up her body, he cupped her tits.

"I don't deserve you."

She relaxed against him.

"But I'm not going to let you go. I'm keeping you as my prize."

****

Caleb's touch was setting her on fire. Faith was so wet, and all he did was touch her breasts and she wanted so much more. He had a day's worth of stubble around his lips, and the light scratchiness was driving her crazy for his touch.

Reaching behind her, she sank her fingers into his hair, needing him. Both of his hands were working her tits, and it wasn't enough.

"What do you want?" he asked, breathing the words against her neck.

"You, I want you. I need you." She didn't care if she had to beg. She'd willingly do it for him.

"Are you wet for me?"

"Yes."

One of his hands left her breasts, and he touched between her thighs. She spread herself open, and he slid a finger between her slit. He stroked her clit, and it made her cry out, desperate for more of his touch. Caleb tortured her, though, as he glided down, and even she could tell how wet she was and it had nothing to do with the shower.

He plunged inside her, adding a second finger. There was a slight burn from his fingers, and he groaned inside her ear. "You're so tight."

She'd been with one guy before she'd even met him, and even then, just one experience.

"Please."

"You want me to stop?"

"No!" She yelled the word. The last thing she wanted him to do was stop. She wouldn't be able to handle him stopping.

He chuckled. "You sound like a little slut, baby. Do you want my cock?"

The moment he called her slut, she shouldn't have been aroused. She couldn't help tensing in his arms.

"What's the matter?"

"I'm only *your* slut." She glanced behind her, needing to look him in the eye.

"You're mine, Faith. I don't share." The hand that had been playing with her tit wrapped around her, holding her close. "If you don't want me to say stuff like that, I won't."

"I don't mind just so long as you know I'm not like that. I've never responded this way to anyone else."

"Good. I don't want you to. You're all mine." He bit her neck, his tongue trailing up to her ear as he sucked on her lobe. "And you can be a slut for me all night long."

This time she did whimper. Even though she didn't want him to get the wrong idea, the names only served to arouse her even more.

"Do you want my cock, Faith? Do you want it slamming inside you?"

"Yes."

Her pussy clenched, and the arousal almost too

painful for her to bear. The desire for him was unlike anything she'd ever experienced. Caleb broke down her walls and made her desperate for him.

"I love your body, Faith. You'll be able to take the fucking that I want to give you. I don't feel in a good mood right now. I never do when I've had to take a life, and right now, all I want to do is hear you scream my name as I take you, giving you pleasure, but above all else, taking my own."

"Then do it." She reached behind her, gripping the back of his neck and turning her head slightly so that she could look at him. "I won't break."

When she was in Caleb's arms she felt safe, safer than she'd ever felt in her entire life, even around her father.

Caleb released a little growl, pressing her against the shower. He took hold of her hands and placed them on the wall.

She stared at the black tiles as his hands glided down her back, holding onto her hips. His thumbs pressed against the base of her back, and suddenly his lips were at her neck, trailing down.

Closing her eyes, she felt the stubble as it scratched down her back. She didn't care. He placed a kiss near each of his thumbs.

His hands moved, and she gasped as he spread open the cheeks of her ass. His touch was incredible. "Open your legs a little."

She did as he asked, and then his fingers were working her flesh, and she couldn't focus or think on anything else. All that mattered was Caleb and his wicked caresses.

"You're so wet for me, Faith."

All too soon his fingers left, and she wanted him. She wanted his touch more than anything.

He moved her so that she bent forward just a little.

Then the hard ridge of his cock pressed against her entrance, and she lost all focus. "You can back out right now, Faith," he said. "Just tell me to stop and I will."

She didn't want him to stop, so she didn't say a single word.

"Fuck, baby."

He slammed every inch inside her, and her entire world went off kilter, and she lost focus to the pleasure of his touch, needing him more than anything. His hands returned to her hips, his cock pulsing inside her.

She'd never felt so full in her life. He was so hard.

Caleb's hands went from her hips to cup her tits, squeezing them. He pinched the nipples before moving down between her thighs, teasing her clit.

She cried out as he stroked her nub.

Pleasure shot through her in all different directions, making her ache for more.

She didn't want him to stop what he was doing but to keep going, and for the pleasure to never end. She couldn't handle it, not for a second, yet she couldn't imagine not having his touch.

"I want you to come on my cock, Faith. Then I'm going to fuck you hard. I'm not going to be able to go slow this time. Maybe next, but not this one. I need to feel your cunt, and watch as I fill your pussy with my cum."

His dirty words drove her need higher.

"I see you like that. You just got tighter around my dick. You want me to fuck you harder, don't you?"

She whimpered in response, and he chuckled.

"All you ever have to do to get what you want is

ask me, Faith. You like it hard, I'll give it to you. You like me to treat you like a lady outside of our bedroom, I will. You want to be my dirty little slut inside the bedroom where no one can see, I'll grant your wish."

"Please," she said.

"Please what?"

"Make me come. Please."

She'd never experienced it like this, and he was keeping her at the peak. His skill surprised and delighted her. She didn't want him to stop, and as he stroked her clit with two fingers while his cock stayed hard within her, she felt overwhelmed.

Her nipples tightened, and she fisted her hands as her orgasm struck her hard. She screamed his name as her body tightened around him, and stars seemed to explode around her temples.

His lips pressed against her neck, and she shook within his arms. Caleb, as always, was in control, and she didn't have a problem with that.

Her orgasm slowly ebbed away, and Caleb's grip returned to her hips. She opened her eyes, and moaned as he slowly began to pull out of her until only the tip of his dick remained. She didn't want him to pull out or stop, so when he drove inside her, she called his name. Even as he fucked her, the pleasure was unlike anything she'd ever experienced.

His cock was so long and thick as he took what he wanted.

"You feel so fucking tight, Faith. I'm going to have to fuck you regularly to get you used to having me inside you."

"I don't mind." She panted out the words and heard him chuckle once again.

Over and over he fucked her hard, the sound of flesh hitting flesh echoing around the shower stall. He drove to the hilt each time, and her own pleasure began to build.

Caleb took his time, working her body, stroking her, bringing her to new heights as he found his release, his cock throbbing as he pulsed deep inside her.

"I'm protected," she said.

"What?"

"I'm on the pill. I take them regularly." One of the women her father had been with had helped take her to a family clinic. She'd recently gotten a prescription when her father had given her to Caleb. They were mostly to help her periods. She turned her head, and saw him staring at her. "What's wrong?"

"I don't know if I'm happy about that or not."

"I'm not ready for kids." He didn't do love, and she didn't believe in it. She didn't want a kid in that kind of environment. "This is fun, right?"

The wicked smile on his lips let her know he was in agreement.

"You've got the tightest pussy, baby. I'm already addicted to you."

"Good." She didn't want him going anywhere else. For the first time in her life, Faith wanted to keep him all to herself.

Did that make her selfish?

She didn't care if it did.

Chapter Seven

"I like your ink," Faith said, stroking his back, and Caleb smiled. He found himself doing that a lot more with her around. Her fingers traced down his spine, and his cock began to respond to the touch. He'd already fucked her in the shower, and afterward, she'd been so exhausted he'd carried her to bed and demanded that she sleep.

Faith followed instruction really well.

Now they were both awake, and it was late.

Rolling over, he stared at her body. She had the sheet wrapped around her, and he gave it a tug, releasing it.

Cupping one of her heavy breasts, he fingered her nipple and watched the pleasure cross her face. He pinched the hard bud before moving down to touch her clit.

He'd already washed his cum from her body in the shower.

When she said that she was on the pill he didn't know if he was happy or sad about that. There really wasn't much for him to say. It was her body to do with as she wished, even if he didn't like it.

"I'm hungry." Pulling his fingers from her pussy, he climbed off the bed. "Come on, I'll go and fix us something to eat."

"I'll just get dressed," Faith said.

He reached for her hand, pulling her to her feet. "Nope. Come down with me."

"But what if your men—"

"They're not here, so they won't see you. Don't worry, I won't let anyone see you, and if they do, they've left their post and will be dead long before they can say that they ever saw you."

"You're really deadly, aren't you?"

"I command respect, and my men give it to me as I've earned it."

"It feels kind of naughty to be in Anne's kitchen naked."

He laughed as they walked down the long staircase.

Caleb didn't let go of her hand, and the few mirrors he passed, he couldn't help but look at her. To some men, her curvy body would offend, but to him, she was perfect. He'd fucked her hard in the shower, and she'd taken every single thrust without complaint. There were a couple of bruises on her hips, but they made him feel possessive as fuck.

He loved the sight of them, and wanted to see more of his pleasure marks on her.

They entered the kitchen, and he released her hand as he went to the fridge. He found everything to make them a cheese and pickle sandwich.

"I like Anne," she said, drawing his attention to her.

She was staring at one of the pictures Anne kept with her. It was one of his brother and himself, along with his other brother.

"Who is that?" she asked, pointing at the guy in the middle.

"He's one of my older brothers. He's been dead a few years."

He didn't speak his name as it was a wasted effort as far as he was concerned.

"Oh, I'm sorry," she said.

"Don't be. He was a fucking asshole that would have easily shot you in the back. He wasn't a good man."

"Wow." She tucked some hair behind her ear. "Do you think people ever really live normal lives?"

"Yeah, but I bet they're boring."

He cut the sandwich in half and offered her one. She took it as he bit into his half, watching her.

Her cheeks were on fire, and he noticed she kept turning her body away from him.

"Look at me," he said. She did as he asked, and her cheeks were a beautiful shade of red. "I like looking at you." He stared down the length of her body, admiring her rounded hips and stomach. Her thighs were nice and juicy as well.

He liked that she was all his.

Finishing off his sandwich, he waited for her. "Another?"

"Yes, please."

"You don't talk a lot, do you?" he asked.

She chuckled. "I thought men didn't like to hear women talk."

"I guess some guys don't. I want you to talk to me. Tell me about your day."

"I've not got a lot to tell, to be honest. I'm either in the garden or the library. My studies are going slowly. I forgot how hard it was to learn. Hope is an amazing tutor though. She seems to know everything."

He smiled. "My brother would like any compliment about his woman."

This brought a smile to her, and he liked staring at her.

"She's really nice."

"I know. It's one of the many things that my brother adores about her. What about you? What do you hope to be?" he asked, curious about her.

"What do you mean? Like when I grow up?"

"Pretty much."

"I don't really know. I always kind of thought I'd get a job, work my way up, have a stable apartment or something like that."

"A man? Kids?"

She scrunched up her nose. "Not really. The only real example of a male figure was my dad, and he sucked at it big time. I didn't want that kind of life for myself. I didn't really think much else after that, I'm afraid. I know, I'm such a bore."

This made him smile. "You're not a bore."

"I don't know. When you're worried about men coming to beat you up because your father couldn't pay or to run you down it takes something out of life." She pointed at her scar, and it made him want to kill the fuckers.

"What happened about that?"

"About what?"

"The people who did your scar?" he asked.

She shrugged. "Not a lot. One moment I was in the hospital, and then Dad came to pick me up, and we were suddenly moving. I don't know. It hurt like hell."

"I bet."

He cut their next sandwich in half and offered her one half while taking the other for himself.

"Did you always want to be part of this world? Being a crime lord, drug lord, I don't know."

"I'm a Carson. I'm an everything kind of guy. I'm my brother's right-hand man, and I make sure I get the job done."

"But growing up? Did you want to do anything else?"

He stared at her for the longest time. "I never wanted to do anything else because it was never an option for me. It was always this life. Our father made sure that we were trained at a young age." They'd all been beaten and forced to learn how to hold and shoot a gun, handle a knife, and to kill someone.

"There's something there though," she said. "You wanted to do something."

"I do what I want to do."

She frowned.

"I like to spend some time every single year where I get away from it all. No cell phones, no luxury, I just hike, take in the sights, and get back to nature."

"Really?"

"Yep. It's what I do every single year around October. It's just a little colder, which means I don't bump into people."

"That sounds … amazing."

"You think so?" he asked, shocked.

"Well, yeah. I can't for a second imagine that. I bet it's so relaxing."

"It is. No one around you for miles. A few years ago, I visited a lake, and I can't even remember which one. I tend to just start walking. I was so quiet, just sitting, looking around me, and I watched a family of deer come to the lake and drink the water. It was so cold, and they were so beautiful, you know."

"Wow."

"Yeah, it was amazing. Moments like that make me realize how small we are in the real world. No one can ever take that away from us. Then of course I get home. Back to reality where I have to kill people and shit."

"Do you hunt when you do these trips?"

He shook his head. "Nope. I'm in their domain. There's always a risk of being attacked by a bear or a pack of wolves. So far, nothing. Still sound good?"

"Yeah, it really does. When you live in the city, worried every single night by a knock on the door, that does sound a lot like heaven." She smiled at him.

"If you want, I can take you with me this year."

"You'd do that?"

"If you'd want to go, that is."

"Hell, yeah. Get away from everything. Hike, travel, see some amazing sights. Absolutely. Consider it a date."

"It'll be a very sexy date." He reached out, taking her hand and pulling her close. "You'll be a delightful distraction."

"I've never been called delightful before. I kind of like it."

Placing his hand on her hip, he pressed his cock against her stomach. With his other hand, he sank his fingers into her hair, tilting her head back.

"You're beautiful," he said.

The smile slipped from her face.

"One day I'm going to say that and you're going to believe me."

"I know I'm not."

He stared at her, seeing the sadness in her eyes, and only wanted it to go away. "Because of your scar?" He traced a finger over the line. It wasn't neat, but it looked like it hurt. "You're a beautiful woman who has been through hell. This scar, it's nothing."

****

Tears filled Faith's eyes. The look Caleb was giving her made her believe every single word he spoke. Could it be true that he thought she looked beautiful? It seemed too surreal to her to believe.

His thumb went to her chin, and once again he tilted her head back. "Don't let what others think ever touch you, Faith. You're better than most people."

When his lips crashed down on hers, she closed her eyes, moaning as his hand gripped the back of her neck, holding her in place. She didn't want to move. His touch was so intimate, and the control he showed only

187

served to turn her on.

His hand moved down her body, and he lifted her up in his arms. Wrapping her legs around his waist, she held onto his shoulders. In a few quick steps they were in his dining room, and he placed her on the table.

"I was going to put you on the counter in the kitchen, but that's a little too high for what I want to do to you."

Caleb pressed her back so that she lay on the table, waiting for him to have his way with her.

He stepped away, and she watched as he pulled each of the chairs away from the table. Her gaze landed on his cock, which was already erect.

"You want to suck my cock, don't you?"

She nodded. He stepped closer to the table, and she wriggled toward the edge. She wrapped her fingers around his length, but Caleb grabbed her hand and pressed it against the table. "No hands. Only your mouth."

Opening her lips, she stared up at him as he slowly fed his cock into her mouth. She tasted them both on his length, and she couldn't help but shut her eyes at the pleasure.

"Look at me," he said.

His voice commanded obedience, and she followed his instructions.

He thrust his hips forward and backward, the tip of his cock brushing the back of her throat before he withdrew.

After she got used to him fucking her mouth, he went a little deeper, to the point that she nearly gagged, but he pulled away, giving her time to get used to the feel before doing it again.

As she sucked his dick, one of his hands moved down her body. He stroked her tight nipples, over her stomach, settling between her thighs.

Two fingers slid in deep, and she had to force herself to keep her eyes focused on him, and not on what he was doing.

The pleasure was intense and drove her wild with more need.

He added a third finger to her pussy, and his thumb stroked across her clit.

"Your cunt wants my dick, baby. I can feel it. You want to be fucked?"

She nodded her head.

He pulled out of her mouth, and in the next second, he had her at the edge of the table. She watched as he ran his cock between her slit, bumping against her clit before he finally pressed the entire length inside.

Caleb ordered her to lie back, and she did.

She felt open, vulnerable. He was the one in control, staring down at her body, spread open for him to see.

"Put your hands above your head."

She did as he asked.

His cock stayed still within her.

Caleb placed her knees on the end of the table. The odd angle made her feel surprisingly full. He ran his hands down her thighs then up again. This time, when he stroked down, he did it on the inside, and he stroked over her pussy.

"I can see part of my cock." He pulled out of her. "It's covered in your cum. I bet there's even more of me there as well."

"Do you like to talk dirty?" she asked.

"Yes. Does that surprise you?"

She shook her head.

"I like dirty things. Fucking isn't done right if there's not a bit of mess."

Faith chuckled. She'd never been the kind of person to respond to stuff like this, yet the words coming from his mouth aroused her even more.

He pulled out of her pussy, and she gasped as his fingers filled her. She didn't know what he was going to do as he slid them across her clit then down to her entrance, plunging inside.

She took three of his fingers, and he fucked her hard, his thumb stroking over her clit. She was about to go over that peak into orgasm, but he pulled out. Instead of going to her clit or fucking her, he pulled his fingers back, teasing over her ass.

"Has anyone fucked your ass before?"

She shook her head. "No."

As he teased her anus she couldn't help but tense up. It was so wrong, right?

She panicked a little as the tip of one finger thrust within her. It felt a little too tight, and it burned.

"It's okay, baby. One day I'll take your ass and you'll be begging for it." Caleb didn't press anymore, and only teased against her.

Faith cried out as his cock suddenly slid back inside her pussy.

"So fucking tight." He began to rock inside her, going deep.

She clenched her hands tight, as he fucked her hard.

"I want you to touch your pussy now, Faith. Show me what you do to make yourself get off."

As she stared at him, he stopped, his cock pulsing inside her. Reaching between her thighs, she touched her pussy.

Her cheeks heated up as he watched her do this.

"You have got nothing to be ashamed of, Faith. I like to watch, and I want to see you play."

Sliding her fingers through her slit, she touched her clit, and moved down until she felt his cock, which was still inside her.

He groaned as she teased and played with his cock and where they both connected as one.

"Do you like me inside you?"

"Yes." She licked her lips. "Do you like being inside me?"

His gaze seemed to flare. "Yes."

She liked his answer.

Drawing her fingers up to her clit, she stroked herself. Slowly, Caleb rocked inside her, driving her arousal higher, and closer to the peak.

His hands were on her hips, and she watched him, addicted to everything that he was doing to her.

All too soon, the pleasure reached a fever pitch, and she couldn't hold back another second, nor did she want to.

She came with a cry, and not long after Caleb joined her, groaning as he thrust deep within her, his dick pulsing wave upon wave of his release inside her.

When it was over, neither of them spoke or moved.

Her hand was trapped between them. His head rested against her breasts with his breath fanning her nipple.

"I don't want to move right now."

She chuckled.

"Am I hurting you?" he asked.

"No, you're not hurting me."

"Fuck! I'm so sorry."

She gasped as Caleb sat up.

Tilting her head back to look at the door, she saw a young guy who looked a little like Caleb.

"Get the fuck out!" Caleb yelled. At the same

time, he covered her body with his hands.

She couldn't do much more as he had her hands trapped.

The young man left the room, and she looked back at Caleb, who was glaring at the door. "I'm going to shoot him one of these days."

"Who is he?"

She'd seen him around the house a couple of times, but she'd always been sure to avoid him.

"That's my nephew. He's the same age as you, and believe me, I'm going to beat the shit out of him. I think he needs to go into an early grave."

"He saw us," she said with a groan.

"Don't worry. I'll deal with him." He pressed a kiss to her lips. "Go upstairs and run us both a bath. I'll be there to join you."

"Don't shoot him here, please. Anne would be so pissed," she said.

He burst out laughing. "Don't worry. I'll make sure Anne doesn't find out. I know a cleaning crew." He winked at her.

"I don't need to know these things."

He pulled out of her, and she felt his cum spilling out of her, gliding down her thigh.

Caleb groaned, cupping her pussy. "I'd love to stay and play, but I've got to deal with him. Wait for me."

She followed behind Caleb, and when she saw the coast was clear, she made a run for it upstairs toward his room. Going straight to the bathroom, she started their bath, and giggled. She couldn't believe what had just happened.

Shaking her head, she finished dealing with the bath, and then moved toward the mirror. Staring at her reflection, she ran a finger lightly down her scar. For a long time after she'd gotten it, she hadn't wanted to look in the mirror. She'd felt hideous, ugly, useless. It was around the same time that any love she had for her father left.

Seeing him constantly doing what he wanted and with herself always dealing with the consequences, she'd gotten angry, and through that anger, she'd stopped having any feeling about him whatsoever.

When it came to Caleb, she felt everything.

"Don't do it, Faith. Don't go there."

She spun on her heel and climbed into the bath.

This relationship had no room for change of any kind.

Chapter Eight

A couple weeks later

"How is Dwayne's training?" Beast asked.

Caleb stopped looking around the library and turned to look at his brother. "He's fine. He's stopped moaning at every single request."

"And what are your thoughts on him?"

"You've treated him too soft."

"There are ways to train that don't involve our father's methods, Caleb. I figured you'd appreciate that. Why have you suddenly taken an interest in my book collection?"

"You have more than me."

"That's what happens when you like books more than you do getting one with nature. You own more tents and survival kits than I do," Beast said, a smirk on his lips.

Caleb smiled. His brother had never understood his need to get away from it all. When your every need was catered to, he guessed a lot of people wouldn't like going out near the winter, just to be at peace with oneself. He needed it. Without, he couldn't handle everything he had to do.

"I nearly killed Dwayne, just so you know."

Beast laughed. "Do I even want to know why?"

"He saw my woman naked."

This made Beast's brow rise. "Your woman?"

"You're shocked that I have a woman but not shocked that I tried to kill our nephew."

"I've wanted to kill Dwayne a few times. I think it's the boy's MO, or at least he has a knack for pissing people off. You've decided to take the little debt as your woman?"

"Don't call her that, Beast." He didn't like that.

Faith deserved a lot more than to be viewed as some kind of debt.

"Hope likes her."

"Is that a good thing?"

"Hope likes everyone."

"Exactly."

This made Beast smile. "Are you happy?"

Caleb stared at his brother and saw the concern in Beast's eyes. They were both monsters and beasts within their world, and rarely took the time to talk about their feelings. He'd always assumed Beast didn't have any until Hope came into his brother's life.

"I'm happy."

"I know this life gets to you."

"I'm fine, Beast. I'll never have a problem."

Beast stared at him for several minutes. "You're sure?"

"I'm always here, aren't I?"

"Still, it must … be difficult."

He'd never had a heart-to-heart with his brother. He'd never felt the need to. They were two different people, and each of them had a different way of dealing with the world.

"You don't need to start worrying about me. Just because I like a woman doesn't mean I'm going soft," Caleb said.

"Well, I know what it's like." Beast leaned forward, holding up a file. "I need you to head to Vegas this weekend."

"What for?" He took the file from his brother and opened it. On the first page was a picture of a man, a cop that was on their payroll.

"I see you recognize him. No, he's not offering our secrets to the law, and we're not going to have the FBI knocking down our doors. He's selling our secrets to the highest bidder, or at least, that's the rumor. I had a call this morning that he's setting up an auction, and hopes to have our competitors pay for the privilege of everything he knows."

"That shit isn't happening," Caleb said, flicking over the page. "This is why I don't like dealing with dirty cops."

"Dirty cops have their uses. What I don't like are dirty rat cops. This guy is dangerous."

"You want him dead?"

"Yes."

Caleb saw where he'd set up operations. "How long has he been there?"

"One day. I already have your tickets."

Beast handed over the flight tickets. Caleb studied them then looked at his brother. "Why do I have two?"

"For your woman, of course. Vegas can be such a … wonderful place. You can have wedding ceremonies, gambling."

"I know exactly what you're trying to do, and it's not going to work," Caleb said.

"Well, you could make an honest woman out of her."

"She doesn't do love," Caleb said.

"Neither do you. Besides, it's amazing what happens when you spend time together. Words are spoken, feelings are developed, and before you know where you are, you're a happily married man with lots to live for and a baby on the way."

Now Beast had a full-blown smile on his face, and he looked so damn proud of himself.

"You really do love Hope?" Caleb asked, closing the file.

"More than anything in the world."

"The age gap … doesn't bother you?"

"Nope. It doesn't. I could let it bother me if I sit and think about it all the time, but I refuse to let something so trivial get in the way. She's happy. I'm happy. Together we make each other so, and I'm not going to question that. Maybe you should start thinking about that."

Caleb stared down at the tickets in his hands. "You don't think it's dangerous taking her along for the ride?"

Beast sighed. "Our entire life is dangerous. We could have some kind of magical shield around our woman, and they'd still be in danger. Do I lose sleep at times over the danger my woman is constantly in? Yes. There are times I can't even think straight it bothers me that much. Then I decided that the best way to defend my woman was teach her how to defend herself."

"You're teaching Hope how to defend herself, even when pregnant?" Caleb asked, amazed that his brother would do such a thing.

"There are men and women out there who wouldn't care that she's pregnant. I'm simply taking care of my woman the best way I know how."

Beast got to his feet, which signaled the end of the conversation.

"I hope to hear soon that our problem has been dealt with."

They shook hands, and Caleb left his brother's home.

Sitting in his car, he stared at the plane tickets. He wondered if she'd been to Vegas. There had to have been a chance with her father's gambling problem.

Putting the tickets to one side, he started his car and left the security of his brother's drive.

The journey to his home was a short one. Calling

his personal head of security, Caleb made the arrangements so men were waiting for him at the Vegas airport to take them to their hotel room. They had men all around the world who were more than willing to be on their security detail.

Of course, each man had to go through their screening, and Beast didn't leave anything to chance.

Caleb found Anne in the kitchen making some bread. "She's in the garden, planting a new rose bush."

"Didn't she do much studying today?" Caleb asked.

"Oh, she did. She just likes to unwind in the garden. It's something she has come to enjoy."

"I'll be taking her to Vegas for a couple of days. You can have the house to yourself."

Anne smiled. "Will you be taking advantage of certain … luxuries while you're away?"

"Are you asking me if I'll marry her?"

"Well, you can do it quite easily over there."

Caleb chuckled. "I doubt it."

"Is this because you feel like you don't deserve love?"

Anne paused in kneading the dough. He didn't need fresh bread, but Anne baked it every single day. She also gave several loaves to the men who guarded his home.

"It's not that."

"Sure, it is. I remember you as a young boy when you'd come to the kitchen after one of your father's … punishments. You out of all of your brothers always suffered. Being the youngest, he didn't want you to grow into a baby."

"I never did."

"No, you never did, but I saw what it was doing to you."

"You couldn't stop it."

"And because of that, it made you believe that you're incapable of being loved, Caleb."

He stared at his cook, recalling every single beating he'd been given. From simply asking for a toy, to begging for a cookie, if his father had ever heard him ask for anything, it had been the belt, or some other punishment. He'd even been left out overnight with the dogs in the freezing cold because he'd liked to be warm.

Pushing those memories aside, he moved up toward Anne. "Don't ever feel guilty. He'd have killed you if you tried to step in, and I wouldn't be able to enjoy your bread."

"Don't fight falling in love. It could be the best thing that ever happened to you."

****

It had been a couple of years since Faith had last been in Vegas. Of course, she'd never overlooked the gambling capital of the world from one of its most luxurious hotels. From up here it all looked shiny and dazzling. Everything seemed to sparkle. When she'd been younger, she'd been on the street looking up at the hotels, wondering about the people who were staying inside them.

Caleb was on his phone, and three men outside waited, keeping guard. She'd spotted all of their guns. This was not a social trip; far from it.

She rubbed the back of her neck, feeling a tension building inside her. Anne had told her to have fun and enjoy the trip, but she didn't know how that was possible. Vegas held a great deal of memories for her, and most of them were attached to anger.

Anger at her father, at the casinos, at the capital, at everything.

Deep down, she knew it wasn't anyone's fault but

her father's, but that didn't make it hurt any less.

If it wasn't for your father, you wouldn't be with Caleb now.

The man himself snapped his cell phone closed and moved up behind her. He wrapped an arm around her stomach and pulled her back, resting his chin on her shoulder. "Do you like what you see?"

"Not really."

"It's all way too garish for me, and far too … fake."

She chuckled. "I should have known you'd see past the lies. The man that gets one with nature and all that."

"Yep, and one day you're going to see it."

"I can't wait."

And she couldn't. The thought of being alone with him, away from cell phones and threats, actually filled her with joy.

"I know this isn't a social call," she said. She saw his reflection in the mirror. They'd packed and landed within the same day. She was sure she still had soil beneath her nails, he'd wanted to be gone that quickly.

"It's not. This is business, but once I take care of business, then we can go and have some fun."

"I don't want to be alone in this room," she said.

"It's safe for you to be here. Once I'm done, we'll go to dinner and then go dancing. How does that sound?"

It sounded a little boring and lonely. She didn't tell him that, but simply smiled. "You're killing someone, aren't you?"

"I'm taking care of business." He kissed her neck, and she turned as he left the room.

She'd noticed over the months that whenever he had to kill someone, he always withdrew from her. It was like he had to close everything else off from what he was doing or he couldn't focus.

Staring out at the night sky aglow with all the sights, she frowned. This was not a romantic place.

Stepping away from the window, she was determined to get out of the room. When she opened the door, she found a guard posted there.

He wouldn't let her pass, holding up a hand to stop her, but he didn't actually touch her.

"What the hell are you doing?" she asked.

"Caleb said you're to stay in the room. I'm simply following orders."

"Wow, really?"

"Yes. Please, I don't want any trouble. Your protection means a great deal to him."

"Can you touch me?" she asked. "*Make* me stay?"

The guard looked uncomfortable. She imagined Caleb had told him to keep her in the room but not to lay a hand on her. It was really sweet how much Caleb wanted to protect her.

There was no way she was staying in the room on her own with her thoughts running riot. Not happening. "There's a casino and a bar downstairs, right? They're part of the hotel?"

"Yes."

She brought her knee up, taking him completely off guard. Grabbing his gun, she removed the safety and pointed it at him. Being around her father, she had learned how to protect herself. He didn't always have a lot of good friends, but he had some that found it funny to show a young girl how to hold a gun. Faith didn't like to remember how they taught her to shoot, and watch as her hands shook, but she always did as she was told. This guard wouldn't touch her, and he also couldn't hurt her.

"I really don't want to hurt you, and if you hurt

me, you know Caleb's going to have an issue. Why don't we pretend this didn't happen? You can call Caleb in a couple of minutes and tell him what I did, and that he can meet me at the bar." She forced a smile to her lips and stepped back. "I'll also tell him that I did this on purpose, and I've got no problem with you following me downstairs to keep an eye on me."

She stepped back and pressed the elevator button. The doors opened and she stepped inside, thankful no one was on the damn thing. When the doors closed, she put the gun away, placing the safety back on before tucking it away in her jeans.

Her heart was pounding as excitement rushed through her. Caleb would be pissed, but she'd make sure the guard didn't lose his job.

There was no way she'd spend her life waiting around for Caleb. She wanted to be with him and share his life, but she wouldn't be put away until he decided to play. She had no intention of going around the whole of Vegas.

Staying in the hotel wasn't a problem to her.

The elevator doors opened, and she stepped out.

There was a mass of activity, and she couldn't help but smile.

Of course, she didn't agree with gambling, and as she walked around the main casino, she wasn't all that impressed with what she saw. There were people winning, which was nice to see, but across the room she'd find someone who clearly wasn't winning, and was down on their luck.

This was the problem she had with gambling. Too much risk. Sure, it was all down to probability of winning. A fifty-fifty chance, but that was too much chance of her going without rent or food. She liked being able to sleep in a warm bed at night.

After a few minutes of watching people, she grew bored.

She found the sign for the bar and made her way toward it.

From all the years of moving around with her father, she owned a fake ID, and Caleb hadn't taken it from her. She took a seat at the bar and ordered herself a drink. When the barman asked for ID, she showed it to him, and he nodded.

Licking her lips, she glanced around the bar. The low music had a seductive quality to it.

Tapping her foot on the base of her chair, she watched several couples on the dance floor. The way they were touching was intoxicating. The air was heavy with sex and something else; promise, maybe.

"You shouldn't be here," Caleb said.

She glanced over her shoulder, and he stood close to her.

"I've been out of my room … twenty minutes and you're back."

"I want you to go back to our room."

She shook her head. "I'm bored there, Caleb. I don't mind being here, but I'm not going to wait around for you. I'm content to just sit here, have a drink, and relax. I'll wait for you here."

"I prefer you to stay there."

She spun around in her chair. "Why bring me if all I'm going to do is stay there, Caleb? I may as well be back in your home weeding the damn garden." Her anger spiked. She didn't mind following him around so long as she was able to do something else.

"I've got work to do here."

"And I'm bored. I'm not stopping you from doing whatever it is you're doing. You didn't have to come back."

He grabbed her hand and led her onto the dance floor. His hands moved to her hips, and began to sway. She stayed perfectly still, waiting.

"You don't want to dance with me?"

"I don't want you to manipulate me into getting what you want, so I'm going to stay perfectly still."

"You're so cute when you're being stubborn," he said.

She rested her hands on his shoulders and shook her head. "I'm not doing this."

Pulling out of his arms, she walked away, throwing some bills down onto the bar before leaving without even drinking.

She didn't go back toward her room.

Instead, she walked out of the hotel and completely disregarded her own advice.

"What the hell?" Caleb said, grabbing her arm and dragging her into the nearest alley. "This is fucking dangerous."

She pulled the gun out of the back of her jeans and pointed it at him. "I know how dangerous life can be, Caleb. I've lived it. I've got constant proof of how bad it can get." She pointed at her face. "Don't treat me like a child. Don't treat me like you're afraid to break me. I get it. You're a bad man, and you do bad things. You kill people. I don't care. I'm here and I'm not going to do anything stupid, but I think you need to take this gun, and right now, I want to go back inside to that bar. I'm going to sit there and drink, and I'll wait for you to be done. Is that okay?"

What the hell are you doing?

"I've never had a chick that I'm fucking pull a gun on me before," Caleb said, taking the gun.

"And?"

"It's kind of hot."

"Only someone like you would find a gun being pulled on you kind of hot. I'm freaked out."

She went to walk away, but Caleb pulled her close. He cupped her cheek and tilted her head back. "I only want you to be safe."

"I can take care of myself."

"I'd never forgive myself in anything was to happen to you," he said.

It was the first time that they'd spoken about feelings. If he couldn't forgive himself, didn't that mean he cared about her?

Pushing those thoughts to the back of her mind, she patted his chest. "I'll be waiting for you to dance with me."

She pulled away and made her way back into the bar.

This time, she ordered a stiff drink to help calm herself down.

Chapter Nine

When Caleb had gotten the call about what Faith had done, he'd been pissed. He'd immediately turned around, found her, and was going to force her back to their hotel room. Once she pulled the gun on him, however, something changed.

He realized that he couldn't keep her contained where he wanted. That's not what he wanted for either of them. He didn't know what was going on between the two of them. They were fucking and he enjoyed her company, but there was something else.

"Please, I didn't mean anything by it."

He stared at the man he had tied to a chair. Caleb liked tying men to chairs. It kept them … grounded. He could circle them and think. Only right now he wasn't thinking about the million different ways he could hurt this man.

His thoughts were on his black-haired woman, Faith.

She didn't have a problem with what he did.

There had been more than one occasion when he'd returned home covered in blood, or having to clean up some mess. She rarely asked questions, and helped him clean up.

Faith was different.

She'd seen the monster inside him, or at least what he'd done, and she'd not run away.

Her own father had used her as a tool to get out of paying a debt. What the hell was he doing with her?

Caleb wasn't using her to pay off a debt.

He liked having her around, even if their age gap made him a little uncomfortable. Still, no woman had made him ache or wish to be back in bed with her.

Faith was the one of a kind woman for him.

"Boss?" one of his security detail said.

"What?"

"Have you made a decision yet?" He pointed at the dirty rat.

Caleb looked at the man, who'd already pissed himself.

He was bored with this.

There wasn't anything more to be gained out of hurting him. They had all the information, and all he wanted to do was be with Faith. He'd upset her, and instead of going back inside, he'd come to do his job.

Pulling on the large glove, he grabbed the knife, and plunged it into the man's neck while also staring into his eyes. He held the blade in deep, waiting until he died.

Once that was done, he removed the glove from his hand and stepped back.

Even though blood spilled from the wound, not one drop had made its way onto his clothing.

He nodded. "Clean this mess up."

Leaving the room of the gym, he made his way out to the car and fired up his cell phone. Beast answered on the second ring.

"You're done already."

"Yes. He's gone. I've also got the briefcase full of files. He kept tabs on our bribes for years."

"And you have every single bit of information."

"From him I do. I think we need to send a message out to the men we pay. We won't hesitate to kill if they provoke us," Caleb said. "I'm happy to organize it when I get back."

"Are you okay, brother?"

"I'm more than fine, Beast. I got the job done, didn't I?"

"You didn't play?"

"No. I didn't. I've got things I need to do. Make

sure you have a list of the men on our payroll when I return. I'll pay them a visit and make sure no one tries to sell our secrets." With that, he hung up and tossed his cell phone onto the seat beside him.

He didn't waste any time in parking the car and heading inside.

Nodding at a few of his security detail, he entered the bar, which had a lot more people in it now. He'd been gone a couple of hours, and he didn't like that a guy was talking to Faith as he entered.

Walking up behind her, he was in time to hear her laugh.

When he wrapped an arm around her waist, Faith gasped and glanced up at him. "You're back already."

"That I am." He stared at her friend. "You are?"

"This is just Wayne. He was being polite."

"Good. I'm here now. Thank you for keeping an eye on my woman." He took her hand and led her onto the dance floor.

"That wasn't very nice," she said.

"I've got news for you, baby. I'm not a nice guy."

She chuckled, her arms going around his neck. "I know."

"Do you like me like that?" he asked.

"I don't know. I think I prefer all of your bad guy tendencies to be directed elsewhere. Did you get done what you needed to do?" she asked.

"Yes. Everything is done."

She stared into his eyes, and he didn't look away. "Are you okay?"

"I'm fine."

Faith teased the hair at the back of his neck. "You lie quite easily."

"There's nothing to report, babe." He ran his hand down her back, gripping her ass. "I don't like you in jeans."

"What do you like me in?" she asked.

"Skirts, dresses, nothing. I like anything that makes it easier for me to touch you." He rested his face against her neck, breathing in her scent. "You smell so good."

"I don't think you'd have appreciated me coming here naked."

"No, you're right. No one else gets to see what belongs to me, and you do belong to me, Faith. You're all mine."

She pulled away, and he stared into her green eyes. "I wasn't flirting with him."

"I know."

"I'm pleased you came in when you did. He was kind of boring, and I love to people watch."

"You do?"

She chuckled. "Why do you look so surprised?"

"You've been at my place for so long. Anne told me you weren't into shopping."

Faith wrinkled her nose. "First, I hate shopping for anything. I find it boring and dull. Secondly, I love watching people. You can make up stories or just be curious about what people are thinking about."

He spun her around so that she was facing people. "I'm intrigued."

"What do you see when you look at people?"

Staring straight ahead, he saw a tall man. "One punch in the gut and he'd easily go down."

"We're not talking in a fight."

"How about you do what you think you're doing and I'll listen?"

He was sure she rolled her eyes.

"That table in the corner. It has two men and two women. Now, the guy with the blond hair keeps looking at the redhead like he wants to eat her, and the brunette at his side is giving her deadly looks. They're so having an affair, or they're having a four-way."

"This is lame," he said.

"A lot of people do this, and it's fun. That guy there is having an affair with his dog's groomer. She's totally screwing her kid's teacher."

This time he just laughed. "You're a weird one."

"They're just stories, and they pass the time." This time she turned in his arms. "I was waiting for you."

"When I look at people I find them boring," he said. "I don't care what story they have to tell or even if it's any good."

"What do you care about then?"

"You."

She gasped.

They didn't say anything, and he gripped her ass, pulling her close. "When you're in the room, Faith, you're the only person I care about. Everyone else can go and get fucked." He squeezed her ass and rubbed his cock against her stomach. "Do you hate me now?"

She shook her head. "I really like your answer. Do you hate me?"

"For what?"

"Pulling a gun on you."

"I don't hate you, but I know what you can do to make it all better."

****

Faith collapsed to the bed completely naked as Caleb gripped her hips. She gasped as he spread her open and his cock lay against her pussy. Closing her eyes, she bit her lip as the tip of his dick began to probe her pussy. At the same time, he moved down to her ass, spreading the cheeks wide.

"All I can think about when I'm with you is how

good you're going to feel on my dick." With that he slammed deep inside her, making her moan. The hands on her ass moved around, and he touched her pussy, stroking her clit. "I want you to come all over my cock." He rubbed her nub, and she cried out.

All too soon, he released her and spun her around on the bed, spreading her legs and plunging his cock back inside her. She wrapped her legs around his waist, moaning as his fingers touched her pussy once again.

"I'm so indecisive tonight," he said, pulling out of her again.

She released a whimper. "Please, I need to come."

"I want to taste you." He lifted her hips, and she gasped as his mouth was poised just above her pussy. "If you want I can stop."

"No, don't you dare." She cried out as his tongue attacked her clit. Gripping the sheets beneath her fist, she moaned as he kept working her nub. He circled the bud then slid down to plunge inside her before pulling back and teasing her some more.

She was so close.

Caleb wasn't done with her yet. He had her at the edge, about to hurtle over the peak, but once again he stopped, lowering her down onto the bed.

She felt like she was going crazy, the need consuming her body, making her ache all over.

"Please," she said, not ashamed of begging him.

He thrust inside her, his cock feeling like a dream to her heated flesh.

Caleb stroked her pussy, and this time he didn't stop. When she found that peak, he threw her over the edge as at the same time, he fucked her hard, consuming her with need.

When she finally came down from her orgasm

she realized that Caleb was still very much rock-hard inside her.

Opening her eyes, she stared at him, confused.

"There's something that I want," he said.

"Okay."

He pulled out of her pussy and moved her so that she was on her knees.

Caleb pressed a kiss against her neck as he found her entrance and plunged inside. "I want to own every single inch of you," he said.

"Okay." She felt like a broken record, repeating herself.

His hand traced down her back, going to her ass, and he ran his finger across her anus. "I want to fuck your ass, Faith."

She trusted him more than anyone else in the world. Reaching behind herself, she grabbed her ass cheeks and spread them. "I'm yours, Caleb. You can take what you want. I belong to you."

"You have no idea how fucking hot that is right now."

His fingers stroked across her anus, and she closed her eyes, enjoying his touch. Caleb used some of her release to smear across her ass. His cock slid inside her, and they both moaned. He didn't stay there though.

He pulled out, and the tip of his cock pressed against her anus. She tensed up, and he stroked her back.

"You need to relax."

She didn't think it was possible to relax with a man trying to fuck her ass. For a second, she truly thought it was a bad idea. Then he pushed past the tight ring of muscles that were keeping him out, and she really thought she'd made a mistake.

When he stroked between her thighs and began to tease her clit, however, something changed. She began to feel the rising need for another orgasm, which totally took away the brief shot of pain as he worked every single inch of his cock inside her ass.

"I've got you, baby. You've got all of me now."

He didn't stop stroking her clit.

Caleb worked her ass, pushing in and out at the same time, he teased her, bringing her closer to another orgasm. It wasn't long before she began to thrust toward him, begging for more, not wanting him to stop.

She whimpered as the hand on her hip tightened even more, but it wasn't down to the brief feeling of being completely taken. It was so much more.

Caleb had completely shattered her entire world.

Not only did he possess her, own her body, her heart was also his, and she couldn't keep denying it.

She didn't believe love existed, but right now, with his cock balls deep inside her ass, she couldn't deny that when it came to Caleb, she wanted everything, and that scared her a little.

He teased her toward an orgasm, and as she went over that edge into mind-consuming pleasure, she cried his name, hearing him call hers. His cock pulsed inside her, filling her ass with his cum.

When it was all over, they both collapsed to the bed, panting. His arms wrapped around her, and his breath fanned across her neck.

"You're amazing, Faith," he said.

"You're not too bad yourself." She didn't want him to know that she was reeling from her own revelations. She didn't know what to think right now as everything just seemed to be too much. If she loved Caleb, then she was doomed. He didn't do love, and it would only be a matter of time before she got her heart broken.

He was one of the sweetest guys she'd ever

known, and kinky as well. She knew it was completely stupid to think of him as sweet when he was, in fact, a killer.

Faith wasn't stupid though.

She knew how the world worked.

There were good men.

Bad men.

Corrupt men.

When it came to Caleb though, he was a monster that did bad things to people, but to her, he was so sweet.

He kissed her neck, drawing her out of her thoughts. "Stay here." He pulled out of her ass, and she gave a little wince. "Sorry. I didn't mean to hurt you." He kissed her again, and she turned her head, watching as he entered the bathroom.

Seconds later she heard the sound of water running, and he returned. "What are you doing?"

He lifted her up in his arms, surprising her with his strength.

"It's time for a bath." He claimed her lips, and she wrapped an arm around his neck, holding on as he carried her toward the bathroom. "I'm going to take care of you."

He lowered her into the bath, climbing in behind her and pulling her close so that her back rested against him. "Do you always clean up your women?"

"I always clean up the good girls that hold their ass open for me. You're really something else, babe." He kissed her neck.

She waited as he reached for the soap and began to lather up the sponge.

"You're very quiet," he said, working the sponge over her body.

"I'm fine. I'm just basking in what we just shared."

"I hope I wasn't too rough with you."

"No. It was perfect." She tilted her head back and smiled at him.

He cupped her cheek, running his thumb across her lip. "You're really something else."

He didn't say anything more but continued to soap her body. When he went to rinse it out, she took it from him and spun around, taking care of his body.

"You look like you're enjoying that a little too much."

"Maybe I am," she said with a smile.

"I like that you smile more."

"What?"

"When I first met you, you always looked so sad." He reached out, cupping her cheek. When she was with him it was like her scar didn't exist. At least, he didn't seem to see it with her. "I don't like to see you sad."

"You give me a lot to smile about, Caleb."

"Are you happy, Faith?" he asked.

His question took her by surprise. "Yes, I'm very happy. Are you?"

She loved his wicked smile. "I've never been happier than I am right now."

"Good."

Faith intended to keep him that way. Soaping up his body, she felt possessive of him, and for the first time ever, she didn't want to give him back.

Caleb was hers, and she intended to keep him.

Chapter Ten

When he first got back home from Vegas, Caleb had to deal with sending a message to all the men on their payroll. First, he discovered everything about each of them, especially the men that were close by. He even picked one of their kids up from school and made the man in question meet him in the park, letting him know that he could have buried all of the man's kids, and to make it a warning to all of them. Fuck with the Carsons, and they wouldn't just kill them. They would keep the men responsible alive while they tortured every single family member, and only when they were begging for death, hurting in more ways than they could imagine, would they bring death to them. Caleb had a gift for getting the message across.

After that, he was able to relax, knowing that only a stupid fucker would try to test him. Beast was always the first to know whereas Caleb was just the messenger, and he didn't mind that. He'd never wanted Beast's role in their world.

The days, weeks, and even months blended together, and throughout it all, Caleb's life began to change. It wasn't anything big. Faith stayed in his bed, and was always home when he got there. Hope helped her to catch up on most of her studies. She still had several exams to take in order to actually graduate. Hope and Dwayne already had graduated from high school.

His nephew decided to stick around close to home and go to a local college. He'd also moved out of Beast's home. At first, he asked to move in with Caleb, but Caleb liked dismissing all of his staff so that he could fuck Faith in every single room of the house. He didn't like to do that just once either. He enjoyed doing it regularly.

Anne was all for their relationship, and whenever Faith wasn't around and he stood in the kitchen, she encouraged him to take it to the next level.

"You've got to stop your meddling," he said, taking a grape from the bowl on the counter next to Anne.

She slapped his hand away and he chuckled, moving toward the window to watch as Faith once again replanted another rose bush. She had a love of planting roses. They were her favorite.

"I'm not going to stop until you realize that you love that girl, and that she loves you."

He turned toward the older woman, who was now chopping up some chicken breasts to put into a salad.

"You don't know what you're talking about."

"And you're both blind. She's worried because she was a debt. You can't see past your own nose to what is right in front of you. Both of you are too damn stubborn. Faith could have gone months ago, but she doesn't. She moved into your room, didn't she? She sleeps in your bed every single night, and you wake up with her in your arms. That girl does nothing now but smile, and you're the reason that's happening."

"You're getting way too romantic in your old age."

"It's about time you start to realize that you're lovable, Caleb Carson. Faith is a one of a kind woman. She can handle every single part of you. The soft parts and the hard parts." She finished the salad and served them up. "One day I want to have little Calebs and Faiths running around. You'd make the cutest kids in the world."

He took the salad and joined Faith in the garden. She washed her hands and sat at the table with him.

Caleb watched her. Her dark hair was pulled

back, and she no longer tried to hide that scar, not that he minded. Her scar never bothered him.

He always found her to be utterly breathtaking.

Like now, he could just sit and watch her. She gave him peace when nothing else could.

"Are you happy here?" he asked.

"I'm starting to get a complex with how often you ask that. Do you expect a different answer?"

He chuckled. "You're right. I just … you don't have to stay here if you don't want." He didn't like how his chest seemed to tighten, and there was a spike of pain rushing through him at the thought of her leaving.

Caleb couldn't ever remember wanting someone with the kind of passion he felt for Faith, and this wasn't just about bout sex either. This was about something far more.

For a long time, he'd been denying his feelings for her. He didn't like to get attached to people. When he was younger, he'd found some kittens in an old barn, and brought them home. He took care of them for eight weeks. Then one day he came home, and found they were missing. His father taught him a stern lesson that day as he'd drowned each one of the kittens in the bath, and made Caleb clean them up.

On that day, he'd vowed never to love, never to want, and yet, he sat before a woman who threatened that vow.

"I like it here, Caleb. I like being with you, and I don't want to leave. Please … don't make me."

Staring at her, he remembered feeling so hopeful over those kittens. He wasn't going to be his father. He refused to be like that bastard.

"I'm not going to make you go. I don't want you to leave." He got up from his chair and cupped her face. "I love you being here."

He dropped a kiss to her lips and made his way into the office.

Taking a seat behind his desk, he dropped his head into his hands, knowing that if he wasn't careful, he was going to fuck up. For a long time, he'd not let anyone in. Life had been easier being alone.

Opening his eyes, he stared at the picture on his desk. It was one of Faith in the garden. She wore a white summer dress, one that she hated and Anne made her wear. He'd thrown some water on her, and she'd attacked him right back. They'd had a water fight. He was standing with Faith, and they were both laughing. Anne had taken the picture, and as he stared at the two of them, he saw that he was in love, that he'd fallen for her.

He would do everything in his power to protect her.

Yes, he loved her. There was no denying that.

The life he lived was a dangerous one, but he'd make sure that she was always protected.

For the rest of the day, he had to take care of some business with Beast. His brother was on cloud nine with the birth of his child, and Caleb had to listen as he showed pictures.

"You're in a miserable mood," Beast said.

"Doesn't it bother you that both Hope and your kid are at risk every single day?" He turned toward his brother.

"It does, Caleb. It's why I make sure she's protected at all times. I love Hope. I'm just too much of a selfish bastard to let her go. You can have Faith, you know. You can live in this life, and you can protect her."

"It's too much risk."

"No, it's really not. I know our father did a number on you. He took everything that you've ever cared about away from you. It's given you this complex that you can't have anything without something being taken. Our father's dead and gone. You can have what you want, Caleb. It all depends on how hard you want to fight for it. If you want Faith with every single fiber of your being, then you'll make it work. If you don't, you'll get rid of her."

Later that night, Caleb lay in bed with Faith in his arms. She was sleeping soundly. He listened to her breathing as he stroked her hair.

Happiness was not something he was … used to. Or feeling content.

He'd killed more men than he could count on both of his hands.

Letting Faith go seemed like the safest option, and yet the pain he felt at the thought of letting her go was not something he wanted to think about.

He couldn't let her go, even if it meant she was safe.

Caleb loved having her in his life where her smiles were all his. Sleeping at night without her would be torture. He loved the way she snuggled up against him, and if she wasn't on her cycle, he'd be deep inside her as he slept.

Her stomach had been hurting her when he'd climbed into bed, and he'd stroked her until she fell asleep.

Caleb closed his eyes as he heard the first creak.

All of his senses went on high alert. No one should be coming up his stairs. Slowly, easing out from underneath Faith, he reached into his bedside drawer and grabbed his gun. Faith released a sigh, and he glanced over at her. She rolled, pulling the blanket over her.

Whoever was coming to his bedroom wasn't supposed to be here.

****

Faith sat in Caleb's study waiting for him to arrive. She'd woken up several hours ago to Caleb attacking an intruder. The man had been holding a gun, and for a few seconds she'd been completely scared that Caleb would get killed. He'd overpowered the man, and now Beast was there, and they were in the basement. She'd spotted the cleaning van that had already arrived. She sipped at the strong brandy she'd poured herself, waiting.

She hated waiting.

Whoever the man was, he'd killed one of the guards on the door. There were supposed to be two, so she knew without a doubt that someone was about to have a very bad night, or at least morning.

She turned toward the door when she heard it open, and there her man stood. He'd gotten changed into sweats, and he looked … angry.

Getting up from her seat, she held the glass in her hand, and waited. "Are you okay?" she asked.

"Am I okay?"

She frowned. "Yes."

He chuckled. "A man attacked us and you were in danger, but you want to know if I'm okay?"

"It's a perfectly reasonable question."

"No, it's not. You see, Faith, you're supposed to want a normal life and have one yourself. You're not supposed to be woken up in the middle of the night because I'm pounding the life out of someone." Caleb threw his hand out, his actions jerky and angry.

She watched him, hating that he was feeling this way.

"You're nearly nineteen. This is the last thing you should have to deal with. You're supposed to be having fun, living your life."

"I am having fun, Caleb."

"You're not listening."

"I *am* listening, Caleb. It sounds to me like you want a reason for me to leave."

"You should. If you value your life you should stay far away from me. I can't even take care of kittens. There's no way that I can take care of you."

"Kittens?"

He shook his head. "It's nothing."

"I don't need for you to take care of me."

He snorted.

"No! You don't get to tell me how I'm supposed to live a normal life and expect me to listen to all of your supposed 'good reasons.' They're all bullshit, Caleb. Every single one of them. No one has a normal life. No one. They may go to college and have husbands, but there's no way of defining normal. I grew up with a gambling father. Wow, I mean, I was so worried I even slept with someone so that I knew it would be my choice, that's how much my life has been fucked up. I've gone without food, and I've had to lie under my bed while debt collectors came knocking on the door." She pointed at her face. "I got this because he didn't pay. What part of my fucking life has ever been normal?"

He went to speak, and she held her hand up. For once she was going to be heard. She wasn't going to have a man tell her what she was going to do or what she should be doing.

"My father pulled me out of high school, and I didn't fight him about it because I was tired of always being behind and I hated being the new girl. I hated my life, and I hated him. Then you happened. You came to collect a debt, and he handed me to you. I was so scared. I'd heard about you, but I didn't know what to expect. Caleb Carson, one of the most feared men in the world, and he … he is the kindest man I have ever known."

"I killed your dad."

"I know, and I don't care. That's how much my life is fucked up, Caleb. I don't care. All I know is that when I'm with you, nothing else matters." She shrugged. "I guess I'm just a bit weird. I don't know." This was the biggest chance she had ever taken in her entire life. "If you're wanting me to leave because you think I'm not happy, or that I'm not safe, then I … I don't want to go. I love you, Caleb. But if you're wanting me to go because you can't stand the sight of me, and you're wanting another woma—"

"What did you say?"

"That if you want another woman?"

"No, the bit before that?"

"That I love you."

"I thought you didn't do love."

"So did I. I guess I was wrong. I love you, Caleb. I don't want to go anywhere else. Being with you, it's the happiest I've ever felt." She held the glass tightly in her fingers.

He took a step closer to her.

"I know you're not a fan of love."

"I love you," he said, stepping right up to her.

She tilted her head back, watching him. "What?"

"I've known for quite a while, and I've been fighting it, but I love you. All I want is the best for you."

"There's no one else that will ever give me better than you." She placed the glass on the desk and cupped his face. Staring into his eyes, she felt herself get lost within him. "I know this life is dangerous. I trust you. I'll train. I'll do whatever you need me to do, but please, don't send me away because you think it'll do me good. I don't want to leave you."

He gripped the back of her neck, and in the next second, his lips crashed on hers, and she melted against him.

Wrapping her arms around his neck, she kissed him back with a passion. She didn't hold anything back, letting him know in her kiss how much she wanted him. Not only did she want him, she craved him more than anything else in the world.

The hand at her neck moved down and gripped her ass. Lifting her up, he placed her on the edge of the desk.

She opened her thighs, moaning as he tore at her panties. He threw them to one side.

Pushing down his sweatpants, she gripped his rock-hard erection. Caleb pressed her back, and she moaned as in the next instant, he filled her.

"You're all mine, Faith. You had a chance to leave, and now I'm not ever going to let you go."

"Good. I'm not going anywhere. I'm going to stay yours forever." She cried out as he leaned forward and took one of her nipples. He sucked on the hard bud through her thin negligee.

The pleasure shot straight through to her pussy, and she tightened her grip on him as he rode her hard.

Caleb pushed all of the paperwork off the desk, and she giggled. He moved off her nipple, claiming her lips.

"I love you so fucking much. We're going to get married."

"Is that a proposal or an instruction?"

"It's an order. You're mine, and we both know you want it."

Someone knocked on the door.

"Fuck off," Caleb said.

"Is this a bad time?" a man asked.

"Dwayne, if you don't leave now, I'm going to shoot your dick off. I'm fucking my soon-to-be wife."

"I'm gone."

"Your nephew keeps trying to cock block you," she said, smiling. How could she not be smiling? The man of her dreams loved her, and they were going to get married.

"No one will ever come between me and you. You're mine, Faith, and I swear I'll do everything in my power to keep you safe."

She believed him.

Closing her eyes, she arched up to his touch, feeling the beginnings of her orgasm. When she came, Caleb held her, whispering his words of love and possession.

Giving her to Caleb was the only thing her father had ever done right. She'd found the man of her dreams in her monster.

Epilogue

A few months later

Caleb smiled as he heard Faith gasp. It was fucking freezing, but nothing could take away from the beauty of the waterfall.

"Oh, my," she said, standing next to him.

He held her hand tightly as they both watched the rushing water. "It's beautiful."

It was late October, and so cold for the time of year. He'd been tempted to cancel his trip, but Faith had been packing for a couple of weeks, and the excitement in her eyes at the prospect of getting away had been too good to pass up.

Beast had dropped them off at one of the sites known for hiking and touring. That had been three days ago.

He never for a second thought that his trips to nature could get any better, but having his wife curled up next to him, keeping him company, there was nothing else that was better.

"It's not as beautiful as you," he said, kissing her neck.

Faith giggled. "Please, you cannot even begin to compare me to something like this. I mean … look at it."

They were both silent. The sounds of the water created a feeling of peace in the air.

"It's really deadly though. If someone was to fall in, they'd be killed instantly. Head knocked out on the rocks."

"Trust you to find something dangerous in something so beautiful," she said.

He took her hand and they moved on. Caleb helped her over several of the large tree trunks that had fallen down in some of the storms.

Not once did he let her go, keeping hold of her until they found a good spot to make camp. It was as they were sitting, about to set up a fire, that he heard a twig snap.

He turned and saw a large deer there, watching them. The antlers looked fierce, and for several seconds neither of them moved.

"He's so beautiful," Faith said.

At the sound of her voice, the deer took off.

"I want to come with you every single year," she said.

He set the fire, and Faith placed the small pan they had for their soup to warm up in. He patted the ground between his thighs, and she sat between them. Taking her hands, he stared at the ring that graced her finger. They'd had a very small church wedding, and Dwayne, Beast, Hope, and a couple of the men who worked for them had been there to witness them.

"I love you," he said.

"Oh, there's something I want to show you." She released his hands and held up her phone. There was a picture of a box, and inside there were at least six kittens.

"Cute."

"You like them. They're black and white, and so cute," she said.

"Yeah, they are."

"Good, they're ours."

"What?"

"When you mentioned the kitten thing, I asked Beast about it. He told me what happened. I'm so sorry about your dad. Anyway, I'm not ready for a kid yet, so I was thinking we could start with being the proud parents of pretty kittens."

Caleb was so overcome with emotion that he grabbed her and ravished her mouth. "I love you so damn much. Have I told you that lately?"

"Nope. Not enough," she said with a smile.

"How did I get so lucky?"

"I don't know, but when you find the answer, let me know because I feel the same way." She kissed him back, and there really was no way he could ever let her go.

She was his woman to love, and he intended to spend the rest of their lives showing her in every single way he could.

The End

Sam Crescent

Copyright © 2018

Prologue

Fifteen years after Her Monster

"He has to be stopped," Caleb Carson said, pacing his brother's office.

Beast just sat behind his desk, smiling. "What's the matter, Caleb? Afraid of our little nephew?"

"Will you stop turning this into a fucking joke? This is not a joke, Beast. This is fucking serious. Do you have any idea what they're calling him?" Caleb pointed outside the door, and Beast sat back, watching his brother.

"I'm aware."

"They're calling him a fucking nightmare. That's what he is now. He took out fifty men in a nightclub."

"And dealt with the local cops and the cleanup. I don't see the problem."

"You think cleaning up his own mess is the only problem here?"

"Dwayne has proven himself time and time again.

That's all he ever wanted to do, and as far as I'm concerned, he's done it. He's got himself a reputation, he can handle himself. Considering his start in life, I think he's turned out quite all right."

"And when he takes on too many and either dies or we have new enemies?"

"Then we'll take care of them, Caleb. I'm proud of all that Dwayne has accomplished. You should be too. Go home to your beautiful wife and children. Sleep easier knowing our nightmare is on the streets hunting. I know I certainly do."

Chapter One

The stench in the downtown bar sickened him. Dwayne had seen many places like this; filth everywhere. The stink of piss, sex, and vomit was heavy in the air, and degradation was part of their lives. No one gave a fuck about what happened in this part of the city. The crumbling apartment buildings, the whores on the street, the useless waste of life walking day to day—no one gave a shit. Kids playing out in the street, filthy clothes on their backs, their mothers probably trying to screw their way to making a couple of dollars. Probably not even to feed their own kid but to shoot up.

He fucking hated this place.

He hated the world and all the scum in it.

No one paid him any attention, but that was fine. He had a lead on some fucking pimp who'd been stealing Carson women off the street.

Their family didn't have women working on corners, taking whatever fucking john who wanted to get his dick wet, or finally know what it was like to fuck in the ass. No, Carson women were kept safe. All of their punters were run through a program to make sure they were.

He couldn't stand men who knocked women around.

His father had been one of them.

A wife-beater and child abuser until his Uncle Beast came to get him. Then Dwayne had never heard another word from the man.

There was a time when he was quite young that he believed he'd leave the lifestyle. Beast gave him that option to walk away, but he couldn't do it. Being part of the Carson family was something he craved. Getting up at the early hours of the morning to train every single day gave him a drive. Fighting, learning his weapons, and honing his craft every single day had given him focus.

His uncles were fearless, and their reputations preceded them. He wanted a name, a reputation, but he also wanted to make sure that when he arrived, people fucking shit themselves in fear.

It kind of amused him to sit down at a bar and watch it slowly empty as they waited for him to shoot up the place. No one took the piss out of him, nor did they believe they were safe.

No matter the time.

No matter the place.

His enemies would always be taken down. He'd proven it time and time again, which was why he was in a shitty as fuck bar at two in the morning, sitting on a stool. The bartender was high on something, and Dwayne saw the bruising around his inner arm from the shit he'd injected. He poured him a shot, but Dwayne had no intention of drinking it. He didn't touch the bar, but from his vantage point he saw everything. The bar wasn't that big, but it was crowded. This was a place where Garcia was known for distributing women and girls that he picked up from the street.

This was his own personal task that he'd set himself.

When Williams, their informant in the police force, had told him what was going down, Dwayne couldn't look the other way. Especially as Williams put faces to the names he was spouting out. If Dwayne didn't have to think of the faces, the people, the names, he could carry on with his life without a single fucking thought.

Williams clearly knew this, and now Dwayne was hunting, especially as Beast got a visit from a wealthy family. He'd been in a meeting when one of Beast's men said they were clearly desperate.

To Dwayne, rich people had no emotion. Their only drive was their wealth, but the look on their faces, the devastation, had touched him. Their eighteen-year-old daughter, Charity, had been taken from the street. She'd been gone twenty-four hours, and they were willing to pay anything.

Now, Dwayne was more than happy to do this for free. He hated scum, especially after he saw the security footage of the event. Charity hadn't been clear to see, but they had sound. She'd screamed for help, begging the men to leave her alone.

Her voice, even in panic, had a sweetness to it that called to him. Pushing those thoughts aside, he continued to survey the bar.

There was a woman on the floor, kneeling in dirt as she sucked one guy off, and worked the other with her hand. Both men were smoking, drinking, and laughing as she did this. He saw the wad of cash on the table, clearly payment, which, he knew from seeing this kind of thing, she'd never get. The woman should have taken half before the act, and then just walked away. As it was, they wouldn't even pay her for a job well done.

Moving past that, he saw several men and women dancing, wrapped around each other, but he wasn't buying it.

Then he finally saw the guard. He stood out like a sore fucking thumb. Perfect suit, pristine, clearly cost him a pretty penny, and he stood in front of the door, guarding it.

They always stood out.

Tapping his fingers on his thighs, Dwayne waited, made sure everything was in place, and then he got to his feet.

For the most part people ignored him, and for

that, they'd keep their lives tonight.

"Where the fuck do you think you're going?" the guard asked.

Dwayne stood in front of him, assessing the situation.

"Let me past."

"Fuck off. I've never seen you, and it's for friends only. Now get before I decide to end your life, you fucking idiot."

Dwayne took a deep breath and flicked his arms out. The point of the blade hidden at his wrist came out, and he jammed it into the man's neck. Holding him up with the blade in the neck, he flicked the catch of the door, opening it.

To anyone else nothing looked out of place.

By the time he withdrew the blade, closed and locked the door, the guard was dead on the floor.

"You should have just let me inside."

Wiping the blood on his black jacket, he clicked the blade back into place and walked down the steps toward his destination. The lights were dimmed, and he heard the screaming, the crying, the begging.

In between that, he heard the male laughter.

Pulling his guns out of his back holster, he clicked the safety off both, and then looked through the window in the door.

Charity Frank was clear to see in the center of about six men. Her face was bloodied, her clothes torn, and bruises were already starting to appear from where she'd been fighting them. She kept her arms wrapped around herself and was trying to escape. Every time she kept moving toward the door, someone would push her, another would grab her, squeeze a breast, and then throw her to the ground, where she'd get a kick for her efforts.

They were damaging the merchandise, and he

wondered if this was on purpose and who they were selling her to. Some people loved to see a bruised woman up for purchase.

It went against everything in him to watch them do this. To see one of the men pick her up by her hair and force her to do it again. As she fell down the second time, and they were distracted by kicking her, he made his move.

Opening the door, he didn't ask questions.

He fired his weapon with precision and ease, not even trying to wound them.

Pop.

Pop.

Pop.

By the time they realized that he was there, they were already dead on the floor. Charity was curled up in a ball, her hands over her head, begging them to leave her alone.

The guns he used had silencers on them so she hadn't seen anything, but she would have heard them, being so close. Stepping over the bodies, he saw the blood leaking out, and he had to move otherwise she'd be covered in blood.

Crouching down, he called her name.

"Charity, listen to me," he said.

The crying slowed, and she moved her arm, looking at him from underneath it. Her blue eyes struck him first. They were pained. The innocence he'd seen in them from one of the pictures her parents sent was long gone. In its place were pain, suffering, and fear.

"Your parents sent me. I'm here to save you. No, don't look around you. Look at me. They're not going to hurt you anymore."

"It's a trick. It's always a trick. You're going to hurt me."

He gripped her chin. "I'm not going to hurt you, but we're going to leave here. Do you know of a back entrance anywhere?"

She shook her head. "I don't even know where here is." She sniffled, and her throat sounded hoarse, probably from all the screaming.

"I'm going to pick you up. We're going to go out of that door, and then I'm going to take you back to my home, okay?"

"I want to go back to my home."

"You will. I promise, but you need to be taken care of, okay? A shower, a doctor to make sure you're not hurt."

"You can't pick me up," she said. "I'm too heavy."

Dwayne didn't bother to debate this with her. Sliding his hands underneath her body, he picked her up with ease, holding her against his chest.

She stank of piss, but he didn't release her or let her go. Holding her against him, he stared at the door as she tensed in his arms.

He wondered how long they'd been playing that game with her.

Stepping over the bodies, avoiding the blood, he walked out the door, and he heard her sigh of relief. She gripped his jacket, tucking her head against his chest, and began to sob.

Now, as he left the bar, there was a chance someone else would be waiting. He'd deal with that when it happened. Making sure she couldn't see the other man that he'd killed, he left the bar.

No one stopped him.

No one put up a fight.

No one even acknowledged that he had a beaten-up girl in his arms.

Walking out of the bar, he placed her in the passenger side of his car and rounded toward the front. Firing up his car, he took off back to his own place.

He hated coming here, dealing business. Each time, he always had to take a long, hot shower to wipe the dirt away.

Charity stared back at the bar, and he wondered what she was thinking.

"I couldn't ever leave."

"You're out now. You're safe."

Unlike most girls and women that didn't get home, Charity *was* going home, and glancing over at her, he saw the news still hadn't sunk in.

According to the pictures her parents sent, her hair was blonde, really light in color and soft. Right now, it had dirt in it, and he couldn't make out her hair color at all. It was going to be a long fucking night.

****

The man who'd saved her had a really nice apartment. Charity wrapped her arms around herself, wincing at the pain shooting through her entire body. Stepping a few feet into the apartment, she was aware of her smell. She'd been curled up in a ball begging for the men to leave her alone, but they'd only found it more amusing to piss on her.

She'd never been so dirty before in her life.

The man, whose name she didn't know, closed and locked his door. He placed a hand at her back. "Come on, you must be thirsty and hungry."

"I, erm, could I take a shower?" she asked, hating how nervous she sounded.

He urged her to sit down, and she felt really nervous.

Her hands wouldn't stop shaking.

This wasn't her.

She didn't get nervous or scared.

Most of the people who knew her would describe her as outgoing, fun. Right now, she felt anything but.

"I need to ask you a couple of questions first."

Tears filled her eyes, and she hated them. Hated feeling this way. Open, insecure, broken. It made her sick.

She was away from those men, and she wasn't a fool. This man, whoever he was, had killed them. She'd not seen how he'd done it, only that the men were on the floor and no longer hurting her.

"I smell," she said.

"I know."

"They … they pissed on me."

She saw his jaw clench, and she found it fascinating that he was angry. Was it for her? Because of her?

Being taken and held against her will had hurt, and it had really messed with her head.

"Did they do anything else?"

"They beat me."

"Did they rape you?" he asked.

She shook her head.

"They didn't?"

Charity didn't like the surprise in his voice. "They, they found out that I was a virgin, and then they decided I'd be worth more. Can I please wash now?"

"Yes. I'm going to call a doctor."

"Okay." She didn't know what else to say.

He got to his feet, and she followed him. He made his way past several doors before opening one at the end of the hallway. The light flickered on, and she blinked rapidly. The rest of his apartment wasn't as bright. The lights were dimmed or something.

"If you need any help just give me a shout."

She stepped into the room, and as he walked away, she panicked. "Wait."

He stopped and turned toward her.

"What's your name?" she asked.

"Dwayne. The name's Dwayne. You're safe here. I won't let anything happen to you."

He nodded at her, and she couldn't help the panic from rising up.

Get a grip.

Don't be that needy girl that everyone hates.

She switched on the shower and refused to look at her reflection. It didn't take a genius to realize that she looked a mess.

Pulling her clothes off, or what remained of them, she quickly climbed into the shower, gasping at the warmth of the water. Turning it up to scalding, she bowed her head, eyes closed, allowing it to wash off the filth that covered her body.

"Whoever buys you, sweetheart, is going to use your pussy good. I bet they're going to put your cunt, ass, and mouth to good use."

She ran her hand over her face, wincing as she touched her split lip. Opening her eyes, she picked up his shampoo and began to rub it into her hair, soaping up the length.

One wash wasn't enough for her.

She washed her hair three times and conditioned it three times. Grabbing the sponge, she scrubbed at her body, trying to rid herself of the dirt she felt that clung to her pores.

"That's enough."

She gasped as Dwayne appeared in the shower. He was in black pants and a white shirt. His hand held her arm steady. The strength in his grip shocked her as she couldn't move while he held her.

"Let go."

"No. You need to stop before you hurt yourself."

"I … I have to get the dirt off. I stink. I have to get it off."

"You're not dirty. You're clean." He cupped her face, tilting her head back. "You're clean, Charity. Repeat it. I'm clean."

She shook her head. "No."

"I'm clean."

"They pissed on me."

"I'm clean."

"They kept hurting me when I begged them to stop."

"I'm clean."

She pressed her lips together, hating how sick she felt.

"You going to barf?"

She nodded.

He opened the shower, and within seconds he had her over the toilet, holding her hair back as she threw up everything she'd eaten. Over and over, she emptied out her stomach, gripping the edge of the toilet as she did so.

"It's okay. I've got you. You're going to be fine."

After she threw everything up, Dwayne was mechanical as he wrapped her in a towel, and then told her to swill her mouth out. He had a toothbrush and toothpaste for her.

She followed each of his directions, shaken that she'd been standing before him naked, and he didn't show any sign of caring, not even a smidgen of interest.

Don't panic.

You shouldn't be thinking about that.

She was still a virgin.

There's no way that she could be thinking about something like that at a time like this. No way.

He wrapped her hair up as well. "I'm clean."

She didn't want to say it, but she knew he wouldn't stop.

"I'm clean."

"Good. You're going to keep saying that until you believe it. What those men did was fucking awful. They won't come and hurt you anymore. Don't let them take another moment of your life. They've already taken enough. Are you allergic to anything?"

"What do you mean?"

"Nuts? Gluten? Meat? Food?"

"No, nothing."

"Good. I've bought us both something to eat. Follow me."

She didn't argue with him as he made his way out of the bedroom. The last thing she wanted right now was to be alone in a bedroom with a man she didn't know, even if he had saved her. That didn't mean anything to her, not anymore.

The scents of the food made her stomach ache. She used to love food, but right now, she wasn't sure if she could even stomach anything.

The boxes were Chinese takeout, and as she glanced inside them, she saw noodles, dumplings, rice, and other things.

"You've got to try and eat something."

Picking up the carton with the noodles, she held the chopsticks and tried to eat. The first taste of food made her stomach recoil, but she didn't stop. Taking another bite, she glanced over the rim of the carton to see him staring at her.

"That's good. Don't stop." He urged her to eat more.

"Do you always do this?" she asked.

"Force a woman to eat?"

"No, save women. Take out the bad guys."

"You can't say anything about that to anyone."

The deadly look on his face made her tense up. It was like he was two different people.

"Who would I tell?"

"You're going back to your parents, Charity. Whatever went down here, you don't know. Got it?"

She nodded.

"Say it."

"I got it. I totally get it," she said, nodding her head at the same time. She didn't want to upset him. He'd saved her tonight. The last thing she wanted to do was to tell anyone what had happened here. It was too humiliating. "I promise. I won't tell anyone."

"Good. After tonight you'll never see me again."

"And if I do?"

"Depending on which side you're on, you'll either be dead or wishing you were."

She stared at him, not sure what to make of that.

Clearly being taken against her will had fucked with her head because she wasn't afraid. This man had risked his life and brought her out of that hellhole.

She ate her food, all the time watching him as he ate his. He was fascinating, his large muscles on full display, the fact he'd not changed his pants even though they were wet. It was almost as if he didn't feel it.

"The doctor's going to be arriving soon."

"The doctor?" she asked.

"Yeah. Don't worry. He's a man I trust, and I wouldn't just let anyone alone with you."

That didn't exactly make her feel very comfortable. In fact, it did the exact opposite. "I don't want to be alone with him."

"Just relax, Charity. Nothing is going to happen to you."

She tried to eat more food, but she just couldn't. The thought of anyone else being near her, she couldn't handle anything else. It was all just too much for her.

She gasped and put her carton down as the doorbell rang.

"That's him," Dwayne said.

She stayed perfectly still in her seat, refusing to move. This couldn't be happening. She was panicking about seeing a doctor. A professional who'd taken a vow to care, to do no harm. In the past twenty-four hours, she'd seen an ugly side to life, and the thought of being vulnerable again scared her.

Dwayne returned with a man in his fifties.

"Charity, this is Richard. He's a doctor, and he'll assess all of your wounds."

She shook her head.

"I know you've had a trying time, Charity, but I need to see everything," Richard said.

She didn't give a fuck what the good doctor had to say. The only person she was interested in and trusted was right there in front of her. Dwayne. The man who'd saved her.

"Maybe I should sedate her?"

"No!" she cried out at the same time Dwayne barked it out. That at least made her feel relief.

"You're not sedating her. She's fine. I'll be there. You'll let the doctor see you so long as I'm there."

She nodded. "But ... I don't have any underwear."

Dwayne sighed. "Come on. I've got something. Stay there." He pointed at the doctor as he passed. Rushing to keep up, she tried not to think about the pain in her side.

"Do you always get what you want?" she asked.

"Most of the time. It's a fear thing. People fear

me so I get what I want."

"And you like it."

"What do you think?" He placed his hand on the doorframe and stared down at her. He was so much taller than she was that she just took a deep breath, not knowing what to say. "See, right now you're afraid."

"No, I'm not," she said.

"You're not?" His head tilted to the side.

"I'm curious about you. I'd like to be able to take care of myself, and you seem to be able to do that." She shrugged. "You saved me. Why would I be afraid of you?"

"I could be a bigger monster than the men I brought you from."

"That's not true."

"How do you know?"

She opened her mouth and closed it, not really sure how to answer.

"Just a bit of advice, sweetheart. Don't trust every single guy that saves you. Believe me, some are worse than they look."

She followed him into the room. "Do you know what it's like? To be hurt? To be lost?"

His back was ramrod straight and she wanted to look him in the eye, but she didn't dare demand he turn to look at her. "Let's just say that I know what it's like to be hurt by the people you trust. Now, stop asking questions. Boxers and a shirt. He needs to look around your tits, so just lift your shirt and rest it beneath."

"Don't leave me."

"Want me to watch you getting changed?"

"You were in the shower with me. What difference does it make?"

He didn't say anything, but stood by the door, arms folded. "Get dressed then."

Was he testing her?

It didn't matter as she dropped the towel and did as he asked.

Chapter Two

Dwayne followed the doctor out of the room, and it was hard to decide if he wanted to kill him or let him live, just because of Charity's reaction, which made no sense to him. He didn't even know her, and yet he wanted to take that kind of pain away. He'd seen the way Charity had flinched at every single touch of this man's hands. She'd not wanted the doctor there, and if it hadn't been for her injuries, Dwayne wouldn't have allowed it to continue.

"She has bruising to her ribs, which will make it uncomfortable for her to walk. A possible concussion, so she needs waking up every two hours just to be safe. Quite a few bruises, and I would also recommend a psych evaluation on her."

"Not going to happen."

"Mr. Carson, she's been through a traumatic experience, and that's not going to go away easily. The next couple of months are going to be hard."

"Do you have anything else to add?"

"The rape kit. I need to collect one."

"Not going to happen."

"Look, you're being unreasonable."

"She's still a virgin, Doc. I don't see her wanting you to play that way, not after the fear she's been through. I got to her in time before they did anything or before she slipped through the cracks. You've done what you needed to do, now you can leave."

He saw the doctor out and slammed the door closed. It wouldn't be long before Beast and Caleb knew and they'd be wanting to talk to him again. He was getting used to their *special* talks. For the most part it was where he sat and listened to the two of them tell him he shouldn't do stuff, and then in the next breath congratulate him on a job well done.

The Nightmare.

It's what people called him now.

Not Beast's nephew.

Or Caleb's nephew.

He was his own man and without even his real name.

Dwayne hadn't gone out of his way to earn that name. It had started some time ago, actually. Back when he was eighteen and pissed off with Beast for dating one of the girls he'd brought home. Hope hadn't even been datable as far as he was concerned. She'd been too weird.

His anger had gotten the better of him one night as he walked the streets. He'd been trying to clear his head when he'd heard the feminine cry.

It had been subtle but the pain evident.

"Listen here, whore. You're going to suck my dick. Take it deep into your fucking throat until you gag!"

His curiosity had been piqued. He'd moved down the alleyway, the streetlight casting enough of a glow to see the two people fighting.

The woman couldn't have been any older than twenty, if that. The man, someone much older, was disgusting, and Dwayne had snapped.

In the back of his mind, he recalled all the vile things his own father used to throw at him. The way he'd treated his mother, and yes, he'd seen the way his father treated her. When he'd wanted to run to his room, his father had made him watch as he raped her. He'd never told another living soul the things he'd witnessed.

When Beast came to tell him he was living with him, his mother had been long dead. She'd died during one of his dad's "training sessions" when he said she needed to learn her lesson, his massive hands around her throat, cutting off her air supply. Dwayne had witnessed her death, and it hadn't been the only one either. Over the years, his father had killed several young women, whores, and others.

There had been no stopping him once he got on the warpath.

Again, he didn't say anything.

Watching this woman's abuse though, it was like being back in their home, his mother begging for her husband to stop, crying out, screaming for help.

He'd just stood there, a young kid who didn't know what to do.

She'd told him to run.

His father had said that if he ran, he'd put the strap to him.

He hated that strap.

It hurt so much that it was like fire dancing on his back.

So, he stayed.

That time wasn't the first or last time.

To make his son a man, to make him invincible, he was going to make sure he knew what he was dealing with.

At eighteen, watching a man force a woman who was crying and begging for him to let her go, Dwayne had withdrawn the blade he'd kept in his pocket. Moving toward the man, he didn't make a noise. It was like his heart didn't even beat as everything moved in slow motion. Nothing mattered, no one cared, and as he jammed that blade into the fucker's neck, hearing him gurgle, something came over him.

Something profound.

He was so fucking happy watching the blood drip out of the man's neck from the mark he made. He'd done it again. As the woman ran away, he'd watched the man die, and in doing so, he found his purpose in life.

Dumping the body had been easy. The piece of shit was wanted, as he later found, but that didn't matter.

Every single week on a Friday night, he'd walk the streets, ridding the world of the vermin that walked. Rapists, murderers, child abusers, the works. There was a kid at school, Arnold, he'd gone to him, asking him to find them for him. Every single person who didn't deserve to live on the streets. Some of them had been granted parole because of the people they knew high up.

He'd started to crave the violence, the danger. Training became a way of life, studying a thing of the past. Waking up at four in the morning, running, training, spending his day getting stronger, harder, faster, meaner.

He had no doubt that Caleb and Beast were aware of what they called him, but that didn't matter.

Dwayne had learned the valuable art of not giving a fuck.

"Are you okay?" Charity asked.

He turned to see her in the doorway. The shirt she wore was way too big, but on her it looked really cute.

"Yes. How are you feeling?"

"Sore."

"I think it's time for you to get some rest. Tomorrow I'll take you to your family."

She nodded. "Thank you."

He moved toward the spare bedroom. Pulling back the bedcovers, he turned the nightlight on and patted the bed.

"In you go."

She climbed into the bed, and he tucked the blanket around her.

"Where are you going?" she asked.

"Just across the hall. Get some sleep, Charity. You're going to be fine."

Leaving her bedroom door partially open, he made his way to his room. He left his door wide open just in case. He had several sensors around the apartment so if anyone tried to break in once he set them, he'd be alerted. Checking his stash of guns and knives, he put the ones he'd used today back in place. Tomorrow, when Charity was back with her family, he'd clean them.

Removing his clothes, he took a quick shower, changed into a pair of boxer briefs, and climbed into bed. He had weapons all around his room in case of intrusion. Picking up the reading book from the shelf, he began to read where he left off.

Now, this was a rare pleasure for him. He wouldn't ever admit it to anyone else in the world, but he happened to love reading romance books. It helped him to relax after a long day, and the sex was kind of cool to read as well.

He was settling down for a really kinky bit when the first scream erupted.

Dwayne slid his bookmark into place and put the book on the cabinet beside his lamp. Listening for another scream, he was out of bed the moment he heard it and making his way across the hall just as yet another ear-piercing scream released.

Charity was up in bed, holding the bedding to her, looking panicked.

"They have me," she said.

"They don't have you. It's a bad dream. No one is getting past me." He stepped up to her, cupped her face, and forced her to stare into his eyes. "Look at me, Charity. You're safe."

"I'm safe."

"Yes, you're safe with me. I'm not going to let anyone or anything hurt you."

"You're not going to let anyone hurt me."

He smiled. At least she was repeating everything he said, which had to be a good sign. He was going to see it as such.

"Get some sleep, Charity. It was just a bad dream."

"Wait. Please."

He'd already turned toward the door and paused to look at her.

"Please, stay with me."

He looked at the bed.

"Not for sex. Just to … I don't feel safe."

"I'm just going to get something," he said.

Grabbing his gun from the other room, and his alarm, he made his way back into her room. She was lying down, watching the door.

He placed everything within reach on the cabinet beside the bed and climbed beneath the covers.

Dwayne tensed up as her arms came around him, holding him like a fucking teddy bear. When the fuck did that happen?

He didn't want to push her off, and slowly, as the minutes passed, he felt her fall asleep. *Great, just fucking great.* He was a pillow now.

****

Charity didn't want to leave Dwayne, but she knew he had other things to do than take care of her. Her parents were waiting, and as she sat in his car, she should be running toward them.

"Your family is good, just so you know."

"Good?"

"Yes. They're not going to hurt you."

"I know." She tucked some of her hair behind her ear. It was back to being blonde now after all the dirt had been washed out.

"What's wrong, Charity?" he asked. "They're

251

waiting for you, and you're sitting here."

"I'm scared."

"Of what?"

Her eyes filled with tears, and she hated that as well.

Being weak wasn't her. Far from it.

"What if it happens again?"

"Being taken?"

"Yes. I don't ... next time they may not wait to, erm…"

"Rape you?"

"Yes."

"I'm going to be watching."

She turned to look at him, not liking that sudden jolt in her body. "You are?"

"Yes. You won't notice I'm there, but I'm going to keep an eye on things."

"I'll notice."

He smiled. "Men who are expecting me don't notice I've arrived until it's too late."

"I'm not like most men."

"No, you don't have a cock or balls."

She chuckled. "What am I supposed to do?"

"Get out of the car and go over to them."

"No, I know about that. I mean about the rest. What do I do? I can't ... everything makes no sense to me anymore."

She stared at her lap, not really sure what to say or what to do. Prolonging their time together was important to her.

"You forget about it. It didn't happen."

"But it did."

"Then you've got to learn to ignore it. No one is going to hurt you because I'm going to make sure of it. Your parents got me involved, and they paid me handsomely for the privilege. You're a strong woman, Charity. You can't let them win."

"What if they already have?"

"Not possible. You're alive. You're sitting here about to be reunited with your family. No one else can win. Only you can let that happen. Be strong and fight it."

She nodded her head and released a breath, opening the door of the car at the same time. "Thank you, Dwayne, for everything. Thank you so much."

"Don't mention it. I hope I won't be seeing you again, Charity."

She giggled and climbed out of the car. "I can't believe I just did that. I'm weird. Bye, Dwayne."

He watched her go. She looked so nervous, and he waited to see the reunion. Her parents rushed forward to embrace her, holding her close. There were tears exactly like he expected. Of course there would be.

Charity was a nice girl.

She deserved to go home to a nice, warm bed and to be safe. Her father nodded toward him, and he saw how grateful the man was. Dwayne acknowledged him, and only when the small family was in the car driving away did he leave.

Only he didn't go back home. Instead, he drove back to Beast's place. The home he'd known after his father had died. This was now the home Beast shared with Hope and their five children.

He never thought he'd see the day that Beast allowed himself to have children. There had been many a night that Beast seemed completely clueless about what to do with Dwayne himself. Caleb, not so much. He recalled many times offering to kill him, but that was later in life when he turned eighteen and upwards.

Dwayne smiled, recalling the fond memories.

Caleb wouldn't shoot him. For all of their faults they were a family, and in a way, he'd come to step in for his father.

Caleb and Beast were the only family he had.

Climbing out of the car, he didn't bother going inside but instead walked toward the garden. Hope wasn't much of a gardener, but she liked to make things pretty. The roses were all out in bloom, and as he made his way toward the small swing that was in the garden, he sat down and admired the view. It was the only element of his life that he considered beautiful.

He didn't own a house, preferring the confines of an apartment. With the work he had to do, he wasn't interested in having his home shot up, and he didn't trust guards.

As far as he was concerned, guards could be paid better and their loyalty was down to a cost. He would never allow himself to depend on guards.

"I thought I saw you arrive," Hope said, coming toward him.

She'd been his tutor for a short time in high school, and now it was kind of weird to think of her as his aunt. They were the same age.

"What are you doing out here?"

"I came to see you. You looked troubled."

"Where's Beast? He's not coming to yell at me about something."

"Why do you make it sound like a good thing that he'll yell at you?"

"Because I'm not doing my job properly if he's not got a good reason."

She sighed. "Beast told me about your latest job. The girl."

"Don't worry, Hope. She's home. Safe and sound."

"I'm not an idiot, Dwayne. I know what you're called. I hear the guards whispering your name. The reputation that you have, it's scary."

"Again, nothing to worry about."

Her arms were folded, and she looked the part of the scolding mom.

"What happened to the kid in high school?" she asked.

"You mean the jock that wouldn't give you the time of day until he needed it?"

She rolled her eyes. "I'm talking about the fun guy that just took life and laughed as he did."

"That kid grew up. You can't expect me to live in the past forever, Hope. We all change, and I did as well."

****

Three months later

Everything was different.

Charity wasn't the most popular girl in school, but she was well-liked. She was known for helping out, being there, and offering support to everyone. After coming home, it had been hard to just settle back into a routine. Her parents had made her go to a doctor then to a therapist for her to talk about her ordeal.

She didn't talk about it, no matter how many questions the woman asked.

The only person she wanted to remember from it all was Dwayne. He'd come out of nowhere, risked his life, and saved her.

No one seemed to get that, and when she asked her parents about him, they wouldn't allow her to even call him, which was just so infuriating. She wanted to know that he was okay. That he felt safe, that he was happy.

How messed up was that?

He'd probably forgotten her.

Moved on to some other damsel and here she was worried about him.

It confused her.

Moving down the long hall, she stopped at her locker, grabbing a few books. Everything seemed mechanical now. She went about school, moving from one class to another, and she felt ... withdrawn from it all. Nothing made any sense to her. Not the classes, not her friends, or even her teachers.

Everything no longer mattered. Her life could have been over if it hadn't been for Dwayne. She'd have been sold to the highest bidder, her life filled with rape and misery. The men who'd taken her had taunted her by what would have happened. First, they suggested she'd have to go on a diet. The man who took her would want her to look her best, and being fat was not allowed.

She didn't care about that as she was happy with who she was.

Diets were not her thing, and if she wanted to eat fried chicken, then she would. Or even some salad; no one was ever going to hold her to anything anymore. She was done playing that game.

With her books in her bag for studying over the weekend, she walked outside. Several of her peers were lurking in the parking lot in small groups, laughing and joking, making plans.

In the three months that she'd been back, she'd made every single excuse not to go out. As she walked toward her car, she heard several of the girls whispering.

"Who do you think he is?"

"What's he doing here?"

"I don't care who he is. I'd totally fuck him right now, and he doesn't even have to buy me dinner."

"You're such a slut."

Curious as to who they were talking about, she

spotted Dwayne leaning against his car. His arms were folded, and he looked ready for business.

She couldn't help but smile, especially as she saw the smirk on his face. Should she go to him? Hold back? Wait?

Three months was a long time to wait, so without doubting herself, she made her way over toward him.

"You know, it's kind of creepy for an older guy to be standing outside of a school, watching it."

He smiled. "I wasn't watching the school or the women coming out of it."

"What were you doing?"

"Waiting for one to see that she was okay."

Her heart pounded. Did this mean he cared?

They'd been together for one whole evening, and the next day he took her back to her parents.

"Couldn't you have gotten in touch with her parents?"

"I don't like talking to anyone but the person I'm interested in."

"And are you interested?" she asked. *Wait.* Was this flirting? She didn't know and felt so out of her depth with the whole conversation. Not that this could be deemed a conversation. Not really.

"How have you been?"

She took a deep breath. "Fine. I think."

"Only fine?"

"It's hard to explain."

"Want to go and get some dinner and talk?"

"Yes." She didn't even hesitate. What was the point in doing that when she would love to spend some time with him? "I can follow you."

"Sure."

She wished he'd offered to take her in his car, but a girl couldn't have everything.

Rushing back to her car, she didn't look toward the other girls as she knew they'd be curious, and right now, she didn't want to deal with any of that.

Climbing into her car, she pulled out of the parking lot and followed him. All the questions could wait until she got back to school Monday. Until then, this was her own time.

"Just be cool, Charity. Don't make this weird or anything. Just be cool and act normal. That's all you've got to do."

She tapped her steering wheel, following him out toward a small Italian restaurant, which surprised her. She expected a diner or café, but she was happy with this. She parked her car. The Italian restaurant didn't have valet parking, and that was fine with her.

Dwayne was already near her car as she got out.

"I take it you like Italian?"

"Who doesn't?"

She saw the smile on his lips, and when he held out his hand, she took it. Whenever she was with him, she always felt safe, warm, together. He made her feel this way, and it had been three months since she'd felt anything close to safe.

Her parents tried, but they weren't there when she was walking safely down the street, only in the next second to be taken. Her life had become so predictable that the men knew when to take her.

The last three months, she'd done everything different. No routine to her life, and that felt crazy to her. She never went to the same café twice in the same week, or even on the same day. She was always changing her life around so that no one could ever get the best of her again.

She had also started self-defense classes, and so far, they were not helping.

Dwayne got them a seat somewhere in the back that offered them a great deal of privacy.

"Did you call ahead to get a table?" she asked. The restaurant was busy, and she was surprised they'd gotten a table.

"There's always one reserved for my uncles and me."

"So you have a family."

"I never said I didn't."

She licked her lips and glanced around the luxurious restaurant. Her parents were wealthy and often loved to flaunt it to their friends.

"I'm sorry."

"I'm not angry. I have a family. Two uncles. They have families themselves."

"You don't."

"No."

"How old are you?" she asked.

"Thirty-four. Does that creep you out? To be out to dinner with a man old enough to be your father."

She chuckled. "You're not old enough to be my father. If that was the case you had me at sixteen. My dad is nearly fifty years old."

"Math has never been my strong point."

"No, I don't find you creepy at all, Dwayne. I like you." Her cheeks heated, and she quickly looked down at the table. It was hard enough to admit that she liked him in her head, let alone to his face.

Biting her lip, she grabbed the menu, but before she could withdraw her hand, Dwayne had a hold of her wrist.

For several seconds he simply held her, doing nothing else. It was like their world stood still and they were the only two there, waiting.

Slowly, his fingers slid down to take her hand.

"I like you, too, Charity."

"You don't even know me."

"I know you're hard-working and that you're strong."

"You always said that," she said.

"Because I mean it. You're a strong woman."

"Why were you here?"

"Believe it or not, I don't live too far from here, and I wanted to make sure you were okay. Not by asking your parents. They don't see the truth."

"What truth?" she asked.

"That you don't want to go to someone to talk about your damn feelings. Or that you couldn't give a shit right now about going to the mall. Three months ago, you were taken by men who were going to put you up for auction. Sell you to the man who paid the highest amount for your virginity. What would happen to you after that, you don't know. I don't know, but I've got a pretty good idea that it wouldn't be flowers or romance. They'd have used you. Fucked you until you were nothing but dead meat to them. That's what animals like that do. For a short time that was your reality, and you don't need to be constantly reminded of it by talking about your fucking feelings."

He was so right it was scary.

Chapter Three

Charity ordered some pasta dish while Dwayne settled on the herbed steak and potatoes. He came here often enough to know what he liked. She looked different. He'd noticed that about her when he saw her coming out of school. Her head was downcast, looking at the floor. She didn't pay attention to anyone or anything. She'd also lost some weight as well, which he didn't like.

At first, he was only going to see what was going on with her. What was wrong. One look and he knew he had to talk to her. The giggling schoolgirls held no appeal for him. When he'd been a schoolboy they'd not held much interest then, but he'd been young and wanting to get off, so he used the girls that threw themselves at him. Never did he give any of the girls he was with ideas that it would be forever.

Charity kept looking around the room as if she was waiting for someone or something to jump out at her.

"You don't have to be afraid."

"I know." She ran fingers through her hair. "Sorry. You could tell that I was checking everything?"

"Kind of hard not to."

"I find public places difficult at times. I never know who is watching me."

"You change your routine?"

"All the time," she said.

He tilted his head to the side, watching her. "I heard you were taking self-defense classes."

She blew out a breath and laughed. "Yeah, for what good they're doing me."

"You don't think they're helping?"

"I don't know what's helping or not, to be honest. We've done some moves that are supposed to work, but

I'm not convinced." She nibbled her lip, and his gaze was drawn to that action.

"Want me to help you?"

"Help me?"

"Defend yourself. My ways won't be entirely conventional, but it will help you out if you need it."

She nodded, and he saw that sparkle back in her eye. "Yes. Please. I'd like that."

The waiter interrupted, and he wanted to shoot the bastard for making the shine from her eyes dull just a little. When it came to Charity he was having a lot of murderous tendencies, and he had to keep it under control before Beast or Caleb grounded him. Not that it would help. If they took all of his weapons off him, he still had his hands. His father had taught him long ago that if you had strength then you *were* a weapon.

He'd honed those skills well over the years, and now he was unstoppable.

The nightmare of every man's dreams.

"Will you teach me how to shoot a gun?" she asked, her cheeks a shade of red and the excitement clear in her eyes.

"Do you think you're ready for that?"

"I know I can't keep living like this, and everything they teach us is about running away. I'm not a fast runner and I can scream, sure, but what if no one comes running? I screamed my head off when I got taken, and there wasn't anyone around." She stabbed at her plate, twirling her spaghetti. "I don't want to be taken again, or even have that risk."

He nodded. "The stuff I'll teach you is not conventional. I'm not going to tell you to dodge and run or even to scream. First, I'll make sure you can handle yourself so that if you are taken by surprise, you don't freak out."

"I don't want my parents to know."

He raised a brow.

"They're ... worried."

"They want to protect you. I can understand that."

She groaned, and he smiled. He found her so charming. It was strange. She was eighteen years old, had her whole life ahead of her, and he couldn't stand girls that age when *he* was that age. She wasn't a girl though. Charity was very much a woman.

"You don't have kids or a family."

"I have cousins. Very close and I would do anything to protect them. When you love people, that's what you do, no matter what. You take care of them. That's all your parents are doing for you."

"I want to stop seeing my therapist."

"Then stop," he said.

"You make it sound so easy, but it's not."

"How is it not? You either don't go, cancel your appointment, or sit in complete silence."

She stared at him for several minutes, her fork in her pasta, and she looked deep in thought. "Do you think I need to go?"

He laughed. "I don't know, Charity. Do you need to go?"

"We're not getting anywhere with this."

"How do you feel when you look back on your ordeal?" he asked.

She licked her lips again. He was getting distracted by those lips. "I get angry."

"Why are you angry?"

"Now you're sounding like my therapist."

"Answer the question."

"I was helpless. I was scared. There's no way I can put into words what I felt or what I feel. It just fucking happened. I couldn't do anything about that."

She blew out a breath. "I don't know. I feel like everything is happening all around me. People are moving on, but I'm standing still. I can't move on."

"And why do you think that is?"

"I don't have a clue. Maybe, Mr. Therapist, you could tell me."

He sliced into his steak, closing his eyes as the flavors coated his tongue. It really was a good, juicy, rare steak, which was the best kind.

"Okay, let's put it to you another way," she said. He waited as she took a sip of her water. "If you were in my position and those guys were doing that to you and everything happened the same, what would you feel like?"

"Simple."

"Well…"

He finished his bite and leaned forward. "I would be pissed that someone came and saved me and didn't leave me one person to take care of myself. I'd need to see their blood pouring from their body to know I got the bastard good, but that's me, Charity. I like killing. It's what I do. Now, what about you? Do you wish you could have killed them?"

Tears were in her eyes. He saw them, and what was even more interesting, she didn't look afraid or sick.

"I'm angry that I couldn't fight back. That I was too afraid. I thought about hurting them so much. Of taking the guns and the knives they threatened me with and turning it on them, and just letting go."

"You shouldn't be worried about thinking like that."

"Why? Because it's natural? There's nothing natural about what I wanted to do."

"Isn't it? It's primal. Human survival. You can't control what you wanted to do, Charity, any more than we can deny our basic nature."

"What do you consider our basic nature?"

"We're animals. The only difference is we've created a world that makes us all have to conform. We're the kings of the jungle because we have guns and knives, but this isn't how it's supposed to be. Don't be afraid of what you wanted to do. Accept it."

"They'd have killed me."

"Yes. You pissed them off, didn't do as you were told; they'd have raped you, used you for a few weeks, then killed you. Obviously, death wouldn't have been easy for you if you'd done all that stuff." He leaned over the table. "Don't cry."

"Why can I talk to you about these things and no one else?"

"Because I don't matter. Not really. I'm just a guy that saved you."

"You do matter."

He shrugged. "I've seen you at your worst. Sobbing on the floor. I don't know. I guess you just don't feel the need to hide shit from me. I don't hide myself from you. I never will."

"You're honest."

"That I am."

He took a sip of his water, enjoying her company. She finished off her pasta and sat back with a sigh.

Dwayne watched as she sipped at her drink.

"Would you like dessert?"

"No. I'm full. I couldn't eat another thing."

He had the waiter bring him the check, and after he paid for their meal, he followed her out of the restaurant, noticing her full ass. At least she wasn't losing too much weight.

"You need to start taking care of yourself."

"Excuse me."

"Not eating won't help you. Don't let the bastards win, Charity." He leaned against her car, holding the door open for her. "I'll meet you tomorrow. Come here." He handed her a small card with an address on it. "Drive safely."

****

Charity lied to her parents about where she was going the next day. She told them it was a date at the mall with a few friends and where she intended to meet some guy. There was no guy or any friends. Checking the address on the card, she stared up at an empty building. It was boarded up. She drove around the back where she saw Dwayne's car.

His arms were folded, and he wasn't wearing his normal business suit. Dark glasses covered his eyes, and he had this sexy smirk that made her think of things she really shouldn't. At eighteen she was no stranger to desire. In fact, prior to her kidnapping she'd been very interested in and intrigued by sex. She just hadn't found the right guy to explore what she wanted.

"You made it," he said as she climbed out of the car.

"I don't get it. This place doesn't look like it has been used in years."

"It's the perfect disguise, don't you think?"

There was no one around, and she guessed it was. "Do you come here to work out or something else?"

"I come here to train. I own it."

"You own a useless warehouse."

He held out his hand, and she took it without hesitation. With his other hand, he held a key, and she waited as he opened up the locks and typed in the security codes. Once they were inside, he locked the doors.

Should she be freaking out? Panicking?

Again, she felt safe. *He* made her that way, no one else.

He flicked the lights on, and the entire floor illuminated to showcase a huge gym.

"Why?" she asked.

"I don't like company. This is where I come for peace and quiet, and to just do what I want."

There were a couple of running machines, weights, and lots of other stuff she couldn't think of.

"Come on."

She wore a pair of shorts and a large shirt that ended at her knees.

He moved her away from all of the equipment to the back, which had mirrors all around and mats.

"You train people often?"

"Nope. Told you, never brought anyone here."

"And you own it?"

"Yep. It's a good investment."

She looked around again. "How is this a good investment? I don't get it. To make money you have to sell something."

"I do."

"You're an escort?"

Dwayne laughed. "Damn, you're funny. No, I kill people, Charity. You should know that." He stood way too close, so that she struggled to think.

"Why am I not running away?"

"Because you've seen me kill bad men."

"But … shouldn't you get taken by the cops or something?"

He winked at her. "The first rule you need to learn about the world. It's a bad fucking place filled with shit as fuck people." She watched as he opened his wallet and pulled out several dollar notes. They looked like hundred-dollar bills. "Men, women, even children do crazy fucking shit for this." He screwed it up and tossed it to the floor. "That talks."

"You sound like an asshole."

"You're not impressed?"

"No." She shook her head.

"Well, let's get started. We're going to work on surprise attacks."

"Surprise attacks?"

"Yes. You weren't expecting them to take you, so how about we start with that."

She watched as he removed his sunglasses and moved toward the end of the room. He was ever so sexy to watch. She really liked his ass.

Every inch of him was rock-hard. Even his face looked ready for business. It made her wonder if he even knew how to have fun.

Do you?

Ignoring her own thoughts, she watched as he was distracted.

She couldn't resist. Being as loud as she could, she let out a scream, watching as he suddenly spun, gun in his hand, tensed and ready. She released a giggle, not the least bit frightened about seeing him with a gun.

"What the fuck was that?" he asked.

"You said something about surprise. So, there you have it. Were you scared?"

He rolled his eyes. "What would you have done if I'd shot you?"

"You wouldn't have."

"How can you be so fucking sure?"

"Simple. You promised to protect me always. I believe you."

"You should be scared when you see a gun."

"Oh, I will. Just not with you, it would seem. Are you going to show me how to use a gun?"

"Would you like to know?" he asked.

"Yes. I think I really would. Can I buy myself a gun?"

"You're way off from having a gun, buying a gun, until we get that mouth under control."

"Stop worrying so much."

"What happens when you blow your brains out?" he asked.

"That won't happen."

"It can and it has, so no guns to start with. Let's just get your mouth under control. No screaming at me. It can also piss off the men so that they hurt you."

She rolled her eyes. It was just so funny to watch him react, and it did also kind of thrill her as well. He cared enough to worry.

"Are you worried that someone is going to come in here, ruin it?"

"I'm not worried about that, but you can never be too careful in life. I've made a lot of enemies."

She rubbed her hands together. "You have?"

"Yes. Now," he moved closer to her. "I want you to attack me."

"How does that work?" she asked.

"I want to know your strength and your weaknesses."

"Oh." She had to touch him. "I don't know what to do."

"Push me. Hit me."

"No, I can't do that." She wrapped her arms around herself, feeling really uncomfortable.

"Charity, you're not going to hurt me."

"This isn't about hurting you. I don't want to do that. I like you."

He tilted his head to the side, and she noticed he did that a lot when he was watching her. She hated it, especially as it made her feel like a bug under a microscope.

His hands were on her shoulder, and he gave her a little shove. It didn't hurt, but she knew what he was doing.

"I've got to help you to become stronger. How am I going to do that if you're not willing to attack?"

"You said it was all about surprise attacks. This is not a surprise. This is me attacking you. I don't want to do that. Like, ever."

He took a deep breath, and she knew she was pissing him off.

"Men will take advantage of your good nature." He moved right up close, the look on his face scaring her. It was like he'd changed. The good guy was long gone, and in his place was someone she didn't recognize. "They will use whatever means they can to hurt you."

She cried out as he wrapped his fingers around her neck and suddenly she was pinned against the wall. His hold tightened just a little, and she tried to gasp.

Panicking, she gripped his arms.

"Don't ever assume that men are your friends or women either, Charity. You can only take care of yourself. Only rely on yourself."

He squeezed just a little tighter, and her air cut off.

Do what he wants.

She didn't want to hurt him, but he was doing this to help her. Even as he held her neck, she wasn't afraid of him. Not at all.

There was no other choice. Drawing her leg up, she kneed him in the scrotum, and watched as he loosened his hold and bent forward, cupping his balls. Everything seemed to happen in slow motion. With his hands off her, she shoved him hard, and he fell back. Her heart was racing as she stared down at him. Hands on hips, she glared at him.

She wasn't looking at him for long as he tripped her up and she fell on her back. Dwayne was on her, holding her hands above her head.

"You should fucking run. You leave the mats, you win. You don't, you lose. It's simple. I could do whatever the fuck I wanted to you right now." He covered her mouth with his hand, which was so large it covered her nose and mouth. Her air supply was once again cut off. "You can see that. I can rape you, beat you, hurt you, and you're so small that no one would ever know."

His knee pressed against her core, and she was so startled she cried out just as his hand left her mouth. She didn't pull away. Even as he continued to shock her with how fragile her safety was, she reacted to his touch.

No man or boy had ever made her ache before, but that was exactly what she was doing now, aching for him, desperate, hungry for more.

Dwayne was on his feet again. "Again. You're going to learn to take care of yourself, Charity."

She got to her feet and stared at him, unsure what to do. Her body was something foreign to her right now. She didn't know what the hell to do.

Chapter Four

One week later

Dwayne plunged his knife into the neck of the man who'd been selling Carson family secrets to their enemies. Beast and Caleb were both present as the interrogation had been going, but for some reason, they decided to stick around for what came next. He didn't mind having an audience, but normally, they left him alone to deal with the kill and the clean-up.

When Dwayne pulled the blade out, the man's head dropped to the side, and for a few seconds he stared, making sure he was dead.

With that done, he looked toward his two uncles.

"Anything else?"

"You're leaving a trail of bodies everywhere you go," Caleb said.

"No, I clean them up. It's one of the reasons you guys love me."

"William came to me," Beast said, handing him a newspaper. "Out in the forest near your known dumping ground they've discovered a bunch of bodies. You're either not burying them deep enough or with the flooding that has been going on, they've decided to pop up."

Dwayne removed his rubber gloves and grabbed the paper. It had made headline news. That was a surprise, but as he glanced at the section of the woods, he shook his head. "This isn't me."

"Dwayne, we all know that's where you go to bury a body."

"Wrong. It's not the only place I've buried bodies. I've not been to that forest in years. Whoever is doing this, it ain't me." He handed back the paper.

"Are you lying?" Caleb asked.

He took a deep breath and looked toward his

uncle. Caleb had always been on his case to be better, training him at the early hours of the morning, putting him through hell, and he fucking loved him for it. He wouldn't be who he was today without his uncles, or his father for that matter. "No, I don't lie."

"This is serious, Dwayne," Beast said.

"I've not fucking lied. Have you ever thought about it being the two of you in your old age going fucking senile?" he asked, glaring at the two.

Caleb stared at him for a couple of seconds and shrugged. "It's not him."

"Nope, it's not."

"Are you two being serious right now?"

"You're right. You don't lie."

He rolled his eyes. "I don't have time for this. Do you two want to take over and do some actual work for a change?"

"Nope, you deal with it." Beast patted his arm while Caleb winked at him. "It's up to strapping young men like yourself to do this stuff. We know you didn't do the body dumps, so we're all good. There's nothing that will come back to you."

He watched them both leave, thankful they hadn't lingered.

Putting his earbuds in, he got to work packaging the man. He had no intention of burning this body. This was a message to all their enemies.

Once it was perfectly wrapped, he lifted up the weight and carried it out to the bastard's car. With gloves on his hands again, he drove the car to one of the other warehouses, got out, and left.

He whistled as he walked back to the warehouse where he'd been interrogating. Before he left for the day, he checked to make sure there was no evidence left lying around. Checking the time, he saw it was a little after eleven AM.

Charity would be waiting for him.

Just thinking about her made him smile.

Climbing into his own car, he drove the thirty minutes to see that the woman in question hadn't left. She leaned against her vehicle, checking her watch.

"You're late," she said the moment he joined her.

"Or maybe you're early."

"It's nearly lunchtime."

"So. You got anywhere special to be?" he asked.

"I could. I have friends."

"That are not hanging around with you anymore."

"How do you even know they're not hanging around with me anymore?"

"I was a schoolkid once. I knew someone who went through something like you did. Not on the same scale, but she was considered an outcast." He chuckled. "She's now my auntie."

"Wait? What?"

"My tutor fell for my uncle. They're married now, kids and all that. She's my age. Had a rough time of it when she was younger, a little younger than you. Her father shot her, and she saw him kill her mother and then himself. For a long time, a lot of people gave her a wide berth. Clearly thought something was wrong with her. I know there was. There's no way falling for my uncle is normal."

He couldn't believe he just admitted that to her.

When he discovered Hope and Beast were a thing, he hadn't really cared. Yeah, it was a little weird, but again, he had his own life to live and he wasn't about to tell two people not to be together.

Locking the door behind her, he made his way toward the workout mats. Pulling off his jacket, he removed his shirt and faced her wearing a vest and pants.

"Were you on business or something?" she asked.

"Yeah, why?"

"Your clothes."

He glanced down at his clothes. There hadn't been any blood on them. "What about them?"

"It's nothing. Ignore me."

Folding his arms, he watched as she removed her bag and then turned to face him. Her back was ramrod straight, and neither of them spoke a word. Her hands were clenched at her sides, and he waited.

"Do I need to order you to attack me?" he asked. "Want me to make it easier for you?"

"I don't … can't you just show me how to defend myself?"

"Part of defending yourself is knowing how to attack." He advanced on her, and instead of staying strong, she didn't. She kept backing up until she hit the wall. He was about to wrap his hands around her neck, but she moved, avoiding him. She ducked under his arm.

Her reactions were so slow, but he'd show her in time. For now, he needed her to build her confidence.

"That makes no sense. Most of the time the people being attacked need to defend themselves because they're vulnerable. They're not prepared."

"Everyone who is not used to being on guard will always get taken. Will always get hurt."

"Have you taken classes in this before?" she asked, arms folded, looking rather stern. It was really cute.

"No."

"What can you teach me that no one else can?" She gave him a pointed look.

Dwayne stepped up close to her. "I'm like every other person, but the difference is, I'm not going to teach you how to run away. I'm going to make sure you can take the man down and have plenty of time to get away."

"How is that any different?"

"I've been doing this a long time. Unless you want to be taught how to kill, this is the next best option."

"I don't want to kill."

"Are we going to have this conversation every time you come here? It's taking up time, and I've got better things to do. If you just want to hang out, tell me. I'm not going to waste my time telling you this stuff if you're not interested."

"I am interested."

"Good. Then stop moaning and either start fucking learning or go back home."

She nodded, and he watched her square her shoulders. "I'm ready."

"Today I'm going to attack you. It's going to be random." He moved toward his jacket and removed the blindfold he kept in the pocket. Holding it up, he gave her a wink.

"Kinky."

"What do you know about kink?"

"That it involves handcuffs, whips, and blindfolds. You want to get down and dirty with me, Dwayne?"

He didn't say a word, simply spun her around and placed the blindfold over her eyes. "Most people are surprised when they're attacked. They cannot and will not be able to defend themselves."

"Ah, I understand the blindfold, got it."

"I want to see how you react, and then we'll work from there."

Once he tied the blindfold at the back he spun her around a few times. She lost her footing, and he didn't help her. This was to knock her off balance.

Taking away her sight was the first step.

She turned in a circle, her hands coming out to steady herself as if she was unsure.

"I don't like this," she said.

He kept his footsteps light so she couldn't hear him. It was strange seeing her blindfolded. It made him think of her completely naked, at his mercy, begging for him. Pushing aside the desire that suddenly hit him, he focused on her.

"This is really weird. Are you, like, making faces?" she asked.

She took a deep breath, and her nerves were so clear to see. Her hands clenched into fists, and she held herself quite tight now. She needed to relax, to keep her hands loose so that no one could go up behind her, and simply grab her.

Like he did, banding his arms around her, lifting her up with ease.

She struggled, but he won, drawing her down to the ground and having her hands locked.

"I've taken you now. There's nowhere you can go." He pressed his face against her ear. "You could be dead by now."

With that, he pulled up, getting her to her feet. "Again."

****

Charity lost count of the number of times he won. The ways he came at her. She didn't even feel it until he either surrounded her, yanked, pulled, tugged, whichever seemed to take his fancy. Not that she'd ever admit it but she rather liked it when he held her hair. It wasn't painful, but it made her think of a great deal of naughty things.

The blindfold started it all.

Just because she was eighteen didn't for a second

mean she wasn't aware of men and sex.

Being with Dwayne, it seemed to enhance it all. He was always so quiet, holding himself back, being aloof, and she liked that.

By the end of the day, she was exhausted, and even though he hadn't grabbed her hard she knew there would be bruises. His touch was always firm. He didn't give her the chance to think that her attackers would be weak.

"That was tiring," she said.

"You did good."

"I did? You killed me each and every single time."

He smiled. "Believe me, if I did that, you'd know about it."

"My body feels it. Isn't that enough?" She collapsed onto the mat. It was a little after four, and she didn't want to go home. Not yet. Her parents constantly asked questions, and that was more exhausting than Dwayne's attacks.

"What's wrong?" he asked, standing over her.

"Nothing. Just family stuff. You know, parents."

"Anything I can help you with?"

"Only if you turned up eighteen and were a potential boyfriend or a girl for me to hang out with, we'd be fine."

His arms were folded, and he tilted his head to the side. It was like he was always assessing her, and he wasn't entirely sure what to expect. Did it make her different from everyone else he knew? Special?

"What's going on?" Dwayne asked.

"You want me to talk about my drama?"

"Why not? Clearly you don't want to leave."

"Is that wrong?"

"No. Believe it or not, there was a time when

women liked spending time with me."

"And now?"

"Oh, they still love spending time with me. I just don't care to spend it with them unless I'm getting what I want."

Jealousy sparked inside her, and she didn't like it.

"Do you have a girlfriend?" she asked.

"No."

"Just someone you have casual sex with."

"Now, Charity, that looks and sounds a little like jealousy to me."

"It's not." She completely lied. "I'm not jealous of anyone." That was partially true. She'd never been jealous until today, and it was all because of Dwayne. He didn't even belong to her, and yet, she felt like he was.

Get over yourself.

"Let's move away from your denial. Tell me your troubles, honey," he said, taking a seat.

"Don't call me honey."

Her dad called her that, and she didn't like that word coming from Dwayne's lips, especially as she didn't think about him in any way that would ever be considered fatherly.

He held his hands up. "You're the boss."

"There's no troubles, really. It's my parents. They're worried, like, all the time." She tucked some of her stray hair behind her ear.

"They don't want your kidnapping to take over your whole life. They do have a point."

"And I get that, but being here with you, I have to make up lies, and I hate that. They're talking about college, and prom, and how I'm going to be moving out soon. It's all just too much. Now I have to tell them about my day at the mall with either a friend or they want to know what guy is interested in me."

"Do you have a guy interested in you?"

"No. At least, I don't know. No one has approached me at school, and it sucks. It all just sucks, and I like spending time with you. I know you're, like, an old man now, but I do. You're a lot of fun."

"You didn't insult me at all."

"My parents said you were old. I kept asking about you. How they contacted you in the beginning. They wouldn't tell me a thing and told me I needed to stop thinking about you. You have your own life and don't need a teenage girl bugging you. Am I bugging you?"

"No."

"Really?"

"Do I strike you as the kind of man that would lie?"

"Yeah."

He laughed. "I guess you're right. I wouldn't lie about this."

"But you would lie about everything else?"

"Of course. I'm not a saint. I never claimed to be one either. So, you're tired of all the lies?"

"Yes."

"You can either keep on lying, tell them your day was fun, but you're tired, or stop coming here."

"I'll keep on lying. I don't want to stop coming here." She hated how desperate she sounded. "I find this fun. You know."

"I wouldn't describe this as fun."

"Oh."

"Not that it's a bad thing thinking about it either. You're a little sensitive today."

"I'm sorry. I'm just stressed." She smiled at him.

"I enjoy coming here. It relaxes me."

"Do you work out often?"

"Yes. A lot. I need to. I need to keep in shape."

"Do you rescue other girls like me?" she asked.

"No."

"How come?"

"Your parents paid a lot of money to make sure you returned home safely. You do realize that the chances of finding you alive were slim."

"Yes. Thank you for not giving up."

"I had no intention of giving up. I got paid to do a job."

He glanced down at his watch, and she knew it was now time to leave. "I better start heading back."

"All right."

As she grabbed her bag, they made their way out of the building. He typed in whatever the code was, and then he walked her to her car. She didn't want to leave and would have happily stayed with him, talking.

"Next week?"

"Yes. Drive safely."

"I will."

She smiled at him and climbed behind the wheel. This time she didn't linger. She didn't watch him get into his car.

"You need to put some distance on this."

Tapping her fingers against the steering wheel, she drove home. All the time she kept thinking about the past day. When he'd not turned up on time she'd been worried. What if he was late? What if he forgot?

The thought of not seeing him for another week filled her with a great deal of sadness that she didn't want to talk about.

Arriving home, she pulled up into the large driveway. Her parents' cars were already there, and she took a deep breath before heading inside. Keeping her bag on her shoulder, she entered her home.

Seeing no one around, she was about to make a run up to her room when her mother caught her.

"Hey, honey," she said.

"Hey, Mom." She turned to see her mother in the doorway.

"How was your trip?"

"It was good."

"Buy anything special?"

"Nah. I had a milkshake and a burger, walked a little."

"Who was there?" she asked.

"A couple of friends from school. I kind of broke away from the crowd though. Needed time to think."

"Makes sense. Dad ordered Chinese food."

"I'll take my bag upstairs."

"All right."

This was how every single Saturday evening went. Her father loved Chinese food, and it was his night where he got to order whatever he wanted. Otherwise it was always healthy stuff or something her mother liked.

Putting her bag on the floor, she moved toward her window and looked out over her yard. Since she'd been back nothing had changed. Everything was always in the same position. The swing she used to spend hours on as a little kid in the back yard. The half-built tree house that her father promised her but never finished. All of it used to mean something to her, and now she saw how fragile it all was.

She wasn't the same person that had come back after being taken.

There were times she felt guilty though. She'd not been taken for a long time or been raped. They'd toyed with her, beaten her, pissed on her, and she'd gotten away. The men who dared to take her were dead, rotting somewhere right now, whereas she was alive. Should she be allowed to be different? To feel it? To look at something and see the ugly not just the pretty?

It didn't really matter though anymore.

She couldn't go back to the way things once were.

Even if her parents kept trying to change her, they couldn't take away what had happened to her. She wasn't their little girl anymore.

Chapter Five

Two weeks later

"You ever had anyone shoot you?" Charity asked.

Dwayne finished loading the gun and looked toward her. Her posture was exactly the way he'd left her to start her first shooting lesson. After two weeks of attack and defense he'd believed she was ready for that next step. Like in school, Charity was a fast learner, and it was in fact a privilege to see her constantly achieving, always working to improve.

"What do you think?"

"I don't know. I wonder if you give people the time to realize you're there or if you just go shooting people like crazy." She started to make gun noises with her hands clasped together, one finger pointing forward as she did it.

"I'm not that good."

"You're great though, right? You wouldn't be where you are now without that skill?"

She was always prying into elements of his life, which he didn't mind. He enjoyed listening to her talk. Charity had one of those voices what would make a good storytelling voice. She was the first woman in his life that he actually enjoyed being around. Most women he found irritating. Not this woman though.

"Fine. Fine. Don't tell me." She held her hands up in surrender, swinging from side to side, looking all cute.

He moved toward her and held out the small handgun, which she turned in her hand, pointing the muzzle up at her head.

Quickly grabbing her, he positioned the gun away from her.

"Are you crazy?"

"What? Doesn't it have a safety or anything?"

"What exactly do you know about guns?"

"They go bang."

"You're a pain in the ass." He shook his head. "Right, keep the gun pointed away from you at all times." He moved to stand behind her, positioning her hands and placing her body exactly how he wanted it. He'd already lined up the empty cans he'd found. Her targets.

"How good were you the first time you got a gun?"

"Why do you want to know?"

"I want to know if it's as easy as it looks, or if it's hard."

"It is hard. I couldn't shoot the beer cans for a long time. It felt like a whole year. I trained constantly to be as good as I am now."

He felt her take a deep breath as he placed her hands into position, and then she started to shoot. She fired three times and laughed. The cans were all in position and hadn't been touched.

"Why are you laughing?"

"I fired my first gun. I think that's pretty awesome, don't you?"

Instead of joining her in her mini-victory, he spent the remainder of the day showing her. He didn't stay pressed against her back and stepped away for her to try on her own. As the day wore on and the sun began to set, he saw her frustration start to build. The cans were still in place and hadn't moved once. The bullets, though; she'd used quite a few.

"You know what, this is faulty."

"The gun's not faulty." He stepped forward, taking it from her, aiming and firing. All five cans landed on the floor.

Perfect.

Precision.

His training.

This was his life.

Taking lives was what he was good at. In fact, he would go so far as to call himself a master in the art.

"Fine. It's not faulty."

She wrapped her arms around herself.

"Are you feeling cold?"

"Just a little bit. I'll be fine."

He removed his jacket and draped it across her shoulders.

"You know for a badass, you don't show it."

"How do I not show it?"

"Well, for one, you don't kill me."

He chuckled. "You want me to kill you? It would be very useless training."

"You think I could take you now. I know all your tricks."

"You're not even close to being that good." He put away the gun and cleaned up the mess while Charity watched.

"Really? You're not training me to take you out."

"Charity, I hate to break this to you, but I'm not training you to kill anyone. I'm teaching you how to survive and to have a better chance of making it out alive. This stuff that I teach you will only get you so far. It'll be up to you to figure out the rest."

"Oh."

She was silent for a few seconds, but it was like he could feel her mind working, preparing, getting ready for more questions.

"Why don't you want me to kill anyone?" she asked.

He finished locking up his equipment and turned

toward her. Her hands were by her sides, open. He always noticed a person's stance. It had kept him alive this long. Knowing if you were going to be attacked at any moment was important. At least to him it was.

Reading people came with the territory of being a killer.

"It changes who you are, taking a life. You've got to be prepared to live with the guilt."

"You do?"

"Yeah, you do."

"Do you feel guilt?" she asked.

He thought about it and nodded. "Yeah, I get guilt. The first man I killed was a rapist." He deserved to die, but still Dwayne felt the change inside him.

"He was a monster."

"Yeah. I saw him in the act. To be honest, I can't even remember if he was my first kill or not. They all kind of mingle together right now. I don't know who was first." He shrugged. "I certainly should tell little girls about this."

"I don't feel like a little girl."

She looked away.

"What is it?" he asked.

"It's nothing."

"I don't bullshit you, Charity. Don't start with me."

"Fine. Everyone wants me to forget. They want me to move on and be my happy self."

"You can't."

"Could you?"

"I had a lifetime of pain and suffering even before I took my first life, Charity. You're not like me. You're a woman, and you're not a killer."

"But I think about it."

"You think about killing?"

"Yes. Those men. They took something from me, and now, all I can think about is hurting them."

"They're dead."

"But men like them are still out there. Murderers, rapists, child abusers, people who don't deserve to live."

"I don't play God in my line of work. I do a job. They were hurting you, and it was my job to kill them."

"How many people have you killed in total?" she asked.

"I don't keep count."

He'd stopped counting years ago. When he was at the height of his training with Caleb, he'd gone out hunting for men who he could work and train on. Being a Carson, he had to know when to sniff out the weak, the evil, and the vulnerable. He'd never hurt a man, woman, or child that hadn't deserved it. He'd killed a few women that were evil to the core, protected children, and driven his blade through men's hearts time and time again.

What he didn't realize when he was younger was how valuable the Carson name was. They commanded respect through sheer force and will. No one took a shit without them knowing about it.

Rats, snitches, betrayers, enemies, they were all part of the people he'd taken out. No one was safe as far as he was concerned.

"I think it's time I went home," she said.

He nodded and moved toward the passenger door. Climbing behind the wheel, he started his car and drove them back to his warehouse. Today he'd made her come with him to begin this training.

"Taking a life, it's not easy?"

"No."

"You live with it though."

"It's my job to live with it."

"Thank you for today," she said.

He watched as she left his car and made her way to her own. When she pulled out of his parking lot, he followed her, not wanting to risk her being alone or someone waiting.

She didn't veer off the path, and the moment she was in her home, he drove off, heading to a bar near the center of the city where he could forget all his troubles.

The bar was a strip club. The music was always soft, and normally he liked to look at the women prancing around naked or dancing until they were.

Today he wasn't interested in the women, just the music and the hard liquor that was poured for him. He knew there was a time Beast and Caleb used to come here. Long before they had women and families. Now when they came here it was to deal with the books in the back. No woman was allowed near them.

"Has it been a long day?" Caleb asked, coming to the counter.

"Fuck me, man. Just thinking about you brings you into existence."

"You're the nightmare, not me."

"What are you doing here?" Dwayne asked.

"Got word that you were here and decided to come and see what's wrong with my good nephew."

"Like you give a shit."

"I do give a shit. Don't mistake my lack of caring for not giving a shit."

Dwayne snorted. Of his two uncles, Caleb had been the one who'd come closer to shooting him a lot more often than Beast.

"Well, we've had that pleasant chat."

"Beast wants a word," Caleb said.

"Of course he does. Don't you get tired of being his messenger?" he asked.

Caleb laughed. "We're both his messengers.

When you go on one of your killing sprees, it's not you they fear. It's Beast's tool. Remember that."

He didn't mind.

Dwayne was known as The Nightmare, regardless of who he was working for. It helped him and instilled fear into anyone who was close.

Following Caleb out back to the office, he entered the large, luxurious room. Beast, as always, was behind the desk, looking very royal.

"You had a long day," Beast said.

Dwayne didn't say anything, staring at his uncle who was also his boss.

"I see. We're going to stick with the silent treatment."

"What do you want?"

He took a seat, aware of Caleb sitting back and Beast's focus was on him, yay.

"The Charity girl."

Dwayne hadn't told anyone about his meetings with her. "What about her?"

"We're not idiots, Dwayne. We know you've been seeing her, even though you really shouldn't."

"What I do on my down time is my concern."

"Her family is worried," Beast said. "I got a call from her dad. They were wondering if I'd be willing to find out what's wrong with her."

Caleb laughed.

Dwayne smiled. "We're not security experts."

"It got me thinking about you. You've been seeing her."

"She asked for my help, and I'm providing it."

"What are you charging her?" Beast asked.

Dwayne's jaw clenched.

"You're doing it for free?"

"I think it's safe to say that our boy may be

pussy-whipped," Caleb said. "It had to happen. There's no way he could be doing the shit he does without getting a release anywhere."

"Nothing is happening, and don't even think for a second to lecture me about her age. If my memory serves me well, both of you fell for eighteen-year-olds. Let's just say I'm following in my family's footsteps." Dwayne had no intention of falling for Charity or having anything more with her. She deserved better than a man like him. He liked being around her. She was a sweet woman. Right now, she was struggling with her life and the changes that were happening, but in time she'd be different and she'd no longer need him.

Her company helped him a great deal.

Since seeing her, he was more focused, grounded if that was even possible. His need to kill had lessened. Most nights he went out to find a reason. Now, he didn't need one. Whatever Charity was doing to his head, he needed it to stop. In his world, people preyed on the weak, and he refused to join the ranks.

"I'll stop seeing her," he said.

Even as he spoke the words, he knew the execution of it was going to be torture.

****

The following week, Charity arrived at his private warehouse to continue training, and as she checked her watch, she realized he was over two hours late. Glancing down at her cell phone, she realized she didn't have his number or any way to contact him. Whenever she needed him, he always arrived. After waiting another hour, she knew he wasn't coming.

Dwayne was a lot of things, but being this late wasn't one of them. He wasn't going to show up. Instead of driving back home, she made her way to the forest where he'd taken her not too long ago to shoot some cans.

As she parked, there was no sign of his car, but then she doubted she'd even know if he was following her unless he wanted her to know about it.

Tapping her fingers against her leg, she glanced around, taking deep breaths.

She didn't like this panic that was consuming her.

The days she spent with Dwayne helped her a lot, and right now, he was avoiding her and she was trying not to freak out. What had she done wrong? *Had* she done anything wrong?

When they parted ways last week, everything had been fine, and now, nothing.

She turned in a circle, and she couldn't see any sign of him. Heading back to her car, she glanced around, but there was nothing but the open road and the forest, along with one lonely sign letting travelers know the direction they were heading.

Again, she didn't go home but instead headed to the mall.

She got a ticket and parked. Deciding against the elevator, she took the stairs, going to the third floor of the mall first.

As she entered the large building, noise enveloped her, which she hated. She wasn't a noise person these days, but at least she wouldn't have to lie to her mother when she asked.

Grabbing a chocolate milkshake from one of the stands, she paid, and then began to gaze into the window of each shop. Some of them were designer, and even though her parents could afford it, Charity never liked to spend her money on such luxury clothing. She walked from one shop to another, trying to let the mall distract her in some way. As she rounded a corner she came to a stop when she saw a couple of her old friends.

They'd not hung out in such a long time. Being around them was difficult. In the days after being saved by Dwayne, she'd not wanted to be around anyone, and her friends didn't help.

She always thought she had some amazing friends. Demanding at times but supportive. When she withdrew into herself, they didn't help. No one stuck around to care, and the truth was, she didn't care for their company either. She was a changed person and couldn't go back to the way things were before.

Sipping on her milkshake, she passed them without giving them the time of day. Moving on ahead, she stopped outside of a lingerie shop. The mannequins looked really pretty with the outfits they wore, and she wondered what they would look like on her.

Did Dwayne like sexy lingerie?

Why do you care?

She was attracted to him.

Had been for some time now, but she simply didn't show it.

Finishing off her milkshake, she held it in her hands as she stared at the window knowing deep down she looked like a crazy person just standing there.

Someone took the milkshake out of her hands and tossed the empty carton into the trashcan.

Glancing to her side, she saw it was Dwayne.

Had he been watching her?

Averting her gaze, she stared at the shop window still.

He'd not been there for their appointment.

She wasn't going to be the first one to speak.

How could he just turn up now?

She was annoyed and happy to see him, which only confused her more.

"You're late." She gritted her teeth, hating that

she spoke first. He should have been the one to cave, not her.

"I wasn't late, because I had no intention of turning up."

She laughed. "Of course. Just keep me waiting for three hours as if I have nothing more important to do with my time. Thanks for that. Wow, I can't even believe you did that." She shook her head and moved on, not wanting to talk to him anymore.

"Did you like anything you saw in that window?"

"I liked a whole lot of things, but it doesn't matter now." She didn't pause to look at another window. Instead, she made her way toward the stairs, not expecting him to follow her. Why would he? He'd just admitted to leaving her waiting for three hours. What kind of asshole did that? Not one she wanted to speak with that was for sure.

He didn't yell her name or tell her stop, but he kept on following her. Grabbing the rail, she made her way down the stairs.

"You can keep running if you want to."

"Don't talk to me," she said.

"You're mad."

She stopped on the step and whirled around. "My time may not mean anything to you, but it does to me. You could have told me or done anything to reach out and tell me you weren't going to be there today. I mean, come on, Dwayne. I thought you were better than that."

He stepped down until he was right in front of her and she had no choice but to back up until she hit the wall. Dwayne didn't step down. He advanced toward her, and she stared at him. Was this some kind of test? Did he expect her to attack him?

She wasn't afraid of him.

Far from it.

Her body was on fire for him, with her dreams being completely devoted to him and him alone. He was messing with her head.

"That was your first mistake, thinking I'm a better person. I'm not a good person, Charity. Never have been and never claimed to be. Don't sit around waiting for me to fall for you. It's not going to happen, ever."

She knew her eyes went wide in shock and her cheeks heated. "I'm not waiting for you, Dwayne. I have no idea what you're talking about."

"You and I will never happen."

"Go fuck yourself." The moment she said the words she hated them.

His blatant rejection stung, and right now she just wanted to get to her car and head home.

"You and I, we're done. No more training. No more nothing."

"Fine with me."

She shoved him away hard and rushed away, hoping the tears would stay at bay long enough. Once inside her car, she pushed the key into the ignition, trying hard to ignore her shaking hand. Her car started, and without a backward glance, she headed on home. The journey back was completely blank. She hoped she didn't run any red lights or knock anyone down. She was tempted to pull out and drive the same path just to make sure.

Then shaking her doubts to one side, she made her way inside. It had started to rain, and she stood in the driveway looking up at the sky.

"Honey, what on earth are you doing?" her mother said.

"Nothing."

"Get inside before you catch something. You're

going to be completely frozen to the bone if you're not careful."

It may be raining, but it was warm. She wasn't about to tell her mother that though. Putting her bag on the floor near the door, she stared at her mother.

"How was your day?"

"Fine. I went to the mall. Had a shake. It was nice." *Saw Dwayne, a guy I've been crushing on but you don't need to know that. He rejected me.* "I'm going to go and get washed and changed."

"Okay, honey."

She didn't linger and made her way toward her room. Even as she took a shower, the tears didn't fall. It was only as she sat on the edge of the bed, a towel around her body and one wrapped in her hair, that she allowed the tears. Saying nasty things to him didn't help, and now she had no way of apologizing.

Dropping her head into her hands, she wondered what the hell she was going to do.

Chapter Six

The following week, Dwayne stared at his warehouse door to see the letter taped there. It had his name on the letter, and he lifted it up.

He knew instantly it had to be from Charity, and he didn't like the twisting that he got in his gut. He'd not followed or seen her since the day in the mall. She'd looked so fucking upset, as if he'd shattered her entire world with saying that he didn't want her.

She was a beautiful woman and so easy to talk to. It had been a nightmare to him saying that shit to her. Still, his uncles had backed off, so whatever he said must have worked. He didn't know how they knew everything, just that they had eyes everywhere.

"Charity dropped that off a few days ago," Beast said, suddenly appearing at his side.

Dwayne stared at his uncle, not surprised by his appearance.

"Do you have some special device that gets you around?" he asked.

"Yeah, I have a car and a pair of legs. You're becoming sloppy in observation. Not good for you, Dwayne." Beast's arms were folded, and he looked disappointed.

"I'm at the top of my game." He opened up his jacket, showing everything he carried. Six guns, two knives, and his cell phone. He never went anywhere without them.

"Someone sneaks up on you though, injects you with some drug that puts you to sleep, all that shit is useless to you."

"Do you have a point being here?" This was the first time he'd been caught being distracted in a long time. Not since he was teenager had he been this careless.

"I was worried about you."

"You don't need to be."

"Okay, reports are that you killed fifty people this week."

"What? Is my quota down?" Dwayne asked.

They were at the docks, interfering with a Carson shipment. He was bored of the complaints, so he broke in, waited until shit went down, saw what was happening with his own eyes, and dealt with the problem.

That was what he was, a problem solver.

"Quite the opposite, really. At this rate we'll need to go to another country to help with their overpopulation process."

He sighed. "You're going to complain about how I do business?"

"I worry about you."

He laughed. "Yeah, right."

"I hate to remind you of this, Dwayne. You've turned into a man that I am proud of. Your reputation rivals even mine, and I'm happy about that. Don't forget, I was the one that came for you. I was the one that stopped my brother from his abuse."

"Yeah, I remember."

"I know I was too late. That you had already suffered a great deal."

"Look, Beast, what do you want?"

"I care about you. I worry about you constantly. You think it's easy for me to know what you do, to remember everything you went through?"

"No, I don't spend my time thinking about all that, Beast."

"You don't?"

Dwayne stared at his uncle, waiting for whatever he was about to say next. "No."

"I do," Beast said. "I think about what I could have done if I'd gotten to you sooner. If I'd not taken my time to get my shit together. What he did, the person he was, he should have been stopped."

He stared at his uncle, seeing the regret in his eyes. "It wasn't your fault."

"No, and yet I think about what would have happened if I'd gotten to you sooner. You think I don't know about the time you killed when you were younger. When you saw men beating the shit out of women, out of kids. How you didn't just snap one time but a few times."

This time Dwayne didn't say anything.

"These bodies that are being uncovered, I know you buried a couple there."

"What have they found?" Dwayne asked.

"Two women have been uncovered."

"I never buried women there, Beast. I was only after men at that point. Everyone else could eat shit for all I cared."

"Just men?"

"Yeah, just men. Women … I only started killing women that betrayed us, Beast. That sold out the Carson name."

"Someone is burying or uncovering bodies, and I need you to find out who."

"What exactly do you want me to do?" Dwayne asked. "It's a prime fucking dumping ground for that shit. No one goes there unless they're some sick fuck looking for a high."

"Either someone is trying to get a message to you or send you one, or they are just using it as a dumping ground and it's completely unrelated to you. Whoever it is, I think you need to find them. Maybe compile a list of people you've pissed off."

"That will be a pretty big list."

"Just do what you have to do and get the job done."

Beast spun on his heel and started to walk away.

"What is all this shit with Charity?" Dwayne asked. "I wasn't doing her any harm."

"Did you fight for her?"

"What?"

"You heard me. All I did was pass on a message to you about Charity. You didn't put up a fight. Do you want her?" Beast asked.

"When you were with Hope, what was it like?"

"I'm still with Hope, Dwayne." Beast's arms were folded. "She became everything I thought about. In fact, I couldn't go or do anything without wondering if she was okay. She consumed every single thought that I had and then some. I wanted to know she'd be fine without me. If her day was any better. The truth was and still is, that she became my whole world overnight and I couldn't for a second imagine life without her. I wanted to kill anyone that hurt her, and for a while that meant myself. By giving her father the gun, I felt like I'd taken everything away from her."

"It's not how it works."

"I get it, but it doesn't make the guilt go away. This past week without Charity, what has it been like?"

"It has been torture. I've wanted to reach out, to make sure she's safe. I can't just ignore these feelings that she inspires inside me."

"Then don't, but be prepared to have to fight for her. Are we done with the man-to-man talk?"

"Yeah, we're done."

"Good. Come to dinner on Sunday."

He watched Beast leave first before checking the time. It would be touch and go to make it to her school, but he was willing to risk it. Glancing down at the letter in his hand, he quickly tore into it. It was just a single page, folded.

To Dwayne,

I'm sorry. I know this is lame and you probably hear this a lot, but I am sorry for everything. For saying those things. You didn't deserve them and I hope you can forgive me. Thank you for coming to save me. For helping me. It means a lot to me.

Love, Charity

Love, Charity?

The fact she'd taken the time to come and deliver a letter had to mean something. Now he just felt like an asshole for pushing her aside.

Climbing into his car, he put the letter in his jacket and turned over the ignition. He had time to make it to the high school.

This time when he finally arrived, he didn't just wait beside his car. He got out and moved toward Charity's car. There were students milling around, trying to look cool. There was a time he'd been part of all that. Leaning against cars, laughing with girls. Doing everything he could to get in their pants and to hide the darkness within his soul.

When he was with Charity, she made him forget who he was. The killing, the need for blood was nothing more than a distant, faraway memory, but still there. He could remember the look on his father's face when he got angry. When the need to hurt, to put him and his mom in their places was present in his mind. Damn, it seemed so long ago to even remember that.

He'd often have to wait, staring out of his bedroom window, watching to see which man came back home. The monster, or the man that wished to be a good man. It would always be in that vicious cycle. One, then the other, sometimes just one.

Girls passed him, pushing out their tits as if that would get his attention. They'd already shortened their skirts, and he wasn't interested. A couple of the men were trying to appear cool and calm, but he made them nervous. It reminded him a little of when Beast would come to the school over some misdemeanor. His friends would pretend that they were all cool and tight with Beast. The truth was, his uncle only ever spoke to him, and then of course there was Hope.

Pushing those thoughts aside, he watched as Charity left the school. She was staring down at her bag, shoving something inside it. She hadn't seen him yet, and for now that was a good thing. He wanted it to be a bit of a surprise. Not that he anticipated this being a *good* surprise. They hadn't parted on good terms.

When she finally flung her bag on one shoulder and looked up, the instant she clocked him, he knew. Her walking slowed, coming to a stop, and she looked a little uncomfortable. Her eyes turned to slits as she glared at him, and then she finally started walking again toward him.

He stayed still, arms folded, waiting for her.

"What are you doing here?" she asked. "I should call security." He saw how nervous she was even, not afraid, but clearly upset and not wanting to show him.

"Not going to happen."

"Why not?"

"You're pissed at me now and I get it, but deep down, you're pleased to see me."

"Wow, I had no idea your ego was so big."

"You did. Don't forget I was one of these punk asses at some point."

"Yay for you. Can you move?"

"I got your letter."

"Oh." She instantly seemed to relax. "You did. I

didn't think you'd read it."

"I did."

****

Charity felt nervous. It had been a week without seeing him, and she'd felt gutted on Saturday not going to his warehouse to train. Sticking the letter to his door had felt right to her. Of course, he'd have read the letter.

She wasn't the greatest writer of all time and didn't have a clue what to actually write, so she went for the next best thing, just to apologize for her behavior.

"What are you doing here, Dwayne?"

"I didn't want to stop your training, Charity. I was following orders. Your parents were worried, and my uncles interfered."

"So you did as you were told?"

"Yes."

"Oh, you're not much of a rebel then, are you?" she asked.

Behind her, she heard the giggle of schoolgirls and with one glance at them, she saw they were in her year, the cheerleading squad that had been drooling over him the last time he was here.

"Do you want to get out of here?" she asked.

"Yeah, I really do. Follow me."

She didn't even question it as she climbed into her car and pulled out of the parking lot. Dwayne was waiting for her, and when she was ready, he pulled out, and she followed him. Her hands felt a little clammy, and she was nervous.

Most of her nights had been filled with thoughts of him.

When he'd saved her, she'd felt this connection with him. Like he knew a little of what she went through, only it wasn't just that. She was attracted to him.

She knew he was a killer, that he took lives as

part of his job. She accepted that, and even though it wasn't something she could do herself, she knew that some lives had to be taken. There were monsters out there, and then there were the good bad guys. That's how she saw Dwayne. He was a good bad guy.

He didn't leave her to rot, nor did he take his turn.

Dwayne had been nothing but sweet to her.

Graduation was coming up. In a few short weeks she'd have to make a decision. College, or taking a gap year. With being kidnapped, she'd been reassessing her priorities, and going away to college just didn't seem like the right thing to do.

He parked near a place that used to be a well-known tourist attraction until people were found dead after being mauled by animals. It stopped being such a well-known spot. It didn't stop people from visiting though, clearly wanting to test themselves or something stupid like that. She pulled her car in beside his and climbed out. Dwayne took her hand, and without saying another word, headed into the woods. She didn't fight him and ran to keep up with his long steps.

The touch of his hand around hers felt so good. He had nice hands, large hands. They were rough, and she knew they'd feel good running down her body.

Get your head out of the gutter.

He veered off the path, moving down a creek. She caught sight of the lake up ahead. There were always a lot of rumors about the woods being haunted by the ghosts of dead men and women.

She'd never believed it, but she had also never gone looking for it either. There was no way she'd be caught here after dark.

"What are we doing here?" she asked when they finally came to a stop.

Tucking some of her hair behind her ears, she

watched him as he moved down the lake, and then stepped over.

"You coming?" he asked.

"I don't know. Are you planning on burying me alive?"

"Nope. I just want to check something."

She rolled her eyes, but her curiosity was piqued. So, she stepped across the boulders to the other side of the lake and followed him. Dwayne took her hand, and she got a little thrill, which was kind of weird, seeing as they were in a known haunted wood.

Whatever, she was never going to be normal anymore.

The world around her had been lit up, and now there was no hiding from it.

They made their way through several trees. Dwayne kicked down some thorns and other debris until he made the spot clear for her to see.

When they came to a log, he stopped and stared at the ground.

She kept her hand within his and looked around. "Are we supposed to be here?"

"No. This part of the forest is known for the wild wolves that live here."

"Do you know about the ghost stories?" she asked.

"Yeah, they're not ghosts. Just wolves. A few years ago, hikers were banned from crossing the river and abandoning the beaten path. Too many deaths."

"So, there could be ghosts."

Dwayne laughed.

She pressed herself against his side.

"Believe me, there are no ghosts."

"How do you know?"

"I came here a lot when I was your age."

"Dwayne, don't try to make out I'm a child."

"When I was eighteen years old, I killed someone," he said, turning toward her.

She was surprised by his words, but seeing the seriousness in his gaze, she knew he wasn't lying.

"Oh."

"I buried him right here."

She stepped back, looking down at the ground. "Okay, that's not creepy at all." Again, she started to think she had to see a doctor as her brain wasn't firing right. He'd just admitted to killing someone.

"I'm not a good person, Charity."

"I know that."

"You shouldn't want to be around me."

"I know that." She repeated the same words as anything else failed her. What was she supposed to say? So? I don't care?

"I get why a lot of people think you're weird."

"Hey! That's not very nice."

"I'm showing you the place that I killed someone and you're not running away."

"Is that what you're trying to do? Make me terrified so I feel I have no choice but to run? But to be scared?"

"You shouldn't be standing there as if this is a date."

"I know this is not a date. Far from it, in fact."

"Then why are you here, Charity?"

"You asked me to come with you. I followed you, and this is where you wanted to take me."

He shook his head, and she found it infuriating that he wasn't making any sense.

"I mean this with me. You should have pushed me away. Told me I was an asshole and you didn't want anything to do with me."

"I couldn't."

"Why not?"

"I don't know. I like you, okay? Being around you feels normal to me, and yeah, *that* terrifies me so damn much, you have no idea. A few months ago, I was normal. I had a bunch of friends, and going to the mall was actually a lot of fun. Now, I can't do it. Being with them, trying to fit in. There is a whole world out there, and it is terrifying. You kill people that are dangerous or whatever, and no one cares. I know I should be running. Screaming for someone to come and save me. You're the thing that nightmares are made of. I get that. I know that I shouldn't be so happy when I see you, or feel safe. You've proven to me more than once how dangerous you are. How easily you can kill me and dispose of the body. Yeah, I should be scared. Screaming for my very life, but I can't seem to start moving, Dwayne. You saved me. When no one else did. You came for me. Killed all those men and then carried me out, and I know I'm not light, okay? You still did all of that for me, and I don't know. Maybe I've got a loose wire in my brain somewhere, but it's not going to stop, okay? I like being around you, even when you are being an asshole, and I really need to stop talking right now."

She'd started to scream as she spoke, and she was panting.

"Okay then," he said.

"What?"

"I just wanted to make sure you were here because you wanted to be. Not that I had you so scared that you felt you had to be around me or risk me killing you."

"That makes absolutely no sense."

"Does to me." He shrugged.

She shook her head. There was no way she'd ever

make sense of him, not in a million years.

"Do you have more bodies?"

"Yes. I dumped quite a few here."

"Do you feel nothing?"

"I did feel nothing when I started. They were not good men."

"How do you know?"

"Because I only hurt them when I caught them doing bad things," he said, winking at her.

She rolled her eyes, wondering if getting her head tested was a good idea. She was clearly going crazy right now.

"So why come here?"

"Someone has been uncovering old bodies. The latest is a woman."

"What does that mean?"

"Either someone had the same idea as me back then, or I'm being sent a message."

"How could you be sent a message?"

"This is where I buried my first kills nearly fifteen years ago, Charity."

"And?"

"I don't know. Something seems off with all of this."

She watched him as he moved across the wood, looking at the ground.

"What are you hoping to find?"

"Answers? Clues? I don't know. Something that would help me remember."

"You don't remember killing these people?"

"I do. It's everything after that is a bit of a blur." He sighed and turned. "What are you doing after you graduate?"

"You know that's coming up?"

"Yeah, it happens to us all."

"Did you graduate?"

"Yep. With the help of my aunt, I aced that shit, why?"

"I just, it seems odd for you to even go to high school. You have this presence around you that makes you dangerous. Scary?"

"I am dangerous and scary. Doesn't mean I didn't have a normal life for a time."

"What changed, Dwayne?" she asked.

He walked back toward her. "I grew up."

"When boys grow up they want normal things. A family, a good job, sex, and you know, not to kill people."

Dwayne laughed. "I was having sex all the time. I had a job, and I happen to like killing people."

"I'm starting to think you say things to see how I react."

"It's refreshing. A lot of women would be running away scared."

"Are we talking about the kinds of women you've not saved?"

"Pretty much."

"Come back to me when they've been rescued by you." *When they've had you standing in the shower, helping wash the crazy away, then come back and talk to me.*

Dwayne took her hand, and once again they were walking back toward the beaten path.

"What college are you going to?"

"I don't know. I'm thinking a gap year is more important, seeing as I missed all the enrollment times and I don't just want to be one of these that pick one after my grades come in. You know, when they're moving people around because grades have been less than perfect. My parents are pressuring me to either do that or go to

Europe for the year. To explore."

"What do you want to do?"

"Work, take some time, think about my life, you know."

"I may be able to help you with that."

"Not get killed before I turn nineteen," she said.

"Damn, you take all the fun out of everything."

"Was that a joke? Did Dwayne just make a joke?"

"You bet I did. Also, how do you feel about meeting my uncles this Sunday?"

This made her stop and pause. As she did, Dwayne also couldn't go anywhere as she tugged on her hand.

"What?"

"Will they kill me?"

"Nope. Their wives will be present, so you'll be safe. Also, kids will be there as well. You'll be safe."

Chapter Seven

Charity may be safe, but he sure as hell wasn't. Caleb and Beast looked like they had itchy trigger fingers right now, and if it wasn't for Hope serving up the mashed potatoes, Dwayne's brains would be splattered across the dining room wall.

"Where are the kids, honey?" Hope asked.

"In the yard. Probably fighting with water," Beast said.

"Want to go and give them a call?" Faith asked, looking toward Caleb.

"Just need to talk to Dwayne about something, babe. Will you do it? I'll make it up to you later."

"Charity?" Hope asked. "Would you like to come along? We'll bring out drinks when we get back."

"It's okay, I can—okay, that wasn't a suggestion. I'll be back," she said, smiling at him. Dwayne winked at her, trying to show her that he was fine.

Beast had told him to go after her, so he didn't see what the problem was.

"What have I done now?" Dwayne asked. He may as well just get down to business, as otherwise they'd never eat.

"You brought her here?" Caleb asked.

"Beast encouraged me to go after her."

"I don't have a problem with you coming here."

"What's the problem now?" Dwayne asked, bored with Caleb's attitude.

Beast looked toward Caleb. "What *is* your problem with the girl?"

"She knows nothing about our life. For all you know, she could be feeding this crap to the cops."

"You need to learn to relax."

"Relax? He's going across the city, killing a lot of

people—"

"People that would quite happily take your family out, might I add. Faith, your kids, you want that?"

"What I don't want is to keep on cleaning up your messes."

"Uncle Caleb, you've not cleaned up one of my messes in a long time, so don't start trying to play that card with me."

"What is it with this girl?"

He glanced in the direction of the kitchen, but he didn't catch a single sight of her. "What about Faith? What was it about her?" He stared at Caleb. His uncle showed no signs of backing down. "Wasn't it just a feeling? Something that you seemed to crave, that just made you tick over and over again? I don't know what it is about Charity. I can't shake her, and I don't want to either. I like being around her. She makes me forget all the horrible shit I've done, and she doesn't care. She knows the worst of what I've done. I'm sorry I can't be this picture-perfect killer for you, Caleb. It doesn't fucking work that way. You want to argue with me about all the men I've killed, go right ahead. The last group of men I killed were heading toward your house, did you know that?" He saw Caleb visibly pale. "I got a call about a group of men wanting to take out a Carson. Going for what they considered the weakest when it came to security. I intercepted their van, took them out. There were ten of them, heavily armed, and two vans. I don't think you'd have been sitting down to this dinner with Faith getting your kids. You may hate me, Caleb, and the numbers I kill, but I do what I have to do to keep this family safe." He slammed his hand down on the table, his point finally made.

Silence fell around the table for a few minutes. Dwayne didn't have anything more to say.

"I wasn't aware," Caleb said.

"I don't go out killing people for the fun of it. I grew out of that." He turned his attention toward Beast. "I went back and checked. Where I buried bodies, none of the ground has been disturbed. Those killings are not mine."

Before they could say anything else, kids began to run in. Beast's and Caleb's youngest girls came running toward them, squealing.

He laughed and hugged them close.

Hope, Faith, and Charity walked back into the room, carrying drinks.

Charity frowned at him, clearly confused by what was going on, but he simply smiled at her to let her know that everything was okay. It would be. He knew how to deal with his uncles.

Dinner went by without a hitch. The kids made it so easy to just sit and eat lunch. They talked constantly. It was kind of strange to see both Beast and Caleb relaxed, laughing, happy.

His own father had never allowed for such noise around the table.

Food had been just another form of punishment. If Dwayne did something to annoy him, he went to bed without food. His mother would try to feed him, but if she was ever caught disobeying his father, then there was always hell to pay. He hated his early years, and watching Beast and Caleb's kids, he felt envious of them.

He knew he was never going to have kids. There was no way in hell that he'd ever risk turning into his father, and the only way to guarantee that was to never have kids. He watched Charity talk with Hope and Faith. The three women had clearly hit it off, and it was also confirmed when they exchanged numbers before heading out.

Faith and Hope both gave him a hug and told him not to be a stranger. Of course, his cousins rushed around him, hugging, or fist-bumping him before he headed out.

Charity was giving him strange looks.

"What?" he asked, staring at her across the hood of his car.

"Nothing. I just, your family is pretty awesome."

"You really think so?"

"Yeah. I mean, come on, don't you see that?"

He glanced back at the house. "Never really thought about it."

"I don't know what went on between you and your uncles, but that was pretty amazing. They care about you, and you can see that."

He saw the envy in her eyes, and he didn't like it.

"Your family cares about you. They paid a fortune for you to be rescued."

"I always wanted a brother or a sister. My parents were too busy to let that happen." She shrugged. "You're lucky."

"I don't have any brothers or sisters, Charity. That's all the family I'll have."

He opened his door, climbing inside.

"You're not going to have a family of your own?"

"No."

"You don't know that."

"I'm not going to have kids. There's no way I'd ever hurt them," he said.

"I'm starting to think you need a therapist more than I do."

"Keep your thoughts to yourself."

He started up the car, and Charity burst out laughing. "Wow, you have got one serious attitude. What is your problem?"

"I don't have a problem."

"It sounds to me like you do. You can talk to me about this. You've talked to me about killing people, so this should be a piece of cake."

He glanced over at her and sighed. "You know who I am. I've got a reputation. Throughout high school I was known as a stud, but now, I'm known as The Nightmare. That when I come visit, everyone is going to end up dead."

"Like the night you came for me."

"Yes. Killing is what I'm good at. My dad, I don't even remember what he looks like. I just remember that feeling that I always got whenever he was home. It's fear, no doubt about it, fear of what is going to happen when he finds me. Hiding was never an option, nor was fighting it. I only had to wait, and he'd be there. My worst enemy, my own personal nightmare."

"You're afraid of being that way for another human being?"

"As far as I'm concerned, the Carson blood is tainted. I won't ever run that risk of being something that my father was to me."

"Dwayne, you're not like that."

"You don't know me. Not the real me. You don't know what it's like."

"I know you're my friend," she said. "When I'm with you, there's no safer place to be than with you. I like being around you, Dwayne. No matter what your father was like, it doesn't mean you'll turn out like him. Your uncles haven't, and they were his brothers."

"Exactly. There's no guarantee their mother was faithful. I've got his blood, and no matter what I'm not going to risk it." She went to say something else, but he shook his head. "No more, please. I'm sorry for being a bastard to you. I shouldn't have said those things."

"I forgive you."

"You forgive way too easily."

She chuckled. "For you, yes." She patted his arm, and he didn't like how much he craved that contact.

****

The days passed, and before long it was graduation day. Charity saw her parents, so damn proud, smiling and clapping. Yes, she'd graduated, her grades were good, but again, she didn't know what to do with her life. She'd been looking at tourist spots across Europe, and none of them really appealed. In fact, the only time she really enjoyed anymore was the moments she shared with Dwayne. They didn't speak about his lack of desire to want a family or anything like that. That topic was off the board.

He talked about work, which was refreshing as he didn't hold back nor treat her as a child.

His honesty at times astounded her.

He was also there for prom night. She didn't go to a dance. Instead, she sat outside on the school bleachers while everyone danced the night away inside the building. Dwayne came to her as she sat outside. He sat down beside her, holding out one of those metal flasks that men seemed to love. They'd not even needed to talk.

The music had drifted out, and there on the pitch, with no one around them, he danced with her. It had been a pretty awesome prom night without any friends, just Dwayne. To most people he was a nightmare, but to her, he was so much more. In way, he was her knight with a gun. He'd come for her when no one else could or would. Singlehandedly, he'd taken on the men that kept her captive.

"I'm so proud of you honey," her mother said, drawing her in for another hug and pushing the memory of prom night to the back of her thoughts.

"Thank you."

"So, you're no longer a high school senior. What are you going to do?" Her father wrapped his arms around her shoulders, pulling her in for a hug.

"I don't know, party, get drunk, get arrested." She laughed along with her parents. She played her part well for them and for her therapist. They didn't really want to know the truth. They only wanted to know that she was moving on, that she wasn't struggling. So, she didn't show them that she struggled. Instead, she considered it an acting job, being the perfect daughter around them, and when it came to Dwayne, she was always herself. "I think I'm just going to go and think. Maybe hang out with a few friends. Is that okay?"

"Of course it is, honey." Her parents hugged her again, and she stood, watching as they left the main graduation area.

She was no longer a high school student. Glancing across the grassy area, she saw all of her friends, or the people that used to be her friends. They were having a good time, and looked happy, and she was happy for them, but that wasn't who she was.

"Look at you in your graduation garb."

She spun around, and there Dwayne stood, in the shadows, easily missed if people weren't looking.

"I didn't think you were going to come."

"Why not? This is your big day."

"Did you have a lot of fun on your day?"

"Yeah, partied a lot, had sex, drank a lot." He shrugged his shoulders. "What are your big plans?"

"I don't have any."

"Where are you parents?"

"I asked them for some time. They think I'm going to hang out with my friends."

"I can't give you a lame ass party, but I can give you some fun."

She tilted her head to the side, watching him. "You promise?"

"Hell yeah, but remove the gown. It makes you look like a clown."

She was already taking it off as she followed him across the parking lot toward his car. Climbing in, she breathed in the scent of his leather. He had one awesome car. Sitting back, she turned her head to watch him as he started up the car and pulled out of the parking lot.

"So, do we want to remember everything or not?"

"I don't care. Just make it fun."

"Fun! Got it."

He put his foot on the gas, and she let out a little squeal as the car seemed to go at a speed she wasn't used to. Winding down her window, she stuck her head out and enjoyed the freedom. Her hair was down, and she closed her eyes.

Dwayne put some music on. The sounds of rock filled the air, and she just let loose, allowing the freedom that he granted her to take over, to completely rock her entire world.

"I love this!" She threw her arms out the window and screamed.

She was no long a high school girl.

Her life was changing, as was her world.

Charity didn't know how long they were driving for, but he pulled up outside a bar.

"Am I old enough to be here?"

"You're with me. That's all they need to know." He took hold of her hand, and she felt giddy from that touch alone. Everything seemed to be hyper-sensitive at the moment. She followed his lead, and they entered the busy bar. There were several men playing pool. Some of them had leather cuts on that claimed them to be part of some club. Dwayne didn't seem to mind, and as they sat at a table, a waitress was already there to take their order.

It wasn't long before they both had a beer and a couple of shots lined up on the table. Music filtered throughout the whole of the bar. Dwayne didn't even seem to care that people were glancing at him with the odd few whispers.

"Dwayne, are you sure this is a safe place?"

"Yeah, nowhere safer. A lot of people here have their own problems, and don't worry, if a fight starts, I'm here to protect you."

"That doesn't make me feel any better." She glanced left and right, and people were watching him as if he was going to explode or something. It made a change to be sitting with someone who was the one getting pointed or laughed at. Pushing some hair back off her shoulder, she decided to ignore all the stares and focus on Dwayne.

He was, after all, the only reason she was here.

"What are we going to do?" she asked.

"We are going to play a game."

"Oh, yeah, like what?"

"Answer a question and if you've not done it, drink; if you have, don't drink," he said.

"Wait, isn't that wrong how you play it?" she asked.

"Don't care. It's how we're going to play it. Ready?"

"I have no idea."

"Okay, here goes. Have you ever pranked your parents?" he asked.

She rolled her eyes. "Which kid hasn't?" She was shocked when he downed a shot, but then she recalled him talking about his dad. "My turn?"

"Yes."

"Have you ever kissed a girl you've not met?"

She picked up a shot watching as his brow rose up.

"You're a virgin, Charity. You're going to get very drunk very quickly, so let's see if we can make this game more interesting. I'll drink a shot if I've done something that I love doing, and you drink if you'd like for it to happen to you."

Her cheeks heated. He sounded so sexy, so sensual.

"All right, go ahead."

"I love getting head."

"Wow, this is just—"

"You ever thought about it?" he asked, cutting her off.

She rolled her eyes and tipped back her shot. "Fine, sex in a public place, have you ever done it?"

He knocked back a shot. "What about you? Thought about it?"

She shook her head. "Nope, not thought about it once."

"Not even in a park or beneath the stars?"

"I'm not that romantic, Dwayne Carson."

"Huh," he said, watching her.

"What?"

"I don't know. I guess I did have you as the romantic sort."

"Not even close, buddy, not even close." She didn't have romantic ideas. Her parents were always talking about marriage and kids, and a family. She thought about it, but it wasn't something that filled her with excitement or made her ache or want it.

No, she wanted something more.

Passion.

Excitement.

Something that was completely unpredictable but so exciting as well.

This was what she loved about being with Dwayne. He made life fun, and she loved being around him.

"Have you ever thought about having sex?"

She took a deep breath and knocked back a shot. "I'm going to have to slow down, and, yes, I've thought about it. Why are you suddenly so interested in sex?"

"It has been a long day."

"It's not that late."

"I've not gone to bed yet." He knocked back two more shots and then took a long swig of beer. "Let's dance."

She didn't argue, stepping into his arms as they made their way onto the dance floor.

"What were you doing?" she asked, wanting to know why he seemed so strange.

"I had a bad night. That's all you need to know."

"Talk to me, Dwayne."

He held her a little tighter, and she closed her eyes, loving his scent even if he hadn't showered or changed.

"There's a lot of bad people in the world. Fucking animals."

She held him, too, not caring anymore about anything else but being there for him.

Chapter Eight

Dwayne inhaled the sweet scent of Charity in his arms. Last night Beast had gotten in touch asking for his help, so he'd met Caleb and Beast at the office downtown. It was a tape that had been sent to them that showed something that made him want to vomit. The abuse of children, sexual and physical. Dwayne didn't even need to be told what to do. He asked for the contact details and proceeded to hunt those bastards down.

Both of his uncles had joined him as he went after them. The children had been so scared, but with Beast and Caleb's help, along with their contacts in law enforcement, they were going to live happy lives soon.

"It's okay. You're fine. I'm here," Charity said.

Beast had wanted Dwayne to go home with him.

Dwayne had other ideas. Charity was the only one he wanted to see. When he saw the graduation ceremony, he'd wanted to go and steal her from the stage, to take her away. He'd watched her with her family, and he'd yearned for that kind of love.

It had been a long time since he'd ever wanted anything in his life, but when it came to Charity, he found himself wanting something. When she'd been standing alone, looking a little lost, he knew he had to help her. To take her away from feeling alone. He understood it, and he didn't feel she needed to change at all.

You're supposed to be making her love tonight, not hate it.

"Let's get out of here," he said.

"You're sure?"

"Yeah, this place sucks." He pulled out some dollar bills, dropping them down onto the table. It was more than they needed for the price of the shots and beer, so it wasn't a problem. Keeping hold of Charity's hand, he made his way back out to the car.

It was a crazy fucking day already, but he opened the door for her.

"Are you sure you're okay to drive? You've had a few shots."

"I'll be fine. Don't worry." He closed her door, got behind the wheel, and took off back to his apartment. The drive helped to clear his mind, and he gripped the steering wheel tighter than he needed to.

"Thank you," she said.

"What for?"

"For coming today. For taking me out and, I don't know, just not leaving me there all alone."

He didn't say anything as there wasn't anything that he could. She needed someone, and like all parents, hers failed to see the problem, or didn't want to.

Driving across town, he slowed down his speed as he made his way toward his apartment. The music was turned down low, and he breathed out a sigh of relief when he finally pulled into his parking lot.

By the time he was out of the car, Charity was already standing beside him, a slight smile on her lips.

With her hand in his, he made his way to the elevator.

"Is this where you brought me that night?" she asked, referring to the night he saved her.

"Yes."

"Oh."

"You don't remember?"

"Vaguely. I've wondered where you've lived for a few months now."

He chuckled. "Have I got a little stalker now?"

"When I'm with you, I like that you're not always telling me about how I should be or what I should be doing. There's no pretending with you, and I love that."

"Your parents love you, Charity."

"I know they do. They just want everything to be normal, and that's fine. I don't feel normal anymore."

"You are to me." The elevator doors opened, and he made his way toward his apartment. Opening the door, he allowed her to enter, watching as she pulled her hand away, holding it close to her chest.

Over the past few weeks, he'd found himself getting more curious about her. He expected his honesty to push her away, but nothing he said seemed to do that. She was still here, and nothing seemed to scare her. She saw every single part of him, the good and bad, and still, she was here.

Closing the door, he followed her inside, going to his kitchen.

"Are you hungry?" he asked.

"A little."

"I can cook you something, pasta maybe, or we can order in." He held up the Chinese menu.

"I could eat Chinese."

He grabbed the cell phone and handed her the menu. "Order what you want. Do you want a beer?"

"Sure."

He pulled two beers out of the fridge as she ordered.

"What do you want?"

"Tell them it's for Dwayne, and they know what I like." He winked at her and made his way toward the sofa. Collapsing on the soft throw, he rested his head back and closed his eyes. He loved the calmness that came over him as he listened to Charity while she finished the order. She came into the room, and he opened his eyes, watching her. Her gaze was on his body, and he knew exactly what was going on in her head.

"You want to see me naked?" he asked.

Her cheeks went red as her eyes finally looked at him.

"You totally need to drink, you dirty woman."

"Stop it."

She moved past him, but he caught her wrist and pulled her down into his lap. The way she landed, her hand went to his stomach, and he loved it when she touched him. Staring into her eyes, he gripped her full hip. She'd started to put back some of the weight that she'd lost. He liked that. It meant she was no longer scared or fearing for her life.

"What are you doing?"

"Why don't you tell me what you want?" he said.

She licked her lips, and he couldn't help but moan as her tongue peeked out. He wanted to taste her.

Running his hand up her back, he couldn't think of a single reason why he shouldn't touch her. He'd been wanting to do this for some time, to feel her against him.

"Dwayne?"

"Tell me to stop, Charity. Tell me to fucking stop."

She didn't say a thing as he gripped the back of her head and tugged her down. The moment her lips touched his, Dwayne felt like he'd finally found heaven. She was so soft, and she gasped, giving him access as he plunged his tongue into her mouth. Her hands gripped his shoulders.

Part of him expected her to push him away, but suddenly, she was moving closer, straddling his waist.

Putting his beer down, he held her hips as her pussy rode his cock, her fingers sinking into his hair as he held her close, refusing to back down.

Wrapping her blonde hair around his fist, he pulled her head back and started to kiss her neck.

Sucking on the pulse, he nipped and kissed down to her chest. The shirt she wore was in the way. Running his hands down her back to her ribs, he slowly slid up to cup her tits, holding them as if they were a gift to be presented to him.

She moaned, especially when he took her first beaded nipple into his mouth. Her bra and shirt were in the way, but he was too impatient to wait to get her naked.

"Oh, yes," she said, moaning as she did.

He moved onto the next nipple, doing the same to her other as he ran his hands down her body to her ass.

She cupped his face and tilted his head back, kissing him.

He felt the passion and the need inside her.

Pulling her shirt out of her jeans, he was about to pull it over her head when the buzz of his apartment door echoed through the room. They were both panting but not loud enough to ignore.

"Food is here," he said.

"I don't care about food."

Her stomach growled, and he chuckled.

"I'll feed you first." He patted her ass, and she crawled off his lap.

Dwayne didn't have any intention of kissing her, but once it had started, there was no way of stopping.

His dick was so hard it was almost impossible for him to move, but first he had to feed her, and then he'd see what would happen.

****

Charity's lips tingled from Dwayne's kiss. She watched him leave the room, and she glanced down, seeing the wet marks of his mouth against her breasts. When he'd pulled her down into his lap, she hadn't known what to do.

Over the past few weeks, it had been getting harder to ignore these feelings that he inspired inside her. She liked him a lot and was attracted to him. That was never going to change. She knew that.

There were nights she lay awake trying to convince herself that she shouldn't be attracted to him, or even want him.

No matter what logic she tried to think about or talk about, she couldn't help the way she felt.

The scents of Chinese food filled the air, and her mouth watered. She couldn't believe her stomach growled at her when she'd been more interested in what his hands were doing.

"Hungry?"

"Yes."

She was a lot hungrier for his touch, but she didn't say so. Sipping at her beer, she watched as he opened up cartons of food and handed her one with chopsticks. Inside the first were some prawn toasts. She didn't even need the dipping sauce.

Taking a bite, she closed her eyes at the flavor, which was mouthwatering. Neither of them spoke as they started to enjoy their food. She couldn't help but glance down at his lap and saw his cock was rock-hard, pressing against the front of his pants.

"You're a little obsessed with my cock, baby," he said.

She gasped with some food in her mouth and started to cough, choking on it. Putting a hand in front of her face, she coughed as Dwayne rubbed her back.

"You okay?"

"Yes, yes, I'm fine." Her cheeks were on fire. There was no way she could act all seductive after that.

"I never had a woman die from embarrassment."

"Don't you have any filter at all?"

"Not with you, it would seem."

"You talk about killing people as if it was a sport."

"It is to me, Charity." Silence fell between them, and she moved a few of the toasts around in the carton. The feel of his lips was still clear in her mind, and she also thought about his hands. He'd never hurt her. "I'm not going to pretend for you. I'm not a good guy. I saved you, yes, but that doesn't make me a good man. You need to understand that."

"I know."

"You need someone better."

She stared past his shoulder, hating how desperate she sounded. "There's no one else that I want. Don't try and tell me something different. I know what you are, what you do, and I still don't care. Does that make me a bad person?"

"There's not a bad bone in your body."

She smiled. "Then don't try and be like my parents, telling me what you think I want or need." She put down the carton of food she was holding and moved to straddle his lap. Her hands were shaking a little bit. She'd never been this forward with anyone in her life. No heavy petting, no kissing, nothing. Staring into Dwayne's eyes, she felt ... empowered. His hands went to her ass, and just from that touch alone, she felt on fire.

Today she had graduated, and everything felt different to her.

Nothing that she could make sense of.

She'd jumped through everyone else's hurdles, and now all that was left was her and Dwayne, sitting in his apartment, with her straddling his lap. She felt the hard ridge of his erection pressing against her core, and she bit her lip to try to contain the moan.

"Let it out, Charity. Whenever you're with me, I

want to hear you scream, to yell, to give me everything that you've got."

She moaned.

It was hard, guttural, but she didn't care.

Dwayne squeezed her ass just a little tighter, and she closed her eyes, basking in his touch. His hands moved, stroking over her, pulling her against him, gripping her tightly, teasing and playing at the same time.

"Kiss me, Charity."

She cupped his face and slammed her lips down on his. One of his hands gripped the back of her head, holding her in place, and she was addicted. Grasping his shoulders, she didn't want to let go, not once.

His hands went from her ass and her head, to all over, touching, stroking, and she couldn't handle it anymore. She needed him naked. Tugging his shirt off, she found him in a white vest and frowned. When she tried to remove that, he grabbed her hands, and suddenly she was on her back. Her legs wrapped around his waist as she held her wrists tightly, pulling them up above her head. She couldn't move, not that she wanted to, far from it.

"How about I show you some attention?"

With both of her hands banded together in the grip of one of his, she stared up into his eyes, seeing the deadly intent there. She licked her lips. He pulled her shirt off, and it felt good to no longer be trapped beneath the fabric. Now, all that kept her covered was her jeans and a lacy bra.

"I like this. It's pretty, but it doesn't cover up those pretty pink nipples." His finger traced across one of the hard buds. "Look at that, beautiful. You want me, don't you?"

"Yes."

"Is your pussy wet for me?"

She loved his dirty talk, and she nodded.

"Good, because that's how I want you, Charity. You want me to be the first guy to fuck you, I will. I'll show you things some men in the world couldn't even begin to do."

"Like what?" she asked.

"First, make you come, screaming my name. Keep your hands above your head."

She shouldn't follow his orders, but they were too tempting, too hot, too sexy, not to. With her hands above her head, she watched him, moaning and gasping as he began to kiss down her neck, sucking at her pulse before moving down. The bra had a catch in the front, and once he flicked it, her body seemed to have a mind of its own. All she wanted was to feel his touch, beg for him.

His lips covered one nipple, while at the same time he worked the button of her jeans and began to pull them down. His nails dug into her flesh, shocking her by the dual feel as he completely consumed her.

She helped him to kick off her jeans, all the time keeping her hands above her head. Charity liked his control, relished it, was desperate for it, and as he spread her legs wide, pulling away from her nipple to stare down at her body, she didn't care. She didn't care that she had cellulite on her legs, or her stomach rolled up, showing off her extra pounds. This was her, and from the look in his eye, he wanted her just as much as she did him.

He pressed his palm between her thighs, and she cried out.

"Do you know how fucking beautiful it is to know that no other man has ever touched you here? That you've not had another dick inside you? I shouldn't care. Before you, I wasn't a monk. I took what I wanted and women were willing to give me everything, but now,

now I fucking need you."

"Has there been anyone else?"

"No."

"Have you been tempted?"

"No. It's like you've put a fucking curse on my dick, and now I can't stand the thought of being with anyone else." He tugged the material from her pussy, and his finger touched her slit.

One stroke over her clit had her gasping, arching up, shocked by the sudden pleasure of his touch.

"Wow, you get like that from just my finger, wait until you get my mouth on you."

He withdrew his finger and tugged the lingerie from her body, throwing it to the ground. While he still wore a white vest and a pair of pants, she was completely naked, at his mercy.

She relished it more than anything else in the world.

Putting her hands back over her head, she smiled up at him.

"Well, Dwayne, you've got me exactly where you want me. Now tell me what you're going to do with me."

She wanted him so badly.

She'd do whatever he asked, just so long as he never stopped looking at her like she was the only woman in the world.

Chapter Nine

Charity lay beneath him like a sacrifice. A very beautiful, sweet, sexy, curvy sacrifice, and one that he was finding it hard to ignore. Damn, he wanted her so badly. His cock pressed against his pants, and it was taking every bit of restraint not to fuck her, take what he wanted, and rut away.

He didn't want to make this awful for her.

When Charity thought of this moment, the night she lost her virginity, he wanted it to be the most beautiful and amazing time of her life. Something precious that he could give to this woman that had entered his life during a time of chaos and pain.

Taking her lips, he stroked his tongue across the plump flesh. She yielded to his kiss, opening up, and he took what she gave, sliding his tongue inside, tasting her, loving every second of it.

She kissed him back with a passion that quite simply took his breath away. He couldn't get enough of her.

Breaking from the kiss was hard, but he wanted every inch of her, to taste her sweet pussy, to relish in being the only man between her thighs. He felt fucking possessed, desperate, aching to be the only man with her.

You could keep her as your own.

He wanted to.

He really fucking wanted to.

Each second was like a yearning deep inside him for more, a hunger that kept possessing him, begging him to take her, to make her want no one else but him.

Sucking on her neck, nipping, kissing, working his way down to her large tits, he pressed them together. Flicking each beaded nipple with his tongue, he heard her gasp. Her legs opened even wider, her pussy wanting him next.

Only when he was ready would he touch her, taste her, know every single inch of her perfect body.

Once he'd given each nipple equal attention, licking the hard tips, biting them, soothing out the pain with a nice, hard suck, he kissed down her body. He didn't care how much time had gone by. All he cared about was having her pussy soaking wet.

When he finally put his cock within her, she was going to hurt. It would be painful, but so long as she was prepared for him, that pain wouldn't last, not even for a moment.

Kissing down her body, he dipped his tongue into her belly button, hearing her giggle. He smiled against her flesh, teasing her even more as he moved down. His face was above her pussy.

She had a small smattering of curls that covered her sex. He didn't mind. To him that showcased how womanly she was.

When he opened the lips of her pussy, her clit was swollen, peeking out of its hood, wanting his mouth. She was already wet, her cream glistening.

The scent of sex was heavy in the air, and he just couldn't wait to have a taste. Using the tip of his tongue, he teased across her clit, hearing her sudden gasp. Out of the corner of his eye, he saw her grip the sofa, her knuckles white.

"Am I hurting you?" he asked.

"No."

He smiled. "Can't stand it?"

"I need more."

So, he gave her more. Not holding back, he pressed his tongue against her clit, and she cried out, arching up, her pelvis shooting off the sofa. He gripped her hips, holding her down, keeping her in place as he teased her clit.

"Oh, my," she said.

He didn't even allow himself the chance to tease her entrance. Only his dick would take care of her virginity. Sucking on the bud, he used his teeth to create just a little pain, which he noticed that she loved.

The pain was almost too much for her, but yet not enough. She was always screaming for more, desperate for whatever he could give her. Soon he'd tease her pussy and her little asshole, get them both ready to one day take him.

Her pussy was going to take him tonight, but her asshole was going to have to wait. She'd need priming for that.

Teasing her nub, he saw the change in her body, the way her stomach quivered, the way she wriggled, and her breaths grew deeper, more erratic. He kept her in place, and when she came, it was a beautiful sound.

His name echoed off the walls, and still he held her in place as pleasure consumed her. He continued to lick her pussy until he knew she couldn't handle anymore. Her entire body was shaking, the intense climax going to the next level where she couldn't bear to be touched. He brought her down slowly. She was so wet.

He wouldn't forget this moment. The way she looked at him was if he was a god. He liked that. Considering most people looked at him with fear, to Charity he was anything but frightening.

There was no death between them, no destruction or pain.

Only pleasure.

He intended to keep it that way.

"How are you feeling?" he asked.

"That was amazing."

He smiled.

"I'll take that as a compliment."

"Is it always like that?"

"Only if the man, or yourself, know what you're doing." He took her hand, pressing it between her thighs. "There's nothing to stop you from doing that. Touching yourself. One day, I'd love to see you do it."

Even now, just with her fingers on her pussy, he found the view highly arousing. His cock pressed against the front of his pants, the tip already slick. Pre-cum was probably already leaking out. It had been a long time since he'd been with anyone. He wanted Charity, had denied himself for so long, and now he wanted his fill.

"You'd like to watch me do what you do?"

"Yeah, I can do the same."

"I'd like that."

He'd like that just as much.

There was no way he was going to make her first time be on this sofa. He was many things, but not a fucking animal, not when it came to Charity. As he picked her up in his arms, she released a little squeal, which he ignored, and carried her to his bedroom.

"You shouldn't do that. I'm too heavy."

"As far as I'm concerned, you're just right."

He lowered her to the bed, and the sight took his breath away. She'd been in one of his beds before, but not like this.

Opening the belt of his pants, he slowly lowered them. He was tempted to keep his vest on, but he knew she'd ask questions. Charity being the curious woman that she was would want to know everything, and he wasn't prepared to talk tonight.

Pulling his clothes off, he stared down at her, wrapping his fingers around his cock, feeling how hard he was. He wanted to be inside her so desperately.

Moving toward his drawer beside his bed, he pulled it open and grabbed a condom out from inside. Tearing into the foil, he pulled out the condom and rolled it over his dick. There were not going to be any consequences tonight, none at all.

He climbed onto the bed and crawled between her legs. Taking her hands, he locked them together.

"You can stop this at any time."

"Why would I want to do that?"

"I'm about to take something precious from you, Charity."

"You're not taking it, Dwayne. I'm giving it to you."

When Beast came to get him, he'd felt he'd been offered a gift, a second chance. When Caleb offered to help him, well, more like threatened, he knew he'd found his calling. With Charity giving him this gift, offering herself to him, it was like he'd finally found heaven and he'd been living in hell until this very moment.

Dropping his lips, he claimed her mouth, consuming her kiss. She moaned, wrapping her arms around his neck, holding him close, and he didn't want to let go. Her fingers tightened around his, and he released her hands to hold her. Running one hand down her body, he cupped her leg, drawing it up over his hip, pressing his against her naked core. She felt so fucking good in his arms, and he didn't want to ever let her go.

It was moments like these that scared him.

Never had he wanted anything to belong to him and him alone.

Charity wasn't a thing. She was a person.

A person he cared so fucking much about, and the thought of never being with her, not seeing her, it tore him up inside. She was his reason for breathing, for fighting.

Breaking from the kiss, he reached between their bodies, grabbing his cock. Placing the head at her slit, he bumped her clit a couple of times before moving down to her entrance.

She panted, moaned, whimpered, begged, and he loved every single word.

Staring into her eyes, he waited, to be sure that she wanted this. Only when he saw the desire, the need in her eyes, did he thrust forward, filling her pussy, breaking through the thin barrier of her virginity.

He saw the pain, and he hated it more than anything else. She released a little whimper, and he wanted to fucking hurt something, but he didn't. With his dick balls deep inside her, he took hold of her hands, wrapping them around his body as he held her close.

"It hurts. I didn't expect it to hurt this much."

"I know. I'm sorry, baby." He'd heard of the first time being painful, and he hoped he'd been wrong, but the look in her eyes, it cut a part of him just seeing that. He didn't want to hurt her. "If I could take the pain from you, I would. I don't want you to hurt at all."

"It's fine. This is supposed to happen." Her hands stroked up and down his back. "It's not really that bad."

"Would you like me to move?"

She chuckled. Even with tears in her eyes, she seemed to find the will to smile.

This woman, she was something else as far as he was concerned.

"Yes."

Slowly pulling out of her pussy, he watched her eyes, knowing it stung just a little from her expression, and he hated it. He hated seeing that look in her eye. With just the tip inside her, he waited, and she nodded at him to keep going.

Hurting her was the worst feeling in the world, so

when he thrust back inside, going as deep as he could go, and she moaned, the sound was like a winning bell in his mind.

Taking possession of her lips, he stayed inside her, not wanting to move, but the moment she started to wriggle, trying to get him to do something, he lost all the fight. Pulling out of her tight heat, he slowly rocked back and forth, taking his time, making love to her, making it good for her just as it was for him.

She moaned, her nails scoring his back, and he groaned out, wanting more of her. She was so beautiful, so open, so amazing. He felt completely possessed to have her.

"Please, Dwayne, I need more."

Hearing her beg like that, he gave her exactly what she wanted, making love to her, driving harder and deeper. There would be a time for fucking, but that wasn't tonight. This was all about her, and he wanted her to love every single second of what he was doing to her.

Holding her down, he thrust in deep, taking every single part of her, bringing her close to orgasm, and when he finally pushed her over the edge, she let out a cry of his name. Only then did he follow her with his own release, filling the condom, claiming her as his own.

****

The following morning, Charity opened her eyes and was a little confused by where she was. Turning her head, she felt the change within her body, the rawness between her thighs from finally having sex last night with Dwayne.

Dwayne!

She turned her head, and he lay on his side, his back facing her. The light filtering in from the curtain shocked her as she saw what he'd been trying to hide last night. There was no hiding in the cold light of the morning, nor keeping anything a secret.

The scars were all faint, but they were there. Signs of a boy that had been whipped, beaten, his skin broken and marred, only to be fixed together by alcohol maybe. These scars didn't show the repair of love but of someone who clearly didn't give a fuck what they were doing.

She recalled his confession about his father, how he would hit him, hurt him. This though, this was something else, and it sickened her to think of the kind of abuse he must have gone through when he was younger.

The scars were so faint that anyone seeing them from a distance wouldn't be able to make them out. She wanted to touch them, but she didn't want to wake him up. This was what he'd been hiding from her last night. The first night he'd rescued her all those months ago, she wouldn't have even noticed these, so taken by her own fear of what had happened to her that nothing else would have even registered in her mind.

Did he mean for her to see them?

Had he fallen asleep not long after he'd pulled out of her, like she had?

She had so many questions, but not one slipped from her lips.

All she wanted to do was hold him, to let him know everything would be okay. That he wasn't alone anymore.

She wanted to find his dead father and kill him all over again. The thought of anyone hurting Dwayne, it filled her with so much hate that she wanted to spit.

"You're trembling," Dwayne said, shocking her. "Are you okay?"

"I'm fine."

He rolled over, and she watched him sigh. "They're just scars."

"I … I don't care about them being on you. Well, I do care, but I want to hurt whoever did them, Dwayne."

"You're never going to get to do that, so don't even waste a moment thinking about it."

"Your dad did that."

"It was all part of his lessons."

"Why didn't you show me them last night?"

"It was your first time. I didn't for a second want those scars, my old man, to be even a memory for you. They're nothing."

"He was a monster."

"I'm not going to deny that, but there's nothing you can do. Stop thinking about them."

"You were a little boy. I saw the pictures of you in Beast's home, Dwayne. He had you from a young age, and even before then, your dad was beating you."

"It was all part of his training, Charity. Don't worry about it."

"You shouldn't have gone through something like that."

"I know, but you don't have to worry about it. The scars don't hurt me." He cupped her cheek, his thumb stroking back and forth. "What about you? How are you feeling?"

"I don't care about me."

She cupped his face, holding him between her hands, and pressed a hard kiss to his lips. She wanted him to know what no matter what he was loved, and she would do everything to take care of him. He deserved happiness, love, someone to always have his back.

He pressed his head against hers. "*I* care about you. How do you feel?"

"I'm fine." She really was. A few little aches were nothing.

"Don't lie to me."

"Okay, it's a little achy, but nothing to worry about."

He ran his thumb across her lip. "You were so tired last night that I didn't even run you a bath. It should have helped with the pain."

"So, it's really not that bad."

"Still, it's my job to take care of you. Stay here."

"Your job. I don't like the sound of that."

He chuckled. "You know what I mean. Stop being a pain in the ass." He winked at her.

"I like being a pain." She watched him walk toward the bathroom. "I mean it, Dwayne."

"Mean what?"

"I'd have killed him for hurting you. I want to hurt him."

"Nothing can be done, but the thought means a lot to me."

She smiled and watched him leave. He had a really nice ass, and he'd not put on any sweatpants to cover himself. She liked that. Lying down on the bed, she stared up at the ceiling, completely blown away by the fact she was here, on his bed, no longer a virgin. After everything that had happened to her, this had overtaken the night she'd met him as the best night of her life.

When he saved her, she always remembered that moment with happiness. He'd protected her, and now he'd made love to her.

For a long time, Charity didn't want to think about her feelings or what it all meant. It couldn't mean anything, not really. He was older than she was, not that she cared about the age difference. Number had no meaning to her, not when it came to Dwayne.

Most of her nights and days were filled with thoughts of him, her curiosity, her concern about what he was doing. She wasn't a fool. She knew what he did on a daily basis, but the thought of never seeing him again filled her with dread.

"Come on," he said, coming back in moments later, still completely naked and looking sexy as ever. She couldn't believe how confident he was, his flaccid cock hanging between his legs, not a care in the world. There was no fighting it for her. She was completely addicted to him, needing more of him with every single second that passed.

Climbing off the bed, she walked toward him, trying to cover her nakedness. When she stood before him, he took hold of her wrists, holding them a little away from her body.

"You don't need to hide from me, Charity." He leaned in close and kissed each nipple, then her stomach, before moving down to between her thighs. "Never hide from me. I like every single inch of you and then more, got it?"

"Yes."

She was thinking of him doing something a lot dirtier than just kissing her.

Get your head out of the gutter.

"I know what you want. I can see it in your eyes, and don't worry, after you rest, I'll be making sure every single one of those fantasies come true." He winked at her, and she couldn't help but think of something highly sexual.

What was it that Dwayne did to her?

Wave a magic wand?

Pushing those thoughts aside, she entered the bathroom and saw he'd lit a couple of candles, and the water in the bath was filled with bubbles. She was overcome with so much emotion that she couldn't even think straight. In a few short moments, he'd done something so incredibly romantic.

He took her hand and helped her into the bath.

Easing back, she closed her eyes, basking in the feel of the water, which soothed her aching muscles.

"Good?"

"Very good."

"How did you know?"

"I had a hunch."

He sat on the edge of the bath, looking down at her. She liked it when she was his primary focus.

"What are your plans this summer?"

"I don't have any. Apart from trying to figure out what the hell to do with my life, that is." She tilted her head to the side. "Do you have any plans?"

"How would you feel about moving in? I know it's quite sudden, but it'll give you a chance to figure out what you want to do. What you want to be? No pressure."

She couldn't believe he was asking her that. Her parents were always on her case so that at times she felt she couldn't breathe.

"Yes."

"You don't want to think about it?"

"I don't need to think about it. Yes, yes, yes." She jumped out of the bath and hugged him tightly. "Thank you."

"Don't thank me yet. You may hate living with me."

She doubted that for even a second she would have regrets. It was Dwayne, the man she'd been wanting for a long time. There's no way in hell that she'd ever hate living with him.

Chapter Ten

One week later

"What exactly are you looking for?" Beast asked.

Dwayne looked up from Beast's office to see his uncle leaning against the doorframe. He'd snuck in early so that he could get started on what Williams, the police informant they paid, had for him. "I'm looking at most of the unsolved cases or the guys that were caught when I was eighteen."

"At seven in the morning?"

"I started around four, why? I didn't wake anyone."

"Yeah, and if you did, I would have blown your fucking head off." Beast entered the room. "Why unsolved cases and assholes that were caught?" He lifted up one file, glancing through it.

"The bodies that you brought to my attention. The women. I didn't kill women. I was attempting to save them with my mission."

"Mission?"

"You can mock it all you want, but it meant something to me."

"I'm not mocking it. Just seems strange to call it a mission."

"It's exactly what it was."

"Fine. So, this *mission*, what were you hoping to achieve going through hundreds of files?"

"To see if someone rang a bell. If I knew someone. Nothing matches."

"Someone clearly thinks like you."

"It's not hard to see a forest that is completely off-limits to everyone, and think, oh, this is a good place to bury a body. I'm only doing this because you two can't."

"In our world, if you don't think about everything and all the consequences of what you do, it gets you killed. Gets people you love killed. Don't take that chance, Dwayne. Anything you see, anything that gives you even a smidgen of doubt, you double-check, triple-check, and make sure you wipe it out of your mind before moving on. Otherwise, people you love could end up dead."

"Got it." He glanced down at the file in his hands. The man had a shaved head, was known for racial attacks, and was still locked in prison. Just seeing the face of the man made Dwayne sick to his stomach.

There was a time he'd have been afraid, scared, and allow that fear to manifest. Not anymore. *He* was the thing that people had nightmares about.

"I heard Charity moved in."

"Can't anyone have a secret from you?" Dwayne asked, opening another file.

"She's young."

"Don't even get me started on her age. Look at Hope. She should have been dating someone like me, not you."

"Still, she wouldn't have gone for your lame ass. Moving in is a big step."

"I know."

"You like her?" Beast asked.

Seeing as his uncle was clearly going to stick around and have this conversation, Dwayne closed the file and focused on his pain in the ass. "Why are you suddenly interested in my love life?"

"You're getting older. Some men, they have certain needs."

"If you're talking about sex, don't go there. I don't need to know."

"I'm talking about settling down, Dwayne. Not

all of us think with our head in the trash. Sex is great, but grow past that," Beast said.

Rolling his eyes, he stared at Beast. The man was huge, scary, and a force to be reckoned with. When he'd come to take him away from his father, Dwayne had considered him Santa Claus, taking him away from the nightmare that had become his life.

"I love her," Dwayne said.

He'd never said that to anyone else before. Staring at his uncle, he saw that he'd surprised him.

"You love her?"

"Yeah, I do."

He opened the file again, about to get back to work.

"Whoa, whoa, whoa, you can't just drop something like that and pretend nothing has changed."

"Nothing has changed."

"Dwayne, you've just said that you love Charity and you don't think that's a big deal?"

"No."

"Does she know?"

"Why do I feel like we're attempting to gossip or something?"

"Dwayne, I know we've not always seen eye to eye, but I do love you."

"I know that." Dwayne stared at his uncle, not really sure what to say to make him seem less enthusiastic. "She's different. I don't want to live without her."

Being inside her, claiming her virginity, he felt … everything with her. She'd seen his scars, knew his story, and she hadn't run away.

"Can we not talk about this right now? I don't want you dropping by and making a big deal of this when there doesn't need to be."

"Okay, but if I ask Hope and Faith, they'd both say loving a woman was a big deal."

"Which is why you're never going to tell them, or Caleb. He can't keep a secret for anyone," he said, looking back at the files. "What if this is completely unrelated?"

"Charity moving in?"

"We're assuming that this guy knew me, but he couldn't have known me. These are all fresh bodies. This has nothing to do with me, so why bring me into this?" Dwayne asked.

"Dwayne, if he keeps dumping bodies near where you put yours, that can come back to you. There's only so much we can do to keep you safe. This guy has to be stopped. Do you have any leads yet on who it could be?" Beast asked.

Dwayne shook his head. "I don't know. Your informant was the one to tell us about them. He's kept a lot of details to himself." He glanced down at his watch. "I need to stop for coffee."

"Dwayne, be careful," Beast said. "Whoever this guy is, he could be dangerous."

He couldn't help but laugh. "You know what they call me, right?"

"I know what they call you. I also know what they call me, and it doesn't make us invincible. We can still take a bullet, a knife, we can still die. Don't let your reputation go to your head. Always remember, someone will happily take your place and throw you off that throne that you've built for yourself."

Dwayne took the warning. Over the years he'd been many things, but stupid wasn't one of them. His reputation had been something other people had made around him, not something that he'd willingly done himself.

"Dwayne," Hope said, surprising him that she was on the stairs in the hallway. He'd always liked her, not sexually either. She'd been a weirdo, but a nice one, when they were at school.

"What's up, Hope?"

She glanced toward the office, and he nodded. "You heard."

"You weren't exactly being quiet."

"I'll remember to keep my voice down next time."

"I'm sorry. I shouldn't have been listening."

"It's completely fine. Just don't tell anyone, okay? I like to keep my secrets a little while longer."

"I won't say anything. She's nice though, sweet. You're good for her."

"Thank you."

He didn't linger. He walked out to his car, climbed inside, and took off toward his apartment. He made a pit stop at a coffee shop that he loved, grabbing some cinnamon buns and coffee before heading back home.

Entering their apartment, he heard Charity in the kitchen.

Putting the baked goods and coffee onto the counter, he moved up behind her, pulling her against him for a hug.

"You're awake," he said.

She chuckled. "Well, yeah, I'm not sleepwalking, silly. I was wondering where you were."

"Sorry, I had a couple of errands to run, but I stopped off, got us a few things." He pointed at the coffee and buns. "It's to make up for not being here this morning."

She cupped his face and kissed him hard. "You're an angel."

Sitting opposite her at the kitchen counter, he admired her curves in his long shirt. It looked good on her.

He liked seeing her in clothes he owned. Her blonde hair tumbled around her, and her blue eyes seemed to sparkle as she licked the frosting off her fingers.

"This is so good."

"How are you settling in?" he asked.

"I put my clothes away in your closet. I hope that's okay." She was nibbling her lip, looking a little nervous.

Her parents hadn't wanted her to move in with him. He'd sat while they tried to encourage their daughter to stay with them. Her father asked him if he was going to argue, and he shook his head, telling them that as far as he was concerned it was Charity's decision. When they saw that he wasn't forcing their daughter to do anything she didn't want, it seemed to help them relax with her moving out. Of course, they hated that she'd moved in with a man so much older than she was, but parents couldn't have everything they wanted. Not on his watch.

Taking a bite of his cinnamon bun, he noticed a couple of buttons of her shirt had slipped open, showing a tempting curve of her breast. He didn't look away. Every time she moved, the shirt would either open or close, offering him more temptation or shutting him out. Since he'd taken her virginity, he'd not made love to her again. He'd not wanted her to ache when they were together again. Also, work and moving her into his apartment had gotten in the way.

"Take off the shirt," he said.

Her chest was flushed, and her eyes looked so beautiful as her cheeks went red. She didn't deny him though. She opened the buttons, sliding each one through the tiny slit, spreading the shirt wide as she dropped it from her arms, her tits on glorious display. His cock hardened instantly. He couldn't deny himself a taste of her for another second. He needed her more than he had ever wanted anything else in his life.

There would be no holding back, not now, not ever again.

Charity belonged to him, and he was going to treasure her.

****

Finally!

Charity had been hoping for more, for Dwayne to take her, to fuck her, to do all the wicked, wonderful things she'd read about in books, and for the past week, it was like they were more friends than anything else. They slept in the same bed, but every time he left early, she was awake. She didn't want to beg him or anything or appear desperate.

"I love your tits," he said. "Lean back a bit in your chair, push them out."

Putting her hands behind her, she thrust her chest out, watching him as his gaze moved down her body. She loved his eyes on her, the way he seemed to eat her up just by looking.

"Have you been thinking about me?" he asked.

"Yes."

"You want me inside you?"

"Yes."

"Touch yourself, Charity. Show me how wet you are?"

It felt so natural to reach between her thighs, to lift her legs up so that she could spread herself wide for him. Sliding a finger between her slit, she stared at him, watching him, unable to look away as she started to tease herself.

Stroking her clit, she stared at him. He sat back in his chair, and he could clearly see her as he removed his jacket, then his shirt, before moving around the counter so that he stood in front of her. She'd pushed away from the counter so that he'd been able to see.

"Put your fingers inside your pussy. Two of them."

Plunging two fingers inside herself, she gasped, especially as Dwayne reached out, teasing her clit as she did so.

"Feel good?" he asked.

"Yes."

"Good. It's going to get even better. I want to taste you."

Pulling her fingers out of her pussy, she held them up for him to take. With his other hand, he gripped her wrist and licked her fingers. At the same time, he kept on teasing her clit, stroking her, driving her crazy with need, and she did not want him to stop, not for a single second.

"I want you, Charity. I want you sliding on my cock, and I want to watch you take me."

"I want that too."

He stepped away from her, and she watched him remove the last of his clothing until he stood before her completely naked. His cock was out, long, thick, with pre-cum leaking out of the head.

Before he removed his pants, he'd gotten a condom, and now he tore into it, sliding it over his dick. She was surprised it fit, his cock seemed so big.

He took hold of her hand, and he moved her toward the dinner table. He sat down in one of the chairs that didn't have any arms.

"I want you to sit on my cock. Slowly, I want to

watch you take me."

She licked her lips and nodded her head, so turned on by what he wanted. As she straddled his thighs, Dwayne held his cock, and she moved so that her pussy was aligned to the tip.

"Look at me when you do."

Gripping his shoulders, she watched him, unable to look away as she slowly sank down on his length. The width of him, everything, took her breath away as she took him into her body.

"That is so fucking hot."

His gaze kept moving from her eyes to between her thighs, watching as she sank down on his cock.

"Oh, wow," she said, moaning.

"That's right." His hands were suddenly on her hips, and he pulled her down, making them both cry out as he slammed to the hilt inside her, shocking her with the power of his thrust. "Fuck, yes, that felt so good." He stroked around her ass, back up, and covered her hips once again.

Cupping his face, she tilted his head back so that she could kiss him. She couldn't get enough of this man, not that she wanted to.

One of his hands caressed up her back, going to her hair, holding her in place as he kissed her lips.

She sucked his bottom lip into her mouth. They both moaned, and he lifted her up, placing her on the edge of the table. He pulled out of her so only the tip of him remained and slammed in deep.

Meeting him thrust for thrust, she took whatever he had to give and gave a part of herself as well, desperate for more. He lifted her legs up over his shoulders, his hands gripping her hips as he pounded away inside her. She loved every second as he took her. She didn't want it to end, nor for him to stop.

Touching her clit, she saw and felt his approval as he seemed to go crazy, fucking her hard. Over and over, he slammed in deep, and she screamed his name, wanting more, needing it.

She'd been a virgin a long time, and that one night, he'd awakened her and now there was no going back, not ever.

"So fucking good. That's it, Charity, fuck my cock. I want you to come all over it. I want it, give it to me."

She whimpered, moaned, and gasped as the feel of him inside her, along with the pleasure of his touch went into another dimension. Nothing made sense to her, and yet, everything felt clear. Dwayne was hers, all hers, and she was going to do everything to keep him. She loved him more than anything else in the world, and it hadn't started when he took her virginity, or danced with her beneath the stars. It had happened when he came for her, carried her out from a room known for death and carnage.

"You feel so good," he said.

Teasing her clit, the sweet build of her orgasm started, and as it did, Dwayne fucked her harder. The sounds of flesh hitting flesh filled the air, along with their heavy panting. She couldn't get enough, and as she came, she screamed his name, wanting more, and he gave it to her.

"Fuck, yes, that feels so good. Yes, yes, yes!" He pounded inside her, and she felt his cock harden as he tensed up, moaning as he came. The pulse of his release surprised her as she felt every little kick.

The bite of his fingers in her flesh would leave marks, but she didn't care. She wanted to wear his marks more than anything else.

"I only intended to eat breakfast with you," he

said.

She chuckled. "I don't mind. You can eat breakfast any way that you want. I'm here no matter what." She winked at him, and he rolled his eyes.

"You're a bad girl."

"Ah, but don't you like that?"

She ran her fingers down his back.

"Yeah, I kind of do." He dropped a kiss to her lips. "Do you want to come out with me today?"

"Are we going to kill people?"

He laughed. "No killing people. Just normal stuff."

"Sounds kind of boring, but I like spending time with you. You'll do."

He rolled his eyes.

He pulled out of her, and she let out a gasp. "Did I hurt you?"

"No, it feels so good. I like you inside me."

He kissed her hard. "You're going to be the death of me."

"Admit it, it'll be a good death."

He sank his fingers into her hair, and she held him tightly, not wanting this moment to end, but also wanting to go out with him.

"I think it's time to shower first."

"Sounds tempting."

He kissed her again, and they didn't make it to the shower for another two hours as they made love once again on the table, and then he couldn't get enough as he pushed her to her knees on the bed. She wasn't going to complain as she loved how insatiable he was when it came to her.

Chapter Eleven

Dwayne closed his eyes as Charity took his cock to the back of her throat and then pulled out until only the tip remained. He didn't know what to fucking do. He was so close, but he didn't want to blow just yet. She'd been wanting to suck his cock for a few days now, and he'd been putting her off. Not because he didn't want her lips around his dick, but because he didn't know if he'd be able to last with his dick in her mouth.

She moaned, and he gripped the chair that he sat on as the vibration traveled up his dick. Some program that they'd been watching played in the background, and he didn't give a shit what was going on. All he cared about was how good her lips felt. He was so close to coming.

You're not a damn teenager.

Running his fingers in her hair, he pumped into her mouth.

When he heard her gag, he eased back, not wanting her to be put off by his desperate need. Her hand covered his cock, and he watched her build up a pace, working his dick at the same time as sucking on him, her lips taking more and more of his cock, her fingers slick from her own saliva.

One, two, three, four, five, six.

Don't blow.

Think of something.

Not her pussy.

Damn, I want to taste her pussy.

It was that time of the month, so she wouldn't let him. She'd started this morning as it had been an interesting trip to the grocery store. He didn't have a clue what he was looking for, and before he'd allow her to move on, he read every single box to understand what she needed in case she ever needed any. A couple of women had stood and watched him. All the time he asked questions, Charity was so embarrassed, but he didn't mind. Some men were freaked out by menstruation, but not him. It was natural, like breastfeeding.

Fuck!

He shouldn't think about that. The thought of Charity, pregnant, her tits leaking milk. Yeah, he was seriously fucking disturbed.

She did that moaning thing again, and he just couldn't contain himself.

"I'm going to come," he said.

Charity didn't pull away, and he couldn't stop it. He came.

"Charity, fuck, baby." He closed his eyes, the pleasure gripping him as wave upon wave of his cum filled her mouth.

He felt her swallow, and as he opened his eyes, he saw her as she took every single drop of his cum. It was so sexy to watch, and when she finished, he was too sensitive for her to touch, and he pulled away, taking hold of her face and kissing her. He didn't care that he tasted himself.

He wanted to kiss her.

"I did it right?" she asked, when he trailed his lips down her neck.

"Hell, yeah. You did it right. I want to fuck you so bad."

"Not long. A couple more days."

He groaned but didn't press the issue. Yes, he was twisted enough to see if they could fuck while she was on her period. They totally could, but some of the boards he'd read were not that promising.

He wasn't about to tell Charity all the things he

checked since she'd moved in with him. They'd been living together now for about a month now. During that time, she'd gone to visit her parents a couple of times. After the first, not so successful visit, he'd opted to stay at home so she wasn't embarrassed.

Dwayne didn't like her being away from home. He enjoyed having her around the house, watching her cook, smile, and just be herself. There were moments when that happiness would fade, and he knew without a doubt what she was thinking. She would always apologize, which again, he hated. She didn't need to apologize for anything.

"I liked that," she said, sitting in his lap. Her head resting against his chest. "Any news on the missing bodies?"

Since she moved in with him, he made a vow to never keep anything from her so she was always prepared for the worst. She was now named in his will, and he'd also made both of his uncles agree that she'd be taken care of, no matter what. He wouldn't allow anything to happen to her, not even for a second.

Planning for the worst was something he'd gotten into years ago.

A week ago, there had been another body uncovered not too far from where he used to bury his own. Caleb and Beast wanted him to move the bodies that he killed fifteen years ago, but he refused. Told them they could, by all means, go and do it themselves. Dwayne wasn't convinced this guy was anything more than an opportunist. The place he put bodies was a really good hiding spot. The guy wasn't dumping them in the same spot twice, and he was using different forests as Williams, their police informant, had let him know. It was so notorious for animal attacks and hikers getting lost that it had been closed off from the public from entering.

He'd been there many times himself when he was much younger, and yes, there were wolves, but with a couple of guns, they never attacked, and of course, he sometimes used to feed them. A quality steak per dig kept the wolves at bay.

"There's security footage that I went back and set up near the drop zone, and I've been able to see his back." He was not about to tell her that the ink on the guy's neck was from a notorious gang known on the streets for pimping women, raping them, allowing men to kill them, and recording it. He'd been investigating the gang for some time as a complaint via Williams, who had asked for help.

Girls as young as fifteen were going missing. Most of them were suspected runaways, but it would seem the woods wasn't the only place that was getting dead bodies to appear. They were cropping all over the city, women facedown in the water, the marks and abuse on their bodies making clear that they hadn't been having fun prior to the attack.

"I hope this matter can be resolved quickly. I don't like the thought of anyone breaking bodies, or hurting anyone, you know. It scares me."

He kissed her lips. "You've got nothing to worry about, baby. I will always take care of you."

"I know." She was about to say something else, he saw it clearly, but then she pressed her lips together and forced a smile, dropping her head back down onto his chest.

He wanted her to talk to him. It was on the tip of his tongue to tell her that he loved her, but each time, the moment didn't seem to be fucking right, and it was killing him.

****

Charity stared across the street. The doors in her car were all locked, and she only wished that the windows were bulletproof. This part of the city was never on the brochures. Women walked around semi-naked, men with their dicks hanging out. The scent of sewage backed up heavy in the air, so much so that it turned her stomach.

It had been several months since Dwayne had come for her. He'd stormed that bar, killed those men, and then taken her home.

She gripped the steering wheel tightly, hating the sickness that rolled through her. She couldn't bring herself to drive away.

In the past few months it had been surreal. She'd graduated and was now living with Dwayne. She had even begun applying for work, which he told her she didn't need to do, but she didn't want to spend all the time at home doing nothing. She was a woman who wanted to work, or at least occupy herself while Dwayne was out of the house.

She knew what he did on a regular basis, and, being home while he was putting his life at risk, she would go insane.

He was her life.

Her parents had wanted her to move back home, but she refused. She didn't want to go back home. The last time she visited them she told them she loved Dwayne. Of course, they didn't think it was love but had to do with the fact that he'd come for her when no one else did. They didn't seem to understand that she'd been falling in love with him for a long time.

Yes, he was a monster.

Yes, he killed people.

He was so many bad things rolled into one package, but she knew the real man. Not the man that could kill a dozen people without caring. She knew he was a good man, someone who at times had nightmares about his past.

She was pleased his father was dead as she'd woken up the other night to hear Dwayne whimpering, begging for him to stop, twitching in such a way that she knew he was being whipped in the dream. It had broken her heart to witness. When she finally got him awake, he'd held her tightly, kissing her, and it wasn't long before he was making love to her. She'd been able to chase the nightmares away for him, and it had twisted her heart so much.

There was a knock at her window, and she gasped as she looked up to see Dwayne by her passenger window. Flicking open the locks, he climbed inside, taking a seat beside her.

"What are we doing?" he asked.

"How did you know where I was?"

"I put a tracker on your cell phone, car, and also in your bag so I know where you are at all times."

"Holy crap! Like, really!" She turned to look at him, not sure if she was happy or angry at him.

"Yes, I told you I'd do whatever I could to protect you. You also have a guard, but seeing as you didn't see him, I'm not telling you who he is."

She couldn't believe he was saying this, but she didn't argue.

"So, why are you here?" he asked.

Charity laughed. "Believe it or not, it's the exact day of the month you came for me."

"I know, which is why I got you this." He held out a small velvet box, and her heart started to pound.

"I didn't get you anything."

"Finding you is all the gift I need."

She opened the box, and there was a ring nestled

in the dark fabric. She didn't know what to say. It was so beautiful.

"I was hoping you'd consider marrying me, Charity. I did have a big dinner planned. A fancy restaurant, nice wine, we could talk, but then … you didn't come home, and you came here."

"You want to marry me?"

"I'm in love with you, Charity. Have been for a long time now. I know I'm not the most ideal person to have as a husband, but I promise you that there will never be another woman for me. I love you more than anything in the world, and if you give me the chance, I know I'll be here for you, always. You'll want for nothing in your life."

"Yes," she said.

"What?"

"I said yes."

"But, I have dinner set up at home."

"I don't care. I love you too." She reached over and caressed his face. "So much, I love you." She chuckled. "Even if this isn't the most romantic place, to me it's perfect."

"A good memory from a bad place?" he asked.

"Yes. I'll always remember this moment, no matter what."

He sank his fingers into her hair and kissed her hard. She melted against him, knowing that it didn't matter if he was the worst romantic in the world. Dwayne made her feel alive. He gave her so much, and there was no way she was ever going to let that feeling go, not even for a second.

****

Charity released a gasp, and Dwayne smiled as he spread the cheeks of her ass. All day long he'd been tasting cakes, and even though he'd picked the lemon cake, she'd gone for the vanilla. Of course, both cakes tasted amazing together, and as his treat for allowing her to join the two together, he'd asked to take her ass, the only place he'd not been allowed to go.

Of course, he'd been prepping her for this for a few weeks now, maybe even longer, but he couldn't get enough of her ass. Today had been a good day. He, Beast, and Caleb had a meeting with the leader of the gang he'd recognized from the footage of the gravesite that he'd secretly installed and didn't allow the police to see. They were known for killing people and burying them. Striking a deal meant they were going to take care of the man bringing heat from the law enforcement.

She moaned as he slid his fingers down the seam of her ass, pressing against her little asshole. Grabbing the lube, he slicked up her anus, coating his fingers to coat her puckered hole.

The tight ring of muscles kept him out, but he pushed past to fill her ass. She cried out, and he thrust his finger in and out of her, spreading her open. It wasn't long before he added a second finger and started to stretch her out even more.

"You want my dick, baby?" he asked.

"Will it fit? I know how big you are."

He chuckled. "We'll take it slow."

His cock was already covered in a condom and slicked up with lube. Putting the tip against her ass, he pulled out his fingers and, holding his length, he began to press against her ass.

Her hands gripped the sheet beneath her. The glint of the ring he'd given her caught his attention.

Charity belonged to him, and their wedding prep was going really well. Caleb and Beast had been surprised by his announcement. Of course, Hope and Faith had soon taken Charity under their wings, and been more than happy to help with the wedding prep. While she was focused on getting married, he didn't have to worry about her wanting to take a job. Of course, there would come a time when she'd want to go out to work, but for now, he was happy keeping her close.

Once he got past those tight muscles, she gasped, and her hand lifted for him to stop, and she whimpered. He stroked her back, giving her time to get accustomed to his dick in her ass.

Slowly, her hand lowered, and inch by inch, he thrust inside her. It took all of his control not to fuck her hard and to take her ass, claiming her completely as his woman. He wouldn't hurt her though. He couldn't hurt her.

Seated to the hilt in her ass, he gripped her hips, holding her tight against him, giving her a few seconds.

"You have no idea how hot this is, seeing your ass open, taking my cock. How does it feel?"

"Weird, good, bad, I don't know. It's ... I don't want you to stop."

"Good, because I have no intention of stopping." He slowly eased out of her ass until only the tip of him was inside her.

When he thrust back inside, they both cried out together.

"Fuck, you feel good," he said.

"Yes, yes." She reached back, and he caught her hand, holding her as he took her ass, thrusting in deeply, watching his cock as she opened up around his dick. Holding both of her hands at the base of her back, he reached between her thighs and started to stroke her clit. "Oh, my."

"Fuck, yeah, baby, I want you to scream for me. Don't hold back. Give me everything that you've got. You like that?"

"Yeah."

He slid his fingers down into her pussy before drawing them back to tease her clit. He wanted to hear her scream for him. Kissing her neck, he felt her ass squeezing him. Closing his eyes, he focused on her, wanting to hear her come, to hear her scream before he even thought about his own pleasure.

Her orgasm built, and he didn't rush it, stroking her clit, building up the pleasure until she screamed his name, moaning, whimpering, thrusting back against his cock. While she was coming, he began to thrust inside her. He kept on teasing her clit at the same time as riding her ass.

Her asshole tightened around him, his own pleasure building. When he brought her down from her release, he cupped her hips and started to thrust, taking her just a little harder, going a little deeper each time until he was sliding balls deep within her, keeping her in place, holding her steady as he fucked her. He couldn't get enough of her curves, her body. He wanted to own every single inch of her. To claim her as his always.

Soon, you will.

She'll have your name.

Your kid.

Everything.

"I love you, Charity. So fucking much," he said.

"I love you too. More than anything in the world."

It was those words that threw him over the edge, and he came with a growl, pumping his cum into the condom, and holding her close as he did.

Chapter Twelve

"You're settling down," Caleb said. "How did that happen? When did The *Nightmare* become a husband? A fiancé? All that good stuff."

Dwayne rolled his eyes as he looked at his uncle. "You sound jealous."

"Nah, he's not jealous, he's just worried that he's going to have to pick up the slack when you go on your honeymoon," Beast said. "Do you know where you're going?"

"Not a clue." Dwayne stared at his reflection. The tailor would be back in no time to finish up his tux for the wedding. He'd not wanted to just buy any suit. This one felt special.

"So, you really love her? I didn't think you had a heart."

"I have a heart, Caleb. You just don't always get to see it." He smiled at his uncle. He and Caleb had that love/hate relationship. There were times they hated each other, but they always had each other's back. He wouldn't let anything happen to Caleb or to Beast. "Yes, I love her. I'm not marrying her to fill some void or whatever. I love her more than anything in the world. Being without her, it was like a part of me was missing."

"That we can understand," Beast said. "I wouldn't be anywhere without Hope."

"Neither I with Faith. They certainly came into our lives with a bit of a shock." Caleb stood up and circled Dwayne. "Marriage is a big step though. You've not dated a woman before in your life."

"I've been dating Charity for some time now. There hasn't been any other woman for me and there never will."

"Does she know everything that you do? The

killing?" Caleb asked. "Some women will find that hard to deal with."

"Charity will surprise you. She knows what I do and what I'm capable of doing. She's seen it firsthand, and without me being who I am, she wouldn't have ever gotten free."

"I get that, Dwayne, but this life is not for everyone. I just want to make sure you've been up front and honest with her about everything," Caleb said, the concerned uncle suddenly stepping up.

"I have. She knows everything."

"I don't keep secrets from Hope. They're the curse of a marriage. Once you start lying there's no way out, and besides, when you're with the right woman, it doesn't matter what you do. Love is more important," Beast said.

Dwayne wasn't about to upset him on that score. He believed that honesty was indeed the best policy, but he also knew that sometimes the truth can unravel every single couple. He'd be honest with Charity, but he would always make sure he knew her thoughts as well. This marriage, he wanted it to work. He liked waking up in the morning, Charity in his arms, the sun shining on both of them. There were moments when he truly believed he'd fallen in love with an angel. When they were apart, he wanted to be with her.

She was looking for places to work and colleges to attend, and the fact he got to help her with that meant everything to him. The little moments they shared, like the food fight they had; they'd burst out laughing because they had to clean up their apartment.

The fact she always came back on a Saturday from doing laundry, and he'd watch her fold it or iron it.

The small domestic things that he once didn't think had any place in his world were some of what he lived for.

When they were married, and after their honeymoon, he wanted to go house hunting. That wasn't a huge need until they started a family, and Charity wasn't ready to start a family yet. Even though she loved kids and had become close with Hope and Faith, she didn't want to start having babies immediately.

He didn't completely mind that either as he wanted to spend some time with her first before they had kids. Children would draw her away from him at times, and even though he did want to see a tiny Charity or a tiny son running around, he could wait.

With Charity, he'd wait forever. She was worth waiting for.

Patience was one of his strong suits when he needed it.

For the next hour he stood in one place as the tailor made changes to the length, and used his tape measure. Staring in the mirror, Dwayne tried to keep his impatience in check. He hated standing for so long while another man touched him, even if it was for a suit.

This is for your wedding. It'll be fine.

However, by the time the tailor said he'd have everything done for when he needed, Dwayne couldn't wait to get the fuck out of there.

After changing back into his clothes, he met Beast and Caleb on the street.

"Are you guys ready to go? Charity wants me to pick out some flowers next." He pulled out his cell phone and saw there wasn't a message from his woman. She wanted to meet him at the florist.

Glancing up he saw Caleb and Beast looking a little worried.

"What's up with you two? I've not killed anyone today or when that guy was taking forever!"

Beast turned his cell phone around, and Dwayne's world shattered.

****

An hour earlier

"Are you sure you don't want company?" Hope asked.

Charity smiled as she crossed the road. She knew it wouldn't be long before it was Dwayne's birthday, and she had sneaked out of the apartment, hoping to get something that he wouldn't know about. She still didn't know where her guard was nor could she spot him in a crowd, but she knew without a doubt he was there. Dwayne didn't say stuff he didn't mean, and she liked that about him.

There was no bullshit when it came to him.

"Nah, you told me when his birthday was, and I don't get why he doesn't celebrate it."

"I know. He's a pain in the ass when he wants to be, but Beast always buys him a present. He doesn't like his day to be a big deal. I'll make him a cake, and he always stops by for dinner."

"I better go. I'll talk soon."

"Okay."

She was going to make Dwayne like his birthday. There was no way that she wasn't going to celebrate his day. He meant a great deal to her, and that meant birthdays were really important.

"Take care," she said, disconnecting the call.

Walking down the street, she hummed to herself, glancing at a couple of the windows to see if there was anything that screamed for it to be Dwayne's.

As she passed an alleyway, she glanced down at her cell phone, and someone covered her mouth. His hold was so tight that it scared her instantly. Dropping her cell phone to the ground, she tried to fight, but whoever had taken her had shocked her. She did everything Dwayne told her not to do. There was no one else in sight, and the man pulled her into the alleyway.

Screaming against his hand, she tried to fight him, clawing at his hands, but he wouldn't let go. She tried to fling her head back to stop him from taking her.

Dwayne's warnings in her head, and as she stamped her foot down on her assailant's, he released her long enough to get away. Just as she was about to scream, her hair was pulled, and she whimpered. She was thrown against the car, her face slammed against the hood. She felt a little dizzy, and as she was dumped inside the trunk of a car, he punched her in the face, stopping her from attacking him as she covered her head.

Pain exploded behind her ears, and suddenly she was in the dark. She didn't know how much time had passed before she realized she was in the trunk of a car and that it was moving. She whimpered and started to attack the hood. It was so dark and so tight. Her heart raced as she kept slamming her hand to the hood.

"Let me out. Let me out. He'll come for you if something happens to me. He'll come and he'll kill you. Dwayne! Dwayne!" She screamed his name, hoping that he'd come for her, that he'd save her.

She cried out as they moved over a bump in the road.

She curled up into a ball, and sobs tore from her throat as she realized that Dwayne was at a fitting for his tux. She covered her face with her hands.

"Please, Dwayne. Please, come for me."

She didn't know who this man was or why he'd taken her. She didn't care either. Dwayne would come. She knew he would. There was no way he wouldn't. He loved her, and if anything was to happen to her, he wouldn't stop until his kind of justice had been served.

They were supposed to be checking flowers today.

Their wedding was only a couple of weeks away. Beast's yard was already getting transformed so they could get married there.

Dwayne had told her how much he'd come to love Beast's yard when his uncle first took him. For hours at a time, he'd lie on the grass staring up at the stars. The love in his words had made it clear to her that Beast's yard was where they were going to start the rest of their life.

Closing her eyes, time passed, and throughout it all, she thought about Dwayne. She wanted to be with him more than anything. Her parents thought he was too old for her. To her, Dwayne was everything.

The car suddenly came to a stop.

She gasped, covering her mouth, finding it ridiculous that she was trying to be quiet. He already knew where she was. He'd taken her.

Where was the guard that was supposed to be on her?

She'd gotten too confident, believing she'd be safe with someone watching her.

The trunk of the car opened up.

"Hello, sweetheart. Did you have a nice ride?" he asked.

She didn't recognize the man at all. She'd never seen him before in her life. He wasn't there when she'd been taken last year, nor was he someone she'd seen since.

"Please, if you let me go, *he* won't come for you."

"You think I'm afraid of your man, huh? Please, he's nothing. He thinks because he can bury bodies that makes him a tough guy? He doesn't even know what real darkness is." He pulled her out of the trunk of the car. "Now, let's go and have a little party."

She cried out as he pulled her across the wood. From the last time she was here with Dwayne, she recognized where they were going, and no matter what she did, he kept a firm hold on her.

Deep down, she knew Dwayne would come.

She only hoped that he didn't take too long.

If I die tonight I hope you know how much I love you.

I'd have done anything for you.

I love you, Dwayne Carson.

She released a whimper as he pulled her along the edge of the lake, water splashing at her feet, and he dragged her deeper through the woods. She recognized the spot where Dwayne had said he'd buried someone.

This man didn't stop there. Instead, he kept pulling her along until they came to a spot where all the grass and brambles were pulled back. He shoved her to the ground next to a shovel.

"Start to dig, whore."

Her hands were shaking. "What? Why?"

He landed a blow to her stomach, ceasing all fight from her. She grabbed her stomach as he pulled her head back. "I said fucking dig." He shoved her face against the mud, and she reached out, grabbing the shovel.

Even though she wanted to fight him, to kick him in the balls, to hurt him, she started to dig, feeling sick. Pain flooded her entire body, and she dug. Even though she wanted to fight him, she knew she was no match for him. Then she saw the gun in his hand and knew there was no chance of her getting out of this alive unless Dwayne got to her.

"You know, I've heard of a lot of people who make their victims dig their own grave. Apparently, it makes them a little fucked up in the head, you know what I'm saying?"

She didn't respond.

What the hell was she supposed to say?

Hell, yeah, I know.

She pushed the shovel into the dirt and started to move the soil. She felt sick to her stomach, but she kept on doing it, wanting nothing more than to spit in his face and tell him to go fuck himself.

The man, she didn't know his name, kept on rambling about how he was going to kill her, or maybe he'd toy with her a little first. She hated every single second of it. Time passed. She didn't know how long she was there, only that the patch of dirt was getting bigger and deeper.

Her body ached, and sweat covered her flesh.

"I wonder who will find you first. The wolves, the cops, or your man."

"Well, I can answer that one right now," Dwayne said, startling the two of them. She turned to see him coming in the opposite direction from the one he'd showed her. He had something in his hand, which he tossed over to the man who'd taken her. "Didn't your mother ever tell you about taking things that don't belong to you?"

Charity stared at the man who once again was here to save her.

"This wasn't about him."

She glanced back to see the man kick the severed head that Dwayne had thrown at him. She was so not getting involved in this right now.

"No, you're right, it wasn't, but seeing as they didn't put you to ground, I considered that a personal slight. So now your little gang is no more. Your leader is right there. You're the only one left. You know who I am. You know what I'm capable of, and still you came after my woman, you sick piece of shit." Dwayne raised his gun, and she covered her ears as there was gunfire.

Dropping to her knees, she watched as Dwayne approached, and suddenly he was on the man who'd taken her. Dwayne had a blade in his hand, and she didn't know how he had it. Only that it had to have been on him to kill the man, stabbing him in the throat, before plunging the blade into his eye.

She covered her mouth, and as Dwayne released the blade, the man dropped to the ground.

Beast and Caleb suddenly came out of the shadows and Dwayne was in front of her. She didn't care what she'd just witnessed. As he touched her face, tilting her head back, she wrapped her arms around him, holding him as close as she could.

"You came. You came. You came."

"Of course I did. I wouldn't ever *not* come for you, Charity. You're mine, and I love you more than anything. I will always come."

"How did you know?"

"The guard I had on your ass. This fucker shot him in the stomach, but he was able to show me who it was."

"Will he be all right?"

"Of course. He's in the hospital now, but he won't be guarding you again. Someone got the jump on him, and there's no way I'm risking your safety." He stroked her cheek, and tears filled her eyes.

"I knew you'd come. I was so afraid you'd be too late."

"No, never." He kissed her lips, and she held onto him, not wanting to let him go. "I'll never leave you, and if I don't ever make it, Charity, I won't be far behind you. I'll avenge your death, and then I'll be coming to be with you. That's how I love you, baby. Nothing else in this world is worth loving. You are. You always will be." He stroked her hair back. "Fuck, I don't even want to think about how I nearly lost you."

"Do you know who he was?"

"He was part of some gang. He was paying cops to look the other way, even had a different informant who was dumping evidence, which is why it was so hard to find him. The truth is, he wasn't anyone to us. Just in his little gang. They were supposed to deal with him, but they didn't."

"Why do you think he came for me?"

"He was pissed that I made his leader pick between his own head, his club, or the guy dumping bodies. He didn't do as I asked, so he took you. Clearly trying to send me a message. Well, now I took the leader, the gang, and that sick fucker. We don't have to worry about them anymore."

"Yeah, when The *Nightmare* gets onto something, he doesn't ever let it go," Caleb said.

"I will understand if you want to … pull out of the wedding," Dwayne said.

She caught him rolling his eyes at his uncle, and she frowned. "Huh? What?"

"After what you just saw. I know it's—"

She pressed her lips against his, silencing him with a single kiss. Taking hold of his shirt, she held him in a death grip. "Nothing is ever going to change the way I feel about you, Dwayne. I know more than anything that you have to do what you do. I love you, no one else, you. I want to marry you."

"Then, let's get this show on the road. I want to get home tonight, and we still have a job to do, so can you two, I don't know, move this along?" Beast said.

Before she could stop him, Dwayne picked her up

and carried her out of the woods. She wrapped her arms around him, not wanting to let him go.

"I will understand if you don't want to."

"Will you shut up, silly? I don't care. I was waiting for you, Dwayne. I don't care what you had to do. I know deep down you're a good person that has to do bad things. I love you. I want you, and there's no way you're going to get rid of me that easily."

"I don't want to get rid of you, not ever. I'm going to cherish you always."

And as he carried her to the car, Charity felt his love, his protection, his warmth, and there was no way she was ever going to let him go. Dwayne belonged to her, just as she did to him.

Epilogue

Ten years later

"You know, at times I don't know who is the bigger child, you or Ben," Charity said.

Dwayne smiled as he sat down next to his glorious, sexy as fuck wife, who also happened to be heavily pregnant with their third child. He reached over, kissing her lips and running his hand across her swollen stomach. Damn, he didn't know if he loved her more pregnant. She was always heavier, but he loved seeing their baby grow. Her stomach was swollen, her tits heavy, and it was because he fucked her.

Yes, he felt so possessive of her.

They'd been happily married for ten years, and even though it took the birth of their first grandchild, Charity's parents had finally come around and were happy for them. They always had their opinions, but he'd been told that they were allowed to have them, and he wasn't to shoot them for it.

The moment they made Charity cry, he wasn't going to make any promises.

"Dwayne, of course," Beast said, sipping his water. They were all at Dwayne and Charity's home. Caleb stood at the barbeque pit pretending he was king of the food, but every now and then Faith and Hope would stand with him, guiding him.

This was his home, his family, filled with his loved ones. Over the past few years, his reputation had remained, but of course, between Beast and Caleb, there was a new generation of Carson men who wanted to make a reputation for themselves. None of them would ever be able to rival him, but he didn't mind.

Beast hadn't trained his boys to be monsters, but thinkers. Men who knew when to strike at the right moment.

"You're happy," Charity said.

He smiled down at his adoring wife.

Her cheeks were nice and flushed, and he kissed her again, unable to resist. "You know I am."

"Even though you wanted to cancel."

He loved his family more than anything. His uncles were important to him, but he also found family events tiring, stressful, and he always wanted to cancel them, be it Thanksgiving, Christmas, birthdays, or anniversaries. He always found an excuse, but Charity would always make him go.

"Yeah, I'm glad you sent me to the kitchen to cool the beers. You guys happy to watch the kids?" Dwayne asked.

"Yeah, go, go," Beast said.

He helped Charity to her feet, and together they walked past the small garden, out toward the pond he'd had installed. He'd done this after Charity mentioned that she loved to watch the still water and if there were frogs, how they jumped, and fish.

Dwayne would do anything for his wife.

"What's up, babe?" she said.

He stopped at the edge of the pond and cupped her face, tilting her head back. Even after ten years, she was still the most beautiful woman he had ever seen. Coming home, it made him excited to see her. His heart raced for her. He wanted her all the time. Not a single moment went by when he didn't want her.

His love for her was the one thing that made him feel alive, as well as the love he had for their children. The night she gave birth to their son, he couldn't recall ever being more afraid of anything in his life.

"I want to know if you're happy," he said.

"Of course I'm happy." She covered his hands

with hers. "How can you even for a moment doubt that?"

"I didn't doubt it. I just needed to *hear* that you're happy. I want you to be. I'll give you the world if you asked for it."

She chuckled. "Dwayne, there's nothing else I want in this world. I love you more than anything. Our family, our life, to everyone else you're their nightmare. That is not what you are to me, nor will you ever be. You were and are and will always be my knight."

He kissed her lips, holding her close.

All those nights ago when he was a kid, he prayed all night long for someone to come, to love him, and to make him feel as if he was the only person alive that she could ever love. Charity was that woman. She was his soul mate, and as they walked hand in hand, they stood at the edge of the garden, watching his family.

The Carson men.

Beasts, Monsters, and Nightmares, but at the heart of it, they were still men. They still had a heart, and they had all found their women that would accept them for who they were.

The End

www.samcrescent.com

BESTSELLING BBW ROMANCE
SPICY ROMANCE FOR REAL WOMEN